FLIGHT
OF THE
WHITE WOLF

D0035439

TERRY
SPEAR

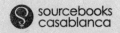

sourcebooks
casablanca

Published by Sourcebooks Casablanca, an imprint of Sourcebooks, Inc.
P.O. Box 4410, Naperville, Illinois 60567-4410
(630) 961-3900
Fax: (630) 961-2168
sourcebooks.com

Printed and bound in the United States of America.
OPM 10 9 8 7 6 5 4 3 2 1

*To Rebecca Jones-Stepp, who succumbed
to a rare form of cancer, late daughter
of my beta reader, Dottie Jones.*

Prologue

THE CASE JUST HAD TO INVOLVE FLYING.

On his first day as a private investigator in Seattle, Gavin Summerfield had gotten a case that made him want to string the thieves up. Stolen pets had become a lucrative market for criminals. In this case, two male, champion-sired Samoyed pups, worth nearly three thousand apiece, had been stolen from their owner's fenced-in backyard. The woman and her two teen daughters were in tears.

"I vow I'll find Kodi and Shiloh and bring them home safe," Gavin told the trio. He hoped he wouldn't fail them. Sometimes, pets ended up in lab experiments or were sold to breeders or puppy mills. Sometimes, the criminals who stole them were looking to return them for a reward.

Soon after he left the family's home with pictures of the pups and their favorite fetch toys, he had discovered that a white van had been sighted at the owner's house and also in the vicinity of four other dognappings. One of the neighbors had captured a photograph of the Alaska license plate on the same van parked in a friend's driveway when the friend wasn't home.

Then Gavin had gotten a lead that the dogs had been flown to Alaska.

Now, he was trying to settle his stomach and pretend he wasn't flying high above the world on his way to see London Lanier, a retired police detective in Big Lake. Gavin's fear of crashing wasn't just a figment of his imagination. Six months earlier, while he was still a Seattle cop, he'd survived a plane crash after jewelry-store robbers had taken him hostage.

The Alaska-bound plane hit more turbulence, and his stomach dropped. He closed his eyes, telling himself he wasn't going to crash. Not this time. That wasn't the only reason he hated to fly. He liked to be in control, and flying left him with no control over anything.

At least he had a lead on the pups. He wanted more than anything to return them to the family, safe and sound. The Samoyeds' pictures reminded him of the dogs his family had raised when he was growing up. Their German shepherds had been as much family to him as his human family had been.

As soon as Gavin's plane landed, he picked up a rental car and drove to the town where his contact was located.

London Lanier was an animal rights activist, primarily concerned with the illegal hunting of wildlife in Alaska. Gavin had called to tell him the pups had been flown to his neck of the woods, and London had begun to check into it.

When Gavin met London at his Big Lake home, he thought the retiree looked like Santa Claus, with the white beard and hair, though he was a trim version of jolly old Saint Nick. He was tall, fit, and eager to take on hunters with his bare hands.

"You look like a cop," London said, shaking Gavin's hand.

Gavin took the remark as a compliment. Now that

he was a PI, his hair wasn't as short as when he was on the force. Today, he looked more like a SWAT team member, with a black T-shirt, black cargo pants, and heavy-duty black boots. He was in a no-nonsense mood and ready to take the bastards down.

London served them both cups of coffee, and then he got down to business. "From what I've learned, a home near here has lots of dogs barking all day long, and then a few days later, most of them are gone. Shortly after that, they have a new batch of dogs. Some of their neighbors are suspicious. Since I don't work on the police force anymore, you'll need to do some canvassing. If you learn anything that proves they really are involved in trafficking pets, let me know, and I'll call the police. I'm still friends with several on the force."

London handed Gavin a hand-drawn map, saying, "I talked to the locals, but everyone knows who I am. Maybe a new guy, just looking for his pups, could convince someone to share something they didn't tell me. Or maybe they've seen something new or remembered something they hadn't thought of before. Good luck."

"Thanks, London. I'll let you know what happens. And I owe you."

London smiled. "Never know when I might need a PI. Besides, if you can help us take these bastards down, you've done me a favor."

Afterward, Gavin headed over to the Big Lake housing area with its high-income homes, lakefront property, trees all around, and large yards for hiding a slew of runs for stolen pets.

He pulled into the driveway of the home three doors down from the suspect's house, parked, and went to the door. When he knocked, a gray-haired woman with bright-blue eyes greeted him with a smile.

"Ma'am, I'm a private investigator, searching for these two missing pups. They were stolen from the backyard while they were outside playing. Have you seen them? Or know anyone who might have them?"

"Oh yes, of course." Her eyes were rounded, and she licked her lips. "She's my next-door neighbor."

He frowned and glanced at his map. That wasn't the correct house. At least, not according to London. "Are you sure?"

"Yes. She has dogs all the time. Not the same ones though. I see her out walking them along the road in the late spring, summer, early fall. Even in the winter when we're buried in snow. Always different dogs. I figured she fostered them or something. I saw her with two of the cutest little Samoyed pups earlier, maybe six months old? Not sure. They look exactly like yours."

"Do you know her name?"

"Amelia White. She lives alone. Well, except for the revolving door of dogs. I never considered that any of the dogs could have been stolen."

"What about the people at this place?" Gavin pointed to the house on the map that London had targeted.

"Oh yeah, sure. Did London send you? He already asked me."

"You didn't mention Amelia to him?"

"No. She's so sweet. I really didn't think she could be involved in anything so nefarious. But she does have two Samoyed puppies. And that's what you're looking for, right? I hadn't seen them with her before yesterday morning."

"And the other people?"

"Oh, the Michaelses? Asher and Mindy? Yes, I wouldn't be surprised at all about them. Not sure what he does. They don't seem to have a regular occupation, just…money and lots of dogs. They don't walk them. The dogs just bark most of the time, and I've seen all of them rushing to the chain-link fence when I've taken strolls past the place. Different dogs all the time."

"What does Miss White do?"

"She's a seaplane pilot. Her family owns the business."

"Thanks." It would be easy to move stolen pets around as a pilot, wouldn't it? No paperwork hassle. Just fly them where they needed to go. What were the chances that both people were involved in the illegal trade of pets? Maybe Amelia took care of the overflow and the transportation. It would be convenient, with her living so close to the Michaelses.

Gavin drove to Amelia's house first, since she apparently had dogs like the ones he was looking for. He'd start surveillance on the Michaelses after that.

He parked and headed for the large, blue-vinyl-sided home, where he climbed the porch stairs. No dogs barked as he approached, and the front door was slightly ajar. That's when two curious little Samoyed pups poked their noses out, probably hearing his footsteps.

Before Gavin could stop them, they nudged the door open, and one raced down the steps. *Hell!*

The second pup ran to join the first, and Gavin was led on a merry chase. He managed to scoop up the one closest to him and finally reached the other, grabbing him up in his left arm. The puppies licked him as if this was just part of their playtime.

The problem was that Samoyed puppies all looked the same to him. These two were both white, identical to each other. And they looked just like the photos he had of Kodi and Shiloh.

One pup secure in each arm, he hurried back to the house, ran up the steps, and hollered through the open door, "Miss White? Your front door was open, and your pups ran off." If they weren't the right pups, he wasn't about to confiscate them and be accused of stealing *her* pets! On the other hand, he worried about foul play because the door was slightly ajar and no one was answering. What if something had happened to her?

Suddenly, a wet, naked woman streaked across the living room, glancing at him for a second as she ran, and disappeared down a hall. "Put them down, get out, and close the door," she called out.

Shocked, he just stood there, his mouth hanging agape, the image of the gorgeous blond in the raw still imprinted on his brain. She was in great shape, her hands covering her bouncing breasts as she'd dashed down the hall. He closed the front door so the puppies wouldn't run out of the house again and set them down on the hardwood floor. "I'm leaving," he called. "Sorry... Your door was open, and I was worried something might be wrong."

He needed to question her about the pups...maybe later. He started to back away from them slowly and had almost reached the door when they came bounding after him. He was trying to figure out how to keep them from dashing out again as soon as he opened the door, when suddenly the woman reappeared with a blue towel wrapped around her curvy body and a Taser in her hand—and shot him.

—◊◊◊—

After taking down the man, who was unlawfully in her house, Arctic wolf shifter Amelia Marie White knew she recognized him—the uniformed, human cop from Seattle. The man who'd been taken hostage on the plane she'd been forced to fly as the getaway pilot. What angered her also was that the man in charge of the heist, Clayton Drummer, the gray wolf she'd been dating, had been a Seattle cop too. She knew now that he'd only been dating her because he wanted to use her to fly him out of Seattle after stealing the jewels.

Had the two men known each other?

Possibly. What if this one was really here to take her down for killing Clayton? Not arrest her, as she'd thought initially.

"Stay there. Don't move a muscle. I have another Taser all ready and fired up to use on you. And the police are on their way."

Not that the guy was moving. He lay prone on her floor near the door, watching her, groaning. *In her home*. He was half-dazed and looked like he was having trouble focusing. Maybe he hadn't seen enough of her to recognize her as the pilot of the plane that day. But if not, why would he be here?

Confident he wasn't going anywhere, Amelia rushed back to her bedroom, her foster pups running after her. She pulled on a T-shirt and a pair of jeans, then grabbed her phone to call the police.

Wouldn't you know, of all the times her front door hadn't locked properly, she'd stripped to take a shower, and the faucet handle had fallen off in her hand—probably due to mineral water corrosion. She'd had to use the guest bathroom and remembered only after she showered that she'd washed all the towels in there. Which were still in the dryer. And she hadn't brought clothes with her because she normally just walked from her master bathroom to her dresser.

When she'd heard the deep-voiced male calling out her name inside her house, shocking her, she'd had a split-second decision to make. She could shift into her wolf and scare the guy off, but she worried she'd scare her foster pups too. Or she could dash through the house naked, grab a towel and her Taser from the master bathroom, and take care of the guy. Dashing through the house as a naked woman had seemed to throw him off guard, at least long enough for her to tase him.

She'd hoped he would be gone by the time she returned. When he hadn't been, she'd had to take action.

Once the police were on their way, she hurried back into the room where the guy was still lying on the floor, stunned. She wasn't sure if he was staying put because she told him to or if he really was still incapacitated. Too bad he wasn't a wolf, as sexy as he was.

"Who are you, and why didn't you leave when I told you to?" She prayed he didn't say he was still a cop and investigating her leaving the scene of a crime.

"Gavin Summerfield," he managed to get out. "Former Seattle police, private investigator now, looking into the theft of a pair of Samoyeds in Seattle, which led me here to Big Lake. And your place."

Now that she could really observe him—unlike the first time she'd seen him, when he'd been hustled into the back of the plane and she'd been forced into the cockpit, or when he was lying on the ground half-conscious after the crash—Amelia couldn't believe the hot-looking man she'd just tased was now a PI. Dazed green eyes, red hair, all dressed in black, his T-shirt showing off his nice muscles.

She'd really thought he'd been in on the heist, offering himself as a hostage as a cover. When Clayton had tried to kill him, she'd taken her boyfriend out, mainly for trying to kill the cop, but also because as a wolf, Clayton couldn't go to jail. And because Clayton had used her and would have killed her if she hadn't gone along with the program.

"Stolen Samoyeds?" What Gavin said wasn't registering because all she could think of were the jewelry heist and the downed plane. Sure, she was taking care of a couple of Samoyed puppies. She was fostering them, for heaven's sake. Just like she fostered tons of dogs until she could find them good homes.

Then she worried. What if Molly and Snowflake *were* the stolen pups he was searching for?

Two cop cars pulled into her driveway, and she met the uniformed men at the door. She prayed Gavin hadn't recognized her and wouldn't say anything about the Seattle business to them.

Brenham, one of the cops, began checking Gavin over and verifying his identity, ready to take him into custody.

"Call London Lanier, the retired police detective who worked in your department. He gave me the information about the pet theft ring in this area," Gavin gritted out.

The other cop called London to see if Gavin's story checked out.

"Do you want to press charges?" Brenham asked Amelia.

"No," she said. "He shouldn't have stayed in the house when I told him to leave, but he did return my pups when I could have lost them for good."

"I was working my way toward the door, and the pups were following me. I was afraid they'd dash out again," Gavin said.

She liked his deep, manly voice, though it was a little rough around the edges right now, different from when she'd first heard him talking to her from the foyer.

"*Was* your front door open?" Brenham asked Amelia, a black brow arched.

"Yeah, I'm having trouble getting it to seat properly, and though I locked it, apparently it wasn't shut all the way. I have a carpenter coming to check it this afternoon."

She couldn't believe Gavin hadn't told the cops who she was. Maybe he truly hadn't seen her face before, and he really was only here about the missing pups. If that was the case, she hoped he found them for the puppies' and the family's sake.

Brenham helped Gavin to his feet. Frowning, Gavin asked her, "Have we met before?"

Her heart pounded. The police waited for her to answer him. She quickly shook her head. "Everyone says that."

"You look familiar," Gavin insisted. "Have you ever been to Seattle?"

She felt light-headed all of a sudden and was afraid the color had drained from her face. "No." She hated to lie. Since she hadn't reported what had happened to her six months ago, she was afraid the police would believe she'd willingly been the robbers' getaway pilot. Especially if they learned she had been dating the dead wolf.

"Okay, my mistake. It's probably like you said. You just look like someone else." Gavin didn't sound like he truly believed that.

Which reminded her he was a former cop—like these two here who were watching her behavior. She was trying to look perfectly innocent. She wasn't sure Gavin was buying it.

Brenham began looking at the pups' photos that Gavin had, and then he carefully considered Amelia's pups. "The ones in the photo and the ones you have look the same to me. Are you sure the pups you're fostering hadn't been stolen before they were taken to the shelter where you picked them up?"

The police were thorough, so one got in contact with the animal shelter to verify her story. Especially since her neighbor had told Gavin the pups had arrived about the same time he learned the Seattle pups had been stolen.

Fearing that they might be, Amelia took the photo from the officer and really studied it. The Samoyed pups did look very much like hers. Except for one thing. The ones in the photo were wearing blue leopard-print collars.

She frowned at Gavin, who was leaning against the wall, still looking like she'd just tased him. "Are the two puppies you're looking for males?"

———

Once Gavin was feeling more like himself—though still having visions of a beautiful, naked, blond female streaking across her living room—he set up surveillance to watch Asher and Mindy Michaels's home, the place

London had originally steered him to check out. Gavin still swore he'd seen Amelia White before—in the commission of a crime. A flashback of the blond wearing a blue dress flitted across his brain for a couple of seconds. The experience was like when he'd see a bank teller at the grocery store. Because she wasn't where he normally saw her, he couldn't quite make the connection. Yet due to having been both a cop and a private investigator, he was good at remembering faces.

Still, he needed to get his mind on his work and off the woman.

Early in the evening three days later, a new vanload of dogs arrived. Gavin quickly made a call to coordinate with the police. Once they were on their way, he went to talk to Asher Michaels, the man getting out of the van, to delay him until the police arrived.

"Hey, excuse me. You're Asher Michaels, right?" Gavin asked, stalking up the driveway and getting close to the man. He was dark haired and clean shaven, his square jaw tight with a cleft in the center of the chin. His hard, gray eyes narrowed at Gavin.

Gavin knew Asher wanted to secure the dogs pronto before anyone began asking questions. He kept looking back at the house as if expecting someone to come out and help him.

"I've got work to take care of. I don't allow solicitors on my property," Asher said.

"I'm not trying to sell anything. I'm just looking for these two little fellas. Kodi and Shiloh. They got out on me, and I heard you took in dogs sometimes. Your neighbor fosters dogs, and she thought you did too. Our family has been devastated by the loss. Can you look at the picture and tell me if you've seen them? Or have them?"

"Look, I don't have your dogs. Now get off my property."

Asher refused to look at the picture. Gavin shoved it under his nose, trying to stall him, but also wanting to get a reaction. "*Please*, take a look."

Asher did, only because it was hard not to since the photo was so close to his face. His eyes widened fractionally. Either he had a couple of Samoyeds he'd stolen, or he'd already gotten rid of them.

"I'm an undercover cop," Asher said. "Get out of here before you blow my cover."

Gavin hesitated, processing that information. Then he assumed Asher was spinning a tale to serve as a cover for his illegal business. "If you know anything at all about them, I'm willing to pay a big reward for their return," Gavin told him.

Asher moved his jacket aside and reached for a holstered gun. *Ah, hell.*

Gavin hadn't expected the guy to pull a gun on him. He grappled with the man, hearing the cops pulling up street side. Gavin was glad for his police training as he struggled with Asher, trying to wrest the gun away before it went off. He hoped the police didn't think he was assaulting Asher for just suspecting he had stolen the dogs.

Gavin called out to the cops, "He's got a gun!"

The cops ran toward them, yelling at Asher to drop the weapon.

Gavin finally managed to trip Asher and take the perp down. When a shot fired, just missing Gavin's head, he was thinking this PI work could be damn dangerous. At the same time, a woman raced out of the house and began beating on Gavin with her fists, trying to free Asher. Gavin wouldn't let go for anything. He was just glad the woman hadn't gone for the gun.

The police finally reached them and arrested Asher and Mindy, a petite brunette with catlike green eyes. Another couple of police vehicles arrived. The police officers hauled the couple off to jail. London even showed up with a list of dog thefts in Alaska to see if any of the dogs matched those that had been recently stolen.

"Hell, you need to come work for us," London told Gavin.

"I thought you were retired."

"Just got rehired to be on a special unit that deals with stolen pets and illegal hunting. Come on inside. Let's see if we can find those pups of yours."

"Asher said he was an undercover cop," Gavin told him as they found kennels full of dogs of every size and breed in the backyard. He would guess the Michaelses had well over a hundred, not including the ones in the van.

"Yeah, like I'm a strip-club dancer. He didn't fool you, did he?" London asked, smiling.

"No. I figured he thought I really was looking for my missing pups and he could convince me to go away. Then he must have realized I wasn't buying his story and thought a gun would change my mind."

Brenham, one of the officers who had gone to Amelia White's home to arrest Gavin, called out to him, "Hey,

Summerfield. You might be interested in looking at a couple of Samoyed puppies in the bedroom up front." Brenham smiled. "They even have blue collars, just like the ones the pups in the picture were wearing."

Hoping they were the pups he was looking for, Gavin hurried into the house and found Kodi and Shiloh in a crate together. They were watching the other dogs being rounded up, excited, wanting to play. Gavin called their names, and they both turned, wagging their tails.

He checked them over. Their microchips had been removed, but he made sure they were both males. They were wearing the same blue leopard-print collars too. Thankfully, they were in good condition.

Gavin was glad to be going home with the two pups but found himself thinking about the naked woman who'd had two Samoyed pups. He hoped she'd hear that he'd broken up a pet theft ring so she knew he'd been completely honest with her.

After the terrifying plane ride back to Seattle and the return of the pups to their grateful family, Gavin went in to the PI agency, where his partners, all former police officers, were eager to hear how the agency's first case had gone.

He told his story, not leaving any detail out. Owen Nottingham whistled when Gavin mentioned the part about Amelia. David Davis laughed. Smiling, Cameron MacPherson slapped him on the back. "Hell, Gavin, you have all the luck."

Chapter 1

Nearly seven years later
Northern Minnesota

GAVIN HATED ONE THING MORE THAN ANYTHING ELSE IN THE world—flying. And that's just what he was going to have to do for this mission.

Eleanor Dylan was a cosmetic heiress, though she also had other kinds of businesses, and she was certain her husband was having an affair. She needed proof to start divorce proceedings and keep her inheritance intact. "Conrad is going on a fly-in company canoe trip to the Boundary Waters Canoe Area Wilderness, the BWCA, and your agency is the closest to that location. They'll be in the wilderness, so you'll have to take a seaplane to get there. Well, I guess you could just paddle in, but it would take you too long to catch up to them. Wouldn't it? I mean, if you only have a day and a half to get ready and be there?"

"Yes, ma'am." Gavin grimaced, glad they were speaking on the phone.

"I would have called sooner if I had thought of doing this earlier. But it's the perfect way to catch them at it, I think. They'll be there for nine days. The tour package includes food and all the equipment they need, so they won't be stopping for supplies anywhere. Can you do it?"

"Yes, ma'am. Our agency can definitely take care of it."

All of Gavin's PI partners and their mates were Arctic wolf shifters who had been turned a few years ago. As wolves, they had enhanced night vision, and their hearing was superior whether they were in their wolf coats or human form. They had settled in Minnesota and their PI business was booming, which meant Gavin was the only one available for this job. A trip to the Boundary Waters totally appealed. More so if he could have just paddled in.

"Not your agency. *You*. I've looked into your background already, and from everything I've seen, you've got an outstanding track record."

"Thanks. All of my partners are also well qualified." Gavin didn't want her to believe that they couldn't handle the case if one of them had to take over for him.

"You, or no deal."

"Yes, ma'am. I'll head up there and check it out." His pack had already reserved permits for him and two of his partners to go to the Boundary Waters later in the summer. He checked on his computer for the availability of a different entry point, and he found one. Some canoeists must have canceled their trip because of the bad weather expected over the next couple of days. Gavin was able to switch his time and port of entry without any trouble.

"Conrad gave me a copy of their trip itinerary in case anything happened," Eleanor said. "It shows their route and where they intend to set up camp. He'll never suspect a lone canoeist is doing surveillance on him, will he?"

"No, ma'am. Does he often give you the detailed itinerary for his trips?" Gavin couldn't help but think that if her husband were having an affair, he'd keep his wife *out* of the loop.

"Always. I would have been suspicious if he hadn't."

Okay, that explained it. Though Gavin wondered if Conrad would have given her a fake itinerary if he thought his wife was having him watched.

"Have you been in the Boundary Waters before?" she asked.

"Yes, ma'am. Several times." Especially once they had more control over their shifting. The wilderness had been the perfect, close getaway for them.

"Oh good," she said with relief.

"How many are on this company trip?" As a wolf, he could get up close to the campsite, and Conrad and his party would never know he was there.

"Four executives from various departments. Lee Struthers, the CEO, likes to chill out with her executives on adventure tours a couple of times a year instead of always conducting business in the boardroom. It's supposed to be a team-building trip. One of the executives is a woman. And the two sales associates going with them are women too."

"You suspect your husband is having an affair with someone in the group, then?"

"A top sales associate. She's in her late twenties. He's forty-five now. I know Orwell Johnston, who's also on this trip, is having an affair with the other sales associate. Conrad told me all about their antics. The long lunch hours at a nearby hotel. The gifts he gives her, even at work."

"How did you learn who would be going?" Gavin wondered why Conrad would tell his wife, if the guy was having an affair with someone at work.

"I asked. And Conrad told me."

That sounded like he was open about things with his wife. "Have you had other investigators checking into his activities?"

"Yes, before we were married eight years ago. I had inherited quite a large estate before I met him, and I wanted to make sure he wasn't marrying me just for my money."

"You must have learned he was a good prospect, since you married him."

"No skeletons in his closet. He worked his way up in the greeting-card business and is now one of their executives. I didn't suspect anything was wrong between us until he came home from the last trip. He acted distant and aloof, and he didn't seem to be his cheerful self for several weeks. I asked what was wrong, but he said nothing was. Which I knew was a lie. He wouldn't tell me what had happened."

"The sales associate had been with him that time too?"

"Yes. They seemed close when I attended the company Christmas party. She was sweet and got me refills on my drinks, and she was trying to be careful about not showing any overt affection toward Conrad. But there were coy smiles, and she patted his hand and ran hers over his back in a way that led me to believe there was more intimacy going on between them."

"How did he react to her attentions?"

"Like he was used to it. He didn't make her stop.

I didn't see him treat her in the same way, but that could just mean he was being more discreet at the party because I was there. After the way he acted following the last team-building trip, and with Cheryl part of the group again, I want to know what's really going on."

"Okay, so anything else that raises your suspicions? Like he's taking more care with his appearance? Staying away from home later, leaving home earlier? Evasiveness? Defensiveness?"

"He has been working later. If you must know, our sex life is nil. He's always taken care of his appearance. Evasiveness? Yes, especially after the last trip. And defensiveness, yes. He's received calls he's secretive about. I haven't smelled a woman's perfume on his clothes though—and I haven't seen any receipts that would make me suspicious. Of course, he could be using a separate account that I don't know about for more… personal business."

"You have a prenuptial agreement, right?"

"Yes. If he's having an affair and we divorce, he doesn't get a cent from me. To be fair, if I divorced him and he wasn't at fault, he'd receive a settlement. I do love him, and I was willing to make that concession."

"Okay. I'll get right on this." Gavin didn't know what to think. If Conrad was telling his wife about his coworker's affair, was he trying to get a reaction out of her? Maybe. One of the cops Gavin knew on the Seattle force had done that. His wife thought it was amusing, until she learned her husband was having an affair with a nurse at one of the local hospitals.

"Thank you. I'm emailing you pictures of Conrad and Cheryl. I trust you'll be inconspicuous."

"Guaranteed."

They finished the call, and Gavin studied the photos Eleanor had sent, apparently taken at the company Christmas party. There was a Christmas tree in the background, and both Conrad and Cheryl were holding glasses of champagne.

Conrad was dark-haired, dark-eyed, and had a manicured, pampered appearance. He didn't appear to be the type who was ready to rough it. Cheryl had dark roots, but the rest of her hair was pale blond, and she had light-green eyes. She looked like the girl next door, sweet and innocent.

Gavin called Faith MacPherson, one partner's mate, to let her know he had a job and would be leaving as soon as he could. She managed the calls for their business while taking care of her six-year-old triplets. Her husband, Cameron, and their other two partners were out on jobs of their own.

"Oh, Gavin, I'm so sorry you had to be the one to take this particular case," Faith said.

He wished no one knew about his fear of flying. Faith had learned the truth when Cameron had needed his help to locate their missing friends, and he'd had to fly from Seattle to Maine to aid them.

"No problem. I'll let you know what's going on when I locate the group and tell you if I learn anything."

"Be careful."

"I will."

Like everyone else at the agency, Faith knew how things could go wrong at a moment's notice. Gavin called Adventure Seaplane Tours and got the owner, Henry White.

"Yeah, I had a last-minute sightseeing tour cancellation," Henry said. "Do you need all the outfitting equipment? Will it be just you?"

"Just me, and I'm bringing my own gear. Thanks."

"All right. Drive up here, and I'll fly you out. My son and I are taking a group out there a couple of hours before your flight. We'll be back well before you arrive. It's a popular time of year. Though a storm's coming in tomorrow. So we've had a few cancellations."

Gavin wondered if the earlier group was Conrad's. It would have worked out time-wise, from the itinerary Eleanor had, and Conrad's company was also using White's tour service. "Yeah, thanks. See you soon."

He was relieved he wouldn't be too far behind the company's canoeists, if that's who White and his son were taking. He'd be able to begin surveillance right away. Getting the job done meant he'd be available for another. He and his partners had accumulated lots of great reviews, and they believed that's why business had really picked up.

If time hadn't been against him, Gavin would have just paddled in from Ely and not bothered with the plane trip. But the group would only be out there for nine days, and a thunderstorm was rolling in the night after he arrived. By flying in, he'd be hunkered down well before the storm hit. If they didn't have too much lightning, the storm shouldn't hinder him much. In fact, it could provide him cover.

A day and a half later, Gavin loaded his canoe on his Suburban and finished packing his waterproof bags, cooler, and rain gear. He headed out thinking that, despite the storm and the fact that he had to fly there, he was going to enjoy this trip.

Amelia Marie White glowered at the group of male tourists who were waiting to take a plane up for sightseeing. One of the men had refused to go if a woman was piloting the plane. Was he a throwback to cavemen or what? She'd already had a day of it, so she wasn't in the mood for any more trouble. They'd loaded all their gear into her plane while she was away taking a call about placing a foster dog, so they'd thought her dad or brother would be the pilot.

The guy's arms were folded across his chest in a defiant way, his blue eyes narrowed in contempt. He was around forty, red hair cut in a short burr. He looked like he could be ex-military. Yet something about him seemed *so* familiar. She couldn't place where she'd seen him before though.

If they didn't want her to fly them, no problem. They could go somewhere else, though at this late date, the other seaplane services might be booked. Unless they also had cancellations because of the coming storm. Her dad wouldn't want to get bad publicity out of this though. The other two companies provided the same services and were already annoyed that her family had settled here and taken some of their business. She was certain they would jump at the chance to take these guys up and bad-mouth her company.

Her dad quickly took her aside to defuse the situation. "You know the other group canceled on me because of the iffy weather. Now I've got to take another paddler out to the Boundary Waters. You're scheduled to fly Winston to Saint Paul. Taking the paddler will give you more time to do that, and you'll be way ahead of the deadline. Just drop this guy off, take Winston to the shelter, and come back here—or stay there and do some shopping. I'll take these people up and see you the day after tomorrow."

Wishing he'd back her in telling the redhead either to fly with her or find another service, Amelia frowned at her dad.

"Listen, maybe the guy was involved in a plane crash where a woman pilot was at the controls. Who knows?"

"All right, Dad. It still irks me." Especially since she'd crashed a plane—on purpose—to give herself and the heist gang's possible hostage a chance to live. That still troubled her. No decent pilot should ever be forced to do such a thing.

Her father knew that was why the passenger's attitude bothered her and was empathetic. "I don't blame you. I have to take this group up and I'll just use your plane. If you have any trouble with anything, call me."

"Sure will." This was going to be one of those days, Amelia thought. First, she'd been running late because of car trouble. Then, while she was loading Winston's dog food in the car, he'd made a mad dash out the door of her duplex to chase a cat. She knew he'd just wanted to make friends with it—not that the cat would understand. She'd wasted a good twenty minutes chasing after him. Even her electric teapot had decided to conk out right before she had her first cup of tea. Now this.

Her dad headed out with his passengers, and she hoped the disagreeable man wouldn't give her dad grief. Her brother had already taken up another group.

Amelia was getting ready to pack Winston's container

of kibble in the plane when a black SUV pulled into the parking area and the driver cut the engine. An orange canoe was secured on top. He must be the guy wanting the trip into the Boundary Waters. When a redheaded man exited the car and hurried to grab a couple of bags, her jaw dropped. *Gavin Summerfield.* In the flesh. *No way!*

Her heart raced. How could he keep showing up in her life?

Was this karma or what? It was like the gods had decided she was going to have to deal with this man, one way or another. After the issue with her first wolf boyfriend, she always carried a Taser gun. So she was ready if Gavin gave her any real trouble.

He turned to ask, "Is Henry White here?" Bags in hand, Gavin stopped dead in his tracks, frowning, looking just as shocked to see her as she was about seeing him here.

Amelia couldn't pretend she didn't remember him, at least not the time she'd knocked him flat on his back in her home. The other time, the crashed-plane time... She wasn't going to reveal anything about that. He didn't act like he knew where he'd seen her before, which had to be a good sign. She needed at least one today. She was eager to drop him off and leave him far behind. Hopefully, the time he'd scheduled for pickup would be when she wasn't available. Though she'd need to remind her dad and brother to watch what they said if the guy asked *them* if she'd ever been to Seattle.

"Are you the one who needs to get to the Boundary Waters?" she asked, almost growling.

"Yeah, I am." He seemed to want to say something

else but hesitated, glancing at the plane and then back at her. "Is Henry ready to fly?"

Could the day get any worse than this? "He had to fly another group out. I'll take you instead. Are you ready to go?"

Gavin frowned.

She folded her arms. She supposed, after their second meeting, Gavin was afraid she would dump him in the rapids instead of docking where she was scheduled to go. Or if he did recall she'd flown the plane she'd crashed during their first meeting, maybe he thought she was a bad pilot. Of course, if he knew about that, he'd probably figure she was a criminal.

Fine, she could just take Winston to Saint Paul, and the paddler could find his own way to the Boundary Waters. She wasn't about to deal with more disagreeable men. "Okay, listen, do you want to come with me or not?"

"Yeah, sure." Gavin hurried to join her.

Though her dad would want the income, she would have been just as happy to not take this fare anywhere. "Did you find your lost Samoyeds?" She asked because she'd always worried about whether he'd located them and returned them to their family.

"Yeah, at the house London had indicated."

"Male, right?" She swore Gavin's ears tinged red.

"Yeah."

"I saw that the police took the Michaelses into custody that day. I didn't know they had the puppies you were looking for. I'm glad."

"Where did you hear that?"

She raised a brow at him. "The newspapers."

"Michaels was armed and nearly shot me when I questioned him about the stolen dogs. And then his rabid wife came out and began beating on me, trying to get me off him. That's when the police took them into custody."

"Huh."

"You don't believe me?"

She smiled. "Don't believe everything you read and half of what you hear."

"Well, it doesn't matter how it went down. All that's important is that the pups were returned to their owners. Did you find foster homes for the two female Samoyeds you were caring for?"

"Yeah. My mom took Molly and Snowflake. She could never foster pets. She'd keep all of them. She works out of the main office, making the reservations for flights, and she often takes them with her."

"I'm glad to hear it."

As soon as the wind carried Gavin's scent to her, Amelia smelled that he was a wolf like her. Shocked to the core—because when she'd seen him before, he'd been human—she couldn't help but catalog more about him. Figuring he had to be fairly newly turned, she wondered just *how* newly turned. She was a royal—no strictly human genes for generations—so she had complete control over her shifting. Because of that, she didn't pay much attention to the phases of the moon. Now she wondered... Was he worrying he would shift? He had to be. And she was wondering when the full moon would make its appearance.

Wearing a T-shirt and stonewashed jeans that fit over nice muscles and hiking boots, he was in great shape. No matter what he'd been before, he was still tall, strong, and imposing. He held his head high, no slumping over, and his green eyes held her gaze, full of surprise, intrigue, and question.

She pegged him for an alpha gray wolf. Now she wondered if he had a pack. If so, she hoped they wouldn't have an issue with her family settling in their territory, *if* he was from this area. Then again, the last time she'd seen him, he was from Seattle. His license plate on the vehicle here indicated Minnesota, but maybe it was a rental car. She'd thought her last boyfriend was a lone gray wolf living in this area, but now she wondered if maybe he'd been in this guy's pack. What were the chances that two wolves would be in the same area and not belong to the same pack?

Then again, she and her family didn't belong to a pack either.

When Gavin set his gear down to shake her hand, he hesitated, his eyes suddenly widening, and Amelia was sure he had smelled she was a wolf. He took in her appearance again, not so casually this time, recognizing she was one of them—and that was important. His smile indicated he was more than interested in what he was seeing. Which surprised her.

He wouldn't have known she was a wolf before because he hadn't been one, so she realized what a shock this must be to him.

He asked, "You and your family are—"

"Arctic *lupus garous*." She wanted to set him straight right away. If he didn't like that she was an Arctic wolf, he could figure out another way to get to the Boundary Waters. She knew her dad would be annoyed if she pissed off a paying customer. Still, if Gavin didn't like

Arctic wolves—and they'd run into some grays who didn't—her dad couldn't fault her too much.

Amelia lifted her chin farther in a way that challenged Gavin to deal with it or find another ride.

Eyes sparkling, he cast her an elusive smile and stretched his hand out. "Well, hell, you have made my day."

She frowned, not understanding why he'd feel that way. "Wait, you're not an Arctic wolf, are you?" That would be too weird to be true.

"Yep. Along with all of my packmates."

"Oh." This could be a real problem. "Here? You live *here*? In the area? Permanently?"

When she didn't shake his hand, Gavin dropped the offer. "Uh, yeah, but we have no problem with other Arctic wolves living in the area, if you don't have any problem with us being here."

She did.

Great. Just great. Then again, he didn't seem to recall the plane incident, and the business of tasing him didn't seem to be an issue. He still appeared interested in her in a wolfish way. Too bad she'd already had a couple of bad experiences with wolves: one recently, and the earlier one with the robber who was also a cop. Not to mention she'd killed that boyfriend! Under acceptable circumstances, as far as she was concerned. But that didn't mean Mr. Cop Turned PI would feel the same way.

"So you moved here from Alaska?" he asked.

"Yeah. A couple of months ago."

Amelia had thought she and her brother would never meet prospective mates down here. Not that she was looking anytime soon. And this guy could be a mated wolf, though the way he was smiling at her said otherwise.

She and her father and her brother all flew. They didn't want to break up the family business, and they were wolves, so family meant everything. Her mom had wanted to live in an area that had a shorter winter. More than that, her mother had been worried about them flying in the dark, which was necessary for part of the year in Alaska, particularly on rescue missions. Seaplane landings at night could be much more dangerous. Doable. But dangerous.

"You don't happen to have a sister, do you?" Gavin asked.

What did he mean by that? "Just a brother."

"Well, that's great news too. We'd love to meet him and the rest of your family. We need to stick together."

No, no, no. This was so not what she wanted to hear. She and her family needed to stay far away from this guy.

"We'll help any of you out anytime you or your family need it."

Never, ever, ever. Though her mother had often said *Never say never*. Even so, as a wolf, Amelia was curious who was in Gavin's pack. A single she-wolf maybe, someone her brother could date?

"You know London Lanier, that retired police detective you met in Alaska?" she asked.

"Yeah? He was a great help to me in solving the case."

"He's an Arctic wolf too. That's why he went on a crusade about illegal hunting once he retired."

"He's working for the police again. Well, I'll be. *A wolf*. No wonder he didn't believe you were involved in trafficking dogs."

"Nope. He's my uncle."

Gavin didn't say anything about that for a moment. Then he frowned. "Your uncle."

"Yep."

Which meant her uncle knew she had tased Gavin.

"I knew there was something I liked about him."

"He liked what you were doing. He asked me, after the police and you left, why I'd tased you. He knew I wouldn't have unless I felt I had to."

"You told him you were running through the house naked and feared for your life?"

"Of course not. I didn't fear for my life. If you'd come into the bedroom, I would have tased you, or if I hadn't had time, I would have shifted into the wolf. As for the rest, only you and I know about that."

He studied her hard again. "I still say you look like someone I've seen in Seattle."

That's what she was afraid of.

Chapter 2

WHAT WERE THE ODDS THAT THE WOMAN GAVIN HAD accused of stealing Samoyeds would be the one piloting the plane he had to take today? He recalled that was her occupation in Big Lake and how he'd thought she could be smuggling stolen pets across the border.

He still felt like he'd met her in Seattle. Which was why he'd asked if she had a sister. Since wolves often had multiple births, maybe he'd seen her twin instead.

All decked out in a leather flight jacket and black, skintight pants and laced-up boots, her blond hair cut shoulder length and her green eyes fixed on him, the Arctic wolf was just as beautiful as when he'd met her in Alaska. He wondered how she'd feel if she knew he hated to fly. She'd looked highly annoyed that she had to fly him anywhere and probably wanted to kick him out somewhere over the Boundary Waters—until she'd discovered he was a wolf like her. Not just any kind of wolf. A white wolf too.

Even so, she was…prickly. Holding a grudge against him for entering her home and seeing her naked, maybe. He didn't entirely blame her there. His cop training told him she was hiding something else. Something about having been in Seattle.

"Have you been flying for long?" he asked, stowing his gear in the seaplane and hoping to get her mind off how they'd met before, because he was certain she was thinking of that meeting between them in Alaska, like he was.

"Since I was sixteen. So for twelve years." She motioned to a building. "I need you to fill out a couple of forms and make the payment."

Inside the office, a huge dog greeted them. A brown-and-white Saint Bernard, amber eyes smiling as he hurried to nuzzle Amelia. He licked her hands and then crossed the floor to greet Gavin.

"Hey, fella." Gavin loved dogs and scratched his head, making the dog's long tail wag.

"That's Winston. He's going with us."

"He must weigh about the same as a man," Gavin said, filling out the forms. "He'll burn more fuel." He couldn't imagine why she'd want to take the dog on a trip like that.

"Yeah, you're right. He's only a year old but weighs a hundred and fifty pounds. I need to take him with me." She didn't offer a reason why, only gave Winston a hug and then waited while Gavin filled out the paperwork.

"I take it Henry is your dad."

"He is."

"Well, your dad said he and your brother took a group out earlier." Gavin was hoping he'd learn something about the company group before he and Amelia even took off. He'd managed to get here only an hour after they left. Perfect, so he could locate them without looking like he was following them.

"Yeah, a couple of hours ago. A greeting-card company team out of Seattle. Don't tell me you missed your party and are trying to catch up with them!"

A couple of hours ago? They must have left ahead of

schedule. "No, I'm not with them. I just wondered where they'll be staying, hoping I can find more solitude." Gavin wanted to tell her the truth, but he couldn't. Work ethics prevented it. "Did they show up early then?"

"Yeah. Dad and Slade were glad because they had to take two planes to carry them there. They took them earlier than planned so Slade could return and take another group up. Since you said you helped the police take down Asher and Mindy Michaels, I wondered if you were here concerning Mindy."

"What do you mean?" Gavin asked, not following her.

"She was one of the passengers that my brother took to the drop-off point in the Boundary Waters."

Gavin rubbed his smooth chin. That was a new wrinkle in the situation. Was Mindy Michaels involved in criminal activities again, or had she cleaned up her act? "No, I didn't have any idea she was here. She's with the greeting-card company now?"

"She's a sales associate, I think. Well, believe me, it surprised me to see her here." Amelia took a deep breath.

Probably as much as he'd surprised Amelia by being here.

"You can't be a lone wolf, not if you're with a pack. So why would you be here alone? *Oh*, you want to run in the wilderness as a wolf. Gotcha."

"Right." Gavin paid her and then headed out to the SUV to get his canoe. Though he was glad to meet the she-wolf, he really needed to hurry so he could reach Conrad and his group as soon as possible.

She was beautiful, sexy, and...hell, she was a wolf. Gavin was always mission first, but...he cast another glance her way. She caught his gaze, then quickly looked away.

She loaded Winston, a huge, brown dog bed, his leather leash, a bag of treats, and chew toys while Gavin carried the canoe.

"So, you've only been here for two months and are fairly new to the area." Gavin helped her to secure the canoe on the plane.

"Yeah, we moved straight here from Alaska. We have to be careful about being seen in our wolf forms. We do much better in winter, though we have lots of wilderness out here too, so we've been enjoying the change."

"Same with us as far as blending with the snow as Arctic wolves. Were you born that way? Since I wasn't a wolf when I met you the first time, I didn't have a clue if you were one before." He retrieved his cooler and set it inside the plane.

"We were born that way. What happened to you?"

"We were turned by an Arctic wolf pack from Canada while we were in Maine. Long story. You wouldn't have any Canadian kin, would you?" Gavin figured it would be a good idea not to insult any of her family members if some of them were from the pack that had turned him and his partners.

"Some. Are you newly turned? Or were you changed some time ago? The full moon won't be a problem for you for a couple of weeks. Then the new moon means you won't be able to shift at all."

"We're not real new. There are nine of us…four adult males, two of whom are mated; their mates; and one of the couples has six-year-old triplets, two boys and a girl, born *lupus garous*. I'll be well out of the

Boundary Waters and home before I have trouble with shifting."

"You have another bachelor male in the pack? That's why you asked if I had a sister."

"Yeah. For the other guy." And to know if she had a sister who was such a look-alike that he'd mistaken Amelia for the one he'd seen in Seattle. "Are you single?"

"I am, and so is my brother. You don't have any single women in your pack?"

"No." He wondered if she believed his pack being more newly turned could be a problem for them. Some wolves who were born that way—like the pack in Seattle—really didn't like newly turned wolves. That made him think about the issue of Amelia being in Seattle. She wasn't newly turned, but he suspected the gray pack there wouldn't like any Arctic wolf encroaching on their territory.

The Seattle gray pack had figured the Arctic wolves would be nothing but trouble for their pack, too easily seen when running around Washington State as wolves, too much of a risk for the others.

Amelia finished tying stuff down. "Are you ready to go?"

"Yeah, sure." Gavin didn't sound sure at all, despite trying his darnedest to pretend otherwise. He looked at the plane for a moment, telling himself he wasn't going to crash this time, no matter how much he felt that any flight he took would end up that way.

She frowned at him. "Don't tell me you're afraid I can't fly you there."

She'd put Winston in a dog life jacket and had harnessed him in, which Gavin knew was a safety precaution. It didn't make him feel any less worried about it.

"It's not you." Gavin had no intention of telling her he hated to fly and ruin any chance he might have to date her.

———

Gavin seemed sincere that he wasn't worried about Amelia's ability to get him there in one piece. Then she wondered if he had a fear of flying, and she was the reason for it. She hated to think she might be. "You… you're afraid of flying." Not that she had any plans to date the wolf. She could see him turning her over to the police! Despite that trouble, if he hated what she loved to do most, that could cause issues—especially if *she* was the reason he hated to fly.

That was one thing she'd liked about her former boyfriend Heaton Compton, who lived in the area. He was a gray wolf, and he was also a pilot. If he hadn't been drinking bourbon while flying, they might have had a real start to a relationship. As it was, they didn't last long.

She handed Gavin an inflatable personal flotation device, a PFD, their hands touching, and their gazes caught for an instant. "Put that on. We'll be there in no time. Just climb aboard, strap yourself in, and close your eyes." Sometimes, she had to transport someone who was so terrified of flying that the passenger would have to take pills to relax.

"A life preserver." He got in and strapped himself in but didn't confirm his fear of flying. Which was a typical response from an alpha wolf who didn't want to appear weak.

"Yeah, we're not going to crash. If we did, everyone who is seat belted in and wearing a life preserver has a better chance at survival."

"Uh, yeah. My seat belt is on. I'm a good swimmer though. We didn't know any other Arctic wolf shifters were in the area, living only about two hours from us."

"Same here. You must run in different woods and have no need to come up to our area." She taxied out onto the runway, then took off. They were flying now, headed for the Boundary Waters, and Gavin sat back in his seat, seeming more at ease.

It appeared he wasn't going to talk about his flying phobia, which was probably best.

"We came because my mom wanted to be closer to civilization, as if we're at the center of any hot spot once we moved to this location. We're happy doing our business out here though. I was afraid there weren't any Arctic wolves in the area. What made you choose this area?"

"We're from Seattle originally, born and raised. Once we were turned, we couldn't return there. A gray pack had claimed the territory and threatened to kill us. Being newly turned, we didn't really have any recourse. We sold our business office and our homes, and we kept searching for a place that wasn't populated by wolf shifters. We needed to be up north so we had snow at least part of the year and found this place."

"That's awful that you had trouble with another pack! We've been lucky. We haven't had problems with any gray wolf packs. I guess none live in the area. Have you ever seen a guy by the name of Heaton Compton? He's a gray wolf. A loner. I dated him a couple of times. When I realized you were a wolf, I thought you might know him."

"No. Never heard of him. He probably has never traveled through our area." Gavin glanced back at Winston. He was peering out the window. "Your dog appears to love flying."

"Winston? First trip up. Yeah, he does seem to enjoy it. He's not my dog though. He was dropped off at a shelter because the owner got laid off and couldn't afford to feed him."

"That's a shame. I can't imagine anything harder than having to give up your dog."

"I agree."

"You're still fostering pets, like you were with the Samoyeds when I first saw you."

She felt her face heat. "I took him in. He's way too big for my duplex and its small yard for me to keep him. I was fostering him while looking for a home for him. With such a lightly populated area, I couldn't find anyone who wanted him. I fly pets to other shelters sometimes through a nonprofit volunteer service. I'm taking him to a bigger shelter in Saint Paul, where a couple want to adopt him for their ten-year-old boy's birthday. The caveat is that they need him by late this afternoon. The birthday party is tomorrow morning. If I don't get him there in time, they'll find another pet locally. That's why I'm flying him out. I'll have plenty of time to get him there, well before the deadline after I drop you off."

"Sounds like a good cause. Do you think he'll work out for the family?"

"Pilots for Pets is an excellent cause. I hope Winston will be good with the family. He's a real sweetheart. This breed loves families, other dogs, and strangers.

They're intelligent. That means they need a lot of mental stimulation. And they love to play. The family has a large fenced-in yard. Hopefully, they'll give him plenty of exercise and teach him all kinds of things."

Air turbulence caused the plane to drop, and Gavin grabbed his seat.

"Sorry," she said.

"It's not you. I was in a plane crash once. I was a police officer in Seattle at the time. I was the first to arrive at the scene of a jewelry-store robbery and offered to take the place of a woman they were holding hostage. She appeared to be around eight or nine months pregnant. They readily agreed."

Amelia hadn't known Gavin had taken the place of a pregnant store clerk. Had he done so as a good cop, or had he been in on the crime?

"I thought my fellow officers would rescue me. Instead, the robbers made off with the jewelry and me. What I hadn't expected was to end up at a small airfield and then be forced onto a plane that took off for Canada. Except we didn't make it. Wind shear probably caused the plane to hit the tops of the trees, and we ended up crashing. I was given a commendation for taking the jewelry-store clerk's place as a hostage. We all assumed she wouldn't have survived, had she been forced to go with them, between the plane crash and being left to fend for herself in the wilderness. I was out there four days before rescuers found me. I was lucky."

Amelia's heart was thundering, and she was glad he wouldn't be able to hear it over the engine noise. He hadn't mentioned a woman flying the plane or shown any indication he knew she'd been the one flying it.

Which she was grateful for. The men hadn't blindfolded Gavin, and most of the robbers had worn masks only part of the time, so she'd suspected Gavin might have been in on the heist. Or, they'd planned to kill him.

"That's awful. I'm so sorry to hear it. At least you survived."

"Uh, yeah, with two cracked ribs, a broken leg, and a concussion. And the trepidation of getting onto another plane after that."

"I'm so sorry," she said again. "You are a true hero." If he hadn't been in cahoots with her dead boyfriend. "What about the men who committed the heist?" What about Clayton? Had Gavin known him? They must have known each other if they were on the same police force.

"One of the robbers, the guy who seemed to be in charge—at least he was giving all the orders—died in the accident. Two of the other three were caught a few days later, one with a broken wrist, the other with cracked ribs. One got away scot-free. The robbers had been trying to make their way to the Canadian border, lugging the bags of jewelry. Some of it was never found. Either the one that got away had all the rest, or speculation was that the guy in charge had hidden his share before he died, knowing he couldn't hike it out of there like the other men thought they could.

"He must have convinced them to move on, or why wouldn't they have taken his share? We speculated that he hid it, thinking he'd retrieve it when he was feeling better, only he never got any better. He was armed with a gun, which is probably why the other robbers didn't take the jewelry from him. They wanted to get out of there before anyone located them. Unless the other man had the lion's share, and that seems unlikely."

Her jaw dropped. Clayton had hidden some of the jewels nearby? He must have done it when she was unconscious. She didn't know how long she'd been out of it. Once she was aware of her surroundings, she'd chosen to stay quiet, half hidden in brush, cautious, wanting to know what was going on before she made a move. She'd planned to take them out as a wolf, if anyone had discovered she was still alive. It was the only protection she'd had against them. All the men had been armed with guns, and she hadn't wanted to risk getting shot.

The woods had been filled with woodland noises— birds singing, bugs chirping—but no human sounds at all. Either everyone had perished, was unconscious, or had left the area. She'd finally decided she had to see who had survived and noticed Clayton on his knees, readying his gun to shoot Gavin. She'd grabbed a sturdy branch lying on the ground, rushed forth, and swung it at Clayton, thanking God he hadn't smelled her first. He'd heard her footfalls though and had turned to shoot her. She had gotten close to him and swung at him, connecting with him just as he'd fired a round. Thankfully, that had ruined his aim, the bullet missing her and hitting a tree behind her.

Gavin looked at her. "Oh, I forgot to mention the pilot."

Chills raced up her spine.

"The pilot got away," Gavin said.

"Out in the wilderness?" she asked, trying to feign real surprise, despite knowing that one of the robbers had made it out alive. But maybe not. Just because they hadn't captured him didn't mean he'd actually survived.

"Yeah. It was odd too. Searchers found her clothes buried some distance from the plane wreckage. The bloodhounds lost her trail. They easily tracked down two of the robbers' trails. The other guy must have had some wilderness savvy. The police figured the pilot must have dressed in a change of clothes—something more suitable for the weather and terrain—and torn off. Maybe *she* even took the loot. She would have been getting a cut, unless they'd paid her a set amount to fly the plane."

"*Oh right*. When most of the men couldn't survive out there on their own or get away without a trace, a woman had no trouble? Sounds like a stretch to me."

"She might have hooked up with the guy who disappeared. The men they caught would never tell investigators the whole story…who he was, who she was. We figure someday someone will find her and the other guy's remains. They suspect she didn't survive. Unless she was a rugged mountain woman or had friends who were able to pick them both up somewhere. As many days as it took rescuers to come for me that far out in the wilderness, that would be an unlikely scenario."

It was way past time to change the subject. "Why did you leave the force?"

"We just needed a change of pace."

Or he was on the take and he had to leave before the police found out about it? "Are you still a PI?"

"Yeah. My buddies and I grew up together, and after we did our time on the police force, we went into the PI business together. Which was a good thing, considering what happened to us. As newly turned wolves, we had a really hard time keeping our shifting under control for quite a while."

"I can only imagine. My family are royals, pure *lupus garous* for many generations, so we're fortunate that we can shift anytime we want."

Gavin glanced out the window at the view of the Boundary Waters. "It must be nice having control over your shifting at all times. I'd sure love to have that ability."

"It is. I guess you're planning to get a ride back to our hangar later to pick up your vehicle. You weren't going to get a flight back?"

"I'll be paddling to Ely. The guys were all on jobs, or I would have asked one of them to drive me there. Cameron's mate is minding the shop and the triplets so she couldn't drive me either. And Owen's mate is much more newly turned than us, so she sticks closer to the cabin."

"How did that happen?"

"One of Cameron's pups bit her when she fed him at a campsite near where we live."

"Oh no, that's not good."

"In the end, it all worked out great for Owen." A breeze was beginning to pick up, and Gavin frowned, feeling anxious. "We're not going to have trouble landing, are we?"

"The bay where I land should be sheltered enough if the wind doesn't pick up any more than this. It can be dangerous landing when the water is glassy too. Um, I guess I shouldn't have mentioned that part."

"I didn't think you'd have to worry about water that's too smooth." Gavin noticed she was frowning, and he smelled her anxiousness too, which didn't bode well. The smell of electrical charges and the rain in the air warned of an impending storm. It wasn't supposed to storm until tomorrow and then continue for a couple of days.

"Yeah, it's hard to tell you're close to the water when it looks like glass. I hate to mention this. Can you smell and feel the electrical charges in the air?" Amelia asked.

"Yeah. Are we going to make it?" He hoped they didn't have to return. He'd have to wait a couple of days to come back out here. He wanted every day to count during his investigation.

"If the bay's too choppy, no. I can't risk the plane or us. I'll have to take us back."

"Wouldn't that be risky for us too?" And if she managed to drop him off in the Boundary Waters, then tried to fly in the storm, she would continue to be at risk. He didn't want that.

"I'll take you with me to Saint Paul. That's saying the weather is better there. You can help me take Winston to the new shelter. We'd be ahead of the storm and just leave the plane there for the night."

He glanced at her. "And stay the night there together somewhere?"

"Let's just see what happens here. Hopefully, I can drop you off, no problem, and continue on my way."

"How far is it to the bay?" He hoped they would be there soon.

"Another twenty minutes. Just enjoy the view. Think of yourself as a wolf with wings, soaring high above two thousand lakes connected by rivers, all that beautiful forested land, islands, pristine. Pine, spruce, and fir make up the forests, along with birch, aspen, and maple. One million acres of woodlands and waterways. Couldn't be more perfect for a paddler. Or a wolf."

They suddenly heard a loud popping sound over the noise of the single-engine plane.

Fearing the worse, Gavin gritted his teeth. He knew that wasn't a sound he should be hearing.

The engine began making a grinding noise, a sputtering sound next, and then a final death rattle.

Amelia considered the instrument panels, then began looking at the area they were flying over.

The smell of smoke and burning fuel filled the air.

Gavin was sure this was bad. He wasn't going to comment, certain Amelia knew what she had to do, and he didn't want to interrupt her concentration by stating his biggest fear: they were going to crash.

The emergency light came on, indicating an engine fire. The propeller ground to a standstill. The plane grew eerily quiet.

Another pop sounded. Calm and in control, Amelia tried to call a Mayday. When she keyed the radio in and hit the transmission button, no squelch sounded to indicate it was working. She quickly ran through her checklist. The lights on the instrument panel all went dark. "Emergency backup battery should come on."

It didn't.

She glided the plane over a frothing river filled with rocks and rapids, cliffs on one side of the river, trees on the other. She couldn't land here. "Under normal conditions, we can land a seaplane either with the power off or the power on. With the power on, the pilot has better control of the plane."

Gavin couldn't believe it. He hoped they'd make it

safely when they landed. With choppy water and no power, he didn't think they would.

———

Amelia prayed she'd reach the lake, even if she couldn't make it to the more sheltered bay. The land was covered in trees, so she couldn't attempt to land anywhere else, and the surrounding lakes were too small to land on.

"The transponder," Gavin said, looking like he'd prefer jumping from the aircraft than landing in it on the rough water that was getting rougher as the winds picked up.

"Electrical system is out, and the emergency backup battery didn't come on. I would have set the transponder to Mode A Code 7700 to let everyone know we have a state of emergency, but I can't."

"What's the next step?" he asked.

She was glad he wasn't panicking, despite his fear of flying. She couldn't believe she could be crashing a second plane with him on board. "I'm gliding us in. If I do this right and we're lucky, we'll be fine. If we flip, the plane will fill with water. *Quickly*. If that happens, unfasten your harness. You have to find the door and swim out. It'll be dark in the cabin. With our wolf's night vision, you should be able to make out some things."

"What about Winston?"

"I'll get him. You just get yourself out of the plane." The pup was *her* concern. She didn't want to lose a passenger too.

Gavin unbuckled his harness and reached back to get one of his bags.

"What are you doing? Stay buckled in. I've got to land the plane."

"I've got to grab my satellite phone and let people know where we are, if you don't have any other way to do it."

She glanced at the pocket where she normally kept her own sat phone and realized she was flying her dad's plane and her sat phone was in the seat pocket on her plane.

"Hurry then."

The lake came into view, and she flew into the wind to slow the plane down, which would hopefully cause the lowest impact damage if she ran into trouble. She could easily lose control of the seaplane if she didn't compensate for the shifts in wind, with the gusts picking up.

Amelia began looking for a smoother area in the water to land. She'd never had to do this without power and with the water as choppy as this. From her training, she knew she had to put the plane down in the valley of the waves, landing on the crest of the wave and nosing in to go down into the valley. She only wished she could land under full control. She had to make do with what she had.

As she went over the landing checklist mentally, she realized the gear warning system was not working. She did a quick visual check to make sure. The landing gear was up.

"I'm landing. Return to your seat, and strap yourself in. As soon as we land, if we need to quickly evacuate, open the door to the aircraft, and get out."

"My sat phone is in one of my bags. I've almost got it." He buckled himself in, then pulled out the phone.

She landed on the crest of a wave. A gust of wind lifted the left wing, making the right wing clip the water and breaking it off with a crack. Her heart stuttered.

The plane flipped so quickly that she felt like she was on a roller-coaster ride, sideways, up, down, holding on for dear life, trying to recall what she needed to do. Make sure Gavin got out ahead of her, unharness Winston, help him out of the plane, then inflate the dog's life vest. She'd have to get the raft after that.

The plane had flipped upside down and was taking on water.

"Gavin, are you okay?" She hurried to unhook her harness. Every second counted.

It was dark inside as she unfastened her belt and heard Gavin unlocking his.

"Yeah. Door to my right. I'll get Winston. Do you have a life raft?"

"Back there with Winston, under his seat." Amelia headed back to Winston. "Don't inflate your PFD until you're outside the plane. I'll get—"

"Do you have another preserver?"

"Yeah. All the seat cushions are."

"Can you attach the carabineer from my bags to one of the seat cushions and shove it outside the plane?"

"Yeah." She was supposed to be in charge, but she was glad Gavin was good at coordinating an escape under pressure too.

"Let me help you unharness Winston," he said.

She unfastened the harness, and Gavin helped the dog to his feet.

"I'm taking him out now. Winston, come on, boy. You can do this." Gavin swam out of the plane, pulling Winston by the collar.

She hooked Gavin's bags to the seat-cushion flotation device and pushed them out through the open door.

Before she could swim out, Gavin returned and took a breath of the air in the cabin. "Go, I'll get the raft. See to Winston. We're a long way from shore, so we could have a problem with hypothermia. Maybe not Winston though. His fur coat might protect him. The raft should help us get in safely. I'm afraid the pup wouldn't make that long swim."

Gavin shoved the raft out, and Amelia reached around. She couldn't locate Winston's waterproof container of kibble. She swam out to join Gavin and the dog. She'd thought of getting out of the water and sitting on top of the seaplane's floats. But they might not get rescued until the storms died down, and the wind and cold air and their wet clothes would be worse. Plus, with a thunderstorm approaching, staying out on the water was much too dangerous. Not to mention that the seaplane was sinking.

The winds were whipping up the waves even worse now, and the sky was growing dark, thunder grumbling off in the distance, the storm headed their way. And they were a long damn way from shore. They needed to use the raft to get there as quickly as they could.

———

Gavin was tying the box-shaped form of the raft to one of the floats. Starting to feel the effects of the chilly air and water, he fumbled with the rope on the raft. If he could shift, his muscles would heat up significantly, and his wolf coat would help to warm him. But he needed to do this as a human.

The raft secured, he yanked the cord to inflate it. Nothing. *Hell*. He yanked again, and then with one last jerk on the cord, the raft popped open with such force that it knocked him back a foot in the water.

He was damn grateful the raft was intact, with no tears that he could see. He lifted his bags into the raft with them still hooked to the seat cushion. "My cooler's still inside the seaplane. Maybe we should get it in case we don't get rescued for a while," he said. "Do you want to get in and pull Winston while I push from behind?"

"Yeah, sure."

Amelia swam around to the other side, searching, and finally found the rope ladder, then climbed in while Gavin held on to the raft to stabilize it. She crawled across the floor of the raft to reach for Winston's collar. He was dog-paddling next to the raft.

As soon as she had hold of him and started pulling, Gavin began trying to push the heavy dog. "Up, up," Gavin said, straining to push the deadweight into the raft.

"Come up here, Winston. Come on."

The plane was groaning and sinking more.

Gavin was beginning to think he wasn't going to get the dog in the raft. Hopefully, Winston's claws wouldn't rip it. With Amelia pulling, the dog trying to gain purchase, and Gavin pushing from behind, Winston finally scrambled into the life raft and collapsed.

"Is he okay?"

"Yeah," Amelia said, checking him over. "He looks fine."

"You?"

"Yeah."

They needed to untie the rope before the plane sank. Gavin thought about the cooler. "I'm going for the food."

"The plane is going under. Maybe it's not such a good idea now. You could be trapped."

"Untie the rope before it goes down. I'll get free."

"Gavin, we need warmth and shelter first and foremost. We can survive without food until someone comes for us."

"It won't take but a minute." He still had a mission, and he planned to accomplish it, despite the setback. He'd need food and all his equipment. And his canoe. It had been secured upside down under the plane. That meant it would be right side up now. The canoe was so versatile that he could convert it to paddle like a kayak, a canoe, or a dinghy. It was virtually unsinkable and untippable. He really wanted to cut it loose.

He swam back to the open door and dove back into the plane, feeling his way around until he reached the cooler. At least it would float on its own. The plane was creaking, and he felt it shift. *Hell.* He grabbed the handle of the ice chest and shoved it out the door. The chest went straight to the surface of the water.

Gavin went up for air again. Amelia was holding on to his cooler, tying it to the raft.

He wasn't sure his canoe had made it unscathed, but he wanted to try to release it. He pulled a pocketknife out of his zippered pants pocket and dove down, feeling his way around the canoe until he could grab hold of the rope and begin to cut. It was taking too long. He swam to the surface and took a deep breath of air, and then dove down again. This time, he tried to pull one of the knots free. He felt the plane shifting lower again.

He felt panicked, concerned Amelia hadn't untied the raft in time before the plane sank completely.

When he went back up for air, he saw that the raft had floated away. Amelia was paddling back toward him.

"What are you doing?" She sounded highly annoyed with him.

"Getting my canoe. Be back in a sec."

Then he dove under, determined to free his canoe. This time, he felt it give. He tugged and tugged and felt it loosening further. He needed air again, and the plane was sinking. He would lose the canoe if he didn't keep trying. With a final tug, he felt it come free and shoot to the surface of the lake while he swam to join it.

He finally surfaced and took in great gulps of air. The winds and waves had pushed the raft maybe an eighth of a mile away. He had the canoe but no paddles. His lucky paddle was gone.

"We're coming for you!" Amelia yelled out to him. They were a little closer to shore.

"I'll paddle to you." He finally inflated his life vest. He was so cold that he was having a terrible time getting into the canoe. He finally managed and lay there, exhausted.

―――∾∾―――

Amelia paddled as fast as she could against the wind and the waves. She was elated that Gavin had freed his canoe, but she was angry with him too. Did he still want to paddle around the Boundary Waters just for fun after this disaster? He could have drowned. In his human form and not wearing cold-weather gear, he had to be freezing after being in the water for so long. She hoped he wouldn't become hypothermic before he could get into dry clothes and warm up. She was chilled to the bone, and she'd gotten out much quicker than him. If she could strip off her clothes and wear her wolf coat, she'd be fine.

Winston was sitting, panting, and watching Gavin paddle with his hand toward them. The cooler was slowing Amelia down, and she felt she wasn't making much progress at all.

"Are your paddles with your other gear?" She was glad her family had rafts in each of the planes and PFDs for everyone, including the dog. She was certain Winston couldn't have swum all the way to shore on his own. And she wasn't a really good swimmer.

"I think it was left behind."

"I'm coming and will tow you in."

The emergency locator transmitter, the ELT, should automatically come on. Then rescuers would know where the plane had gone down. That made Amelia feel slightly better as she continued to paddle toward Gavin. She and Gavin were ten miles at least from the bay where she should have set the plane down.

She kept trying to figure out what had happened to the plane. Why the engine had quit, everything electrical had shorted out, and the emergency backup battery hadn't come online. She didn't want to think it was sabotage. If it had been, then had the ELT been disabled too?

Great.

Why would anyone want to crash her plane?

Chapter 3

AS A WOLF, GAVIN WOULDN'T FEEL THE COLD LIKE HE DID AS a human. But he couldn't remove his clothes right now and shift. Besides, as soon as he was in the raft, he had every intention of taking over the paddling so Amelia could strip and shift to warm up.

At least he had clothes in the dry packs that they could wear, plus two single sleeping bags—in case one got wet—a tent, a tarp, and food to keep them going until someone came and picked up Amelia. He still had a mission. He was damn glad he'd rescued his canoe. He looked back at the plane that could no longer be seen. It could still be just below the surface, but with the roughness of the waves and the darkness of the day, it was impossible for him to tell.

"Gavin, you've got to be freezing."

"The storm's coming in fast and furious. You know how they are. It isn't safe out here with the lightning closing in on us. We need to take cover." He was stuttering a bit from the cold. "How do you feel? Are you sure you're okay?" She was cut up and bruised. As long as she wasn't badly injured, she'd heal quickly with their enhanced wolf healing genetics.

"I'm good. What about you? You look a little banged up." Amelia finally reached him and tossed him a rope.

He tied his canoe to the raft and then figured it would be just as difficult to climb from the canoe into the raft as it would be to jump into the water and use the ladder to climb into the raft. Since he hated to get into the cold lake again, he opted for showing off his agility skills— which, as cold as he was, were sorely lacking. "Nothing that won't heal soon. Besides, I'm used to roughing it."

With an arm and leg over the raft and the rest of his body in the canoe, Gavin struggled to get into the raft while Amelia steadied the canoe. In the middle of making the move, he wondered if he should have just pulled the raft behind the canoe.

Once he collapsed in the bottom of the raft, he said, "Go ahead and take off your clothes and shift."

"No. You've been in the water far too long. You need to shift first."

Gavin was going to argue that with the water temperature between 68 and 70 degrees, they could have lasted twelve hours if they were floating in the lake the whole time. Amelia picked up the paddle again and headed toward shore.

"All right. For a few minutes, and then I'll take over." He began to remove his clothes. He was having so much trouble untying his boots that she set the paddle down and began to help him. They finished untying the boots, and she pulled them off. She tugged off his socks, and then helped him out of his life vest.

Her fingers were numb too, and she was having trouble with his zipper. She finally managed to unzip his cargo pants, while he removed his T-shirt. Finally, he tugged off his cargo pants. "This life vest won't fit right on a wolf," Amelia said.

"I can swim without it if I need to." Gavin pulled off his boxer briefs. He wasn't planning on being a wolf for very long. Off in the distance, streaks of lightning struck the ground, and thunder boomed only a mile away. "We need to take cover from the thunderstorm. Maybe I should just skip shifting."

"One of us needs to be a wolf to warm up. We can switch off after a while."

He wanted her to warm up, so he'd paddle the rest of the way after he changed back. Between the cold-water shock to their systems, the terror of experiencing the plane crash, the struggle of pulling Winston into the raft, and all the paddling she'd already done, Amelia had to be exhausted. He was naked now and calling on the shift, feeling the heat suffuse every cell in his body, warming him like a hot bath deep inside. And then he was a wolf, his thick, double coat of fur able to deflect the water.

"I'm glad you rescued your canoe, but I'm *not* happy with the way you could have drowned yourself."

He'd had to try, though she was right.

She began to paddle again. "I have to say, you're beautiful as a wolf."

He moved toward her, licked her cheek, and settled next to her to share his heat, his head resting on her lap.

"Now, *that's* nice."

He woofed in agreement. He still didn't like that she was so cold, but he was glad to help her any way that he could. He hoped she didn't believe she had to save the day now that the plane had crashed. Looking down at his wolf nails and the raft, Gavin hoped he didn't puncture the rubber. He glanced at Winston, whose nails were neatly trimmed. He was sitting up, ears perked, nose sniffing at the wind. He seemed to be happy with the rafting excursion now, out in the wilderness, smelling all the interesting scents. Gavin couldn't imagine the dog had ever been here before, so everything was new to him.

Rain began to fall on them, and Gavin wished it had held off a bit. It wouldn't reach his skin. He needed to shift and take over. Then he had an idea. His rain gear was in one of the bags. He could shift, dress in dry clothes, and put the rain gear on, and then Amelia could shift into her wolf. Why hadn't he thought of that before he shifted and it began to rain? He was certain hypothermia had messed with his thought processes.

Amelia had been paddling for some time when he finally shifted. "I'll take us the rest of the way now. You need to wear your wolf coat and warm up."

"All right." She kept paddling while he dug out some of his clothes.

"Good thing you have rain gear."

"Yeah. I sure wish I'd thought of it earlier. Rain jacket too, for lighter rains. You need to just shift and get warm."

"I will, as soon as you're dressed. We're drifting back out because the wind has shifted, so I'm fighting against it to keep us going in the right direction."

"Do you see the cliffs? Where there's a rock ledge for shelter?" He pulled on some board shorts—at least they would dry out fast and were meant for the water—a T-shirt, and the rain jacket and pants to keep him warmer in the chilly breeze.

"Yeah. It should give us some protection from the elements."

"Agreed. Okay, I'll take over. Go ahead and strip."

Shivering from the cold, Amelia let out her breath. "I bet you say that to all the women you see."

"You're the first." Gavin still couldn't believe the woman streaking across her house in front of him had been a wolf all along. A white wolf.

He paddled harder and faster than she had and was making some real progress.

She was struggling to remove her clothes in the raft, which was rocking and rolling with the wave movement. "You made this look so much easier."

"You helped me when I was so cold the first time." He set the paddle on the floor of the raft and moved over to help her undress. "I hate to say this"—he untied one of her boots, and then the other—"but I should have left the sat phone in the bag when you told me to stay in my seat."

"Don't tell me. It's at the bottom of the lake with the plane."

"Yeah. I have a cell phone too, and it's in my pocket. I doubt it'll work."

"Even if it wasn't waterlogged, you can't get any reception out here." She pulled out her cell phone. "Mine is waterproof, though I don't think they had swimming in mind. In this waterproof case, it'll probably be okay. The problem still is no cell reception. I had already packed my bags and my sat phone on my plane and forgot about them when we switched planes."

She pulled off her shirt, and he waited to see if she needed any help with anything else. She was wearing a hot-pink sports bra and bikini panties, and she fumbled with the back hooks on the bra. Her fingers had to be numb.

"Here, let me." He stayed in front of her, because

moving around in the raft was unsettling everyone. He felt around the back of her bra until he found the hooks and unfastened them. After slipping her bra off, he reached down to help pull off her panties.

Once she was naked, she immediately shifted. Even though the temperature was normally around seventy-five during the day in the summertime, the storm had cooled the temperature to around sixty, with a wind chill of lower than that.

Amelia woofed at Gavin, thanking him for helping her, and when he began paddling again, she curled up next to him. He reached down and rubbed his cold hand over her head. They had taken on so much water—from the wind-swept waves and trying to get Winston into the raft, from Amelia and Gavin climbing aboard, and now from the rain—that he wished one of them could begin bailing out the raft. The water in it was slowing them down. So was the headwind.

Lightning flashed across the darkening sky. Gavin didn't like that they were still so far from shore while the storm raged overhead. Then the rain came down in a deluge. *Great*. More water in the raft. That's all they needed. He couldn't paddle and bail at the same time.

Amelia moved closer to him and rested her body against his leg as he continued to stroke the water with the paddle. The rigorous exercise was the only thing halfway warming him until she cuddled up next to him, and that helped too. He wanted to just shift and curl up with her in the raft and let the wind and the waves take them where they would. But the electrical storm made it too dangerous for them to be out on the water longer than necessary.

Gavin was still aiming for the cliffs where the rocky shelf jutted out. It appeared to be high enough that they could sit underneath for protection from the rain, wind, and lightning.

After another hour, he was finally able to say, "We're almost there."

In her wolf form, Amelia sat up to get a look.

As soon as he reached the rocky shore, she jumped out of the raft. Gavin climbed out and pulled it in to shore. Then he climbed back into the raft and grabbed hold of Winston's collar, urging, "Come on, boy. We need to get out of this weather." They needed to hurry. "Just a few more steps."

The raft was rocking, and Winston seemed happy to remain where he was.

Amelia leaped back into the raft and nuzzled Winston to get him to move with her, and then they both jumped out. She coaxed him to the safety of the rock alcove under the ledge overhang. Gavin began unloading his gear from the raft.

Once the canoe was empty and he'd untied it and the cooler from the raft, he carried the raft into the woods and tied it to a tree so the wind wouldn't catch it and carry it off. Afterward, he hauled the canoe up into the woods and secured it between tree branches. Then he grabbed his bags and joined Amelia and Winston under the rock ledge.

The two of them were sitting together, warming each other and wagging their tails. Winston was still wearing his life jacket. "Hey, fella, guess you can get out of this," Gavin said as he unfastened the preserver and set it aside.

Then he headed back out into the storm to retrieve the
cooler and the other containers that Amelia had rescued
and set them at one end of the alcove. He needed to dress
in warmer clothes and boots so he could make a real
shelter for them. As humans, they could last for days
without water, even longer without food. As wolves,
they could try to catch meals, drink water from the lake,
and sleep in their fur coats for warmth. With a shelter,
they could stay here nice and safe as humans.

Gavin began stripping out of his rain jacket, and to
his surprise, Amelia shifted. Naked, she began pulling
off his rain pants.

"You don't need to help me. You'll be cold all over
again," he warned, removing his board shorts.

"*You're* too cold. Are you going to shift?" She was
beginning to tremble already.

"I'm going to dress in something warmer and hang up
the tarp to make a real shelter to keep us warm and dry."

"Okay, I'm helping."

Gavin appreciated it, though he'd had every intention of doing this on his own so she could stay with
Winston under the shelter. "I've got several days' worth
of clothes, including some sweats you can wear until
your clothes are dry." He dumped out the contents of
one of the waterproof bags, while she pulled the sleeping bags out of another.

Amelia spread out the sleeping bags. "Two singles?"
She said it as if she thought he often took a girlfriend
with him. If he had, he would have just had a double.
She could smell the bags, and though he'd washed them
after the last trip, she would only smell a faint residue
of his scent. No woman's scent. He was glad for that.

"Yeah, I take two in case one gets wet. Then hopefully I still have a dry one. I learned that lesson when freezing fog blew through the tent vents in the middle of the night and got my sleeping bag all wet. Since then, I usually keep a spare sleeping bag in a dry pack, just in case." He pulled out a pair of gray sweats.

"Uh-oh." Amelia was eyeing the sleeping bags as if she'd done the wrong thing.

He shook his head. "They're here for us to use. I'll make a fire once it stops raining. We can hang the tarp to block some of the wind that's whipping around in here. Once we've set up housekeeping, we can strip and shift."

"Okay, or if we're warm enough by then, we could stay as we are." She hurried to pull on the sweats. "Maybe I can wear a pair of your dry socks and then put on my wet boots."

"Yeah, sure. Here." He handed her a pair of black socks.

She sat down on the pebble-covered floor of the alcove to pull them on.

"So what do you think happened?" Gavin asked, sitting next to her while Winston lay down on the floor and closed his eyes.

"For everything to go wrong?" She shook her head.

"Sabotage?" Gavin finally tied on his spare pair of hiking boots.

"Maybe. I can't imagine how every system went down a few seconds after each other. I'd say it could be sabotage." Amelia sighed. "I don't think I have ever been so cold and wet in my life."

He glanced at her. "You don't need to help. I can do this on my own."

"We can get it done quicker if we both do it."

"You look damn good in my sweats. Much better than I do." He hurried to pull on jeans and then a blue sweatshirt.

"Thanks." She tied on her boots.

"You can wear the rubber rain suit to keep you dry."

"What about you?"

"I have a lightweight rain jacket."

The wind was whipping around their sheltered area, and he needed to get the tarp up now. He slipped on the rain jacket, while she put on the rain suit. She was swallowed up in it.

He began to tie the tarp to a tree jutting out of the side of the rocks. Then he secured the other end with stones from the beach a few feet away, both on the top edge of the ledge and on the floor of their shelter. Amelia helped him move the smooth stones, making a pile of them for him to use. They made a good team.

He paused to watch her, and an elusive memory of being in the woods with her made him wonder again why she seemed so familiar. Not that he'd known her for more than a passing experience. Still, he just remembered seeing her face, and then she was gone.

She glanced up at him. "What's wrong?"

"Are you sure you were never in Seattle? I had the strangest notion I saw you in the woods somewhere when I was still living in the area."

"In the woods?" Amelia continued bringing rocks over. This time, she was making a fire ring.

"I don't know. I went camping with the guys a few times. Saw horseback riders once, other campers and hikers…" He shook his head. "I don't know."

"I've never ridden a horse. And I've never camped in the woods anywhere near Seattle. Alaska? Yes. Lots."

Gavin knew he'd recall where he'd seen her if he thought about it long enough.

He wished it would stop raining, but he didn't voice his opinion. "Okay, the tarp is secure enough unless the winds get much higher. Why don't you take off your clothes—"

She began stripping. "Believe me, I never get naked in front of a wolf I barely know. Especially this often."

"Except the one time."

"That was different. You *weren't* a wolf that time, and you weren't supposed to be in my house."

He zipped the two sleeping bags together, then spread them out so the inside was facedown to keep Amelia and him dry. They could wrap themselves up in the bags later, if they felt warm enough to shift into their human forms and were still stuck here. "I have to say, I'm still puzzled why you flashed me in your house in Alaska. If you were trying to get my attention, you sure had it."

"Uh, yeah. Well, it was either that or shift into my Arctic wolf half. I didn't want to scare the puppies." She explained to him about the front door not shutting properly. The faucet in her master bathroom not working. The towels in the guest bathroom washed and in the dryer. It was just one of those days, Amelia told him.

"And you had left your clothes in the bedroom," Gavin said.

"Right. I mean, I never take them in the bathroom with me. Then I heard you, and I figured I'd need to grab my Taser and my cell phone, which were both in the bedroom."

"And if I had tried to grab you—"

"I would have turned into a vicious Arctic wolf. I could have flown you off to the wilderness, somewhere no one would ever have found you."

He couldn't imagine what he would have thought if she had turned into a wolf. "Good thing you only tased me."

"You probably never figured me tasing you could be a good thing."

"You're right."

She removed her clothes again, and he did too, thinking he should start a fire. In their wolf coats, they would be fine—as long as no one came upon them and saw a couple of wolves and one Saint Bernard, with no humans in sight.

Gavin wondered what his pack would think of him now. He knew his friend David Davis would be wishing he had this job himself, although he'd probably prefer to skip the ditching-the-plane-in-the-water scenario.

Chapter 4

AFTER SHIFTING INTO HER WOLF, AMELIA STARED AT GAVIN'S sexy physique for a moment before he shifted too. He was beautifully muscled and truly hot, hard all over, and she couldn't help noticing he was well-endowed. Nothing little about him. Red hair trailed down his belly to his half-aroused cock, despite the chilliness. He smiled at her perusal before he shifted into his white wolf. He was taller than her, his tail fluffy, his coat fully fluffed—impressive. Even with the shift, their muscles would heat, so by wearing their warm, dry fur coats, they stopped shivering. She was grateful to have an Arctic wolf coat and Gavin to curl up with.

Amelia reminded herself she didn't go out with cops any longer, wolf or otherwise. Now she was sure he knew he'd seen her. He was just confused about exactly when or where. He had to have been in pain when they'd crashed, and she'd tried to keep out of his sight, though he'd had his eyes closed when she struck Clayton with the stout tree branch. She knew from the way Clayton had been giving orders that he'd been in charge of the heist. That hadn't lasted long when he was so badly injured and couldn't tell his cohorts what to do.

She was dying to ask Gavin if he knew the cop. Had they been friends? Had they been partners in the crime?

Amelia hadn't thought she'd mate Clayton, but he'd been fun to date while it lasted. She'd been one growly wolf when he'd threatened her with his gun and forced her to help with their getaway.

Gavin suddenly sat up on the sleeping bags as if he'd heard something, and she sat up too, listening to the rain and wind and thunder.

He nuzzled her face, then went out into the rain, returning a few minutes later to curl up with her again. She wondered why he'd left so suddenly. Maybe to relieve himself.

Winston seemed to think the sleeping bag had been laid out to serve as the canine bed. Though Amelia couldn't blame him, since she and Gavin were both wolves and sleeping on it. And Winston's own dog bed was still in the plane. Winston rose to his feet, stretched, then joined them and snuggled, treating them like they were his wolf pack. She'd never let any of the dogs she'd owned or fostered sleep with her. Not because she wanted to show who was alpha and king of the roost, but because she was such a light sleeper that a restless dog would wake her all night. Also because dogs got their feet dirty or wet, and she could just see them coming to bed with her and leaving paw prints all over her bedding.

It wasn't long before Winston began kicking his legs in his dream world. Which was another reason not to take a dog to bed. Amelia had imagined he'd sleep the night and hadn't counted on dog dreams. As exhausted as she was and Gavin had to be, she'd figured they'd sleep like the dead too. She'd camped several times, but never quite like this—with a bachelor male wolf, a huge dog, and a stormy night in a little cave-like alcove after crashing a plane.

With all the time it had taken for them to paddle to

shore, it was now late evening. Though the sun was already setting this late in the summer, the sky still looked much darker than normal because of the storms in the area.

She began to think about the business of sabotage again. And Gavin's job—he was a PI. What was the chance he was really on a mission out here? Not just here to enjoy the solitude and get in a little paddling and fishing and running as a wolf. He was part of a pack. Why wouldn't one of his pack members come here with him? She had been the one who had said he was here to run in the wilderness as a wolf, thereby giving him an alibi, when that might not be the case at all.

Had he lied to her? He'd better not have. Though she couldn't really blame him, since she'd lied about seeing him before.

She thought back to when he'd asked if they'd dropped off any other party earlier, saying he wanted solitude. What if he really was on a spy mission concerning the earlier group they'd ferried out here? Mindy Michaels had been with that group. What if he'd been investigating her after the earlier situation with having her arrested? What if the plane losing all its power had to do with a PI job Gavin was on?

Amelia ground her teeth.

She considered the business with the plane again and all the trouble that had befallen it. It might not have anything to do with Gavin. Her dad had fired a man recently. The same man she'd dated. The gray wolf by the name of Heaton Compton.

Still as a wolf, Gavin rose to his feet, and she wondered what he was doing now. He shifted, then grabbed

a camp blanket from his bag and covered her with it.
Then he shifted again and curled up against her as a
wolf, maybe thinking if one of them wanted to shift
later, they wouldn't have to find a blanket. She thought
about that—them lying naked together as humans. She
admitted the notion had appeal. Was it because he was
an Arctic wolf and the only one she'd met in this area?

She knew that wasn't so. She'd dated several Arctic
wolves in Alaska, and she hadn't felt that way about
any of them. She believed the attraction was due to a
combination of reasons. First, he was sexy as hell. Then,
he'd gone after pet traffickers, risking his own life, and
he'd offered himself as a hostage in the jewelry heist.
He'd even rescued her pups. He was also good with
animals. The first thing he did after they crashed was
free Winston from the plane. Being an animal lover was
a big plus in her book. Sure, the Arctic wolves she'd
known cared about other wolves. Not all the men she'd
known had loved other kinds of animals. Two of them
didn't like that she was fostering dogs. Some of her
foster dogs didn't like them either. She'd hoped they'd
learn to like one another, but it didn't happen.

The part about Gavin not liking flying… Well, she
could understand his reasoning on that. Especially when
she probably had a hand in his phobia. But she didn't
think he'd be happy when he found out the truth.

If she hadn't been as comfortable in her fur coat as
she was right now, she would have shifted and questioned Gavin about what he was really doing here. She
was warm with him like this, the wind howling, the rain
slowing to a constant patter, and rumbles of thunder still
grumbling away. She cuddled against him further.

She slept for a time, then at some point, she felt his arm wrapped around her. She realized her wolf's head was resting on Gavin's naked, muscled chest, and he had shifted. He was under the blanket with her.

As much as Amelia knew she shouldn't do this without knowing him better, and not while she still felt so at odds over the heist situation, she shifted too, snuggling her whole body against his. She'd never imagined she'd be doing this with a hot Arctic *lupus garou* who had been her passenger—when she had only meant to drop him off in the bay and then get on her way. Winston was curled up on the other side of Gavin now, his head on Gavin's legs.

She groaned to herself, remembering she'd missed the deadline to drop the dog off at the shelter. She felt bad that he didn't have a home to go to now. Brushing her arm against Gavin's warm abs, she reached out and petted Winston on the head, loving the big pup. Sometimes, she had a hard time remembering he was just a young'un, as big as he was. She wished she had a big enough place. If she did, she'd keep Winston in a heartbeat.

Her thoughts shifted to the plane and seeing it flounder until it sank.

She couldn't help thinking of her dad and how angry he would be about the plane. Well, alarmed about her first, of course. And her passengers. Then he'd be furious regarding the cause of the wreck. As much as she hated to have to go through that, she was glad her father hadn't had to. She was glad she was the one here with Gavin instead of her dad. Was she nuts or what?

Gavin caressed her hair, and she sighed against his chest. She breathed in his spicy, male scent and that of the stormy rain. The sound of his heartbeat against her ear and of the rain falling all around them soothed her. She shouldn't be feeling anything for this wolf. It could only hurt her if he learned the truth about her.

He leaned down and pressed his mouth to her forehead and kissed her. She knew she shouldn't do this. Every human part of her brain shouted: don't feed into this intimate moment. The wolfish side craved to make the connection. To see if they were meant to have something deeper.

Amelia wrestled with her feelings. Logically, after what they'd been through, she felt closer to him than to guys she'd only dated a couple of times. Going through a life-threatening crisis with a guy, and seeing how he handled it, showed a lot about character. Certainly more than if she were just eating in a restaurant and having a conversation with a date where each of them was careful to say the right things and act the right way to help decide if they were the right ones for each other.

Emotionally, she was torn. No way should she kiss him back. But she wanted to see if his kiss matched her expectations. Logically, it made sense—as far as her wolf half was concerned. As far as her human half was concerned, it made no sense when she considered what he would think if he learned the truth about her.

So why in the hell did she tilt her head up, wanting to kiss him back? Her wolf feelings were running amok.

He angled his head down, and she moved higher on his body to reach his mouth, rubbing her scent over him as if claiming him, melting against him. She pressed her lips against his hot mouth. That quickly escalated to them parting their lips and deepening the kiss. Their tongues stroked, and their bodies writhed against each other's, her whole body craving more, her nether region already aching with need.

Winston suddenly moved his head off Gavin's legs and resettled to sleep some more, which immediately brought Amelia to her senses.

Breathless, she pulled her mouth from Gavin's and sank against his body again. "My God, Gavin… You are a…wolf." He was; there was no denying that. For being a much more newly turned wolf, he surprised her. He had all the right wolf moves where she was concerned.

He chuckled and kissed her hair, his hands stroking down her back, his touch gentle but heating her up all over again. "So…are…you."

She'd never felt like this with another wolf. As if she'd known him for much longer than she had. She wondered if this was like what had happened between her parents—two wolves meeting, sensing they were the ones for each other. She knew that in the wild, wolves didn't take months to decide such a thing. That was why the shifters often mated as soon as they found a wolf who felt totally right to them. It wasn't something they took lightly because wolves, shifters included, mated for life. Boy, would she be screwed if she told him of her connection to the dirty cop.

Winston whimpered in his sleep. Gavin reached down and petted his head. "It's okay, boy. We're here to protect you."

"You're good with Winston. Have you had a dog before?"

"We had German shepherds growing up. That was when I was a kid. They were like part of the pack. I learned a lot about canine behavior from them. It helped me when I became a part-time wolf. What about you? Have any dogs?"

"Yeah, Alaskan malamutes when we were growing up. We went sledding, took them snowshoeing with us, and ran with them as wolves sometimes."

It was still raining and dark out, not time to get up. And then, enjoying the feel of his hard body beneath hers and the sexy smell of him, Amelia listened to his heartbeat drumming against her ear and the rain falling in a steady stream outside their protected alcove and fell back to sleep.

Although it rained off and on all night, the rock overhang and tarp protected them, and they stayed dry. Thunder boomed right overhead and everyone jumped a little bit, their sleep disturbed. Amelia swore she saw the shadow of a man silhouetted against the tarp, illuminated in a second flash of lightning. She barely breathed, watching, waiting, not about to wake Gavin when it was most likely nothing. Another flash of lightning lit the sky, and there was no shadow. It had to have been her imagination. She'd watched way too many scary thrillers.

Yet she couldn't sleep. Trying not to disturb Gavin, she left the sleeping bag and shifted into her wolf, then went out into the storm, breathing in the smells. Luckily, scents lasted longer in cool, damp forested areas. In fact, scents needed moisture to survive, so rain wouldn't destroy them. Wind and rain could disburse them. The wind was blowing, and she did smell the scent of a man and bears. Four wild black bears. A sow and her cubs?

Might be. The sleuth of bears could be unrelated males. Though bears didn't live in family packs like wolves, sometimes males of varying ages would live in close proximity. Not hunt or live together, but they could be in the same area with the older males serving at the top of the hierarchy. She still suspected the group was a mother and cubs.

Amelia relieved herself in the woods, listening for any sign of the bears or a man. Had they been there earlier? She wasn't certain. Cold and wet and concerned about the lightning all around them, she had been too busy trying to get Winston into the alcove and set up their shelter, then sleep. She hadn't been trying to catalog scents. Maybe Gavin had noticed.

She returned to the alcove, and standing just outside it, she shook off the excess raindrops collected on her outer fur before she stepped inside and shifted.

Gavin, the fierce-looking Arctic wolf, nearly ran into her, looking like he was ready to find and protect her. She hadn't expected that. She licked his face in greeting and thanks and entered the alcove. He turned to watch while she shifted and climbed into the sleeping bag. "I smelled bears and a man out there. The scents could be from several days ago. I have no way of knowing," she said.

He shifted and joined her. "I thought I heard a bear, which is why I left earlier."

"Then that's what I saw. A bear silhouetted against the tarp when lightning lit up the whole sky. She probably smelled the food you have."

"She?"

"She or he was standing up. Since I smelled four bears, I was thinking the one was a sow and the other three might be her cubs."

"Okay. We'll have to safeguard our food when we get up in the morning. All we'd need is to have bears steal it."

"They'd better not even think about messing with our food," Amelia said, sounding all growly.

Gavin pulled her into his arms. "I'll protect you, Winston, and the food."

But she had every intention of making such a racket if the bears came back. They would need protection from her, not the other way around.

Chapter 5

A GLIMMER OF LIGHT FINALLY WOKE AMELIA EARLY THE next morning, and she ran her hand over Gavin's chest, loving that she'd had his warm body to sleep against but knowing she shouldn't. "Are you awake?" she asked.

"Yeah." He rubbed her arm with a light caress, then took a deep breath, his chest rising and falling. "It's times like these I'm glad I'm a *lupus garou.* Especially when I was lucky enough to share my sleeping bag with you." Then he frowned. "How old are you, really?"

She snorted. Of all the things to ask her! "You know a man is never supposed to ask a woman her age." But she knew what he was getting at. She was a royal, her wolf lineage not diluted by a lot of strictly human genes for generations. When she turned twenty, she began aging one year for every five, so she wasn't really old, like some who had aged even more slowly before the great Time Collapse, as wolves were now calling it. She didn't have the life experiences of wolves who might be decades older in human years, having lived through all kinds of wars and technological changes in the time before the change. But they were much younger in every physical aspect.

"I'm twenty-eight based on a human's actual life span, but because of the extended wolf genetics, I'm physically twenty-one. And you?" she said.

"I was twenty-five when I first met you in Alaska,

then I was turned the next year. That means I'm twenty-six in wolf-aged years, thirty-two in real human years."

"Okay, so we're four years apart in human years, and—"

"A year apart in wolf years. What do you think about that?" Gavin twisted a curl of her hair between his fingers.

"I'm glad I'm not robbing the cradle. Are you glad you're not hooking up with an ancient wolf?" Not that she was really "hooking up" with him.

He laughed. "It's one of those things I forget about, usually because we aren't around wolves that have lived for so many years. The ones we've met don't talk about their historical pasts, but even if they did, it would sound like they were just talking about historical facts, not about their own pasts. I was just curious."

"I don't blame you. If you hadn't told me you'd been turned a few years ago, I would have wondered the same thing about you. The historical past is still just the historical past to me."

Winston lifted his head as if he thought maybe it was time to get up, but when he saw that Gavin and Amelia weren't moving, he laid his head down and fell back to sleep.

"If it wasn't still raining, I'd start a fire." Gavin let out his breath. "I've been thinking about the situation with the plane. If it was sabotaged to the extent that the electrical system was shorted out and the emergency battery didn't work, then the ELT was probably disabled. When will anyone miss you?"

"Not for another day, unless the weather continues to be bad. And then no one would miss me for a couple of days. We weren't flying anywhere today because of the weather, which means I'd just chill out at home, catching up on the next show in my conspiracy theory series. If the weather continues to be bad tomorrow, the same thing. What about you?"

"No one will expect me back until I'm ready to return in about nine days or so. Unless I had some news to share."

"Well, they'll miss me before that. Maybe everyone will worry about us because the weather turned so..." She paused. "God, I hope my dad and brother are all right. What if someone actually did sabotage my dad's plane, and the bastard did the same to all our planes? If not, I hope my brother and dad landed safely before the storm caused problems for them."

Gavin ran his hand over her shoulder. "We need to get you out of here."

"You're staying?"

"Yeah."

"I think we're going to need a private investigator to look into this matter, by the way." Every time she woke last night, she'd been thinking about it. It would take months for aviation accident investigators to sort this out. They needed results faster. "I didn't thank you for everything you did. I don't believe I would have gotten Winston out on my own or into the raft by myself. Certainly, I couldn't have retrieved everything else out of the plane like you did. If we hadn't had the raft, we probably wouldn't have made it. You must have been half-frozen swimming in the water, as cold as it was with the wind chill and rain."

"Shifting into the wolf for a while made all the difference."

Amelia agreed. "Is work slow, and that's why you've taken a vacation?" She figured it was time to learn the truth about why he was here.

"I'm…not on vacation. The truth is, I'm on a case."

"What if the plane going down had something to do with what you're investigating?" She'd been thinking it had something to do with her or her family's company. But what if Gavin was investigating someone and *that* was the reason for the sabotage? They had to consider all plausible or even seemingly unlikely avenues.

Gavin raised his brows at her, appearing as though he didn't think *he* could have had anything to do with the disaster. "Normally, I never discuss a case I'm on with anyone other than my partners. It's a matter of ethics. We don't share what we're doing with anyone, or clients won't feel their cases are being handled confidentially. Since we're in a bit of a quandary over this situation with your plane, in the unlikely event my case has anything to do with what happened to it, if you can keep this a secret—"

"I can. What if it had *everything* to do with it? What exactly are you working on? It's about the other party my brother and dad brought out here yesterday, isn't it? The ones you were interested in, though you had said you were just concerned there'd be too many people around." She climbed out of the sleeping bag and began pulling on the sweatpants.

Gavin was still lying in the sleeping bag, his arms behind his head, looking up at her as she yanked the sweatshirt over her head.

"Yeah, it's about them. Or actually a man who's with the group."

"Man?" Amelia had immediately assumed it was about the woman he'd helped to arrest before. She sat on the edge of the sleeping bag and pulled on her socks. "Not Mindy Michaels?"

"Mindy Michaels? I told you I didn't know she was out here."

"Let me guess. The perp you're after is cheating, or supposedly cheating, on his wife."

"That's the gist of it. You didn't hear it from me. It's possible he isn't. I just have to learn whether he is or isn't." Gavin climbed out of the sleeping bag and fished out a pair of fresh boxer briefs.

Amelia let out her breath. "Okay, so your case is kind of blown, isn't it? You're a whole day late in following them. You've lost your paddle, though if I can get picked up, you're welcome to mine. I imagine you would need a camera to take pictures to have proof of his infidelity. Just your word wouldn't be good enough."

"I have a waterproof camera in a waterproof bag, so I'm good there."

"You were going to surreptitiously take pictures of him?"

"I planned to keep my distance, stay out of sight, and learn what I could. And yes, take compromising pictures, if there are any. It's amazing what people will do when they're away from home and think a spouse can't witness their transgressions." Gavin pulled on a pair of socks, then a shirt and jeans, hiding his spectacular body.

"But it's a company excursion, right? Wouldn't it be difficult for him to be inconspicuous about seeing a woman in front of the others?"

"I would think so. Supposedly, the guy I'm placing under surveillance could be having an affair with one of the sales associates. Sounds to me like the perfect way to have an extramarital affair. If I weren't a wolf, of course. Maybe he doesn't feel any need to hide an affair in front of his coworkers. One of the executives is apparently openly having an affair with one of the sales associates, so maybe on these trips, the guy I plan to investigate can do the same. Maybe everyone already knows about the affair, so he does what he wants."

"That could be. Which guy and which woman?"

Gavin shook his head. "I wasn't supposed to say this much."

She had to admire him for that. "Well, call me your PI assistant, then."

He gave her a dark smile.

But she was *serious*. If someone had tampered with her dad's plane and she'd wrecked it because of that, she had every right to help investigate why and who was involved. "When they were getting ready to leave, a man of about forty to forty-five seemed ultra-friendly with a young woman in her midtwenties, and he wasn't her father. The dark-haired guy was Conrad Dylan, and she was a blond, Cheryl, not sure of her last name. A man named Theodore was joking with them. I didn't catch his last name either. The woman who seemed to be giving all the orders was Lee Struthers, a blond of about thirty. My brother took them up."

"Conrad's my client."

"Okay, well, it's definitely possible they're having an affair. Cheryl tugged on his sleeve in a playful manner. I didn't see what happened after that because I was busy with other things. The other man, Orwell Johnston, was dark-haired too, graying temples, and the woman who appeared to be with him was Mindy Michaels. There was also a redheaded woman named Nina Cavendish. My dad flew them up."

"Nina must be the other executive. I can't believe Mindy's a sales associate with the firm." Gavin still couldn't believe the woman who had been involved in the pet theft ring in Alaska was here. He kept meaning to leave and grab firewood for a fire, but he wanted to hear what else Amelia had observed about the company's party.

"Yeah. Shocker, isn't it? But they didn't get much time in jail for any of it. Typical, when it comes to pet theft. She was out on probation in a flash."

"What about her husband? Did he come on this trip too?" Gavin asked. "I guess not if she's working as a sales associate for the company and he's not one of the executives."

"They're still together, as far as I know. I mean, they moved out of my neighborhood. I never heard where they ended up. He served six months in jail; she did a month. Back to the guy that you're here about. It's possible Conrad could be having an affair with any of them—Cheryl, the CEO, or the female executive. I doubt he was having an affair with Mindy. She appeared to be with Orwell."

Gavin nodded. "It's possible. Or he's not having an affair with any of them."

Amelia frowned a little at him. "When you've looked into cases of infidelity, how often do you find the client was right about his or her suspicions?"

"More often than not. Usually something the spouse

does tips the husband or wife off. On occasion, the spouse is wrong and nothing is going on. Sometimes the spouse who hires me is really having the affair and is projecting on his wife or her husband. You meet all kinds in this business. Did you see anything going on between Conrad and the other women that might have indicated he was having an illicit affair with one of them?" He tugged on his boots.

Amelia tied on her boots. "No. They just seemed excited to be going on the trip, eager to get all their stuff loaded. They wanted to set up camp after paddling to their first location yesterday. I heard them talking about planning some work sessions for a couple of days while the storm passed through. I wondered how well that would go during a storm. Then again, it wasn't supposed to be coming in until today. I thought it was an interesting way to conduct training.

"If I had known to look for something more, I might have seen some indication that Conrad had something going on with one of the other women. I really was more concerned with getting everything loaded and making sure my brother and dad didn't leave anything or anyone behind." She eyed him and sighed. "I'm so sorry you had another plane crash experience. And that I was the one piloting the plane this time."

Gavin caught her hand and pulled her close. "You weren't responsible for what happened to the plane." He might have believed they'd neglected maintenance on it, but she figured he wouldn't think the plane could have so many issues all at once. "The main thing is you got us down. We're all alive. Except for some cuts and bruises, we're okay."

"Thanks, Gavin. I really feel bad about it."

"All I've got to say is that this wolf isn't meant to fly. I've been damn lucky to have survived a plane crash twice now. If the plane was sabotaged, which I believe to be the case, can you think of anyone who could have done it? Any idea?"

Even though the plane had malfunctioned, Amelia was still thinking about what she could have done differently to keep it from wrecking and sinking. She couldn't thank Gavin enough for not being sore with her that she'd messed up his mission.

"I had a couple of thoughts. My dad fired a pilot working for us a couple of weeks ago. He had flown a group of passengers to this area. They complained when they returned, saying the pilot had been drinking alcohol."

"Hell." Gavin's eyes narrowed as he listened.

"Yeah. That's one thing my dad won't allow. No drinking before takeoff, during the flight, or before returning. If you want to drink, you do it on your time."

"I agree with him there."

"The pilot is a gray wolf. A loner. At first I thought you were a gray wolf and could be part of his pack, and he'd lied about being a lone wolf. For all I knew, he'd had trouble with his pack over his drinking. Anyway, I'd only dated him twice when my dad canned him. I assumed he'd realize that was the end of anything between us, but he called me, wanting me to help get his job back and go out again. I lectured him about what he'd done, how he'd jeopardized people's lives and the company's reputation. I had no intention of dating him further. He wasn't happy with me. Swore at me.

I thought that was the last of it though. I figured he'd leave the area to find work somewhere else."

"Revenge is definitely a plausible motive. You said you had another idea about who might have had a reason to sabotage the plane."

"When we moved into the area, two seaplane adventure tour companies were already here. We saw they had enough business for the seasons when we fly paddlers in, or we would have found another place to try. They weren't happy we cut into their business."

"Did they threaten your dad? Or you and your brother?"

"Mostly, there was just competition—everyone trying to outdo each other. Though Slade got into a fight with a pilot who arrived at the same time as my brother at one of the drop-off points. For safety reasons, we coordinate with the other companies to work out schedules so we don't come in on top of each other. Words were spoken, though they waited until the paddlers had taken off, thankfully. The other company's pilot was in the wrong, but he wouldn't admit it. My brother came home with a black eye, but he swore the other pilot looked worse."

"Sounds like a possible motive to me."

"I agree." She sighed. "I'm hungry. Other than chasing down something to eat as a wolf, have you got some food in your bags that we could have for breakfast? I don't want to eat all your provisions, but...anything would be good after all the exercise we had yesterday."

"I was going to cook fresh eggs first thing in the morning."

"Good thing you rescued the cooler. I couldn't find Winston's food in the plane though."

"That blue sealed plastic box you stored in back with him near the dog bed?"

"Yeah."

"I didn't see it in the dark either and wasn't really thinking of it at the time. Sorry, Winston."

Winston lifted his head and wagged his tail.

"We'll have to share some of our food with him. I was worried about what we could feed him that would be safe for a dog. As wolves, we can eat so much more than dogs can. I have fire starter logs, a one-burner stove, a lantern, fuel, and a Dutch oven. Though I had figured on wood for the fire. There's plenty here if we can find some dry kindling beneath the layers of pine needles." Gavin pulled on the rain jacket.

"As to food, I've got ham, bacon, bread, English muffins, oatmeal, brown sugar, peanuts, granola and protein bars, tuna fish, canned hash, mac and cheese, frozen beef stew, and some freeze-dried jerky. And I have a couple of fishing poles. I planned to pretend to be on a vacation in case I got 'caught' in the area where they're staying. I always take two poles, in case somehow I lose one." He set out his knife, hatchet, first aid kit, water, and purifier tablets.

"Great on the food. Do you have a gun with you?"

"Yeah, and a license to carry one and a permit to have it on me in the Boundary Waters."

Amelia breathed a sigh of relief. If someone had really taken down the plane, the guy had to realize the accident could have killed everyone. What if he was out here, making sure they hadn't survived?

She put on the rain gear, and they headed out to bring in firewood and kindling. Winston immediately came with them. It was only lightly raining now.

"My dad was supposed to take you."

"Yeah?" Gavin had his ax with him, but he found enough dead timber to use for the fire.

"If someone sabotaged his plane and wasn't after any of the passengers, he must have been after my dad." Then she had another thought as she gathered kindling that was drier underneath the wet stuff. "You seemed to dismiss my other theory, but what if whoever did this was after *you*? What if the man you're trying to find dirt on knew his wife had hired you? He knew she would have given you his route, and you'd probably have used the same air service that took them there to learn what you could about them."

"But how would he know which plane I'd be on?" His arms wrapped around a couple of logs, Gavin began to head back to their camp.

"Both my brother and I were scheduled to fly a different group of passengers out, and we were taking different routes, if he knew our schedules. That leads me back to the notion that our fired pilot tampered with the plane." She sniffed at the air and smelled nothing new— no fresh bear scents indicating they'd returned, nor any scent making her believe a person had been in the area.

"Which means it has nothing to do with the case I'm on." Gavin set the logs on the drier rocks partly under the tarp cover.

"Right. Heaton knew our schedule and the planes. So yeah, he's my number one suspect." She really believed that if anyone could do it, Heaton could. She handed

Gavin the kindling. "Not only that, but he'd been a mechanic in the Air Force. Still, it's hard to imagine him doing something so awful."

"There have been so many cases of workplace violence that it could easily be that. He's out of a job and will probably have a time getting another one, if anyone looks into his work history with your company. So, good motive. He's thinking he's taking down your dad, owner of the company, and wouldn't know you swapped off with him until it was too late to change anything. I'm going to gather more firewood so it can dry out." Gavin headed back into the woods.

Amelia frowned as she and Winston followed him again. "I agree."

Gavin stared at something on the ground.

Not completely giving up on his case, in the event it had anything to do with what had happened, Amelia joined him and glanced down to see what he was looking at. Fresh piles of bear scat. "Conrad's wife called you how far in advance before you booked with us?"

Armed with another load of wood, Gavin headed back. "A day and a half. Between packing and driving out to your place, I didn't have a lot of time. Maybe Conrad had his wife's phone bugged so he knew who she was calling and learned I was coming up here to follow them. Still, how would he have gotten someone to take care of the plane that quickly? It would have had to be done during the night when none of you were around. And again, how would he have known which plane I'd take?"

Amelia finished gathering more kindling and rushed after Gavin. "Heaton knew the schedule for the next three weeks from the time he was let go. Then things changed at the last minute. So, he wouldn't have known about that unless he'd bugged our phones. I can't imagine he would have done that. Are you sure the wife who hired you isn't involved in this?"

Gavin paused and looked back at her. "Why would you suspect that?"

Amelia caught up to him, and they walked back together. "She hires the pilot, who has an ax to grind, to take down my dad's plane, and you with it. Maybe she planned to pin the crash on her husband somehow. Maybe she's not as concerned about proving he is having an affair as she is about giving him real trouble. She doesn't have to pay him any money if he's in jail when she divorces him, right?"

"Sounds way too fantastic to me. Though she did say she wanted me on the job. No one else." Gavin pulled out one of his fire logs, put it on top of the drier kindling, and used a battery-operated fire starter. A little curl of smoke appeared. He blew on it, protecting it with the tarp.

Amelia frowned at him. "Is that usual, a client asking specifically for one of you?"

"No. We work together or separately, anyone taking on the cases that come to the office. We're all highly trained, and none of us have had any issues with clients before. She said she'd had me investigated and liked what she'd seen, but if I didn't take the job, she'd get someone else to do it—someone not in our agency." He shrugged.

"Okay, well, you might not think it's enough to raise a red flag, but I think it's important to rule out any other possibility."

He poked at the fire for a moment and looked up at

her. "I still don't think she'd have anything to do with this, but she did ask if I'd have to take a plane."

"You mean, that you wouldn't have time enough to paddle out here?"

"Yeah."

"Okay. Even if there's only a slim chance that means anything, it's still something to consider."

"Which means we need to look into her background." Gavin didn't say anything for a moment, then poked at the fire again. "What if she's having an affair and wants a divorce? Then she's stuck with giving him money because that's in the prenup agreement. If he's not guilty of any infidelity and she's the one at fault, she pays."

"Wow, okay. So it's still a possibility."

The flames started licking at the kindling and the starter log. "We need to get word to the authorities. I'm afraid everyone's hunkered down and no one's coming here to drop off or pick up anyone because of the storm."

"Gavin." Amelia moved closer to him, concerned the perp might still be in the area and listening to them. She couldn't help breathing in Gavin's sexy male wolf scent. "What if someone did sabotage the plane, and he came here to make sure the deed was done?"

"That's…possible. As a cop, I watched for suspects who might be observing the scene of a crime. Some run, but some stick around, blend in, pretend to be a morbid spectator to see the reaction of the police and everyone else there. Sometimes to gloat. Sometimes to overhear if the police have any clues." He took hold of her hand and squeezed it with reassurance. Then he released her, walked over to the cooler, and lifted the lid. "Eggs and sausage or bacon?"

"Eggs and bacon, please."

"The bacon and sausage are precooked, so there's no worry about cooking them thoroughly enough, though as wolf shifters, we can manage what humans can't. It's always better to be safe than sorry."

"I agree. What can I do?"

"If you want to get some water for the coffee, that would be great. Purification tablets are in that container over there." Gavin pulled off his rain jacket.

"Are the eggs scrambled, shells and all?"

Smiling, he pulled the container from the cooler. "No shells. I remove them first and keep the eggs refrigerated." He eyed them in the clear plastic container. "Amazingly, they weren't scrambled, so your choice."

"Whatever way is easiest."

She set the coffeepot next to the fire and got a dish and filled it with water for Winston.

Gavin poured a little olive oil into the skillet, then added the eggs and bacon. "Lemon and pepper seasoning all right on the eggs?"

"Yeah. Sounds good."

Gavin considered the eggs. "Well, how about scrambled eggs?"

She glanced at them, saw two of the four yolks had broken, and smiled. "Sure, that works."

"I hadn't expected to have breakfast with a pretty wolf on this mission."

"I hadn't imagined I'd be waking up with a wolf this morning either." She set the coffeepot on the campfire, then brought over a couple of plastic plates for the food. "I would have been sitting out on my small porch, enjoying the flowers, butterflies, and birds... Well, I guess not, because of the storms. I might have been watching a show or reading a book. Never in a million years would I believe Winston would still be with me and I'd be having breakfast on an island in the middle of a lake with a white wolf and sharing a cozy hideaway with him."

Gavin laughed. "At least you had protection."

"Winston? He adores you. No protection there."

"I meant from the wild beasts in the woods."

She chuckled, her stomach beginning to rumble in anticipation of eating a good breakfast.

"You don't have that Taser with you, do you?" Gavin served up the eggs and bacon, then made them cups of coffee.

"No. I had it in the plane." She noticed how his face brightened a bit. "Don't look so relieved. If there's a bad guy nearby, I would have used it on him." She sat down on the sleeping bag and took a bite of her eggs. "This is like a five-star camping trip. Thanks." She began eating a slice of bacon. "Everything is delicious."

"Thanks. My dad loved to cook. He always said if you starve everyone enough before you feed them, they'll love anything you cook for them. He was right." He sat down next to her on the sleeping bag.

Amelia ate another strip of bacon. "Your dad was. Not that what he had to say has anything to do with what you prepared. It's great. We did a lot of camping in Alaska, super place to enjoy the wilderness. We usually didn't have anything this fancy for breakfast, just hot oatmeal and coffee or cocoa to get us started in the morning."

"Oatmeal works. I have that too." He smiled at her, then finished his coffee.

After they ate, she fed Winston some eggs and bacon. "I'll clean up things, but I need to run out to the woods for a minute."

"Good idea. Mark your territory."

She rose from their bedding and hesitated. "You're right. I might as well go as a wolf—lots easier. And I won't get wet all over again." She stripped off her clothes and shifted into her wolf.

Amelia was a beautiful white wolf, all pure white as if she'd had a bleach job, with not a tinge of yellow to her fur like some Arctic wolves had. Gavin couldn't believe she wanted to help him with his case. With all the ideas she had, he thought she'd be a great help.

"Beautiful," he said to her, and she wagged her tail. Then she ran out of their alcove and into the woods. "What about you, Winston?" Gavin asked. The dog had finished every scrap of his meal and was now eyeing the skillet. "Do you need to go for a walk?" Immediately, Winston stood and began wagging his tail. Gavin laughed. "You sure know that phrase."

As soon as he left the alcove with Winston, the Saint Bernard ran into the woods.

"Winston!"

This was not what Gavin had been expecting. Their German shepherds had always minded commands and never run off. He tore after Winston, afraid that the dog would run into a wolf or a bear. Moose even. Any of which could injure him.

"Winston!"

Chapter 6

AMELIA WHIPPED PAST GAVIN IN HER WOLF FORM, CHASING after Winston much faster than Gavin could run as a human. Figuring she'd chase the pup back to their camp, Gavin found a spot to relieve himself. Then he gathered more firewood and took it to the rock shelter to save for cooking meals later.

The rain had stopped and the wind had died down, but the sky was gray and still appeared threatening. Gavin washed his hands in the lake. Then he glanced in the direction of where the plane had gone down and saw something bobbing up and down in the water about an eighth of a mile out. Hot damn! It looked like…his lucky paddle!

Gavin quickly untied the canoe and readied it to take it out, hoping Amelia was doing all right with Winston. The dog had stayed with them in the alcove last night just fine, but they might have to tie him up whenever they didn't want him running off. Gavin hadn't heard him bark once, so that was a good thing.

He remembered camping once when someone's yappy dog barked for hours one night, two miles away. As a human, he still would have heard the dog. As a wolf, it had been worse. And the owner kept yelling at the dog periodically throughout the night to shut up.

After pulling on his rain gear in case it got bad again while he was out on the water, Gavin pushed the canoe out and climbed in, then started paddling out. A woof sounded behind him. He glanced back. Amelia was standing with her charge on the shore at their makeshift campsite, watching him. He was glad they had returned.

"Going after the paddle." He pointed in the direction. She woofed again in acknowledgment.

The early-morning sky was filled with dark-gray clouds, and Gavin knew he didn't have a lot of time before he needed to be back under the safety of the shelter ledge so he didn't get caught out in the storm.

He stroked hard and fast, glancing back to see Amelia and Winston still observing him. Then she and the dog disappeared into the alcove.

It seemed to take him forever, but he finally drew closer to the fluorescent paddle and saw something else floating in the water. At once, he recognized the large, blue plastic box. Hot damn, Winston's kibble. Gavin was glad, not only because he'd worried that feeding Winston some of their food might upset his digestive tract, but also because he'd brought only enough food for himself for the time he'd be here, and now he was sharing it with Amelia too. He just hoped he'd have good luck fishing. Though he could go fishing as a wolf too, and sometimes he was more successful that way.

Glad he'd retrieved his fluorescent paddle, Gavin paddled toward the box. When he was close enough, he lifted it into the canoe and looked around to see if anything else from the plane was floating nearby.

He didn't see anything, but the wind was beginning to pick up, and he smelled the smoke from their campfire.

Turning toward shore, he figured they could have the homemade beef stew for lunch or dinner once it had thawed out enough. Between the hefty chunks of ice he'd made in aluminum pots for the cooler, and the fact that some of his food was also frozen—like the stew—the food should still be refrigerated.

On this mission, part of his cover was to appear prepared for camping for over a week in the wilderness. He was glad to have company. Though he knew that wouldn't last long once someone picked Amelia and Winston up.

Fat raindrops suddenly fell from the sky. *Great.* Gavin paddled even faster, hoping he could help with the fire and keep it from going out so they could dry things out a bit. Amelia had shifted and dressed and was lifting a corner of the tarp high above the fire with tent poles, so she could keep it more sheltered from the rain.

But they'd need more kindling and hardwood.

When he reached the shore, he noticed she was wearing his rain jacket and the sweats as she ran out to greet him. She had laid out their wet clothes in the alcove near the fire to dry them. And she'd already cleaned up everything from breakfast. He appreciated that she was as hard a worker as he was. He'd camped with a woman years earlier, when he was still human, and he swore she'd thought it was supposed to be a five-star camping affair—maid service, room service, hot showers, restrooms, none of which they'd had at the campsite that was as primitive as the one they were making do with here. And man, did she complain the whole time she was out there with him! Which meant cutting his trip short or suffering her complaints. Regrettably, he'd had to cut the trip short.

Then again, wolves were more used to their natural

surroundings and comfortable in them, so he could see why this suited Amelia fine.

Amelia helped him haul the canoe back into the trees to secure it. "Oh, yay, you got Winston's kibble."

"Damn good thing, or Winston would surely eat us out of house and home and still be hungry, as much exercise as he's getting. I don't think the eggs and bacon would have held him over until the next meal."

"You're right." She carried Gavin's paddle back to the camp while he carried the big container of dog food. "He was eyeing the skillet when I was cleaning it, looking for any scrap that might be left over. The container of kibble would be plenty to keep him going for a few weeks. I wanted Winston's new family to have the food he's used to. I often have to get a different kind, depending on the pet I'm fostering—different breed, age, size."

"That's just great."

Amelia hauled the container into the shelter, and Winston started nosing at it. "Yes. That's yours, but you have to wait. I figure I'll feed him his regular food since he's used to that. Otherwise, he doesn't feel he's had his real meal."

"Like the eggs and bacon were a treat."

"Exactly." She poured some kibble for Winston into the lid of the container, which could serve as a dog dish. "Sit… Down… Break…"

At hearing the final command, Winston, who was lying down on the ground in the alcove, scrambled to his feet to rush to eat his kibble.

Gavin admired the pup. "He's well trained."

"When he wants to be. Running off in the woods wasn't part of the training." She filled the dish she was using for Winston's water. "But I didn't have time to work on that before I found new owners for him. Well, *had* found."

The lightning and thunder drew closer.

Gavin ran his hand over Winston's back, seriously thinking of offering to take him in. "Did you see anyone while you were chasing Winston down?" Gavin assumed she would have told him if she had, but he'd smelled a man's scent and still wondered if it was recent or from some time ago—long before they arrived and set up camp.

"No, I didn't see anyone or hear any voices or smell any food. At least not where Winston ran to. I was able to turn him around fairly fast after he did his business."

"You didn't say why your dad canceled on me and took another party instead."

She narrowed her eyes at him.

"I don't mean he had anything to do with tampering with the plane. I don't believe your dad had anything to do with you being targeted. You're a wolf family. Most wolf families take care of each other. Though if you were all humans, the cop in me would consider family and friends as first suspects."

"Heaton would fit the bill as a friend and employee. My father hired him to help fly for us because business has been so brisk this summer. And because Heaton was a wolf, Dad thought he'd be more reliable. If Heaton deliberately incapacitated the plane, he might have been after me, because I had dumped him. He knew my brother was already flying a sightseeing group out, and I was the only one who could switch with my dad."

"Why *did* you switch with your dad?"

"One of the men who was supposed to be in my group refused to fly with a female pilot."

"Ah."

"What's *that* supposed to mean?"

"You seemed ready to blow your top if I told you I didn't want to fly with you. I was just surprised your dad wasn't taking me. It had nothing to do with you flying the plane. I don't blame you for being annoyed with the guy though. I think in this instance, the passenger not wanting you to pilot the plane worked out well for all concerned."

She looked at Gavin like he was crazy. "I crashed the plane."

"Not on purpose, and besides, you found a wolf you can't live without."

Amelia exhaled in a way that said Gavin might have to work harder at convincing her of that. "If someone did sabotage the plane, would he have used a remote controller?"

"That might have been too unpredictable. If he couldn't get enough of a signal, he would have missed the opportunity. Your plane could be out of range, you might take enough of a detour, anything could happen to screw up his plans. More likely, he'd have a timer set."

"Which means he might have done it in anticipation of your arrival. Dad had a couple cancel his flight, which allowed you to take their place."

"What reason did the passengers give for canceling?" It sounded like too far a stretch, but Gavin had learned years ago never to discount anything. He'd seen too many police cases where key evidence was ignored for too long because it seemed too far out to connect to the crime.

"The upcoming storms. We had more than one group cancel because of them."

Which, in Gavin's estimation, was reasonable. "Okay, so we have a couple that canceled, the group that didn't want to go with you, and the disgruntled former employee."

"And the guy you're investigating."

"And the companies you're in competition with. You have a plane go down, it's in the news, and suddenly your adventure tour company sounds too dangerous to fly with."

"Correct. If we're working on conspiracy theories, they'd all be tied in, right?"

Gavin smiled down at her. "Do you watch a lot of conspiracy thrillers?"

"Absolutely. What does the wife get out of it, if you prove her husband is being unfaithful?"

"A divorce. She's worth millions. She has a prenuptial agreement that if he's caught in an extramarital affair, she doesn't have to give him a cent."

"Okay, so let's say he assumes she's got a PI on his case. Getting rid of you wouldn't help him at all. All she'd have to do is send another."

"True, but maybe not soon enough to follow her husband at this point. I can't think of anyone who has a vendetta against me."

"Or your pack? Your PI agency? With the cases you've worked, you might have had issues with someone. Even a man or woman who you proved was cheating on your client? Someone you exposed who had committed a crime and was put in jail? Just all kinds of things."

"I can't imagine anyone going to that much trouble.

And it's got to be someone who did some work on the plane beforehand. You say the fired pilot is a wolf?"

"Yeah, I wasn't really paying much attention to smells in my dad's plane when we boarded it. All of us had been in it at one time or another. His scent around the plane wouldn't have made me suspicious." She sighed. "You're a former cop. What should we do?"

"I was going to say we could pack up the raft and the canoe and head for the bay, where surely someone will be arriving to pick up or drop someone off sooner or later."

"The storm is stationary and no one's going to be paddling in this unless they're nuts. And no planes will be dropping anyone off or picking anyone up either," Amelia added. "Have you paddled through this area before?"

"A few times with David and Owen, two of my partners. We didn't have the brick-and-mortar office going yet, and we came out here once we had more control over our shifting. We could have gone during the new moon, but we still wanted to run as wolves at night once we set up camp."

"Did you ever run into any other wolves?"

"Yeah, a lone gray wolf, but he saw the three of us and took off. Now it makes me wonder if it was Heaton and not just a wild wolf. We saw him on an island while we were paddling, so we didn't stop to check it out, to learn his scent and see if he smelled human too. What about you? Do you ever come out here?"

"No, except to drop off paddlers. I always wanted to, but with running a business, I couldn't go with my family. Someone has to keep up with scheduling and taking flights out. I'm not a lone wolf, so I didn't have any interest in coming out here on my own. It would be more fun to paddle with someone."

"Like me?"

She smiled at him. "Well, despite the harrowing situation we were in getting here, yeah. You seem good at this survival stuff."

"Eagle Scout. My dad had been one too."

"But usually wolves don't join human… Oh, you were human."

"Right."

The rain was still coming down, but lighter now.

"On another subject, while I was trying to grab the paddle and Winston's food container, I was thinking about a canoe trip I made a couple of years ago with the guys and how an obnoxious dog barked for hours one night. We were camped two miles away. With our wolf hearing, we could easily hear what was happening because water carries sound much farther."

"No worries there," Amelia said. "Winston's very quiet."

"He is, but it made me think that if we were about a mile away from someone else on another island, if we shouted for help, they could hear us even if they're strictly humans. They might have a sat phone we could use."

"Or just a mobile phone like mine that won't work." She brought out her phone and checked for a signal anyway. "Nothing. At least it's working."

"That's good. When the storm quits by tomorrow morning or so, that would be a great idea. If we howled, that would really carry."

"But that could keep everyone away." She poured herself another cup of coffee.

"Unless people thought they might be able to see the wolves up close and paddle this way."

"True. With cell phones or cameras in hand. If we saw a paddler, we could hide, shift, and come out, wave our hands, and call out."

"Naked?" It was one thing to shift and be nude in front of other shifters. Sometimes, it was just inevitable, like being here with each other. In front of humans, there was a whole different set of moral codes.

She blushed a little. "Well, okay, one of us could be human and dressed."

The wind began to pick up, and the lightning and thunder were right overhead. The rain came down in a torrent.

"I need to secure the food before it attracts wild animals." Gavin had considered doing it before the storm started up again, but it had looked so dark that he knew the rain would come down any moment.

"Not until the storm stops. It's too dangerous. Then I'll help you."

"All right."

Amelia pulled off her wet boots and set them near the fire, then slipped off her socks and laid them out with their other wet clothes. "What do you want to do now?"

"Take a nap. And then when the weather breaks, I want to explore the island after we secure the food. I need to see if anyone else is staying here."

"Are you going as a wolf?"

"Yes. I can cover a lot more ground and do so much more quietly."

"Do you want me to come with you?"

"It would be best if someone stays with Winston to

make sure he stays put. If we tie him up, he could be in trouble if a wolf or bear came along."

"Agreed." But Amelia sounded like she wished she could go with him.

He wished she could too, but if he found what he was looking for, he'd race back to their camp, and they could return as humans.

They lay down on the sleeping bag, and she rested against him. Even though he closed his eyes, he couldn't stop thinking about how much she looked like the woman he had seen in Seattle. Where had he seen her before? If he could think of the location, he would remember.

Chapter 7

NEITHER AMELIA NOR GAVIN HAD FALLEN ASLEEP WHEN HE suddenly knew where he'd seen Amelia before. He never forgot a face. Especially one as lovely as hers.

"I remember where I saw you," Gavin said, snapping his fingers.

She didn't say anything for a moment, then said, "Really? Where?" She sounded worried that he'd recall he'd truly seen her, and he noted she didn't deny it could be her this time.

"At a café in downtown Seattle. You were with some guy, laughing, and seemed to be having a good time. There you were, a beautiful blue-eyed blond. I'd just broken up with a woman. Or maybe I should say she broke up with me and started seeing another cop on the force." Which was the best thing that could have happened to him. "I thought how fortunate the guy was to have you. The woman I had been dating had become so disagreeable that it was good seeing two people obviously in love." Gavin frowned, noticing Amelia was really quiet, tense, worried.

His cop training made him aware of changes in a person's reactions, but with his wolf senses, he could even smell them now. "Why would you be worried that I'd seen you before?" All he could think of was that she had committed a crime and he had been a cop.

She didn't say anything.

"Hell, the guy you were with? He…he was…" Gavin sat up on the sleeping bag and stared at Amelia, who was sitting up now too, waiting for him to finish what he was going to say. "He was the leader of the men who had committed the jewelry-store heist. And they had a female pilot. She disappeared. They never found her. Damn it, Amelia, you were the pilot? Why didn't you tell me the truth? You were an accessory to the crime."

"You pretend to be the innocent in all that. You knew him too. You could have given yourself up as a hostage to join your crew and get away with the stash, looking like the hero—cop offers to take the place of the · pregnant store clerk—when you were in on it all along."

"What? So that's what you thought?"

"They didn't tie you up or gag you or blindfold you."

"Which had me damn worried. When that happens, they kill the hostage. Besides, the two men sitting in back with me were armed with guns. I just hadn't found the right moment to take them down."

"Right."

"That's right. I knew two of the men had rap sheets. One man always wore a mask. I never saw anything about the other man, Clayton Drummer. No rap sheet at all."

"Clayton Drummer?"

"Yeah, the mastermind, though since he didn't have any arrest record, some thought there might have been someone else who actually paid for this to be done. But Clayton was responsible for coordinating the team to do the heist."

"But how would he have met a crew if he'd never been in prison?"

"He might have been associated with criminals, done crimes but never got caught himself."

Because he was a wolf. And because he was a cop!

"He was a Seattle cop!" She stood and folded her arms, looking down at Gavin with scorn, her brows knitted together.

"A cop? No. We would have known. There wasn't any way that he was. His fingerprints showed he was Clayton Drummer. No criminal record."

Her frown deepened.

"You were dating the guy, and you thought he was a cop?"

She let out her breath in obvious irritation. "Jeez, he played me for such a fool. I guess he pretended to be a cop so I'd think he was a decent guy."

Gavin didn't know what to think. Had she really thought the guy was a cop? But it didn't change the fact that Gavin was certain she had piloted the plane.

"What were you going to get out of it? A pretty good damn cut? But you missed it all when the others got caught. Except for the one who got away. Did you and he escape together? That's how you made it out?"

"I don't know who the man was who got away. He didn't have any scent I could smell, and he wore a ski mask the whole time."

"Hell. *You were a wolf!* That's how you didn't get caught. You ran out of there as a wolf. Every man for himself. You left your injured boyfriend behind and headed for the hills."

"I was a hostage every bit as much as you were, if you truly were," she growled at Gavin. "He was a wolf too and said he was a cop. He had a badge and the uniform and everything. I'd dated him for two months! Bastard. We were supposed to be going on a date. The next thing I know, he's threatening to shoot me, forcing me to pilot a plane that wasn't one of our company's. And his men dragged you on board as a hostage. A cop hostage. So the two of you had to know each other. You never reported he was a cop when you were rescued."

"That's because he wasn't." Gavin stood. "But you left him for dead. Even if he'd lied to you and you'd been taken hostage, why didn't you stay with me and your injured boyfriend? Why run off? It would have all been sorted out then. Your name would have been cleared."

"Do you know why that plane crashed? *I* did it! *On purpose!*"

Gavin stared at her in disbelief. Did she have a death wish? Or did she think because of her healing genetics, she would have made it out alive? The rest of them could have easily been killed. Her wolf boyfriend hadn't been so lucky.

She poked her finger at Gavin's chest. "I saved *your* life!"

He arched his brows. "*How?* You could have killed us all."

She laughed bitterly. "You were a dead man. Clayton had ordered his men to kill you. I took that opportunity to crash the plane. And I didn't do it all just for you *either*. I knew my life would be over once I was no longer useful. Even if Clayton thought he'd keep me around, I wouldn't have gone along with the plan, so he would have had to kill me. I didn't have any choice. I didn't know if you were innocent or part of the team. Both of you were cops, or at least I thought he was one too. And I figured he might have used you, then planned to kill you to cover his tracks so he wouldn't have to share the profits with you."

"You ran off," Gavin reminded her. "If you were innocent, you would've stayed with me. Taken care of me even, if you had been one of the good guys. You can't tell me you were afraid to testify because you are a wolf. You're a royal. You don't have any trouble shifting at any time. You could have gone to trial for weeks, and it wouldn't have mattered."

"I saved your ass twice more. Clayton was in bad shape, but he must have believed he was still going to walk out of there and join his buddies, who had conveniently run off with all the jewelry. He wasn't leaving you behind as a witness. He was going to kill you. He had his gun readied, and I grabbed a sturdy branch and hit him on the head with it."

"Blunt-force trauma," Gavin said, surprised as hell. "The coroner attributed it to the crash."

"Yeah, well, he had a bullet chambered just for you. But he heard me coming up behind him and fired the shot at me! If anyone bothered to really look, they would have found the bullet in a tree trunk nearby. Searchers would never have found you in time if I hadn't shifted and run home. It took me two days to reach home, and believe me, running as an Arctic wolf meant I had enough trouble trying to slip into the neighborhood without making anyone go for their rifles and start shooting. Not to mention I'd been hurt in the crash too. Not as badly as you, obviously, but muscle strains and cuts and bruises."

Okay, so yeah, she couldn't have survived that crash and come out of it unscathed. "You lived in Seattle."

"The countryside outside Seattle. My parents were frantic. I'd just disappeared, and there'd been no word from me. Except they knew I'd had a date with Clayton. We were supposed to meet at a café, but he changed his mind at the last minute and said to meet him at the hangar. He wanted to get some photos of me standing next to my plane. And then we were going out to eat."

"You weren't suspicious?"

"Why should I have been? He'd talked about doing it before because he loved that I could fly. No wonder! But after the accident, I had to reach my dad and tell him where to look for the wreckage and that the cop who'd been taken hostage was injured and needed to be rescued."

"Then you left food and water for me and a couple of blankets and a pillow."

"Yeah, I did. I left all the food and drink that I could find—candy bars, granola bars, bottles of water and beer—in case I didn't make it back home to get help for you. I mean, I could have been shot. I hoped your injuries wouldn't kill you, and you'd have enough food and water to see you through. I guess the men who left had what they thought would be enough supplies to keep them going and didn't take all the food and water. Or maybe they'd left it for Clayton in case he managed to get on his way."

"Thanks. I...was surprised they'd left me anything to drink or eat. It made me believe they hadn't meant to kill me."

"Clayton did. Believe me. Once I told my dad what had happened, he and Slade took off in their planes and located the wreckage first, then relayed the message to the searchers of just where they could find you. If I hadn't told my dad, and he hadn't directed the rescue teams to that location, you would have been a pile of bones."

"You've saved my ass three times, then?" She was a firecracker.

"How do you think I could have explained that I ran all the way back to the outskirts of Seattle to tell my dad where the plane wreckage was because the location was so remote? Where you were? Do you think anyone would have believed a human could run that distance? Hell, even as a wolf, I nearly killed myself trying to get home fast enough so they could search for you. Not only that, but my dad said there was no way I was going to tell anyone I had piloted the plane. If someone had identified me, we would have come up with a story. My family would have been my alibi. No matter what, I couldn't have told anyone what had really happened. And *you* weren't a wolf at the time. So, I couldn't have let you in on the secret, now could I?"

"You were living in the Seattle area for a time."

"My mother worried about us flying so many rescue missions by seaplane in the dark in Alaska. It was the same reason we ended up moving to Minnesota. Dad had a minor accident landing in the water at night one time. Even though it was minor, he was put at big risk—an ice floe tore up a float, and he had to abandon the plane and was taken in by some of the natives there. That's when we moved to Seattle, to try it out there. We had only lived there for a couple of months, and everything was working out well for us. I had begun fostering dogs again. We lived in two separate homes out in the country. We were flying tourists to sites all over the state and beyond."

"And then the heist happened."

"Right. My parents were afraid I'd run into you at some time or another after that." She snorted. "So there I was back in Alaska, and who barges into my house but you."

"Saying I thought I knew you from Seattle." It all made sense now. "You thought I had come to arrest you."

"I had considered the possibility."

"I was only there to find the dogs."

"I didn't know that when I first saw you."

"Then you moved to Minnesota. Not to avoid me though."

"No. We were in Alaska until two months ago."

"You didn't think I knew you piloted the plane."

She shook her head. "I was worried when I saw you again, ready to take a plane ride. I guess that means I'm the one who caused you to have a phobia of flying." It was still pouring rain out, but she said, "Why don't you go look for someone on the island?"

"It's still too stormy out. If you were going to save me all those times, seems a waste to send me out in an electrical storm. Come on. Why don't we lie down and take a nap like we'd planned?"

"All right." But she said it in a hostile way. She grabbed the sleeping bags and unzipped them to separate them, then shoved one of them into his chest.

He smiled. He couldn't help himself. She was a real wolf. "Did London know about your plane crash?"

"Yeah. We told him we were moving back to Alaska, and he put us up until we could get places of our own."

"He didn't suggest you clear your name?"

She frowned at Gavin.

"All right. You're wolves. I'm still thinking with my cop brain," he said.

"You know, insurance can really go up once we've crashed a plane. Not to mention the possibility of losing a license."

"Extenuating circumstances were beyond your control," Gavin said.

She made Winston lie down between them, as if he were the wall she needed to separate them. Gavin sighed. So much for her being his PI assistant and the possibility of courting the she-wolf right away. If ever.

After ending the relationship with Clayton, then Heaton, Amelia believed she might never be interested in another wolf. She couldn't believe Clayton hadn't even been a cop!

She believed Gavin hadn't been on the take, at least. That he'd truly been a hero when he took the clerk's place as a hostage. She wasn't sure what he was feeling about her now, but she figured they needed the distance between them so they could sort out how they felt about each other's involvement in the heist. Her family still could use his services as a PI, and she still wanted to learn the truth about the plane crash, but she was thinking she should pack up Winston and paddle the raft to the bay and wait there until someone, anyone, came to pick up or drop off paddlers.

She still couldn't believe an Arctic wolf pack lived nearby. Or that the human she had tased would turn up in her life again, this time as a wolf. He'd seemed really interested in her, and she had to admit she was feeling the same way about him. She didn't have a great track record with boyfriends.

"For what it's worth, I believe you," he said. He was turned toward her, and she had her back to him. He didn't speak for a while, and she didn't say anything. "You're right. I wouldn't have believed you if you'd told me you had nothing to do with the heist. Not back then. Not when I'd seen you with him in the café as girlfriend and boyfriend. Not when you were flying the plane willingly. As far as I could tell. And then you took off after it crashed. What was I supposed to think?"

That she was guilty? Which is why she couldn't tell him before.

"But I'm a wolf too now. And I understand. Even about killing Clayton."

"I didn't do it out of revenge."

"I wouldn't blame you for that either."

"Yeah, you would. You're a cop. Former cop."

"And a wolf. You did it to save me. We couldn't understand why there were signs he had fired a round. Not when the assumption was that he'd died shortly after the crash. The gun was resting beside him. He must have had it holstered, or he would have lost it when we crashed. It all fits. Him pulling the gun out, then I guess you whacked him on the head, and he dropped the gun and fell back."

"You must have been unconscious. At least you appeared that way to me. You were breathing, heart rate normal."

"I heard something. He was close to some of the plane's wreckage, and you must have slipped around it to avoid me seeing you."

"I had been wearing heels and a dress, but I lost the heels in the crash. I had to locate them, strip out of the clothes far away from the wreckage, and bury them. I didn't want to lose precious time."

"And you left blankets and food and water for me."

"You'd passed out. I knew approximately where we'd crashed and that it would take me at least two days to reach home. I didn't want you expiring before I could get help for you."

"Even if I was a crooked cop."

"I didn't know for sure one way or another. All I knew was you weren't a wolf, so if you were one of the bad guys, your rescuers could sort it out when they got to you. If you were one of the bad guys, you could go to jail."

"I didn't think I'd ever say this, but thanks for crashing the plane to save my life."

She smiled a little, glad this was out in the open between them and that he seemed to have taken it pretty well, which surprised her.

When they woke after taking a nap, Amelia discovered her wall in the form of a Saint Bernard had moved to lie behind Gavin, and Gavin was sleeping in his other bag at her back, keeping her warm, when she'd thought it had been the dog.

She'd been lying there, stewing about the man who had refused to fly with her and how he seemed so familiar. And then it came back to her. "Omigod, I know why that man refused to fly with me."

Gavin opened his eyes and raised a brow. "He had a bad experience with a female pilot."

"With me! He was one of the men on the jewelry heist."

"Are you certain?"

"Yes! He's probably served his time and is out on parole. I recognized his scent, but I couldn't place the face. It was over seven years ago. They were wearing masks most of the time, and he was clean-shaven then and bearded this time."

"He probably worried you might mention he was a felon to his friends. He may have turned over a new leaf, and nobody he associates with knows what he'd done in the past."

"Or he was afraid I would just crash the plane again, as if I was in the habit of doing that."

He smiled a little at her.

She frowned back at him. "I can't believe it. Don't you think it's odd that three of the people who were on that plane—you, me, and the robber—all end up in the same place?"

"Yeah, it does seem like too much of a coincidence. Do you recall his name?"

"Red. That's all I knew."

"That was Ralph Winton. He went by Red because of his red hair. He's been in and out of prison for years. He's about forty now."

"That would be about right. Why would he be here, then? Refusing to fly with me?"

"To ensure you flew your father's plane? But who would know your father and you would switch?"

"Heaton. We had a similar scenario, only someone didn't like my father and we switched planes."

"Because the gear was already loaded up."

"Yeah."

"And Heaton knew."

"Yeah. He was watching the whole scenario and later said he was surprised we didn't just tell the passenger to fly with another company. But we're not a big company, and we can't afford to have a lot of bad reviews. Several of the people scheduled for the flight were his family members, and they would have all canceled on us."

"So the three of us were on the same plane after the heist."

Amelia cleared her throat. "Okay, so Conspiracy Theory 101, how likely would it be mere coincidence that Red maneuvers us to fly on the same sabotaged plane and that the woman who hired you—or possibly her husband—did it so that we'd go down together?"

"I'd say the odds are unlikely. Okay, then that's something else we need to look into further." Gavin climbed out of his bag. "I'll put up the food, then head out. Can you shoot a gun?"

"Uh, yeah. I'll help you with the food though."

"Okay, if someone sabotaged the plane and he shows up while I'm out exploring the island, you protect yourself."

She would, and Winston too. She hoped Gavin wouldn't run into any trouble while she was back at camp. She had to figure out something useful to do while she waited on him. Patience was not her strong suit.

Chapter 8

As a wolf, Gavin ran through the woods, hunting for recent signs of anyone having been on the island. He was sniffing wet leaves, looking for tracks, and watching for any movement. While he was searching, he thought about Amelia and what she'd told him. As a cop, or a PI, instinct told him he needed to investigate every detail of her story to prove she had been telling the truth. Gut instinct, or some lower power, was telling him she was the wolf for him and everything she had told him was true. That she was innocent of any crime, a victim every bit as much as he had been. He wasn't sure he would have ditched a plane to save himself and another passenger. That took real mettle. Even then, she'd managed to do so in a way that allowed everyone to survive. At least initially after they had crashed.

When she'd finally fallen asleep during their nap, her breathing steady and her heartbeat slowed, Gavin had moved Winston over so he could be next to her again. He liked the intimacy they'd already shared. And he wasn't taking any steps back from this. He was certain they could put the past behind them. The thought kept running through his mind that she had saved him three times already. It sure sounded like mate material to him. He did worry she might want to leave for the bay without him to wait for a seaplane to pick her up.

He'd been running about an hour and continued to

move through the spruce trees and check the shoreline so he could see if anyone was camped across the lake on the other island there, about an eighth of a mile away.

He suddenly saw movement across the lake. A soaking-wet black bear was lumbering out of the water. Then the bear saw Gavin and watched him with a wary eye, making Gavin glad the bear was on the other island. Gavin was running along the rocky beach when he saw a bright-yellow canoe on the south side of the other island, the symbol on the canoe indicating it was a Golden rental from Ely.

Glad to observe anyone in the vicinity, Gavin would have to return in his canoe and see if he could locate the paddler. Then he saw a man near the edge of the woods, wearing a camo jacket and pants, boots, and a hat, like he was dressed to hunt. The only reason Gavin even noticed the guy was that he'd turned to head deeper into the woods and out of view, bags in hand. He was probably carrying his gear over a portage. The movement had caught Gavin's eye, but he didn't think the man had seen him, or he would have come out of the woods to get a closer look at the out-of-place Arctic wolf.

This was one time when Gavin wished he was in his human form and could call across the lake to get the man's attention. Motion across the lake caught Gavin's eye, coming from the direction where the bear had been. Sure enough, the bear was heading for the canoe. He must have smelled the scent of food that had been carried in the craft. When the bear finally reached the guy's canoe, he poked his nose into it. Apparently not finding anything, the bear headed into the woods the way the paddler had gone. The guy had to be making a couple of trips to carry all his gear across the portage. With any luck, the man had something to make lots of noise to scare off the bear.

Gavin thought the bear might help to delay the paddler from reaching his canoe on the return trip, which could give Gavin time to come back as a human and meet him. Gavin lifted his chin and howled to Amelia back at their makeshift camp to let her know he'd found something.

She howled from another direction, way on the other side of the island, confusing and concerning him. She was supposed to be staying with Winston as a human at their campsite. What was she doing running as a wolf? Where was Winston? He immediately worried they'd had trouble and she'd felt safer as a wolf.

His heart racing, Gavin tore off toward the direction of her howl, stopping for a moment to howl again to let her know he was coming to her location. She howled back to acknowledge his message. He'd run for about half an hour when he heard something moving in the brush, turned, and saw Winston. The dog ran to greet him, and Gavin greeted him back with licks to the face. Not immediately seeing her, Gavin woofed for Amelia.

She woofed back from twenty or so yards away, hidden in the brush and trees. He and Winston quickly joined her. Gavin nuzzled her face, waiting to see if she had found anything. She led him toward the shore where a fire had burned that morning. Someone had cooked eggs and ham. Gavin didn't smell any sign of people. Someone had camped here under a tent, the grassy area bent where it had been set up. A canoe had rested there too. He didn't like that he couldn't smell anyone there.

No hunting was allowed here. So why would anyone be wearing hunter's spray? He glanced in the direction of the island and the paddler he'd seen. Was he the one who had camped here?

They sniffed around the area, searching for anything the paddler had left behind. They didn't discover anything. Gavin led Amelia to the area where he'd seen the canoe on the shore of the other island.

The canoe was gone. *Damn it!*

He couldn't have gotten the paddler's attention as a wolf anyway. He had to know if the guy was wearing hunter's spray and if he was actually hunting illegally. Though that wasn't Gavin's mission. Finding someone with a sat phone was.

Gavin stared at the beach across the lake where the canoe had been, as if it would suddenly appear. He ran down the beach a little way, but he didn't see any sign of the canoe on the lake. Amelia and Winston chased after him while he observed the lake further. He couldn't imagine paddling in the bad weather. Gavin ran along the shore, looking for any sign of the canoe in the opposite direction. He saw nothing. The paddler had to have carried the canoe up into the woods or paddled around to the other side of the island where they couldn't see him. Maybe the paddler was trying to find a better location to set up his camp. If he had a sat phone, they needed to find him.

Gavin studied the distance to reach the other island. He considered swimming across the lake to explore the area and see if the paddler left a scent. But then he would be a wolf. Gavin needed to cross in the canoe so he could talk to the paddler if he found him.

Gavin, Amelia, and Winston headed back to their camp, and when they reached it, they all walked into the shelter. Both Gavin and Amelia shifted. "What did you see?" She pulled on her panties.

"A yellow canoe beached on the island across from ours. I thought maybe the paddler would have a sat phone, and we could contact your dad." Gavin pulled on his boxer briefs. "I also saw a black bear nearby, and that might have made the guy decide to move to somewhere else. I did see a man wearing camouflage in the woods near where the canoe was beached. He might have carried up his gear first and returned for his canoe, unable to make it in a single portage."

"Yeah, if he was alone. Or had a companion but too much gear." She fastened her bra, then checked the rest of her clothes. They appeared to still be damp, so she slipped his sweats back on.

He liked them on her, making him feel as though he'd claimed her in some way. "Maybe, once we get this situation resolved, you can teach me how to overcome my fear of flying." He finished dressing.

She laughed. "A few more crashes, if you survive them, and you'll either get used to it or have the worst phobia ever." She pulled on socks and her boots. "But you seem to be a really good swimmer. Maybe you can teach me to be a better one."

"It's a deal." He wasn't sure about the flying bit, though he'd heard sometimes doing something over and over helped to reduce the phobia. He liked the idea of teaching her to be comfortable enough in the water to swim to her heart's content. It sounded like she felt she could trust him now. "About what was said earlier—"

"I trust you are one of the good guys," she said. "Don't prove me wrong."

He smiled darkly at her and finished dressing. He was one of the good guys—unless he had to take out a bad guy, and then he was no longer Mr. Affable. "I believe your story."

"And you're going to investigate everything I said when you return home."

"No, I don't need to. I believe you. About all of it. If I'd still been human, I would have had trouble with it."

"If you'd still been human, I wouldn't have told you about the wolf business. Or I would have had to bite you first."

He chuckled. "Been through that already. If you want to bite me, be my guest."

She sighed. "So what's the plan?"

"You stay here while I check out the other island. Uh, by the way, why *did* you leave the camp?" Gavin leaned down to where Winston was sitting on the comforter and scratched his head.

"Winston had to go to the bathroom after eating his kibble. I don't have his leash. When we evacuated the plane, the bag with his leash and dog bowls was left behind. I figured I'd have better control over him as a wolf. When I took him for a walk, he kept running, looking for the perfect spot. I swear we explored half the island before he peed. Then we found the fresh campsite, and I think that's what drew him that way. We heard you howl that you'd found something, and I howled that I had too. It's still stormy out. I can hear the thunder in the west. It's heading this way again. How long would it take you to cross the lake to the other island?" she asked.

"It should take me only an hour or so to reach the island, put up the canoe, and search for the guy. Longer if he already reached the location where he planned to put the canoe back in the water."

"What about your job? Do you think you can skip where the client's husband will be the first couple of days and go straight to his next stop?"

"That's the plan."

"I still say it could be dangerous."

"Which is why I want you to stay here."

"Maybe you should take the gun."

"I want you to be protected. I'm going to get the canoe and head out." He pulled on the rain gear, but before he could leave, she pulled him in for a hug and kiss.

"If you get yourself killed over this, I'll never forgive you."

He smiled. "Especially after you've saved my life so many times. I promise I'll be careful." He kissed her and hugged her right back. Then he left the alcove, but as soon as he reached the trees, he noticed the raft and canoe were gone.

He just stared at the location and then looked around at the woods, as if he might have mistaken where he'd left them. No, both were gone. "We have a problem."

Amelia was right behind him, wearing his rain jacket. "Where's the raft? The canoe? Oh God, Gavin. Who would have taken them?"

"The person who sabotaged the plane? Where's the gun?"

"I hid it underneath the rocks before I ran as a wolf. I didn't check to see if it was still there."

Thank God that she'd hidden it, but Gavin hoped

whoever this was hadn't found it. "Okay. I doubt he could have taken the time to search for it or grab our food. I didn't check. He had to have taken the canoe and raft the opposite way from where I ran, or I would have seen them when I went to the water's edge. Same with you. You headed in the direction I did. Then you veered off to the west."

"Do you think he's still paddling with them in tow?"

"Could be. He might have punctured the raft so it would sink. That way, no one could see it from the air."

"The emergency flares were in one of the raft's pockets."

Gavin had never expected anyone to steal the raft. Or the canoe, for that matter. "Oh, hell yeah. I thought they'd be safe there until we needed them."

"Me too."

He figured they'd been gone a couple of hours or longer when they took off looking for signs of anyone. Plenty of time for someone to slip into camp and steal their transportation.

Gavin ran down the beach to look for someone towing the canoe and raft in the water. Amelia ran after him, observing the water too. He knew whoever took them wouldn't head straight out from the island. He'd go around it so he could distance himself from their view and reach the next land mass while staying out of sight.

The rain started falling, and they heard distant thunder again. "Good thing you hadn't gone anywhere in the canoe," Amelia said.

But if he had, they'd still have it.

As stuck as they were, Gavin reminded himself that they had each other. And she was right. Maybe the person who had taken the raft and canoe would run into serious trouble out on the lake in the approaching thunderstorm. He could only hope.

"Oh." Amelia was looking out at the lake and started pointing out at something. "There. Do you see something?"

He couldn't be certain, but he thought he saw something yellow floating on the water, something flattened, like a raft that had lost most of its air, lifted on the crest of waves and momentarily visible, then falling into the troughs and hidden from view. No canoe was in sight.

"The raft, maybe? It's hard to see, as dark as the water and sky are. If I had to guess, I'd say it's the raft and it's lost a lot of air. I don't see any sign of the canoe. It won't sink, so unless he's ditched it somewhere else, we'd see it. Let's check the rest of our supplies and make sure they're all there."

They ran back to the trees where Gavin had hauled their food high into the branches to keep it away from bears. It was still there.

"Oh good," she said.

They entered the alcove.

"Gun's here." She pulled it from where she'd wrapped it in one of Gavin's socks and buried it underneath the rocks. "I hid it there just in case someone with kids came along while I was out running with Winston or a bad guy showed up."

"Okay, good show. You stay here with Winston and protect our things. I'll look for the paddler out on the lake. It will take him some time to get beyond our sight if he's on the lake, pulling my canoe in this choppy water. He'll have to hide it up in the brush on land."

"You don't think he's already done that? And he didn't take it into the lake with him?"

Gavin considered the possibility. "Maybe. I'll check the lake first before he can get out of range. He could have a couple of hours on us. After that, I'll look for any trail inland." He was glad she'd left with Winston and hadn't had a confrontation with whoever this turned out to be.

He ran along the beach, looking out across the lake, trying to see any sign of his orange canoe. He didn't see anyone out there, and the rain was really coming down now. He ran back toward the camp. Amelia was looking out at the lake, but she turned to observe him. "Anything?"

"I didn't see any sign of his canoe or mine. The rain is coming down so heavily now that it looks like the sky and lake are all blended into one gray mass. I'm going to search the area near where we tied up the canoe, in case he moved it and didn't have time to come back and take it yet."

"All right." Amelia had the gun in hand, standing under the rock ledge with Winston. The dog looked like he wanted to go with Gavin. But he wanted Winston to stay with Amelia.

His heart pounding with anger, Gavin checked the area where the canoe and raft had been tied. He discovered someone had walked from where they had been stowed, and he followed the trail in that direction for a few hundred yards.

Lightning lit up the sky. Gavin was ticked off that he had risked his neck to save his canoe and the raft, and whoever this bastard was had made them both vanish. The footprints on the tromped-on underbrush indicated

the man had moved away from both of them and…
hallelujah! Gavin's canoe came into view, left on the
ground in a thicket of shrubs. There was no one in sight.
Thrilled they still had transportation, Gavin smiled and
did a fist pump. The guy had abandoned the canoe and
taken off. Unless it was a trap.

But the man couldn't have had enough time to take
the raft out and dump the canoe at the same time. Unless
he was working with someone else. The winds began to
pick up as Gavin carried the canoe back to the camp and
secured it.

"Canoe's safe and sound," Gavin called out, and
Amelia came out to give him a hug. "Hopefully, the
storms will move out of the area by tomorrow. The
rain's letting up again. I'm going to check out the paddler and see if he left a scent behind."

"But what if you run into trouble over there?"

"I have a couple of knives. I'll be fine." He hated to
leave her and Winston behind, but if he could locate
the man and discovered he was wearing hunter's spray,
Gavin was questioning him. If not, Gavin was still
hoping to connect with someone who had a sat phone
out here.

He carried the canoe into the water, got in, and
paddled as fast as he could to reach the island. When
he finally arrived at the other island, he pulled his canoe
onto the shore. He carried it into the woods, then set it
down and quickly began tracking the man's scent. This
wasn't the man who had been wearing hunter's spray.
This man's scent was fresh and the same as the male
scent Gavin had smelled near the alcove. Winds had
shifted it around, so he was having a time locating the

direction in which the man had gone, though if he was carrying all his gear and the canoe, he must have made the portage here. The trail was well worn.

The guy must have been at their location sometime earlier. Gavin couldn't pinpoint the time any better than that. Hours, a couple of days? He didn't have a clue.

He recalled Amelia saying she'd seen a bear standing upright outside the tarp, silhouetted when lightning lit up the sky. What if it hadn't been a bear, but a man?

Amelia paced across the alcove, unable to wait any longer. Even though it would take Gavin a considerable amount of time to paddle to the location on the other island and then to search for the man, she couldn't sit still any longer. It could take him hours.

She decided the best thing they could have done was all stick together, paddle out to the location, and search for the man as a team. Gun holstered, she put on the holster, then got dressed in the rain gear. "Come on, Winston."

Amelia doubted anyone would come back for anything at the camp, since the really important thing was the canoe. She wanted to go to the beach across from where Gavin had said the other paddler's canoe had been so she didn't have to wait as long for him to return.

She jogged through the trees as fast as she could with Winston at her heels. She encouraged him to stay with her the whole way, and he didn't wander off to explore.

As soon as Amelia reached the shore where Gavin had taken her earlier as a wolf, she saw Gavin's orange canoe up in the trees near the shore on the other island. At least he'd made it there. She considered swimming across to search for him, but she wasn't a really good swimmer, and she was afraid Winston might tire out before they made it. So now what?

She began to pace again, but the whole time, she watched the trees where the canoe was, just in case Gavin or someone else showed up. She was glad she was wearing the rain gear, but she knew it would take her a little longer to reach the gun if she had to use it. She hoped she wouldn't need to. She also had it in mind to protect the canoe if anyone turned up and thought to move it.

Then she saw movement in the bushes on the other island. She was unfastening the rain jacket so she could grab the gun when she saw Gavin lifting the canoe and carrying it out of the woods.

"Gavin!"

He quickly lifted the canoe in front to look across the water and saw her and Winston beside her, wagging his tail vigorously. "Is everything all right?" He kept moving toward the water.

"Yes! I just couldn't sit still any longer. Did you find him?"

"His scent. By the time I reached the island and made the portage, he was way the hell downriver, headed for the next lake. I called out to him, but he couldn't hear me. At least, he didn't respond. So I assume he couldn't hear me from that distance."

Gavin put the canoe into the water and climbed aboard. Then he paddled across the lake to where Amelia and Winston waited. Winston was such a mellow dog for being a pup. He waited quietly on the shore with her until Gavin was nearly to the beach, and then he wagged his tail like crazy and ran into the water to greet him.

"Hello, pup. Do you want to go for a ride?" He helped Winston into the canoe, then joined Amelia.

Before she climbed aboard, she let out her breath. "I was worried you were taking so long. What if something happened to you and we were stranded?"

"I worried something was wrong when I saw you and Winston standing on the shore. Then I figured you just couldn't get enough of me."

She cast him a small smile. "Right. I just worried someone got the best of you."

"I'm under your skin, right?"

Her smile broadened. "I hate to admit it, but yeah, whether that's a good thing or bad."

"It's a good thing." He pulled her close, leaned down, and kissed her, long and hard and deep.

His warm lips felt good against hers as they stood in the rain kissing. She was glad to see him, even gladder that she hadn't waited for him to rejoin them.

They came up for air, their hearts beating as one, heat suffusing every cell in her body. Any time she touched the wolf like that, her pheromones kicked in, and she smelled his too. She had never felt that strong of a sensual connection with another wolf.

"Sorry it took me so long. I was running through the woods, afraid I would miss him. It didn't matter, because it had taken me so long to get there that the wind had scattered his scent. I will say it's the same man who had been in our camp. Before we settled or after, I'm not sure."

"Then the bear I thought I saw might have been a man."

"Possibly."

"The same one who took the raft?"

"I didn't smell his scent there. Or on the canoe either. I would have otherwise."

"So, a different man who's wearing hunter's spray?"

"Must be. And the other guy? Most likely just another paddler." He kissed her again and then helped her into the canoe. "In the meantime, I think it's best if we stay put at the camp tonight. Once the weather clears up tomorrow, if it does, we'll head for the bay and wait for the next seaplane to arrive. No more trying to chase down paddlers who might have a sat phone. It could be days before anyone comes though."

"That's true." She thought about their fired pilot again. "I can't believe Heaton would do all this, if he's the one responsible."

"The fact Red wouldn't fly with you—and your father switched places with you—sure makes it appear he's got a stake in this. I still suspect Heaton though." Gavin dipped his paddle into the water. "If your family learned you didn't return with the seaplane once the weather cleared, and there's no sign of it, the raft, or any debris, they won't have any clue where you are. That is until we can get ahold of someone paddling out here or if we can make contact with another seaplane. Were either your brother, you, or your dad bringing anyone out here anytime soon?"

She began paddling back to their camp. "I was. If I don't show up, my dad will know something's wrong. The guy had to have been watching us. He probably saw the plane go down, then maybe he took cover during the storm, or maybe he just kept an eye on what we were doing until we went to sleep."

"I'm glad you had hidden the gun."

"Me too, because if he comes anywhere near here,

I'm shooting him. What are you going to do about your client's request?"

Gavin let out his breath in exasperation. "I need to make sure you are returning home safely, first and foremost. And that your dad is able to have this business investigated so he can catch the bastard who did it."

"No matter who did it, I still believe we need to hire a good private eye to investigate this—one who's a wolf. And I've heard of one who is having trouble getting to his original assignment in the Boundary Waters. He's already seen the whole situation firsthand. So he's in on the ground floor, so to speak." She paddled faster, wanting to get to the safety of their alcove quicker, the rain still coming down fast. "I understand rich heiresses think enough of his agency that he gets hired without hesitation. And that he's already where he needs to be. Well, almost, once he finds the person responsible for this. He's said business is really picking up, so I wouldn't want to lose the opportunity to hire him on the spot."

"You're talking strictly about PI work, right?" Gavin asked. He sounded hopeful she might be talking about something else. Something more to do with them.

She glanced over her shoulder at him. "Depends on how much encouragement you might need."

"To leave here in a plane, lots."

Amelia laughed. "What about your other job, learning whether the executive is having an affair or not?"

"As soon as you and Winston are picked up, I'll catch up to the husband's group and do as much surveillance as I can. Your dad needs to make sure the other seaplanes are in good shape, in case the saboteur messed with any of them."

"Which means we need to get word to him and my brother before they fly again. Then again, if the saboteur was going to do something to each of the planes, he would have sabotaged them before this, at the same time as this one."

"True. So tomorrow, we head for the bay," Gavin said.

Even though she wanted to ensure everyone was okay at home, she didn't want to leave Gavin behind either.

"Or, if we see a canoe or canoeists paddling anywhere nearby, we can try to hail them," Gavin asked.

"What if Heaton is paddling one of them?" Wouldn't that confirm he had everything to do with this? She couldn't imagine he'd be out here otherwise.

"We have the gun, if he tries anything."

"But we stick together from here on out." She wasn't going along with a plan where they were split up again.

"Right. Until you go home."

"I've been thinking about that." She'd been thinking about this a lot, and if he was agreeable, she really wanted to help him. "If you're going to take this job, you'll need a partner. And since I know what Heaton looks like and what he smells like, in the event we run across his scent, and I've seen the people you are going after, I'll stay with you. Besides, if we find the people who are having their company canoe trip, a couple on a trip out here looks a lot less suspicious than one man with a camera. You could even take pictures of me, but instead, you would really be focusing on the husband and his shenanigans, if there are any."

"Well, hell, I think I got myself a new partner." Gavin smiled.

Amelia hadn't been sure how he'd take the news.

She'd thought he might feel she'd be more of a hindrance than anything. She was glad he was agreeable.

"That means sealing the deal." Gavin loved paddling with her, camping with her. He couldn't believe she'd offered to stay with him. And he was more than willing.

"I'm all for it. We work well together."

"We sure do."

"But we'll need someone—my brother or dad—to bring us a sat phone so that if we have an emergency, we can get ahold of someone."

"I agree."

The whole time they paddled, they watched for other paddlers or any sign of smoke curling in the air. All they saw was more rain.

When they could see the cliffs, Amelia perked up. "We're almost home!"

Gavin laughed. She was right. It had become their home away from home.

When they finally landed on the beach, Gavin helped Winston out of the canoe. Amelia hopped out, and they carried the canoe next to the alcove.

"I'm ready for us to seal the deal." Amelia hurried to strip off the rain gear while Gavin pulled off his rain jacket, and they set them near the banked fire. Winston shook all over them. "Oh no, Winston! You could have done that when we were still wearing the rain gear." Then she slid her hands up Gavin's arms and pressed the barest of kisses on his cheek and whispered, "I can't imagine this was how you sealed the deal with your other PI partners."

He pulled her in close and nuzzled her cheek gently. He was aware his stubble could scratch her, so he was trying to be careful, but she wasn't. She dragged her hands through his hair, then pulled his face down to hers, and he kissed her. As if they were on a desert island, never to be rescued. As if their life depended on it.

Gavin didn't know about her, but kissing her was making him react in ways he'd never done with any human woman. He'd never kissed a she-wolf before. Smelling her sweet scent and the way her pheromones were in turmoil kicked his own into action, and he was lost in the kiss. Her heart was thudding as hard as his as she pressed her soft curves against his body, her nipples pebbled, her skin hot.

He kissed her throat, her breastbone, and then he took a deep breath, not about to go any further. Instead, he placed his hands on the sides of her face and kissed her deeply, their tongues colliding. She was as aroused as he was, but he had to put on the brakes.

They came up for air, and he said, "You'll make one hell of a partner."

She smiled up at him. "Flying comes first for me, but yeah, anytime you need some help with pretending to be a couple, I'll be happy to do so."

Despite the rain and thunder overhead, Gavin heard movement in the brush near where the canoe was tied. *Hell.* If someone tried to take it again... He got the gun from Amelia and was about to head out to face the bastard when she grabbed his arm. "Bears. I smell bears."

Chapter 9

A MOTHER BLACK BEAR WEIGHING AROUND FOUR HUNDRED pounds was climbing a tree to get to the food Gavin had tied up there. Three cubs were watching her, waiting for her to bring them their meal, learning just how it was done. Amelia was right behind Gavin, pots in hand, and began banging them together, determined to chase off the bears and not lose the food to her and her cubs.

The mother bear scrambled down from the tree, and Amelia thought she was going to run off with her cubs. Instead, the bear bluff charged Gavin and Amelia.

As terrifying as it looked, Amelia knew the bear was only bluffing, snarling, trying to chase them off.

Amelia and Gavin yelled and stood their ground, clanging the pots and pans. Winston began to bark, wagging his tail.

Worried the dog would stir things up, Gavin said, "No barking, Winston. Quiet." He banged the paddles together and charged the bear in the same way, nearly freaking Amelia out.

Sure, she knew some first aid, but if the bear really tore him up badly…

Realizing Gavin and Amelia weren't running away, the bear and her cubs finally ran off.

Relieved, Amelia relaxed. "That is so not good. She smells our food, and the bears are discovering they can steal from paddlers and don't have to work to scrounge for their own food."

"We'll keep chasing her and her little ones off if they keep coming back. Our shelter is too well protected from the storm to leave it for now. Tomorrow morning after breakfast, we'll head to the place you were going to fly me to. Maybe your competition will be flying some folks in, if neither your dad nor brother show up."

She hoped it would be her dad or Slade. She couldn't tell their competition what had happened. Especially not if they had anything to do with this.

Gavin heated up the stew for dinner and spent the rest of the day watching through the rain for the bears or anyone paddling across the lake, though they didn't see any signs of either.

That night, Gavin lifted one of the sleeping bags. "Separate?"

"Together. In case it gets cold."

Gavin quickly unzipped the bags so he and Amelia could zip them together into a single large one.

While they were zipping the bags together, she said, "I was surprised to find you sleeping next to me and Winston on the other side of you this morning."

"He didn't want to separate us."

She laughed, and they curled up in the bag together.

"You traveled a hell of a way as a wolf to get help after you ditched the plane in the woods after the heist," Gavin said, snuggling with her. "Did you run into anyone while trying to reach your family?"

"Some horseback riders. They didn't see me, and I skirted way around them, afraid I'd spook the horses. They were eight hours or more from where you were. I couldn't have told them about you anyway. Not without clothes and trying to explain how I'd moved so quickly from the crash site. And I came across a couple of camp-sites, but again, I stayed clear of them. It's easier for a gray wolf to blend into the woods. As a white wolf, I have to be much more careful. Though we're shorter legged, so sometimes we can pass as a mixed dog of some sort."

"We've taken some service dog training so we can carry vests with us on trips if we need them," Gavin said.

Amelia laughed. "I'm sorry. We never have trouble like that. But that's a really good idea."

"We've had to resort to it a few times. Sometimes the urge to shift still isn't controllable. And yeah, it works."

The rain was letting up, the thunder moving off in the distance.

Amelia sighed. "Considering how we got here, I feel like this has been the most interesting camping experi-ence I've ever had."

"And I wish it didn't have to end."

"You're not getting rid of me that easily. I'm your PI partner in this venture, right?"

He smiled.

Early the next morning, Gavin was cooking the eggs and sausage before they packed up their camp and left when he heard rustling in the brush. He had his gun with him in case the person had come back for the canoe and quickly pulled it out of the holster, but only ten feet away, the big mother bear stood. "They're back," he warned Amelia, who was unzipping the two sleeping bags, then rolling them up to pack them away in the waterproof bags.

"The bears?" she asked for clarification.

"Yeah. Can you watch the cooking while I chase them away?" He didn't want to burn their breakfast.

"Sure." She came out of their alcove and hurried to grab the pan from him, scrambling the eggs while he picked up a couple of other pots and started banging them together, moving toward the bears a little to intimidate the mother.

The mother bear eyed the container of food and a couple of backpacks Gavin hadn't slipped into the dry packs yet. He could see the thought process. Could the bear grab the pack and get away with it before Gavin could stop her? He'd read several accounts of bears taking off with field packs filled with food, sometimes ripping them apart and eating the contents in front of the surprised paddlers.

He yelled at the bear and growled. If he thought howling would have helped, he would have done that too.

The sow finally turned and ran off, the cubs racing after her.

"They're sneaky," Amelia said. "You saw just what she thought she was going to grab, and she was testing your resolve."

"Yeah, I sure did. They had to kill a bear a while back that bit a woman in the ankle and pulled her from her tent into the woods. She was screaming, and her boyfriend was yelling and hollering, trying to scare the bear off. Once they've begun to attack humans—"

"They don't stop."

After he and Amelia ate and she'd fed Winston, they

washed up and finished packing their camping gear. Once they were done, they both looked at their shelter. Without the tarp to make it home, it seemed part of the wilderness again.

"I'm going to miss it," she admitted.

He wrapped his arm around her shoulders. "Why don't we make a date to return here when we can?"

She smiled up at him. "It's a deal. We'll come when there's no chance of a storm."

"I liked hearing the rain pouring all around us while we kept warm and dry in our little shelter."

"Yeah, it was like an off-and-on waterfall. The thunder and lightning I could do without."

Amelia put on Winston's preserver, and then they each put on their own.

Once they finally managed to get Winston into the canoe, Gavin and Amelia climbed in and headed out. It would take them about six hours of paddling to reach their destination, but they were going to enjoy it while they could. The sun was shining, a smattering of clouds floating across the sky. The day was beginning to heat up, a light breeze barely rippling the water as they dipped the paddles into it.

They first headed for the location in the lake where they'd seen what they thought was the raft. If it had been the raft, it was gone now. They looked for any sign of the plane or anything that might have floated out of it, but they found nothing. Near one of the islands, moose were standing in the water observing them. Amelia and Gavin continued to scan the lake and islands, looking for any sign of humans. They didn't see smoke from campfires or anyone paddling on the water.

A hawk flew overhead, and a flock of geese landed on a sandbar.

It was a pretty day, the sun rising higher in the sky, and if Gavin had just been canoeing with a pretty Arctic wolf, he would have thoroughly enjoyed the day. If it wasn't for the business with the plane.

They heard a seaplane's engine before they were even two hours out from their alcove shelter, and they stopped paddling and looked up to see if they could spy the craft. When they finally did, Amelia began waving her arms, trying to signal to them. The seaplane continued to the dock. If anyone on the plane had seen them, they probably assumed she was just waving hello. Gavin and Amelia still had another four hours to paddle before they reached the location.

"Your plane, or the competition's?" Gavin asked.

"The competition's," Amelia said, sounding disgruntled. "If we still had the flare gun, we could have shot the flares with it."

Gavin smiled at her. "Signaled to them."

She snorted. "I'm afraid we'll never make it in time before they drop their passengers and their gear off and leave again."

"Right, but maybe we can reach some of the canoeists before they paddle away and see if any of them have a sat phone. Then we can call your dad, and I can get ahold of my partners and let them know what's happened."

"Will they join you here?"

"They're all working on cases right now. This wasn't supposed to be a big deal. I just need to update them on what's going on."

"But now you've picked up another case. The

National Transportation Safety Board will investigate the crash, and they'll involve law enforcement officials if it looks like it was sabotage. We'll need more than just aviation accident investigators looking into this though. It can take several months to a year or more to learn the truth. We need to know if Heaton was responsible. And if so, whether he acted alone or was paid to do it."

"He's a wolf. He can't go to prison." That was something Gavin and his partners hadn't had to deal with much—rogue wolves and what to do with them. They'd had trouble with werewolf hunters when they'd been first turned, and that was a whole other story.

"I agree. Which is why we need you to help look into the matter."

The seaplane took off and Amelia tried to signal again, but either they didn't notice or just figured she was waving at them. "Damn it." She began paddling again.

"What's going to happen to Winston?" Gavin couldn't help but feel concerned about the pup.

"He doesn't have a home now." Amelia sounded choked up about it.

"I'll take him."

She turned around, her eyes filled with tears.

"Hey, Amelia, it's all right. It's doable. Faith is home with the kids mostly, and Owen's mate is a writer and home alone working on her books. If I take him in, I'm sure they'll watch him while I'm gone on assignments like this one."

She smiled through her tears.

Not that he'd planned it that way, but Gavin believed if he'd wanted to make some headway with the she-wolf, he'd done the right thing by her. He really couldn't imagine Winston not having a big yard to run in, or kids to play with, or a pack to call his own. He would be much loved. He was a good dog, and he deserved a good family. "Faith and Cameron's kids will love him to pieces. My yard's not fenced, but we live on a lake and all the woods around us are ours. He can go on long walks with us, either when we're wolves or as humans. I'll have to train him to walk with me and not run off."

"If I wasn't afraid I'd tip over the canoe, I'd give you a big hug and kiss."

Gavin smiled. "Keep that thought, and when we reach the dock, I'll be ready for it."

"Thank you," she said. "I really mean it. I've been trying to think of some way I could keep him. I just don't have a big enough place."

"We'll give him the home he deserves."

"Thank you."

They were paddling as fast as they could, hoping to catch up to the canoeists who would be left off at the dock. Amelia and Gavin were still so far out that they couldn't see them or the dock. Amelia knew the canoeists would be on their way, and there was no telling where they'd be by the time she and Gavin got closer. The paddlers could be long gone. She still couldn't believe he'd offered to take Winston, and she thought the world of him for it. Winston would too.

She kept telling herself another seaplane could be along any time. Even her brother's or father's, if they had a change of schedule. As they drew closer to the dock three and a half hours later, they saw the specks of color off in the distance—an orange and a yellow canoe—too far for them to holler out to. Too far for the paddlers to see Amelia and Gavin, even if they were looking this way.

With a heavy heart, and feeling discouraged when they finally reached the dock, Amelia knew she was going to be sore the next day, with as much paddling as they'd done. Now she worried she might not be going anywhere. That they might end up having to set up camp right here and stay for as long as it took for someone to come along.

She and Gavin helped Winston out of the canoe, and then she said, "Listen, you have a job to do. Go do it. Surely someone will come along and—"

"It's true I don't like to miss doing a job when I've signed up for it. But right now, getting you home safely is my priority. I wouldn't leave you out here by yourself—"

"With Winston…"

"With Winston, even if I left most of my gear so you could be comfortable in case a seaplane shows up."

Then she thought she saw something in the distance. A red canoe?

Gavin turned to see what she was watching. He pulled out his binoculars to get a look. "A canoe with a man and a woman. It appears they're headed this way. They should get here in another hour, hour and a half, maybe."

"It's too late in the day for anyone to come pick them up. They must be setting up camp here, and someone will fly them out in the morning."

"That would be good." Gavin handed her the binoculars. "Recognize anyone?"

"They're too far away. Both have billed caps and are wearing sunglasses." She shook her head. "I can't tell. Should we set up camp or leave in case they're trouble?"

"We stay. We'll set up camp, but I want you and Winston out of firing range, just in case. It looks like just a couple."

After they set up camp, Gavin cooked the rest of the stew for dinner, and Amelia fed Winston.

They kept an eye on the approaching canoe. "Anyone you know?" he asked again as the canoe drew closer.

"Oh," she said. "They're two of the people who were with that CEO, the ones doing the team-building trip."

"What?" Gavin took the binoculars from her and looked out at the lake. "Why would they be returning this soon? And only two of them?"

"I don't know. Maybe they have a sat phone. Since they weren't scheduled to return for nine days, we wouldn't be picking them up until then. They must have run into trouble."

"Okay, so at least they're probably not a problem," Gavin said.

They waved at the couple as they neared the dock. "Which ones are they?" Gavin asked Amelia.

"The female executive, Nina, and one of the other male executives, Theodore."

Gavin and Amelia both went to the dock to help them, Winston tagging along to greet them. "You're one of the pilots with the same company that flew us here," Nina Cavendish said.

"Yeah, Amelia White. This is my friend Gavin Summerfield," Amelia said. "And Theodore…"

"Canton," Theodore offered.

Gavin shook Theodore's hand.

"You wouldn't happen to have a sat phone we could borrow, would you?" Amelia asked.

"No. Our CEO has one," Theodore said. "Nina has food poisoning. Lee called for a pickup, and I volunteered to bring Nina here to fly out. Once she's picked up, I'm returning to our campsite."

"You can find your way back okay?" Gavin asked.

"Sure. I got here fine. And this is a test. We come here for team playing and to show our fortitude. Every time we go on these trips, I take on a new challenge. Makes me feel more alive."

He should have been with them when they crashed. "Who's coming to pick you up?" Amelia asked Nina.

"Not sure who. The woman we talked to said she'd send one of you. But you're here," Theodore said.

"Uh, yeah. So it won't be me." Amelia didn't want to tell them her father's plane had been sabotaged and had sunk in the lake. She was afraid they would be scared to fly back with her father or brother if they thought the other planes had been tampered with too.

"Excuse me," Nina said and hurried off to the woods.

Theodore started unloading the canoe, and they helped him. "I'm glad to see you here. I've tried to keep her hydrated, but we've had a real time of it getting here," Theodore said.

"I'm sure she appreciates you for bringing her," Gavin said.

"She's been embarrassed, but we've all been there. So you're not flying, I take it? Just here paddling like the rest of us?"

"Yeah," Amelia said.

"How's everyone else feeling at camp? Are they all right?" Gavin asked.

"Yeah. Nina just ate something that disagreed with her. No one else felt sick."

"That's good. Have you had any trouble with bears?" Amelia asked.

"No. You?"

"A mother and three cubs. We were on the island over there." Gavin pointed in the direction, then asked, "Do you want some of our stew?"

"Sure, I'd love it. I'm not sure that Nina can eat anything."

"How's your team-building going?" Gavin asked. "Amelia told me you were with a company group."

"Well, it's been a little shaky, to say the least. Between the storms and staying in our tents, and now with Nina getting sick just when the weather is clearing. We'll sure miss her."

Nina screamed.

Gavin had his gun out in a flash. "Stay here! Keep Winston here."

"He's got a gun," Theodore said, his eyes rounded.

Gavin hoped Amelia didn't tell the executive he was a PI. He raced into the woods, and not too far from the camp, he saw Nina running for him. "A wolf," she said, breathless, terrified, her skin even paler, and she was trembling.

"All right. Head back to the camp. I'll look for him. They normally won't hurt people." The wolf might be just a regular, old wolf. But what if it was the pilot Amelia's father had fired? Gavin needed to shift to be able to track him. Making sure Nina couldn't see him any longer, he quickly stripped off his clothes and shifted. Then he headed in the direction he thought the wolf had run after he found some gray fur caught on a branch. He kept looking for more signs of fur.

When he tried to find the wolf's scent to track him down, Gavin realized the wolf had left none.

Amelia was never gladder than when Gavin returned to camp. "Nina said she saw a gray wolf."

"Yeah, I chased after him. He was harmless. You know, like wolves are. Bears, moose, that can be another story."

"Oh sure, they won't attack people. Not normally." But Amelia saw the look Gavin gave her, and she worried that Heaton was the wolf.

"Do you think you can eat some beef stew?" Gavin asked Nina.

Nina shook her head. "Thanks, no."

"I've got some medicine that should help." Gavin sorted through one of his bags and brought out a package of pills. "Take one of these, and that should stop it."

"Thanks so much," Nina said. "Lee thought she had some in her first aid kit, but she didn't." Nina took the medicine and washed it down with water.

Gavin helped Theodore set up their tent, eager to learn what he could about the dynamics between Conrad and the sales associate, since he was getting such a late start investigating. "Amelia was telling me her dad and her brother had taken a couple of groups out there to work on team-building. She said the CEO herself came, and then the rest of you are executives?"

"We have two sales associates with us too. They take the notes and make the coffee."

"I was really surprised to see Mindy with the group. She used to live near me when I was in Alaska. How long has she worked for the greeting-card company?" Amelia asked.

Gavin worked on building the fire some more, glad Amelia was helping him with his mission.

"Two years. So, you knew her in Alaska?" Theodore finished his stew.

Amelia set her plate down and drank some water. "Yeah. You know how it is with neighbors. You usually don't know them all that well."

"I agree. It's a small world. You must have heard she and her husband got into some trouble," Theodore said.

"Yep," Amelia said.

Gavin was surprised Amelia didn't tell Theodore all she knew about it, maybe not wanting to talk about someone he worked with if he didn't ask for specifics.

"All I know is based on reading the newspaper accounts," Theodore said. "Our CEO has a habit of hiring women as sales associates who have been in trouble with the law. Nothing major. She likes to give them a second chance."

"Running a pet theft ring isn't a minor offense," Amelia said, her hackles raised.

The courts might see it as nothing major, but Gavin agreed with Amelia.

"Uh, yeah, I didn't mean it that way." Theodore looked at Winston, and Gavin suspected the guy realized pet lovers wouldn't appreciate what Mindy and her husband had done.

Gavin wondered just how much Theodore knew about the situation. The newspaper accounts hadn't mentioned Gavin, as if the police didn't want to let on that they hadn't been doing their jobs. Their hands had been tied. As Joe Civilian, Gavin's hadn't been. He was just a concerned pet owner looking for his missing Samoyeds. And the police were grateful to be his backup in case anything got out of hand, which it did.

But Gavin did wonder if everyone in this select group of executives knew about Mindy's history.

"Are Mindy and her husband still together?" Gavin asked.

Theodore frowned. "She's divorcing him, says she's turning over a new leaf, has a good job, and doesn't want to ruin that. Plus, as far as I can tell, she's really interested in one of our executives." Theodore shrugged. "If her husband is still up to no good, I don't blame her. She didn't give any particulars, but that's the impression I have. I'm not sure Orwell is interested in marrying her either. That's just what it looks like to me from outward appearances. She's easy, and he's having fun with it."

"Is he married?" Amelia asked.

"Separated. Which, once he's divorced, makes him extremely eligible, though I believe the separation might be due to the affair Mindy and Orwell are having. Are you from Alaska too?" Theodore asked Gavin, changing the subject.

Nina was sipping water quietly, but she suddenly stood up and said, "I'll be right back." She hurried off to the woods.

"Will you be all right?" Gavin asked her, worried she might still be scared about the wolf.

"No, I'll be good. If I scream, feel free to rescue me."

"Sure thing." Then Gavin answered Theodore's question. "No, I'm originally from Seattle." Gavin wasn't going to tell him about helping to take Mindy and her husband down.

"That's where our home office is. See? I told you. It's a small world. You live somewhere else now?" Theodore asked.

"Close to here in Minnesota. I love the wilderness."

"Well, I admit I'm more of a five-star hotel guy, but I've been getting better at paddling ever since the CEO began taking us on these trips three years ago. The first year, I thought I'd die, every muscle group contorted in pain. She has it right though. At first, I thought she was just bored and wanted some companionship while she worked out. I learned the hard way she's interested not only in exercising our minds at work, but also in getting us in physical shape. We can work longer hours without feeling the stress because we're keeping in shape. Believe me, my wife loves that I work for the company. We joined a gym and even work out together now. It's been a life changer for us."

Amelia nodded. "Gavin and I like to run together too. It's a nice way to get to know each other and to work out any stress we might be feeling." She reached over and ran her hand over Gavin's thigh.

He smiled at her.

The rumble of a plane's engine caught their attention, well before Theodore heard it with his human hearing. Amelia and Gavin looked in the direction it was coming from, both surprised that anyone would be arriving this late in the day. They'd have a full camp at this rate, with another group of paddlers being dropped off. As they watched for the seaplane, Theodore finally heard it too, and Nina came back from the woods and looked up at the sky.

"More paddlers?" Theodore asked.

"It's my dad's, well, my plane," Amelia said, her brows furrowed, indicating she was worried, but at the same time, Gavin heard the relief in her voice. "He's not carrying any canoes. He must be coming early to pick up Nina."

"Then you can return with him," Gavin said, having mixed feelings about it. He truly enjoyed Amelia's company, but he didn't want her in a bind because she was with him while he tried to track down the person causing all the trouble for them. He didn't want her to feel she was obligated to go with him.

Theodore eyed them, looking as though he thought Gavin and Amelia must be having relationship troubles, if Gavin was suggesting she return with her father.

"I'll tell my dad what happened, but I'm continuing on the vacation paddling with you. He can take Winston with him. Mom can watch him until we return and you can take him home with you."

"Are you sure?" Gavin was surprised she'd really want to stay with him to help. He was concerned for her safety, especially if the wolf that had scared Nina was Heaton. On the other hand, no one would suspect Gavin was doing surveillance. Not when he was paddling with his girlfriend. Theodore would be returning to his company's campsite in the morning, and if he happened to see them later, he would think they were just there having fun on a camping trip.

"Yeah, I want to stay with you." Amelia headed for

the dock, then paced up and down it, anxiously waiting for her dad to land.

"I guess you'll still be staying the night here with us," Gavin said to Theodore, who was near the campfire, waiting, in case Nina had to return to the woods.

"Yeah. I wouldn't attempt to return to the island tonight. It would be dark before I got there. It took me eight hours to reach here."

"I wouldn't either." Though with his wolf's night vision, Gavin could have done it. And he was an expert paddler, so physically, he could have made it. Their present company precluded that. "You can have breakfast with us in the morning, then."

"Thanks, I'd like that. I brought some food with me for tonight and tomorrow, since I wouldn't have been able to rejoin the group until later. I'll share that with you too."

"Sure." Now that Amelia was staying with Gavin longer, they would need more food.

The plane landed on the water, and Henry finally parked it at the dock. Amelia hurried to tie the plane up. Nina was back in the woods, being sick. Gavin hoped the medicine would kick in soon and she'd make it back to the hangar okay.

"I tried getting ahold of you," her father said to Amelia, sounding anxious. "Where's the plane?"

She told him what had happened, and her father's expression was angry.

"I ran by your place, and you weren't there. I checked with the shelter where you were taking Winston, and they said you hadn't arrived. You'd just disappeared off the radar. That and the woman being so sick are why I came tonight instead of waiting until tomorrow."

"We're okay. All three of us." She gave her dad a hug and spoke softly for his ears only, though with his enhanced hearing, Gavin made out her words.

"We think my plane, well, your plane was sabotaged." Then she told Henry the rest, their heads bowed together a little while she explained what had happened. She also told him about Gavin being an Arctic wolf.

Her dad looked over at Gavin, and he wondered if Henry worried about his daughter being alone with the wolf. Or maybe he was just shocked to learn Gavin was an Arctic wolf too. Thankfully, she didn't tell him the rest of their history together.

When she mentioned Gavin was taking Winston, her father smirked at the PI. Gavin seemed to be earning some good points with everyone over that. He knew Winston would appreciate it most, and certainly, he'd missed having a dog all these years. He wondered if Amelia's father believed he was just offering to take in the dog to win over the girl. If it helped, Gavin was all for it.

Once a pale-faced Nina returned from the woods, Gavin and Theodore packed her bags in the plane, while Amelia grabbed Winston's container of kibble and carried it there.

Henry shook Gavin's hand, his handshake firm, as if warning him to take care of his daughter. Not to be bested, Gavin gave Henry just as firm a handshake back, letting him know he was alpha all the way and would take care of Amelia. Henry inclined his head a little to Gavin in approval, his expression still stern. Henry shook Theodore's hand too, but Gavin suspected he didn't use quite the gorilla grip on him.

Amelia's dad helped Nina into the plane. Gavin and

Amelia hugged Winston, then put on his life preserver and loaded him in. Henry exited the plane with a sat phone and a couple of bags in hand. Theodore was still standing on the dock like he was part of the group, but Henry needed to speak to Amelia privately and took her aside.

"I'll see you later," Gavin said to Henry. "Hey, want a cup of coffee?" he asked Theodore to move him away from the father-and-daughter talk.

"Yeah, sure." Theodore and Gavin left the dock and returned to the camp.

Amelia was so glad her father had come and not their competition. "Dad, the man who didn't want me to fly the plane was one of the jewelry-store thieves running with my ex-boyfriend in Seattle. I didn't realize it until after we had crashed."

Her dad's eyes widened.

"What are the odds that a jewel thief shows up and causes a scene, then I end up flying with Gavin on the sabotaged plane?"

"Hell."

"Yeah. It's too much of a coincidence. But we both believe Heaton actually did the sabotage."

"I can believe that. I'll notify the authorities. You just…enjoy yourself. They'll want to speak with you too," Henry told Amelia.

"All right, Dad. I'm so sorry I lost the plane."

"The plane isn't what is important. You are. Are you sure you don't want to return with me?"

"No, I'm certain. Gavin's going to help us with this. And I want to help with his case, since he hasn't been able to do anything on it yet because of what happened.

Plus, even when I suggested just leaving me here while he took care of his business, he wouldn't do it. Are you going to be all right without me flying for a while?"

"Yeah, but you know how I feel about this." He motioned to the bags. "You left your bags and your sat phone in the plane when we switched off. I suspect you'll be wanting these."

"Boy, do I ever."

"You're all right with—"

"My boyfriend? Absolutely."

Her dad raised his brows, glancing back at Gavin as if he couldn't believe it, or maybe he realized she was just saying that for their cover.

"Call me when you arrive safely," Amelia told her dad.

"I will, and I'll have both our planes checked out to make sure they hadn't been tampered with. Though we've had no trouble with them, so I suspect this was meant for either me or our passengers."

Henry wished them all luck, gave Amelia a hug, and climbed back into the plane. "Be careful."

"We will."

After returning to say goodbye, Gavin untied the ropes, and Amelia's father took off across the lake until he was airborne.

Gavin wrapped his arm around Amelia's shoulders as they watched her father flying overhead, wanting the intimacy and not just to take part in some role they were bound to play. Then they left the dock and returned to the campfire.

Pulling out a bag, Gavin asked Amelia and Theodore, "Do you want to roast some marshmallows?"

He wanted to talk to Amelia about what they were going to do tomorrow. They needed to travel in the same direction Theodore would be paddling, but they couldn't just follow him. Well, maybe partway, and then paddle off to another island close by.

"Yeah," Theodore said, and Amelia agreed. "That was damn decent of your dad to make the trip early."

"He was concerned about Nina getting too dehydrated. I'm glad he came tonight too," Amelia said.

"He'll take good care of her. You know, I miss Winston already," Gavin said as he skewered marshmallows on metal rods and handed one to each of them. They began to roast the marshmallows over the campfire, watching the white marshmallows turn golden brown and gooey. "He's so big, he's easy to miss when he's not around."

"He's a beautiful dog," Theodore said. "How big do they get?"

"Almost two hundred pounds when they're full grown," Amelia said. "He's only a year old."

"I have two sons who eat everything in the house and then some. I can't imagine feeding a dog that big too." Theodore looked at the woods nearby. "Do you think the wolf will come back?"

"No. Not if he knows what's good for him. They don't really bother people. And he's a lone wolf."

"Did you track him?" Amelia asked.

"You can track a wolf?" Theodore sounded awed.

"Yeah, but he was super wily, as if he has been around humans a lot," Gavin said.

Amelia's eyes widened fractionally.

Clearly she realized, as he did, that the wolf had to be a shifter.

Chapter 10

"I HOPE YOU WERE ALL RIGHT WITH ME CALLING YOU MY boyfriend," Amelia said in Gavin's ear as they snuggled together in his tent later that night, while Theodore slept in his own tent across the campfire from them.

"Are you kidding? I've been working toward that goal ever since I met you again." Gavin loved the intimacy he shared with Amelia and thought of how much of a void there would be if she wasn't with him now—without her warmth, her soft touch, her whispered breath against his ear, her heart beating in rhythm with his, her scent that made him want her the way a male wolf craves a she-wolf.

"Even after the first time and, technically, second time we met? You're not a glutton for punishment, are you?"

He laughed. "I'm hoping we're beyond that."

She licked his chest. "Maybe I should have made you work harder for it."

He kissed her forehead. "I would have. Believe me. I heard most of what you told your dad and that he's going to get ahold of the accident investigators. I couldn't read his body language from where Theodore and I were standing near the campfire though."

"He's angry. He gets real quiet when he's mad. Before he reacts, he considers all the implications."

"Like a wolf."

"Yeah. And about that… He was shocked you were

one too, and even more shocked to learn you're an Arctic wolf like us."

Gavin traced his fingers over her naked shoulder in a gentle caress, not disturbing the sleeping bag tugged up to cover her back. "Did he believe you about the boyfriend-girlfriend bit?"

She nuzzled his chest. "I'm sure he smelled you all over me, so he wasn't entirely shocked."

Gavin laughed. "I guess it went without saying."

She swept her hand down his bare chest. "You could have just been warming me up after our little swim in the cold lake."

"He's too wily to think that's all there is to it."

"Right. Learning you are a PI and former cop, he probably felt you could protect me if I needed it."

Which was the only downside to having Amelia here. Someone might wish her harm. "Your dad didn't mind that you weren't going to return and help with the sched- uled flights?"

She shook her head. "We're down a plane. So no. He's angry we're going to have to cancel on some flights because we're short a plane though. We have another, but it's undergoing refurbishing."

"He wasn't worried that Heaton might be out here as a wolf?" Gavin was surprised her father wasn't more concerned about that.

She sighed. "I didn't tell my dad that part. He defi- nitely wouldn't have wanted me to stay if I'd told him about that *and* about the raft."

The truth was coming out. Gavin groaned. He'd thought Amelia would be perfectly honest with her dad about the situation.

"What? I can protect you. Don't worry."

"From your father? He will want to kill me if he learns I didn't insist you return home with him for your own safety."

"If I had seen the wolf, I would have known it was Heaton, scent or no."

"All right."

"Besides, you need me for your cover story."

Gavin let out his breath. "As soon as Theodore's asleep, I'm looking for Heaton, if it was him. You just stay here. I'll leave the gun with you."

"Well, don't get yourself killed over it, or my dad will be mad."

"I fully intend to be the one left standing if it comes to that."

"You better be."

An hour later, Gavin kissed Amelia. "I'm heading out."

"Be careful, and if you need me, just howl."

"I need you, all right." Then he dressed, kissed her again, and left the tent. In the woods some way from their tents, he left his clothes and shifted. Adrenaline pumping, he was in hunting mode, praying this wouldn't backfire and put Amelia at risk.

While Gavin was off trying to track down the wolf, Amelia couldn't sleep. She dressed in jeans and her own blue sweatshirt, socks, and boots, then left the tent to make a fire. Once she sat beside it, gun in hand in case Heaton showed up, she watched the woods, listening for sounds of anyone walking about. Or growling in the distance. Theodore was lightly snoring in his tent.

In the romance department, she didn't think Theodore was interested in Nina in an intimate way, beyond being concerned about her health. Just a working relationship. Because he'd paddled all the way here to ensure Nina could go home sooner when she felt so ill, Amelia saw Theodore as a hero.

The sat phone suddenly rang and startled her, giving her a near heart attack. She quickly answered the phone so it wouldn't disturb Theodore. The caller identified himself as Phil Thomas, the man heading the team to investigate her plane crash. "I'm sorry I'm calling you so late. I was just assigned to head up the task force to investigate this. Your father said you were paddling with your boyfriend tomorrow. I need your story concerning the accident, and I'll need to speak with you and your boyfriend tomorrow, face-to-face, before you leave."

"Uh, yes, of course." She didn't want to wake Theodore—if his sleep hadn't already been disturbed—and have him learn the truth. She banked the campfire, then headed into the woods away from camp, as far as she could in the dark with the moon lighting her way, so she could talk privately to the investigator.

Suddenly, she saw the glow of fluorescent eyes in the brush. Gun in one hand, the phone in the other, she said to the caller, "Just a minute. Can I call you back? I see a wolf." She hung up on him before he could say a word.

"Gavin?" she called out to the wolf. Gavin and Heaton were similar in size and build. Their markings were different, but she couldn't really see them that well in the dark.

If it was Gavin, she suspected he would have woofed and come running to join her. This wolf was wary, watchful. What if it was a real wolf, smelling the beef stew they'd cooked earlier and checking it out?

"Heaton? Why would you have sabotaged the plane? Risking killing me and my passengers? Revenge?" She knew he couldn't answer her, but she had to ask the question, if he was the wolf.

They heard noise in the brush, and the wolf turned, then dashed off.

A couple of minutes later, she saw wolf's eyes again. "Gavin?"

He woofed at her. Now she was worried whether it really was him. She couldn't smell him because the breeze was blowing away from her.

He shifted. "Just me," Gavin said, then joined her and caged her with his arms. "What are you doing out here?"

"The accident investigator called, and I didn't want to disturb Theodore's sleep. Then I saw a wolf. He didn't respond to me like you did."

"Hell." Gavin released her and shifted, then sniffed around and headed deeper into the woods. He disappeared from her sight and she waited, listening. Brush crunched nearby, and she heard a zipper sliding up. Gavin must have shifted and was getting dressed. She was glad, but she hoped if the wolf was Heaton, he wouldn't attack Gavin when he was more vulnerable.

Gavin approached and wrapped his arm around her shoulders. "Let's go back to the campsite."

"I promised the investigator I'd call him back. I left him hanging when I told him I saw a wolf."

"Okay." Gavin released her. "Give me the gun, and I'll stand watch while you talk to him. I couldn't locate the wolf, not when he's wearing hunter's spray. He has us at a disadvantage."

"I didn't think of that." Which made her believe the wolf had to be Heaton if there were no other wolf shifters in the area. She called the investigator back and filled him in on the details.

"We'll be out there in the morning, first thing."

She didn't want to delay the plane investigation or surveillance on Gavin's case. She also didn't want Theodore to see the accident investigators arrive and learn what was going on. She knew they needed to talk to the investigators though.

"All right." She just hoped the investigators would finish with them quickly and quietly, and then she and Gavin could be on their way.

After they ended the call, she and Gavin returned to camp. "We'll deal with it. No worries, Amelia," he said. They slipped back inside the tent.

"Since I'm going to be stuck talking to the investigators in the morning, why don't you just go ahead with your case? Maybe you could make sure Theodore's out of here before I have to deal with this." That was her main concern, repercussions about the plane crash for their business. She'd already delayed Gavin enough.

"You forget one thing. I need your help in this case, and the crash investigators are going to want to hear my version of what happened too. Which means you can't get rid of me that easily."

Amelia sighed, really not wanting Theodore to hear what was going on. "What about Heaton?"

"That's another reason for sticking together. I wouldn't leave you here alone."

"Someone would take me home. One of the investigators."

She and Gavin stripped off their clothes and climbed into the sleeping bag together. "You want me to leave before the investigators even get here. Not doing that. Not only because I wouldn't risk your safety, but because they'll want my statement."

With that, they snuggled. Gavin kissed her forehead. "It will be all right. One way or another. If Theodore learns what is going on, we can deal with it. We'll have a busy day tomorrow."

"Hmm," she said, already feeling sleepy and thinking if Gavin wasn't here with her, she wouldn't still be awake. He made her want to enjoy every aspect of being with him until she couldn't stay awake a second longer.

They both slept soundly with no Winston to disturb their sleep, no sounds that indicated a wolf was prowling the campground, no sat phone ringing. It wasn't until they smelled coffee and heard a plane approaching that Amelia stirred. Despite wanting to get this over with and move on with the mission, she didn't want to give up on the plane crash investigation.

Then she remembered Theodore—that he was the one who'd made the coffee—and she groaned. Great. She'd secretly hoped he would have taken off to make the most of the early-morning hours and to reach his group by early evening.

So much for keeping the crash a secret from Theodore.

———※———

Gavin could smell Amelia's anxiousness as they rushed to dress. "You go talk with the investigators. I'll keep

Theodore occupied." Gavin knew she didn't want word to get back to the rest of their passengers about the plane wreck. Her father's arrival last night was sure to garner goodwill because it showed his concern about one of their passengers. He'd risked coming that late in the evening, but this business could cast a bad light on the company.

"All right." Even though she was in a rush, she paused to give Gavin a hug and kiss, then hurried out of the tent. "Good morning, Theo—"

Gavin joined them and saw a tall, blond-haired man, lightly whiskered, sitting beside the fire, sipping coffee with Theodore.

"What are you doing here, Heaton?" Amelia asked, her words hard.

Furious the man was here, Gavin touched her shoulder to remind her she was trying to circumvent Theodore hearing much about the situation with the accident investigators.

She growled under her breath about strangling someone and then smiled sweetly at Theodore. "Be right back."

Theodore was eyeing the three of them. He said good morning to Amelia and Gavin but looked uneasy.

"I'll make us a quick breakfast so Theodore can get on his way," Gavin told Amelia, then gave Heaton a scathing look.

The man just eyed him back, not in the least bit intimidated.

Gavin quickly started some oatmeal, hoping Heaton would leave. Then again, as soon as Theodore left, Gavin could question him.

"Trouble?" Heaton asked, acting mildly concerned.

Amelia looked ready to slug him and stalked off to greet the investigators before she actually did.

Gavin was ready to do the same.

"So, who are you?" Heaton asked Gavin. "Amelia's new boyfriend?"

Theodore thanked Gavin when he handed him a mug of oatmeal. He looked torn between wanting to hear what was going on between the three of them and being sorry he had invited Heaton to have coffee with them because of the obvious animosity Gavin and Amelia were showing toward their uninvited guest.

Gavin didn't offer Heaton a mug of oatmeal and was waiting to make some for Amelia and himself after the investigators took their statements. In the meantime, he poured himself a mug of coffee. He was wondering where Heaton's canoe was. He hadn't seen it when he was searching for the wolf last night.

Theodore scarfed down his oatmeal in record time. He hadn't eaten the beef stew that fast last night, so Gavin assumed he was feeling the need to pack up and go. "Hey, if I'm going to make it early enough to join my group, I need to leave now."

"That's an excellent idea. I can help you pack, and I'll clean up your mug later," Gavin said, taking the mug from him.

"Thanks. I appreciate all you did for me, and for Nina." Theodore cast Heaton an annoyed look, probably figuring the guy was trying to mess up the situation with Amelia's new boyfriend, and Theodore didn't like being used.

Gavin helped him take down his tent. Then they carried

his canoe to the shore and packed it, and Theodore shook Gavin's hand. "Hey, sorry about this Heaton fella. I didn't know he was trying to cause trouble for you folks."

"Nothing we can't handle. We're glad you shared the camp with us last night. Good luck on your team-building from here on out. Safe trip there."

"Thanks." Theodore climbed into his canoe and headed out past the seaplane parked at the dock.

He waved at Amelia, who called out to him, "Safe journey."

"You too, and thanks for everything. I won't forget it."

Gavin hoped that meant Theodore wouldn't share what had happened to them, because though Amelia was keeping her voice low so he wouldn't hear, the investigator wasn't.

"You're welcome!" Amelia turned back to face the investigators and continued talking to them.

When Gavin returned to the campfire, she motioned to him, or maybe to Heaton. Maybe she was implicating her ex-boyfriend in the possible sabotage of the plane. It didn't look right that the guy suddenly showed up unexpectedly when he was the ex and supposedly Gavin was the new boyfriend.

"Looks like she's telling quite a tale," Heaton said, then finished his coffee.

Gavin strongly suspected Heaton had tampered with the plane and wanted to see his reaction when confronted with it. "Why did you sabotage the plane?" Gavin paused, watching Heaton's expression. Heaton gave him a smug smile. "Was it because you were angry with her father for sacking you?" Another pause for effect. When Heaton didn't enlighten Gavin, he continued. "But then her father

didn't fly the plane, and she did instead. Were you surprised she went down with the plane? Worried for her?"

Heaton laughed. "You can't be serious."

Then he sobered and filled his mug with more coffee
as if he was welcome to do it. Which, Gavin hated to
admit, he had been—by Theodore, who was only being
as friendly as Gavin and Amelia had been with him.

"Why would you think I'd tamper with the plane?
Yeah, okay, if you consider her father fired me, maybe
I'd have motive, but it was a wake-up call for me. I'm
grateful he did it."

Gavin snorted. He didn't believe the guy in the least.
Not after knowing his friend and PI partner Cameron
MacPherson's father, who had been a drunk. He'd died
driving under the influence, never having attempted to
take part in a recovery program. If this guy had a problem like that, he might never change.

"What the hell are you doing here? Prowling around
as a wolf wearing hunter's spray? Sneaking around?"
Gavin purposely waited for an answer, not expecting
one but giving Heaton the opportunity to make up something, if nothing else.

"Prowling? I'm a wolf. I was curious when I was
here and heard voices. Since I was already running as a
wolf, I drew closer to see what I could see. I mean, I'd
dated Amelia and heard her voice. Why wouldn't I have
checked to see what was going on? In my place, I'm
sure you would have too."

"Why destroy Amelia's raft? And then attempt to
steal my canoe? If you were just angry with her father,
why harass her? Was it because of me? When you
learned she was with a wolf?"

Heaton looked at the fire, and for an instant, Gavin suspected the guy really was infatuated with Amelia. Considering the way Gavin was feeling about her, he certainly could see why. It probably irked the hell out of Heaton that once he'd learned she was safe, he'd discovered her passenger was a wolf, not just human.

"You know, if you'd managed to get rid of my canoe too, we would have been stuck together. I can't imagine why that would have been your plan. Take down her father's plane, cause trouble for their scheduling, maybe even put her dad out of commission temporarily or, worst-case scenario, permanently. Once you learned he didn't go down with his plane but Amelia did instead, it doesn't make sense for you to get rid of our transportation. She was going to leave when the weather let up. But with the continued harassment, she decided to stay with me." Gavin waited to see what impact that had on Heaton.

"You sound as if I had something to do with this. Which I didn't."

"When we didn't perish after the plane flipped and sank, did you hang around to see how you could eliminate us in some other way? First, get rid of the raft and canoe so we couldn't leave or go for help? Then take care of us?"

Heaton set his empty mug down. "You must be a cop, thinking everyone's a bad guy. Am I right?"

"Only in your case."

"I wasn't anywhere near wherever you were camping before this. If it was any of your business, where I was staying wasn't even close to there."

The investigative officer and Amelia headed their way. Heaton asked Gavin, "Who do you think he's going to question first. You? Or me?"

"I'm sure they know all about your qualifications that would enable you to sabotage the aircraft, your motive, and the fact that you're here now, watching to see what happens next."

"Which, as I said before, would prove my innocence. I've been here all along."

Reaching them, the investigating officer identified himself and then said to Heaton, "I understand you had a grievance with the owner of the plane, and Miss White says you've been stalking her and her new boyfriend out here. Care to give us your story?"

"Yeah, sure. It's a free country. I had no idea..." Heaton paused. "Well, yeah, I saw the schedule before I had to leave Mr. White's employment. They've done a lot of flying since I left. Why wouldn't I have done something before this?"

"Stewing about it maybe? Before you decided to take action?" Gavin asked.

"Why? I'm working for the competition now. Better wages and lots more flying time. Why should I jeopardize that when I've got a second chance?"

"More flying time?" Amelia asked, arms folded, brow raised. "Why are you here, then?"

"I'd planned the trip for months. Easily checked out. The great company I work for now said no problem with taking the five days I requested so I could go on my vacation. Surely you remember I was planning to come out here. Your mom had already scheduled me off for these days."

"I guess so," Amelia said. Gavin was surprised to hear that was the case and she hadn't remembered it.

Then again, when Heaton left, she probably just forgot about it.

"All I know is the schedule had to be changed around a lot when you were fired."

"What's the name of the company you work for now?" Gavin asked, as if he were still a police officer and investigating the crime. He knew the accident investigators couldn't arrest anyone. They only had the authority to turn over evidence to law enforcement agencies. And he wanted all the pertinent information on the guy to prove whether he was lying.

"Flying Right Adventure Tours."

"They still hired you after you told them my dad fired you for drinking on the job?" Amelia asked, sounding surprised.

"Based on a one-time incident? And your dad didn't want to even hear my story? Yeah, they did. I've never lost a plane either." Heaton gave her a small smile.

She took a step forward as if to slap the smirk off his face. Gavin ran his hand over her back in a soothing caress. He didn't want her to be up on battery charges if she socked the guy. Though he doubted Heaton would press charges, given that they were wolves.

She took a deep breath and relaxed some.

"So, you saw the plane in trouble?" the investigator asked Heaton, getting the interview back to the business of the plane crash.

"Nope. I was too far away to even hear it." Heaton pulled out a map. "That's where I was the last few days. I can send you a copy of the map when I get home. I want to keep this one just in case I need it later—for a return trip to make sure I take a different route next time."

"Why are you here now if you have five days to paddle?" Gavin asked. No way in hell did he trust the man. Not with him sneaking around as a wolf. The hunter's spray was the real key. Because he'd left no scent, he was correct in saying that neither Amelia nor Gavin could say he'd come into their camp.

"I've already been out here for five days. I came in as early as I could to make sure I didn't miss my flight back. One of my pilot buddies is picking me up later this afternoon. So, see? When did your plane crash? I couldn't have had anything to do with it."

"Remote control? Timer?" Amelia asked. "Either could have worked. You knew the schedule."

"Right. I knew the schedule. Not that I remember who all was taking what trip when. Why would I when I was no longer with your company? Besides, I only paid attention to where I was supposed to be taking people and when. In any case, even if I'd still been working for your company, I was going to be here during this time."

"Where's your canoe?" Amelia asked.

"Everything's just a little way off in the woods. I didn't want to carry all that stuff into camp without being welcomed first. Then Theodore invited me for coffee, and I took a load off and had some. I didn't suspect the woman whose father fired me was going to be here."

Which was a bald-faced lie, because Heaton would have smelled them, and he'd seen them last night when he was running as a wolf. He was still wearing hunter's spray. Even now, Gavin couldn't smell him. They couldn't mention it in front of the investigators.

"What's the name of the guy who's picking you up? His phone number?" Gavin asked, noting that the investigators weren't asking any questions of their own but were writing down everything that was being said.

"Seriously, are you a police officer?" Heaton laughed.

"Do you have anything else you want to add to your statement?" the investigator asked Heaton.

"All I have to say is I didn't know anything about the seaplane crashing, and I had nothing to do with it."

The investigator turned to Gavin. "What about you? Can you tell us everything that happened that you can recollect?"

Gavin gave them his version of what he'd heard before Amelia had to land on the windswept lake. Amelia moved into the tent, and he heard her unzipping the sleeping bags.

"You know, just because your dad fired me, that doesn't mean we have to stop seeing each other," Heaton called out to Amelia. "I'm really sorry about what happened to the plane, and I'm damn glad you weren't injured."

Gavin was surprised that the man sounded so genuinely concerned for her and that he'd finally said he was sorry about what had happened. He'd thought the guy had no empathy whatsoever. If Heaton did have something to do with the plane crashing, and if he really cared about Amelia, it would make sense that he was upset. Maybe that's why he'd been following them around—to see if she was really all right. Then Gavin turned out to be a wolf, and that had probably irked Heaton.

The business with the raft? That didn't make any sense.

As soon as Gavin was finished giving his statement and telling the investigators where he could be reached, he fixed oatmeal for Amelia and himself. Then he started to haul the packed gear out to the dock, hoping Heaton wouldn't make a nuisance of himself with Amelia. They needed to get on the water if they were going to have any success in seeing what was going on with Conrad.

Did Gavin trust Heaton? Not one bit.

Chapter 11

As soon as Gavin began hauling bags to the canoe, Heaton started helping Amelia with the tent, whether she wanted him to or not. "I've got it, Heaton."

"I didn't have anything to do with this." Heaton was half pleading for her to believe him.

She couldn't believe he would have done something so evil. Yet she hadn't expected her other boyfriend to turn out to be a jewel thief either. "You had the motivation and the means. Maybe you hadn't counted on me flying the plane, but you were still angry about my father firing you and me calling it quits with dating you."

Gavin headed back to get the cooler and more of their gear, his fierce expression asking her if she was all right with Heaton. She inclined her head. She suspected Heaton would speak more freely around her when Gavin wasn't nearby, so she could do this.

Gavin carried the items to the lake and set them down on the beach.

"What's the deal with him? You sink the plane, and then you become bedmates with an Arctic wolf?"

"I'm sure you can guess how that happened." She finished packing the tent away.

Heaton cast Gavin a dark look. "How did another Arctic wolf end up here? Was he someone from Alaska you already knew?"

Didn't Heaton figure she could have been interested

in a wolf that quickly after it was over between him and her? Then again, it would make sense. He'd assume Gavin was from Alaska because he was an Arctic wolf shifter like her.

Figuring it would assuage Heaton's ego to think she'd known Gavin before this, she said, "If you must know, yes, I met him when I was in Alaska." She wasn't going to say *how* she met him, or that the meeting was brief, or that he had been strictly human back then.

Returning, Gavin grabbed the canoe and carried it over his head to the lake.

"Was the meeting at the hangar between the two of you planned?" Heaton looked like it was killing him to not be able to help her with something, anything, to make it up to her for getting fired, as if the plane going down wasn't important.

She'd been so angry with him over drinking on the job. She'd thought someday they might really have a chance to be mated wolves because of their love of flying, though she hadn't felt the pull with him like she did with Gavin. With Heaton, it had been all about their interest in flying. With Gavin? He was wolf-mate material she could really fall for.

"No. I didn't have any idea Gavin lived in this area. He never flies out here. He always paddles. So he's never used our services. We were completely surprised to see each other here." She'd said too much already, she realized as soon as she spoke the words.

"Then you weren't dating before you left Alaska? Or he would have known where you were. Unless that's why he moved to this area. Then again, why wouldn't he have come to see you before this? I know you weren't seeing each other, or you wouldn't have dated me. Unless you're just…friends." Heaton put out the fire.

One of the investigators was talking to Gavin again.

"We're making up for lost time," Amelia said, not in a hurtful way, or at least she didn't mean it that way. Hopefully, her comment would make it sound like she and Gavin had been close in Alaska, but she had left and they'd lost contact. Until he moved into the area. Of course, the timeline was all wrong, but she wasn't about to enlighten Heaton.

"Why did he book a flight this time?"

She grabbed the bagged tent and began walking toward the beach, not answering Heaton.

"But now you're staying with him out here? Not returning home?"

"I have no plane to fly, remember? He's a wolf. I'm due a vacation. I haven't taken one in eons." She stopped and turned to face Heaton. "Listen, you might as well come clean on this. You're wearing hunter's spray, so you're concealing your scent from what? Us? Other animals?"

Because he'd been skulking around their campsite wearing hunter's spray and then had boldly come to see them this morning, she knew he had been up to no good, that he'd sabotaged the plane. She might not have any physical evidence, and the investigators might not be able to prove he was the one who did it, but she was certain he had.

"You've been sneaking around our camp here and at the place we were before this. Why would you do that if you were just out here paddling to your heart's content? Let's say you did have the trip planned all along. When you did, it was just for taking a vacation. When you were fired, you had another reason to come out here. To use it as an alibi. What I can't figure out is why you destroyed our raft and tried to take off with our canoe. To strand us? If you'd just wanted to destroy the plane, maybe kill or seriously injure my dad, why harass us? Me? Dad isn't here. The plane is gone. You've done the damage already."

Gavin returned to take the tent from her.

"I'll help you pack the canoe in just a second, Gavin." She still hoped Heaton would say something to fully incriminate himself if Gavin wasn't within hearing distance.

"No problem, honey." Gavin leaned down and kissed her mouth in a way that told Heaton to take a hike.

She kissed Gavin back as eagerly to prove this wasn't just a show. Heaton would be able to smell Gavin's and her interest in each other, something that hadn't happened between her and Heaton. When they broke free from the kiss, Gavin carried the tent off.

Heaton watched him leave. "He wouldn't have planned to take a camping partner, would he have? Does he even have enough food?"

"We're going fishing." And she meant for more than just the kind they could eat.

Heaton turned his full attention to her again. "What does Gavin Summerfield do? Don't tell me he's a pilot too." Now Heaton sounded angry.

Amelia imagined Gavin could have any occupation but that and Heaton wouldn't care. A pilot taking his place? He would blow his top.

"He's a private investigator and former police officer."

Heaton frowned, glancing in Gavin's direction, looking a little worried. Maybe the notion Gavin was a wolf with investigative skills and trained to take down criminals had Heaton rethinking this whole situation. What if Gavin had only been an accountant, for instance. Or a bank president. Whole other story. "Now I get how come he asked all the questions of me," Heaton finally said.

"Right. You're his number one suspect, so unless you can prove you should be off his radar, you can count on him checking out your story further." Digging deep, she wanted to say.

"Then I'd better have an airtight alibi, hadn't I?"

Gavin returned for her. "Yeah, you'd better."

He sounded like one pissed-off, growly wolf, and she knew Gavin would take care of the man personally— wolf to wolf. He wouldn't be concerned with taking Heaton to court if he really was responsible for this, like Gavin would have if they'd been human and Heaton had too.

"You know you can't have me arrested," Heaton said slyly to Gavin.

"Why would you even consider that if you aren't guilty of anything? But if you are, don't worry about it. Arresting you would be too easy for you," Gavin said. He wrapped his arm around Amelia's waist and walked her to the beach.

She and Gavin finished loading the canoe, but they didn't talk. Not when Heaton might be able to hear them. He was watching them from a distance but still close enough to hear what they might say.

As grim-faced as Gavin looked, Amelia knew he wanted to say something further to Heaton. She suspected with his cop and PI background, Gavin had every intention of proving Heaton's guilt before he did anything to the guy.

Once they were on the water and paddling across the lake, Gavin said, "He's lying. Not about being concerned for you. His concern over that seemed genuine. Maybe he's telling the truth about the scheduled canoe trip he's been on, but he saw the plane go down. He watched it, and he watched us. He tore up the raft and tried to steal the canoe. He's been sniffing around our camps. The chance that he didn't cause the plane's trouble would be slim."

"I agree wholeheartedly. I still think he sabotaged the plane, but why would he show up at our camp while the investigators were there?"

"Do you know how many people who have committed a crime come in to tell us who they think did it but make sure they have an airtight alibi first? Who play a cat-and-mouse game, showing how brilliant they are that they got away with it? I think he also was dying to know who I was and how long I'd known you. He had to meet me face-to-face. To see if I was a beta wolf or alpha enough to take him on. He wondered if he'd been the one to force us to grow close by causing the plane crash."

"I agree. Do you think he acted alone? For revenge against my dad, but it backfired because Dad wasn't flying the plane?"

"Possibly. Unless, because he'd been an inside man in your operations, that was the condition of his employment with the other company. Maybe he even received a bonus for doing it. Take down one of your planes. Cause trouble for you. Maybe encourage your family to pack up and leave if you ended up having so much bad press that you lost enough business. And get back at your dad for firing him. Or somehow he's in cahoots with Red."

"Did you believe him when he said that he's leaving this afternoon?"

"Not entirely. He wouldn't give us the name of the pilot who's picking him up. And he hadn't brought his gear to the place where he would need to be picked up either."

She glanced over her shoulder. "He's moving his stuff there now."

"Okay, so he knows we can still see him. If we continue to paddle beyond that island in the direction we're heading, we won't be able to see if a seaplane picks him up. If we park the canoe at the island over there, we can climb up that hill and watch to see if the plane comes for him."

"You'd delay your own mission even further."

"I would. I want to make sure he's really leaving. I don't trust him to go. And I don't want to worry about watching our backs the whole time we're out here in case he's still stalking us."

"Okay. Why would Heaton be here, taunting us about this?" Amelia asked.

"I've worked cases where the perp was extremely helpful, steering us in the wrong direction or being smugly confident that we couldn't prove he was guilty of the crime, taunting us to just try to trip him up."

"So what ultimately happens? Do you get convictions in either type of case?"

"Yes. And no. Some we do, and some we don't. In Heaton's situation, he may think we can't do anything about it—even if we learn he really did cause the plane crash beyond a shadow of a doubt—because he's a wolf."

"In our Arctic wolf pack back in Alaska, the pack leaders eliminated wolves who were murderers or attempted murderers. Our kind can't go to prison long-term, but they're not going to let one go scot-free either."

"Exactly. He's a lone wolf. Maybe he's never been taught what would happen to someone like that."

"That could be."

They paddled for about twelve miles to the island with a better lookout point, then pulled the canoe out of the water. They made ham sandwiches at the base of the cliff, had lunch, and then climbed up the cliff.

"He said he'd be picked up later in the afternoon, right?" Amelia asked as they found a safe perch on the cliff, binoculars in hand. She'd halfway believed Heaton when he said he was leaving, but Gavin seemed warier.

"Yeah, that's what he said." Gavin was looking over the map. "The fastest way for us to reach the island where the company is staying right now is to cross here. We won't set up our camp too close. We can stay on this island. The river cuts between the two of them. If we camp far enough away, we can slip across the river at night, move in close to their campsite, and watch from the woods to see if we can observe or hear anything."

"Do you think they might have stayed at their last campsite, waiting for Theodore to rejoin them, instead of moving to the next site?"

"Hell, we should have asked him. I was counting on them to stay at the old campsite, since he knew where they'd be and it's much closer."

"Okay, so what if they followed their original plan and met up with him at the new location?"

"We'll paddle upriver here." Gavin pointed to the map. "Portage here and cross another river. They'll be camping here. If they aren't already there by the time we get there, we'll camp on the island here so we can move in close later and listen to what's going on."

"That looks like a good plan." Amelia swore she heard the faint sound of a plane's engine. Not one of her own though. She turned her head to the side and looked up at the sky. "I think I hear a plane coming this way."

"I hear it too. I'm surprised. Do you mind if I use your sat phone?"

"No, go right ahead." She fished it out of one of the bags and handed it to him. "Where are your binoculars?"

"In that first bag."

She pulled out his binoculars so she could see whose plane it was. It was carrying a yellow canoe and a red canoe. So the pilot was dropping more paddlers off.

Gavin called the number for one of the competitor air-travel tour companies in the area. "Hi, I'm calling to make travel arrangements to the Boundary Waters Canoe Area Wilderness. I've heard my old friend Heaton Compton is flying for you now… Okay, well, let me get back with you about some dates, and maybe he can fly me out there… Oh, is he there? No? Okay. Do you know when he'll be returning? Okay, thanks. I'll call back later. Got to ask the missus about the dates of our trip. She keeps track of the schedule. Thanks. Bye."

"I take it Heaton works for them," Amelia said to Gavin when he got off the phone.

"Right. He won't be returning to work for another four days."

"And he's not there because he's here. What does that mean, exactly? He's not leaving here like he said he was?"

"Or he's returning with that plane," Gavin said, motioning to the one landing on the water. "And he's going somewhere else for the rest of his vacation time."

"It's one of the Right Flying Adventure Tours seaplanes. We should have asked him what he was going to do with the rest of his time. So he's lied about the amount of time he had off? Nine days, instead of five, or he's only been here a day and he has four days left?"

"I don't know. I was trying not to sound like a cop."

"You always sound like a cop when you're trying to learn something from someone."

"Even when I entered your house after chasing your runaway pups?"

"That was different. I was naked. You hadn't announced who you were. At that point, I wasn't taking any chances."

"I don't blame you. Did you ever get that front door fixed?"

She squeezed his arm. "Yes. That afternoon, in fact. Probably made the house easier to sell."

They watched the plane park at the dock. The island was about twelve miles from the other, so it was hard to see all that was going on. When the seaplane was airborne, they should have been able to tell if a canoe was secured to it, which most likely would indicate Heaton was leaving. Unless someone else had shown up and was being flown home. They didn't know what color

Heaton's canoe was, since he'd kept it hidden from them. When he'd started to bring his gear to the beach, he hadn't brought his canoe yet.

"Okay, he's leaving. The seaplane, that is. And I see a canoe, a yellow canoe attached. So maybe Heaton was telling the truth."

"*If* that's his canoe."

"You mean someone else might have arrived and was being picked up? You could be right."

They watched while the seaplane took off. The people who had been dropped off appeared to be setting up their camp, smoke already curling up from a campfire. Amelia and Gavin portaged to the other side of the island, put the canoe back in the water, loaded their gear, and paddled to reach the island across the river.

When they reached the end of the second portage, they saw that the greeting-card company group had set up their camp, and Theodore's red canoe wasn't among them.

"I hope he's all right," Gavin said, worried about the executive who, in his own words, wasn't a real outdoorsman. "Let's paddle down the river away from their camp and set up our campsite."

After they moved away from the other island and the campers, they finally reached a point far enough away that their voices wouldn't carry to the other camp.

"Why don't you stay here with our gear, and I'll paddle toward the place where they made camp before and see if I can locate him," Gavin said.

"Sure. I'll set up the tent and build a campfire." She gave Gavin a hug and a kiss that told him she thought the world of him for being concerned about the guy.

"I'll leave the gun with you, just in case you need it."

Then Gavin took off to see if he could locate Theodore, hoping he hadn't lost his way or had a heart attack or something. Gavin couldn't believe how messed up this one little job had become, when he'd thought it would be so easy. Just observe Conrad, see if there was any evidence of his cheating on his wife, document it, end of assignment. Gavin hadn't intended to meet up with a couple of Conrad's coworkers first and then get even more involved in their situation.

When Gavin was closer to where the man should be paddling, if he hadn't gotten lost, he called out Theodore's name.

Gavin didn't get any response. He hoped that didn't mean Theodore had ended up somewhere else. And he hoped Amelia was fine while he was gone.

"Theodore!" Gavin called out again.

Chapter 12

AMELIA BUSIED HERSELF WITH SETTING UP THE TENT AND sleeping bags and then built a campfire. She hoped Gavin would find Theodore quickly and that he was all right. Poor Gavin. At this rate, he was never going to be able to complete the job he'd come here to do.

She called her dad to let him know where she was and what Gavin was doing. And to say that she thought Heaton had left the area.

"Gavin's supposed to be protecting you. When did you learn Heaton was there?"

"I'm fine, Dad. Gavin will be back before we know it. I've got his gun anyway." But now she had to explain to her dad about Heaton. She had forgotten she hadn't told her father about Heaton being out there in the Boundary Waters. She shouldn't have made the slip.

"You shouldn't be there if that maniac is out there too. Just be careful. Are you so sure about Gavin? He's a wolf, and you just met him."

"I met him over seven years ago when he was on a case in Alaska, looking for stolen pets. He's the one who identified the theft ring—Mindy and Asher Michaels?" She figured her dad had to see him as one of the good guys when he'd helped take down a pet theft ring.

"I thought the police were the only ones involved in that."

"That's what the newspaper led everyone to believe.

In truth, Gavin had to take Asher down, even when the crook was armed with a gun."

"You never mentioned anything about Gavin to us before. How did you meet him?"

Amelia stacked more kindling on the fire, looking downriver and trying to spy any sign of Gavin. "Oh, you know Mrs. Primrose? She thought because I was fostering dogs, I might be involved in a pet theft ring. Our Samoyeds looked just like the two Gavin was trying to locate, but they were males, and ours were females. Mrs. Primrose apologized afterward to me. Gavin had spoken to her, then came to my door. And you know how I was trying to get someone to fix it? Well, it was partly open and the puppies had gotten out. He caught them and brought them back. Anyway, that's how I met him. He's always been the most honorable of men."

"Hmm. I should have asked if you had a big enough sleeping bag."

She knew her dad wondered just how close she and Gavin were getting. "He has two single sleeping bags."

"You just tell me if he gets out of line."

She chuckled. "I love you, Dad."

"Love you back, honey. Wait. *Gavin Summerfield*. Hold on."

Uh-oh. What were the chances her dad would make the connection between her and Gavin during the jewelry-store heist?

"You knew him six months before that."

"You mean on the jewelry-store robbery."

"Yeah. It says here he survived the crash and got a commendation for taking the place of the pregnant clerk."

"Yes. See? I told you he was honorable."

"So he knew you were the one piloting the plane? It says in this online newspaper account that he knew the pilot was a woman, but he didn't know what had happened to her."

"No. Well, he put two and two together while we were stranded."

"But he knew you were innocent."

"Yes. I explained what had happened. You have to know I had my doubts about him too. He was a cop, and so was my boyfriend, supposedly. Gavin said that he'd never been a cop."

"Clayton lied to you all along, then."

"He did."

"I'm sorry, Amelia."

"It's not your fault the guy was a bad wolf."

"I should have known."

Her father had always felt bad that she could have easily died that day, that he hadn't read the wolf better. Clayton had been charming, and he'd fooled everyone, including Amelia's whole family. If she hadn't ended his miserable life, both her dad and Slade would have done it. Even her mother would have. Amelia could never see her mother in that role, but she knew in a pinch, her mother and her dad had fought wolves off and she'd killed one. If the price was high enough—her mom had been carrying twins—she would have done anything to protect her mate and offspring.

"You let me know if there's any trouble, and Slade and I will be out there for you."

"All right, Dad. Thanks."

Then they ended the call. Her dad had given her a backup solar-powered battery, so they had to be careful not to use it too much unless they really had an emergency. Four hours of talking time, thirty-six hours of standby. She thought they were going to have mostly sunny days for the next few days though.

Amelia could hear people talking across the river. She didn't have a canoe to paddle over to the other side and do surveillance, but after Gavin had lost the opportunity to work his case two days ago, she wanted to help him with this. It could take him a couple of hours to return, longer if he couldn't locate Theodore. She didn't even know if the voices she'd heard belonged to the company's group.

Swimming across the river as a wolf, she would stay warm and remain unseen as she prowled through the woods and drew close to the camp. And the river wasn't very wide. Maybe she'd hear something that would give Gavin a clue as to whether Conrad Dylan was having an affair. The one female executive was gone. The only females left were the two sales associates and the CEO.

Amelia hurried to bank the fire, then went inside the tent, stripped off her clothes, and shifted. Leaving the tent as a wolf, she ran across the beach and into the water, then swam across to the other island. Once there, she raced through the woods, smelling the aroma of chili and the smoke of a campfire about a mile and a half ahead. She heard a couple of people talking, and she moved closer.

She saw Mindy practically sitting on Orwell's lap, smiling up at him as he drank from a coffee mug. He didn't appear to adore her as much as she seemed to adore him.

Conrad said, "Don't you think that Theodore should

be getting back by now? When Henry White called, he said that he'd picked up Nina late yesterday."

"It took Theodore several hours to get there," Lee said. "He'll be here."

"He's not that good with a compass or with navigation," Orwell warned. "He's gotten a lot better at paddling, but…"

Cheryl was sitting off by herself. She wasn't fawning all over Conrad in the least. The CEO was examining a map. If this was the only time Amelia had to consider Conrad's actions, she'd say he wasn't doing anything extramarital. At least not here. Or now. Then again, when everyone went to bed that night, who knew?

Paddles splashed in the river, and Amelia heard the water slapping at two approaching canoes. She hoped they were Gavin's and Theodore's.

"Oh, oh, there's Theodore and someone else," Mindy said.

"Ahoy," Theodore called out. "I brought company. Or I should say, a fellow paddler. Gavin Summerfield found me and brought me here."

"Well, Theodore, I'm glad you could make it," Lee said, and she sounded genuinely relieved. She set the map down on a log. "I was just trying to figure out how we were going to go back and try to locate you. Join us for dinner, won't you?" she asked Gavin.

"I've got to get back to…" He paused and looked into the woods for a split second, and though the light was fading, Amelia figured Gavin had seen her glowing wolf eyes. "Well, sure, thanks. I'll do that."

"What about your girlfriend?" Theodore asked, sounding surprised Gavin would forget about her.

"She was tired and went to sleep. Long day of paddling and more ahead of us. We're not far from here. I'll just grab a bite to eat and then head back to our camp."

Theodore smiled. "It's all the workouts at night that are wearing her out."

Gavin only smiled in her direction.

As if.

"I have to tell you that Henry coming earlier than expected was a godsend. I wouldn't use any other seaplane service if I came out here again," Theodore said, greatly relieved.

Lee put down her bowl of chili. "Yes, he called me to say he'd taken her to the hospital, and she was staying overnight. They believe it was food poisoning, but she should be all right."

"She ate something that no one else ate?" Gavin asked.

Mindy Michaels glowered at Gavin. Amelia guessed she'd recalled who he was, even though they hadn't seen a lot of each other when she was beating on him before the police arrested her and her husband and when he must have spoken at the trial.

"Yeah," Mindy said. "I brought sausage my husband made for me, but I didn't feel like eating any. I keep telling him it isn't lean enough. Nina wanted to try it. An hour later, she was sick. I figured the sausage either hadn't been cooked thoroughly or it had spoiled, not having been refrigerated enough on the trip. I feel terrible about it. That's all I can think of."

"Your husband and you are on good terms?" Gavin asked.

Amelia's wolf jaw dropped. She couldn't believe what Gavin was thinking, but that had to go back to his cop reasoning. Sure, the plane that had brought Mindy here an hour earlier than scheduled had gone down, and then something intended for Mindy made Nina sick. And here she was hanging all over another man when she was still married to Asher.

"Are…you saying he tried to poison me?" Mindy asked, horrified, her eyes wide.

"The plane that had carried you here earlier crashed," Theodore said as if he had to explain why Gavin thought there might be foul play.

Damn, so he'd seen enough of what was going on, probably overheard some of it, and knew she'd lost her plane.

"Omigod, no," Mindy said, tears filled her eyes. "I-I hinted at wanting a divorce. He was angry, even at just a casual mention of it. How would he have known which plane I was going to take?"

"Two of our executives said they couldn't make it, then at the last minute, they said they could," Lee said. "Initially, we were scheduled to have one plane take us. Two days before our scheduled arrival, I contacted Henry, and he said he could provide two planes, no problem. Due to storms in the area, they'd had some cancellations. We arrived an hour early because of wanting to get started. And Henry and his son, Slade, were eager to bring us out here earlier."

"So, Gavin, you had a canoe trip scheduled, and you came at the time Henry was supposed to fly us in," Theodore said.

"Uh, yeah, and we lost all power. Amelia was able to land it well enough that we got out without too many bruises, but the plane still sank."

"You're sure it has nothing to do with the company? Competition?" Lee asked. "When it comes to competition, some companies will do anything to try to sabotage a competitor's efforts."

"We've considered it could be," Gavin said.

Lee turned to Mindy. "Your husband wouldn't have been able to personally sabotage a plane, would he?"

"He has a lot of shady contacts. No telling who he might know to get the job done. He's still doing illegal stuff. I just didn't want to take part in it, and I haven't for years. I'm happy with your company. I don't want to jeopardize that. I plan to call it quits with him when I return."

Amelia noticed Orwell had stood, then sat on another log across from where Mindy was still sitting, distancing himself from her, as if associating with her could get him into trouble too. If her husband had anything to do with the plane, they could have all perished.

Gavin ate some of the chili, but Amelia was worried that he might get sick too, if any of the rest of the food had been tampered with. Though wolves had stronger digestive systems, so he could probably deal with it better. And their healing genetics enabled them to overcome injuries and sickness faster.

"Does he have an insurance policy on you?" Gavin asked.

Mindy paled at the mention of an insurance policy. "Yes, with a double indemnity clause. Should I die accidentally, he gets double the face amount of the contract. Of course, I have one on him too. He suggested doing that about six months ago. I'm throwing out any of the food Asher packed for me." Mindy started going through the food in her backpack.

Gavin glanced at Conrad, but he was looking across the river. Amelia wondered if he was thinking that his wife might want to eliminate him if she learned he was having an affair. Had the Michaelses bought their insurance policies about the time Mindy started to have the affair with Orwell?

"How long did you know that you were going on this trip?" Gavin asked.

"A couple of weeks ago. Lee usually plans them well in advance and gives us fair warning," Mindy said.

Amelia was dying to know just when Mindy started having the affair.

"Was there a special reason why you got the insurance policies six months ago?" Gavin asked.

Yes! Amelia felt like she was really a PI-in-training, and Gavin was asking all the right questions. She would have just jumped in and asked what she wanted to know without being careful to learn the truth in the most judicious manner. Did Asher know his wife was having an affair?

Mindy glanced at Orwell. He was poking at the fire with a stick, not looking at anyone. All eyes were on Mindy, waiting to hear the truth.

When she didn't offer anything, Lee spoke up. "Unless Mindy started it earlier and we were unaware of it, she was having an affair with Orwell at that time."

Mindy let her breath out in a huff. "Orwell was separated. I planned to divorce Asher when the time was right."

"So he could have learned you were having an affair six months ago?" Gavin said, not truly as a question, but more of an observation.

Again, Mindy didn't reply.

"They weren't being discreet about it, if that's what you mean," Lee said. "They were having long lunches away from work. Asher could have had a private eye following them at any time and learned what they were up to, if they had been up to anything."

"If you were going to divorce Asher, why did you get the life insurance policy?" Gavin asked.

"That's what I wondered," Theodore said.

"Are you a cop?" Mindy suddenly asked Gavin.

"No. Former police officer with the Seattle Police Department."

"I should have known you were a cop."

"Why did you agree to the life insurance policy?" Gavin asked.

"Maybe Asher would have an accident. It could happen, you know. Then I wouldn't have had to divorce him, and I would have been well off." Mindy folded her arms and looked like she was pouting. She was too old for it to look cute on her.

Greed was the reason Mindy had gone along with purchasing the policy, Amelia thought. She also watched the dynamics between Conrad and Cheryl. Unless they were being extremely cautious, nothing seemed to be going on between them. No glances at each other. Just nothing. She wondered if Gavin was seeing this like she was. If he was watching all the dynamics like she was. It helped to be here in the woods as a wolf. No one would know another pair of eyes was observing all.

"Of course, it could have to do with anyone in the group too. For any reason," Gavin said.

"Hmm," Lee said. "You ought to be a private investigator yourself."

Gavin just smiled, waiting for anyone to offer other reasons, but when they didn't, he finished eating his chili. "This was really great. It hit the spot. Thanks so much for dinner."

"Thanks for bringing Theodore safely to us." Lee spooned some of the chili into a plastic container. "This is for Amelia."

"Thanks. She'll love it." Gavin took the plastic container from Lee.

"Yeah, thanks, Gavin. I owe you big time," Theodore said.

Amelia wished Theodore hadn't overheard about the plane going down and then shared it, but she supposed that if whoever sabotaged it wanted to kill someone who took the earlier flight, it was best they were alerted.

"No one else in the group has any reason to sabotage the plane, do they?" Gavin asked, before sliding his canoe into the water.

"I have powerful enemies, my competition," Lee said.

"Have you ever had anyone try to eliminate you permanently?"

Lee smiled. "Not that I know of. Business practices can be brutal sometimes, but they don't go as far as murder."

Everyone else just shook their heads, indicating they hadn't made anyone mad enough to be on someone's hit list.

Amelia wondered about Orwell though. Even though they were separated, what if his wife wanted to exact revenge against both Orwell and Mindy?

"What about you?" Lee asked Gavin shrewdly.

"If someone set a timer, it would have been set to go off when your people took the plane trip," Gavin said.

"Whoever did this had to have known the schedule and set the timer before the plane was in service the next day."

"That means someone who works for Amelia's company," Lee said.

"Possibly a pilot who worked for Amelia's dad and was fired from his job."

"So it could be just a case of revenge against him," Lee said.

"It could be." Gavin shoved his canoe off and climbed into it. "Night, all. And good luck with your training." He started to paddle downriver but heard a splash and looked back to see Amelia swimming after him. He smiled at her and shook his head.

He paused and helped her into the canoe. She shook water all over him. "I'm sorry you couldn't have joined us. I hadn't planned to stay until I saw you in the woods. I had to hang around in case anyone saw you, so I could assure them the wild wolf was just curious about them, not a threat. At least they gave me some of the chili for you, and it's great."

She gave him a little woof.

When they arrived back at their campsite, Amelia jumped out of the canoe. She wasn't sure how Gavin would view her conducting surveillance on her own, without making sure it was the right thing to do. She was a take-action kind of girl, and sitting around waiting for hours for Gavin to return wasn't something she had any interest in doing. Besides, it all worked out.

She ran into the tent to shift and dress while he got the fire started again.

"We make one hell of a team," Gavin said, and she knew he wasn't upset with her.

Then again, if he had any chance of dating her, he had to play his cards right. She smiled and slipped into a pair of fresh jeans, socks, and boots. Then she put on her sweatshirt and headed out of the tent.

He smiled at her as he dumped more kindling on the fire. "I hadn't expected you to do the surveillance without me, but thank you for getting a head start on it. Did you learn anything?"

"They were worried about Theodore." Amelia took the container of chili Gavin offered her. "While you were doing all the questioning, I was watching everyone's reactions. Orwell seemed concerned."

"Hell yeah, if Asher's out to get his wife, taking Orwell down would be a bonus."

Amelia took a spoonful of chili. "This is really good." She was glad they'd sent it along with Gavin.

"It is. We can do some fishing tomorrow and, if we catch anything, have it for one of our meals."

"Works for me." She hadn't gone fishing in eons. Certainly never with a hot wolf. "Do you think that the questioning about affairs made Conrad supercautious about who he might be seeing?"

"Maybe. He seemed cautious about revealing anything. Then again, he may have nothing to reveal."

Amelia figured it could go either way too. She finished her chili.

"Maybe if Conrad is being secretive about his interest in Cheryl, he waits until everyone goes to sleep."

Amelia had thought that too. In the dark of night, no one could see what they were up to. But they'd have to be awfully quiet. "Could be. I wonder what's going on with Orwell? I mean, Mindy was all over him until you arrived, but he moved away from her once he learned she planned to ask for a divorce. It made me think he was not as into her as she was with him. Maybe he was trying to cool it with her. Maybe the notion she's getting a divorce doesn't appeal to him. He separated from his wife recently, so why jump into another relationship?"

"I agree with you there. I know if I had ended a marriage as a human, I wouldn't want to commit to another woman right away."

"Not unless she was the right one for you, and you knew because you'd been seeing her for the last six months." Amelia raised a brow.

Gavin smiled. "As a human, possibly. Particularly if I were the kind of man who couldn't live without a woman for any length of time. It's hard finding the right woman when we're wolves and there aren't any wolves around."

"True." She sighed. "What if Heaton didn't cause the trouble with the plane?"

"Who else do you think could have done it?"

"Maybe our company's competition. Maybe they have some connection with Asher Michaels, and he hired them to disable it. They got the schedule from Heaton, who didn't know why they'd even ask, except maybe to cause trouble for us. But nothing this bad. And Heaton was mad that my dad fired him, so he's not that upset the plane went down." She hated to think it might be their competition. Though if they could prove it, that might be a way to put *them* out of business.

"But he seemed concerned you went down with it."

"Right. And his attitude that he didn't have anything

to do with the sabotage may be because he really didn't have anything to do with it. Then again, even if he did it, he wouldn't want us to believe that."

"Possibly."

"I wish Theodore hadn't brought up the downed-plane business in front of the group. Though I guess if anyone in their group is a target, it's good for them to know. They might even have come up with some ideas after we left, or maybe they will in the morning, after they've slept." She really had mixed feelings about that.

"I agree."

"Where did you find Theodore?"

"He was sitting on the shore, trying to read a map, frowning deeply. I called out to him, and he looked up, startled. Seeing it was me, he jumped up from the ground and began yelling and waving his hands as if he was afraid I would continue past his location and not come to his aid. Poor guy. He was extremely grateful when I told him I had found his group and would lead him there. Of course, then he worried about you. I explained you were setting up camp and then going to bed while I searched for him."

She could just envision Theodore sitting there, trying to read the map, perspiration beaded on his forehead. "He's a sweet man. I bet he was grateful. I sure was. It appeared Lee was too."

"Yes, she seemed to be. He was afraid he'd be stuck alone in the dark on an island and fending off the bears and wolves and moose."

"I thought Conrad looked unsettled about the plane incident. Maybe he was worried his wife might have paid to sabotage the plane. I was thinking we could go back as wolves to see if we can hear any noise coming from his tent," she said.

"Return there as wolves? Sounds like a great idea."

"You know, Conrad might just be worrying about the fact that the plane went down, which may not have anything to do with him feeling guilty."

"You're right. Anyone could feel that way. Are you ready to go on your second PI spy mission?" Gavin asked.

"I sure am."

They quickly banked the fire, cleaned the plastic container, and set it with the other food items high in a tree. Then they stripped in the tent and shifted.

Leaving the tent, they headed out to the river. As they swam next to each other, Amelia didn't think she'd ever done anything as interesting, different, or clandestine.

Chapter 13

ONCE THEY WERE ON THE SHORE, AMELIA AND GAVIN shook the excess water off their fur, then ran through the woods to reach the campsite, carefully listening for any sign that anyone was out in there. The camp was quiet. No one was making a sound, and the campfire was cold. A lantern was on in one of the tents. The wolves prowled around the tents, sniffing for scents to learn who was staying in which one.

Each of the men had a tent of his own. Cheryl and Mindy were staying with the CEO in a larger blue tent.

Gavin smelled that Mindy had been sleeping in the green tent with Orwell. Not now, but maybe they'd get together later. Or maybe the discussion earlier about insurance policies had made Orwell or Mindy—or both—decide it was better to keep their distance.

He hoped Amelia was all right with sitting around on a job like this, listening during the surveillance, possibly for hours. It could be a long wait for nothing. He should have mentioned that to her first, but he suspected she would have come with him no matter what, rather than be left behind. He was glad she was with him. And truly, the idea of snuggling with her while they waited and listened appealed.

After they checked out all the tents, they lay down under the trees in the brush and waited to see what would happen next. They were curled up together, heads raised, listening.

A couple of hours later, Amelia was snuggled next to Gavin, her head resting on his back as he listened, enjoying the wolf closeness they shared. He never imagined being on a stakeout like this with a beautiful wolf and sharing the space as one.

Someone began moving about and Gavin perked up his ears, twisting them this way and that, pinpointing the location of the rustling. Carrying a flashlight, one of the women was leaving Lee's tent. He squinted his eyes to identify which one it was in the dark. The woman was Lee. He frowned. What was *she* doing? Hopefully not walking into the woods to relieve herself close to where he and Amelia were lying down.

Nope. She made a beeline for Conrad's tent, trying to step quietly on the leaf-and-twig-littered ground so she wouldn't disturb anyone's sleep. Gavin's enhanced hearing was something he loved about being a wolf.

Lee slipped into Conrad's tent. They were having an affair? Never having suspected it, Gavin wondered if she'd brought Cheryl on the trip as a cover.

"Lee, please, I don't want to do this," Conrad said as she entered his tent.

Gavin couldn't have been more surprised. Was Lee sexually harassing Conrad? Gavin had to admit he never would have thought it, not after what Conrad's wife suspected was going on.

"You want that promotion, don't you?" Lee said, her voice hushed and annoyed.

"What if Eleanor believes I'm having an affair? What if she's the one involved in the downing of the plane?"

"She wouldn't be. How would she suspect anything? You haven't done anything wrong. *Yet*. Besides, I doubt she'd try to kill you. Unless you have a life insurance policy with a double indemnity clause. Do you?"

Amelia nudged Gavin with her nose, and he realized she was awake and listening in on the conversation.

"No. I won't do this."

"Your loss, Conrad." The flashlight moved toward the opening of the tent, and then Lee left the tent and headed back to her own.

"Crap," Conrad said softly, though the wolves heard.

Gavin and Amelia waited around for another hour. Then the northern lights brightened the night, the greens and purples stretching in colorful bands across the inky black sky. A loon called to its mate; a timber wolf let out a beautiful howl, and a little one answered.

Everyone seemed to be sleeping, and Gavin wanted to take Amelia back to their camp and enjoy the spectacular light display.

He nudged her to let her know they were done for now. She licked his face, and he licked hers back, ready to enjoy the star-filled night, then curl up with her in his sleeping bag. They loped through the woods and back to the river, swimming across to the other side. Once they reached the shore, they shook off the water and ran toward their campsite.

Everything was quiet there, no indication anyone had found the camp. At least not camo man. Heaton was another story, if he hadn't left with the seaplane. Everything was still at their camp, and nothing seemed to have been touched. No smell of bears either, which was a good thing.

They moved into the tent and both shifted.

"Let's get dressed and enjoy the light display," he said.

"We could just be wolves."

"It wouldn't be the same." Not when he wanted to wrap his arms around Amelia and snuggle.

They quickly pulled on clothes, and then sitting outside on the beach, he wrapped her in his arms. They looked heavenward. "Corona Borealis," Gavin whispered against her cheek, the black sky brimming with sparkling stars.

"Beautiful," she said, snuggling against him.

"I'll say. Before I was a wolf, I'd go on a trip like this, and my portages meant getting to the lake or river on the other side of the island, doubling back if I had to so that I could carry another load. When I glided across the lakes or rivers, I'd see moose, bears, loons, eagles, beavers, anything I could observe from the water. On a portage, all I did was check my bearing and count my steps. At night under a star-filled sky, we'd talk about the past, about cases we'd worked on, just all kinds of things, but I never looked up and saw the beauty of the night."

"But now?"

He hugged her tighter. "I enjoy every bit of the walk—the trails, the rocks, the flora, the hills, the birds all around me. Warblers, waxwings, orioles. Before that, I didn't notice. I'd only hear my own heartbeat pounding and think about the wolves and bears that could be watching my every move."

"Which they still could be."

He chuckled. "Yes, but now I'm one of them. One of you. Maybe not a royal like yourself. Sitting here with you makes stargazing truly enjoyable." He took a deep breath and let it out. "Do you believe in fate?"

"That we're meant to keep crashing in planes together?" Amelia lifted her mouth to his, and they kissed under the stars and the dazzling lights, out in the wilderness, two wolf shifters making the most of this, providence or not.

Gavin figured they shouldn't have dressed, because as soon as they began to kiss under the stars, he wanted to move into the tent. He helped her up from the beach. She entered the tent first, and Gavin followed. As soon as he was inside, he caught her in his arms and kissed her again. "How do you feel about your first night of surveillance?"

"If this is the follow-up critique, not bad," she said, running her hands over his chest.

He wanted them both bared to each other. "I want to take this further between us. Not all the way, but—"

"Taking baby steps?" she asked, her chin tilted up, eyeing him as he was studying her back, her expression lustful.

He knew his expression had to mirror hers. "Hell, no way." He slid his hands under her shirt and cupped her naked breasts, his mouth claiming hers. If they hadn't had to be cautious about a mating for life, he was sure they would have made love to each other already.

She had nice-sized breasts that fit perfectly in his large hands. He massaged her soft, warm breasts and felt her nipples pebbling against his palms.

Then he freed her of the sweatshirt and slid his hands down her waist until he reached her jeans. He slipped his hand under the band, molding his fingers to her ass and pulling her tight against his burgeoning arousal.

"Hmm," she said, lifting her head to kiss his mouth as she rubbed her mound against his stiff cock.

He was about to pull off his shirt when she began working on his belt buckle, hurrying to unfasten it. He was amused that she was removing his pants first, getting to the meat of the matter, instead of removing his shirt like he'd done with her. He was going to yank off his shirt, but he liked feeling her undress him, just as he was enjoying undressing her.

He kissed her hair, loving the silkiness, breathing in the tantalizing hint of a floral fragrance scenting it before she unzipped his pants. She drew them down, his fully aroused cock springing free, her cheek brushing it as she leaned down to help free his feet from his jeans.

Her touch made his cock jerk, and he wished he could bury it in her hot, slick heat. For now, he wanted to show her he was the only wolf for her—like animals courting in the wild, making all the right moves to prove to their ladylove they were well-suited.

Her heart was already racing as much as his was. Their pheromones were bouncing off each other's, telling each other they were more than interested.

She brushed her hand over his cock. Tease. And then he pulled off her jeans, trailing kisses down her belly. She moaned, her fingers curled around strands of his hair. She rested her hands on his shoulders to steady herself while he pulled off her jeans.

Then she was helping him out of his shirt, tossing it aside, and running her hands over his bare chest. Everywhere she touched him, his skin sizzled. He did the same to her breasts, cupping, weighing, molding his hands to them and loving the heat between them.

Once they were both naked, he pulled her down to the sleeping bag and covered them because, despite how hot her touches made him, it was cool in the tent and he'd felt her shiver.

They began kissing again, her body half covering his, her breasts settled against his chest, her mouth pressing kisses against his cheek, his jaw, and then his throat. He swept his hands down her back, then cupped her buttocks and squeezed. He wasn't sure if it was the wolfish half of his nature that felt so attuned to her, never having had the opportunity to experiment with a she-wolf, but he sure as hell felt she was the one for him. He was driven to have her, to make this permanent between them. Was he crazy to feel this way? Or was there something to their wilder animal half that allowed them to recognize the truth?

When she ran her hand over his arousal, he moved her against the sleeping bag so he could kiss her breasts and take this further. Not all the way, but…further.

He drew his fingers down her belly to her curly hairs, found her erogenous spot, and began to stroke her. He breathed in her delightful, musky scent of sex and desire. He was circling her feminine nub, then stroking, and her heels dug into the sleeping bag. She was so tense, breathing through the sensations, that he was certain she was about to climax.

If he could have, he would have plunged his cock into her then, but instead, he sank a finger between her legs, as deep as he could, and she cried out. He kissed her mouth and rubbed his cock against her leg, swirling his finger inside her still. She stroked his back and ass as he continued to move against her, until she pushed him onto his back and took hold of matters. With the perfect grip, she stroked his erection and had him coming in record time.

He groaned and relaxed against the sleeping bag. He wanted to wrap her in his arms and pull her close and sleep.

"Come on, let's go out and wash off in the lake under the stars."

He felt bone-tired, but he agreed. They both headed outside and hurried to the water, got in, and washed each other off. Then he swept her up into his arms and carried her back to the tent. Inside, they quickly dried off and slipped into the sleeping bag. He pulled her into his arms and thought about the stakeout tonight, hoping she hadn't minded it too much. He guessed it was like her wanting him to not be afraid of flying. He wanted her to like the kind of work he did.

"So you didn't mind the stakeout too much?" At least not while she was snuggled up next to him as a wolf. He sure liked it.

"No, I didn't think anything was going to happen, but I was glad to be there with you. I…might have drifted off for a moment. I wasn't making little woofy noises, was I? I hadn't thought of that."

He chuckled. Now that would have caused a stir. "No, you were quiet."

"Thank goodness. As soon as I heard Lee making her way to Conrad's tent, I was all ears. At first, I even had the idea she was worried about the plane situation and was seeking his advice. I was sure shocked to learn she was making the moves on him, and he was rejecting her."

Gavin wholeheartedly agreed. "Only this time, maybe because of the plane incident? Worried his wife might be the one responsible? Or has he been rejecting her for a while? His wife did say he'd acted strangely when he returned home from one of these team-building excursions last year."

"Either situation could be the case."

"From what she said, he's not played along with her, even when he could get a promotion out of it," Gavin said. "That says something for his character. If I had to base this on what I saw tonight, and he isn't having an affair with someone else, which could be his real reluctance to have one with Lee, I'd say he's clean."

Amelia shook her head. "Here I figured Cheryl was seeking to elevate her position. In Mindy's case, I believe that's what she was up to, but Orwell's backing off."

"So why would Cheryl have come along?" Gavin asked. "I was thinking she was a cover for Lee's interest in Conrad."

"Could be. Will you really take me up on flying with me?"

"Sure. Maybe I can volunteer for any job that requires I fly out to the location, just to try to overcome my phobia."

"Anytime you're free and I have room, I'll take you up. How far is your pack located from where our company is situated?"

"We're two hours' drive south from there. So close enough to visit and date you."

She leaned into him and kissed his mouth. "You've met my dad. You'll need to meet my mother and brother."

"My pack will be thrilled to meet your family too."

"They won't feel we have to be part of yours, will they?"

"No. We really don't have a pack leader as such. Though Cameron and Faith were turned first, and he's always been sort of in charge of the PI agency. He was the first to have a mate, and we were fine with them serving as pseudo pack leaders. It's much more democratic than in a real wolf pack. We all have a say. No matter what though, we freely offer our services in any way you or your family may need. Wolves need to stick together, and with as few of us as are here, and with us being Arctic wolves, even more so."

"Thanks, Gavin. I offer the same to you and your pack members, though I can't speak for my family. I believe your offer to help us with this crash will be all they need to convince them you're one of the good guys."

"As long as you don't tell your family you tased me when we met in Alaska."

She chuckled. "You will never let me live that down." Then she kissed his mouth again, and he knew they were going to have to do some fast dating if he was going to hold off on a mating.

The sat phone rang, and she fumbled to get it out of the pouch.

Either there was a development in the case—though at this hour, Gavin thought it was unlikely—or there was some other trouble.

"Hello? Dad? Oh no."

"I hate to ask this of you, Amelia, but Slade got into another fight with one of the pilots, and he's a mess," her dad said.

Amelia ground her teeth. "All right. You want me to return to fly Slade's plane." She'd sock him herself for being so pigheaded when it came to fighting the pilots who were with their competition.

"He had just cause," her dad said.

"What could be worth fighting like that?"

"The guy disparaged your name. Said you'd been sleeping with any guy who was available. Slade knew he was just trying to rile him, but he couldn't help himself. One of Slade's eyes is swollen shut. He can't fly in that condition. I'm sorry. I know you wanted to do this with Gavin, and as hard as you always work, we wanted to let you take the break."

She knew her father assumed she wanted to get to know Gavin better. That this was the first time she'd met an Arctic wolf she really, really liked. Or she wouldn't have agreed to stay out in the wilderness with him and assist him.

"Of course I'll return. When do you need me?"

"First thing in the morning."

"I will kill my brother. Okay. I'll be there."

"Thanks, honey. I'll see you in the morning."

When they hung up, Amelia was surprised to see Gavin was already dressed and starting to pack up camp. She appreciated that he'd overheard and was getting ready to leave, not questioning her, but making this happen.

"Thanks, Gavin, and I'm sorry."

"I would have been in the same boat as your brother if anyone had mouthed off in a bad way about you."

She smiled at him. "Thanks. I guess I can't fault him too much. You really don't mind?" She began getting dressed.

"No. I completely understand. That's what wolves do for each other."

"If I can, I want to come back in a couple of days. I'll leave the sat phone for you in case you have an emergency."

"Thanks, I appreciate it."

"I'm so sorry about this," she said again, thinking of how they were going to spend half the night paddling toward the dock again. Forget about getting much sleep. Or anything else.

"Good exercise. If you're too tired of paddling, I can do it."

"No way. Not after putting you out like this." They packed the canoe, and then they were off. "I think we're getting really good at this though. I think that's the fastest we've packed up."

Gavin agreed.

They were quiet on the long trip back, cognizant of how voices could carry across the water in the event they passed islands where people were camped and sleeping. Amelia was tired too. She had every intention of paddling all the way back, relieved when they had to cross land a couple of times, though she was even tired while doing that. She was ready to collapse and sleep until her dad picked her up early in the morning. Then she'd have to fly.

"I didn't even know it was possible to land a seaplane in the dark," Gavin finally said quietly to Amelia as they did another portage.

"The wind has died down, but that means the water is glassy. A light mist will probably cover the lake early in the morning, so if Dad uses his landing lights, they will reflect off the mist and ruin his night vision. He's good at glassy water landings, coming in at a low rate of descent, using a nose-in landing altitude, and watching instruments as well as looking outside the plane for any dangerous obstacles. It's so important to watch for possible debris in the water. Even a moose in the water can cause a hazard. In Alaska, caribou migrated across the rivers and lakes at night. That's where we had to fly a lot of night missions. Otherwise, in the fall and winter, we would have been really limited in the amount of time we could fly. We did a lot of search-and-rescue missions there."

"Good thing I wasn't flying there."

She smiled. "We can make a large campfire to give him a reference point to determine his descent. And we can place a couple of lanterns on the dock. The little beams of light across the water also help as reference points."

"Okay, sounds good."

They were quiet again after that and finally reached the lake where they still had to paddle for some hours.

"How are you doing?" Gavin asked her.

Awful. She wasn't stroking the water half as much as she had been at first. She was so tired that she felt she could keel over and just fall asleep in the middle of paddling. Boy, would she be sore tomorrow.

"I'll make it." Mind over matter, she told herself. She would make it because she said so.

"We're nearly there," Gavin said. "The thing about any kind of boating is that we can run into things at night too."

"You mean the moose?" She'd been watching them from a distance, but as the canoe drew closer, the moose moved off. They could be so cantankerous that if they felt something was in their space, they might charge.

When Gavin and Amelia finally reached the shore, she didn't think she could set up camp. She was so exhausted.

Gavin quickly helped her out of the canoe and then began unloading the gear and setting it on the beach as if he had superhuman energy. Amelia thought he was trying to save her from having to do too much. With lanterns standing nearby, he had the tent up in record time.

Carrying some of the bags, she kept stumbling, annoyed with herself.

"Why don't you make up the bed while I tie up the food and get naked, and I'll join you in a few minutes," he said.

She smiled at him. He was so cute, no matter the hour or how tired he had to be too.

"I should help more." But she was having a time just making up the bed.

He called out to her, "You'd better be in bed by the time I get there."

"If I get into bed first, I'll be out like a light."

"Even better."

She shucked off her clothes and then climbed into the sleeping bag. He soon joined her in the tent and began stripping. She tried to stay awake to say good night to him.

But before she was ready for it, she heard the sound of her plane's engine as her dad flew in to pick her up early the next morning.

—⁓—

As soon as Gavin heard the seaplane's engine, he tried to untangle himself from Amelia, but she was so tired that he hated to wake her. On the other hand, she had to leave quickly, so he hurried to get dressed, and then she finally got up, looking as tired as he felt.

"Are you going to be all right to fly?" Gavin was worried about her. Did she fall asleep at the wheel, so to speak, if she hadn't had enough sleep?

Amelia hurried to dress. "Yeah, I'll be okay. Thanks, Gavin."

"I'll take your bags to the plane and tell your dad you're coming."

"Thanks."

"All right." Dressed in her bra and jeans, she pulled him in for a hug. "I'll call you on the sat phone as soon as I know I can join you."

"That's a deal. I'll paddle back for you."

"Unless you think me returning would be more of a hassle for you than it's worth."

"Are you kidding? No way. Just call me." He pulled her tighter and kissed her mouth, loving the feel of her soft lips against his, her eager tongue quickly engaging his. God, he wanted this and so much more—all that made them mated wolves. Hating for her to go, he said, "I'll go see your dad."

Then Gavin was out of the tent, hauling her bags, while her dad was tying the plane to the dock.

"Mr. White," Gavin called out to announce himself, though he knew the astute wolf had noticed his approach.

"Henry." Her father took Amelia's bags and placed them in the plane.

"She's coming. We paddled most of the night to get here, so she's still tired."

Henry eyed Gavin for a moment as if he wondered if they'd been fooling around.

"Your intentions?"

"To court Amelia. She wants to return to help me with my mission when she can. We're well-suited, and I can't tell you when I've had a better stakeout. She's a real help."

"Okay."

"Any word on the aircraft investigation?"

"Not yet."

Gavin explained about Heaton showing up and how he worked for the competition now.

"Their mistake. You're sure he actually left the area?"

"Fairly certain, unless another paddler arrived and the plane took off with that canoeist instead. Is your son all right?"

"Slade can be a hothead in dealing with the other pilots. The truth is, I would have reacted in the same way."

"And Amelia?"

Henry cast him a dark smile. "She would have tased the guy."

Gavin turned to see Amelia headed for them.

"Tased who?" she asked, looking from her dad to Gavin as if she was afraid he'd told on her.

"If someone had said something derogatory about the family," her dad said.

"Oh yeah." Then she kissed Gavin and headed for the plane.

Her father paused for a minute, as if he wasn't used to seeing Amelia being so affectionate toward anyone in public.

He slapped Gavin on the shoulder. "Take care. We'll talk later."

Gavin suspected Henry meant about his relationship with Amelia. He waved at Amelia and her father before they took off, and then they were sailing across the lake and soon airborne and finally gone from his view.

He missed her at once. Her smiling face, her warm hugs, her snuggles. Her kisses. He couldn't wait for her to return, but for now, he had to get his mind back on the business at hand. He hoped he'd learn for sure whether Conrad was having an affair, and then he would look further into the sabotaging of the plane.

Chapter 14

AMELIA SHOULD HAVE EXPECTED HER FATHER TO GIVE HER the third degree when he took off flying. She really wanted to sleep until he landed at the hangar where she'd pick up a load of passengers.

"Okay, tell me more about how you met Gavin Summerfield in Alaska. I think you're leaving out some of the important details."

Except for the part about her racing through the house naked, she told her dad the whole story, even about tasing Gavin.

Her dad had a good sense of humor and laughed. "Poor guy. And he still wants to see you."

"I don't think he's easily deterred. Though I have to tell you that he and his pack are fairly newly turned. He said they'd help us with anything we need though, he and his pack."

"Newly turned?"

"Nearly seven years."

"Doesn't that worry you? His trouble with shifting?"

"They offered to help us with anything they could, but maybe we can help them, if they need wolves who don't have trouble with shifting at any time of the month."

Her dad sighed. "You know what I mean. As far as hooking up with him permanently. It could take years to get his shifting under control. He won't be able to shift during the new moon. He'll have trouble with shifting during the full moon. That can put a damper on running with him as a wolf at certain times of the month."

She only smiled and closed her eyes.

"You've got it bad for him already, don't you?"

She opened her eyes. "Like you had it for Mom?"

"She's a royal like me, like you. It's not the same."

As if that meant anything when he had fallen so hard for her mom. "I don't mean that. Would you have avoided seeing Mom if she had been newly turned?"

Her dad didn't hesitate to answer, but Amelia already knew what he'd say. "No. Even if she'd only been turned the day before. I fell in love with your mom when I rescued her from being stranded on that iceberg as a wolf. She was so woeful, wet, with her ears flattened and tail down. Of course, some of her concern was because she believed I was human and would harm her. As soon as I was on the iceberg, she growled and crouched as if she was ready to take me down."

"But when she smelled you?"

"Her tail rose, her ears perked, and I could see the pure joy in her eyes. And I had made that happen. She licked me, rubbed against me, and then I quickly got her into the plane before moving ice ripped up our transportation. Can you imagine what would have happened then? I would have had to shift, and there I'd have been, stuck on the iceberg as a wolf too."

"She fell in love with you from the beginning."

"I was a hotshot pilot and landed at risk to myself between ice floes just to rescue the beautiful Arctic wolf, when I didn't even know she was a shifter. So yeah, she thought I was a real heroic wolf."

Amelia would never get tired of her dad and mom telling her their story. It was *so* romantic.

"You seem to like this guy much better than you did Heaton."

"He's fun and fascinating. He's afraid of flying though."

Her father glanced at her as if he thought that would be too much of an obstacle between them.

"We made a pact. He teaches me how to swim better, and I teach him not to fear flying."

"You crashed into the lake."

"Yeah, but this is only the second plane crash experience he's had. Maybe a few more, and he'll get used to them."

Her father nodded. "He seems like a decent guy. So who do you think might have messed with my plane? Heaton tops *my* list. Though this business with that jewelry thief seems damned suspicious too."

"Heaton's at the top of mine too. If he did it, did he do it out of revenge, or was he hired by someone else—like Red—for some other purpose, and revenge played a small part in it?"

"That's what we need to learn."

When they arrived at the hangar, Slade headed out to meet them. His right eye was swollen shut, and he was frowning at their dad and Amelia. "I told you I could do this."

"No, you can't," their dad said, still looking annoyed with Slade. Maybe not so much about getting in the fight but with not being able to fly because of it.

"Sorry, Amelia," her brother said. "I hear you've got something hot going with an Arctic wolf and that he's with a pack. Any single females?"

"Sorry, no. Thanks for defending my honor. You need to learn to duck faster though."

"The other guy looks much worse," Slade said.

"You always say that."

"Hey, he had two black eyes. And we heal faster than humans. He'll be out of work for several days. Serves him and two of his buddies right."

"Two of his buddies?" she asked, not believing her brother took on three pilots.

Slade grinned at her. "Yeah. I got both of them too. Except one got in a lucky punch."

She noted his jaw was purple. "Looks like they got in *two* lucky punches."

"I'm sure the guy who hit my jaw broke a bone in his hand. I heard the crunch."

Smiling, Amelia shook her head.

"But really, I couldn't believe it when Dad said you were staying with an Arctic wolf on his canoe trip. And I still can't believe Dad's plane was tampered with. I'll kill the SOB who did it. Was it Heaton?"

"Maybe. We don't know for certain. When do I need to take a load of passengers up?"

"Half an hour," her dad said. "But your mom wants to talk to you before you go."

Amelia knew the questioning would begin all over again. Why couldn't her dad just tell her mom all she'd told him? But she knew her mom wanted to hear firsthand from her, so Amelia wouldn't leave anything out. Besides, her mom always asked different questions than her dad.

Amelia was walking into the office, ready to deal with the fresh interrogation, when Winston ran to greet her. She was glad he would be staying close by when Gavin took him. Then she wished all over again that she was still with Gavin and hoped he'd stay safe.

Gavin spent all morning heading for where Lee was taking her group, hoping he could rest a little during the day, then conduct surveillance that night.

When he arrived at the location on the itinerary, the group wasn't there. He backtracked to where they'd camped last night, thinking maybe they hadn't left, but they weren't there either. *Hell.* Had they gotten lost? Or did they decide to change their plans for fear someone was out to kill one of them? *Great. Just great.*

He ate beef jerky, potato chips, and a chocolate chip granola bar, not wanting to take the time to cook a meal. He sniffed around the area, in case they'd made portage across the land here, but they hadn't. They had to have left the area by canoe. Gavin headed out again, listening for any talking, the sound of water lapping at the canoes, or paddles dipping into the water. Nothing but the singing of birds in the trees on the island and his own paddling as he searched the river in front of him. Four canoes would be easy to spot. A red, two yellow, and one orange.

He didn't have any luck all day. Early that evening, he saw a lone yellow canoe, just one man paddling. He was wearing camouflaged clothes, which made Gavin think the guy might be the one he'd seen earlier.

Gavin paddled hard after him, trying to catch up, despite how tired he was, both from the long hours of paddling and from the lack of sleep. Maybe the guy had seen the group canoeing somewhere else earlier.

"Hey, excuse me," Gavin called out, afraid he'd never catch up to the man and figuring he'd be better off hailing him and trying to stop him that way.

The guy quit paddling and turned to see him. He wore a beard and a billed hat that shaded his eyes.

"Hi. I'm looking for a group of canoeists. Six of them. I met them last night, and I hope they are all right. None of them are experienced." Not that Gavin really knew if they were or weren't experienced paddlers.

"Are you supposed to be their guide?" the guy asked, sounding sarcastic, as if Gavin had lost them.

Gavin didn't like the dark-haired and bearded man at once. There was something familiar about him. His voice. Something about his posture. And the canoe, a Golden rental. Gavin was certain it was the same canoe that had been parked on the beach across from where he and Amelia had stayed the first night.

Wait! Asher Michaels? Mindy's husband? *Hell.* Gavin couldn't believe it when he realized who the man was. Between the beard, his longer hair, and the shaded bill on his cap, he looked very different from when Gavin had helped the police take him into custody in Alaska.

Gavin wondered if Asher was still involved in a pet theft ring or what he was into now. Attempting to murder his wife for the insurance money?

"Fancy meeting you here. Are you looking for your Samoyeds out here this time?" Asher asked with a sneer.

The guy could very well be armed, like the last time Gavin had questioned him. "What are the chances of running into you out here?" If Asher pulled a gun on him, Gavin wouldn't hesitate to shoot back.

"Are you out here all alone?" The easy manner in which Asher talked made Gavin feel Asher believed he had the situation well in hand. He didn't know Gavin was a former cop or that he had a license to carry a gun and a permit to bring it with him into the Boundary Waters.

If Asher had anything to do with Amelia's plane going down, he could very well have been the one to get rid of their raft. Conrad had given his wife their itinerary, and Mindy could have done the same with her husband. Maybe Asher had hung around to see her perish in the crash.

What if the party truly did fear for their lives and had decided to go somewhere else? Someplace not listed on their itinerary. Maybe they were even headed to the next closest pickup point, which they weren't scheduled to reach for several more days. Paddling there would take them two days though.

"Looking for your wife?" Gavin asked. Why else would Asher be out here? He hadn't come with the company. If he had been involved in the plane crash, he could still be trying to get rid of his wife. Accidentally, of course, so he could get the insurance payout. There were so many in the party that Gavin couldn't see how Asher could do it without getting caught. Killing all of them would be too risky. Not if he was trying to do this sneakily so he'd get the money.

Asher pulled onto the shore, unloaded his bags, and carried them and the canoe into the woods. He was traveling a lot lighter than Gavin was. Though enjoying the trip was Gavin's cover. Moving quickly without being seen was most likely Asher's mission. So he probably assumed he'd have to get rid of his witness too.

Gavin had two choices: follow Asher into the woods and risk being ambushed, or continue to paddle and see if he could locate the party on one of the islands nearby. He suspected Asher didn't know where they were any more than he did. Asher wasn't a wolf. He must have known where they'd be initially. Had he lost them? Maybe he wasn't much of an outdoorsman or tracker.

Had Asher already known that Gavin was the one flying in at the last minute? The only way to know that was to have seen him at the hangar or for Gavin's client to have shared the information with him. Gavin couldn't imagine why Eleanor Dylan would do that, if she even knew the man. But then he recalled how insistent she was that he was the one taking this job, not any of his fellow PIs.

Gavin paddled far enough from the shore to ensure his safety in case Asher was planning to shoot him from the woods. Without any further contact with Asher, Gavin traveled for about an hour downriver, thinking he should call Slade to see if he had the number for Lee, when he smelled smoke drifting on the breeze. He continued to catch whiffs of it and followed it the best he could. Then he finally saw a couple of canoes sitting on a beach. He made his way toward the shore, deciding that if it was the company's group, he'd join them, telling them he'd protect them if they were in danger. He had to tell them that Asher was in the area and see Mindy's reaction. Did she know already? Or was she completely clueless?

He would suggest returning home, if they hadn't planned to do so.

As he drew closer, Gavin saw Theodore coming to move one of the canoes. He stopped and stared in

Gavin's direction. Gavin waved to let him know it was just him. Theodore quickly waved back. Gavin hoped Asher wouldn't discover where Mindy and her party were if he was up to foul play. If Asher had crossed the island to the next waterway, he wouldn't be able to see them, and he'd be too far away to smell their campfire. If he'd been waiting to ambush Gavin, he might have returned to the river and attempted to follow him. That was the problem with open water if someone was trying to be sneaky. It would have been difficult for Asher to come after Gavin without him noticing.

"Hey," Theodore called out, all smiles, looking eager to see him. "We didn't expect to see you again. Where's Amelia?"

"Her dad needed her to fly the other plane, to help out with some flights."

"Bummer. The two of you seemed to really hit it off."

"Yeah. She said if she could, she'd return." Though Gavin was rethinking that idea now that Asher was here. He didn't want her in the crosshairs. He reached the shore, and Theodore steadied the canoe while Gavin climbed out. "Where is everyone?"

"Gathering firewood for the meal and for tonight. We caught some fish! Sunfish. A whole stringer of them." Theodore looked so proud of their accomplishment.

"First time fishing?"

"Yeah, lucky, I guess. So where are you headed now?"

"If Lee and the rest of you don't mind, I'd like to stay here with your group. Safety in numbers. Specifically, I can protect your backs." At least he hoped he could. With this many people, it could be difficult.

"What makes you think we need protecting?" Lee

asked, coming out of the woods carrying a couple of small logs for the campfire.

"I just saw Mindy's husband, Asher, paddling not far from here. Why would he be here unless he wants to cause problems for her or the group?"

"What?" Mindy said, bringing a bunch of kindling. "He can't be."

"Did you give him your itinerary? Where you're going to be every step of the way?"

"No. Not that he couldn't have accessed my email and seen what Lee had sent to me."

"Well, I saw him, so he's definitely here. And he knows I am too. I'm sure his canoe is the one I saw the first day Amelia and I were out here. Unless you have another explanation for why he's here, I'd say he's up to no good."

Mindy's eyes were round. Orwell must have heard, and he looked pale.

Conrad joined the others and said, "I told you we should pack up, call for pickup early, and leave."

"I won't be chased off by whoever did that to the plane," Lee said. "If I tucked tail and ran every time I had trouble, I'd never have made a success of the company. If Gavin Summerfield wants to offer his protection—and I assume he's armed and dangerous—then I'll hire his services. If anyone feels uncomfortable staying here, you're free to leave."

Gavin couldn't tell them he was already hired to watch Conrad. So that he didn't blow his fellow tourist cover, he agreed. He definitely didn't agree with anyone leaving on their own.

"We'll have someone on watch all night long. After

that long trip back with Amelia in the middle of the night and paddling out here, I need to get some sleep or I won't be able to function," he said.

"I'll help you set up your tent," Conrad offered.

Gavin never got close to the people he put under surveillance, afraid it would affect his objectivity, but he had to make an exception in this case. These people's lives were more important than proving a man's infidelity. "Thanks." Gavin was surprised when Conrad set up the tent between his own and the women's while Gavin and Theodore were hauling his gear there.

Gavin rolled out his sleeping bag, and after removing his boots and socks, he climbed into it. He listened as everyone began working on cooking the fish. He was so tired that he'd barely closed his eyes when he smelled Amelia's scent all over the sleeping bag and imagined her in his arms as he fell asleep.

When he got up, they offered him dinner, and he enjoyed the sunfish they'd cooked in foil with potatoes, carrots, and peppers.

"You're a private eye, aren't you?" Lee asked. Before Gavin could come up with another story or repeat how he was out there on a canoe trip, she said, "So who are you investigating on this trip?"

Gavin wanted to protect the group, but he didn't believe telling them why he was here would make any difference. Unless he discovered Conrad's wife had anything to do with the plane crash. For now, he had no intention of revealing her part in him being here.

But it didn't matter if he told them what his true occupation was. "Yeah, I'm a local private investigator. I was a Seattle cop before that. I came to enjoy some paddling. That was before the plane took a dive. And since your group, or someone in your group, could be the reason for that, it puts me in the middle. Not to mention that I've offered my services to the Whites to try to help shed some light on this."

Lee nodded. Gavin wasn't sure she believed him. It didn't matter. Everything he'd said was true, even the part about paddling in the area for enjoyment, because he had thought to enjoy the scenery while he was on the job. He hadn't expected to be with Amelia.

"He had to have been here just for the fun of it," Theodore said. "Why else would he have taken the downed pilot with him and be spending time with her?"

"The storm?" Lee asked.

The woman was shrewd, but she was the CEO of a successful greeting-card and gift company, so Gavin understood how she would be. "True. I couldn't drop Amelia off at the pickup site or even get ahold of anyone to take her out of here, because we'd lost my sat phone and our cell phones couldn't get any reception."

"A new love?" Mindy asked, sounding sarcastic. "Wait, you were the one who came to our house and helped arrest Asher. Amelia lived a couple of houses down from us. Did you know her then?"

"I met her there. I never expected her to be flying planes out here or that I'd end up on the same plane with her for this trip."

"My…my husband didn't hire you to check on me, did he?" Mindy asked, looking horrified.

Gavin snorted. "Hardly. If you recall, when I asked him about the whereabouts of a couple of Samoyeds that were stolen from a woman and her daughters in Seattle, he tried to shoot me. Then I helped to take him into custody and testified against him. So no, he didn't hire me to check up on you."

Mindy looked relieved.

"But he's here anyway, and unless he said something to you about it, I don't think that bodes well, do you?"

She shrugged, but Gavin could tell she was bothered by the notion. "He doesn't tell me what he's going to do half the time. I guess he figured if I was going to be on a trip out here, he'd check it out."

"Does he do a lot of canoeing?"

"No. I don't think he's ever been in one before."

"You don't think he's here to spy on you? To see if you're having an affair?" Gavin asked.

"I don't know."

"Do you think he's armed and dangerous?" Lee asked.

"Possibly. Orwell, you're separated from your wife. Would she have any reason to pay to have the plane crash?" Gavin asked. He might as well question everyone about it.

Orwell stared into the campfire. Finally, he let out his breath. "She said she'd make me pay for my transgressions. When she learned I was having affairs, she was furious. Of course, I thought she meant making me pay for child support and alimony."

"Affairs?" Mindy asked, clearly surprised and angry she wasn't the only one he had been seeing.

"She kicked me out of the house. We've been having a legal battle over the finances. We've had insurance policies from the beginning, when we were married twelve years ago."

"Double indemnity?" Gavin asked.

"Yeah. That way, if anything happened to me, she and the kids would be provided for."

Gavin figured now was the time to flat-out question Conrad, in the guise of trying to solve this mystery. "What about you, Conrad?"

"Life insurance policies? Sure. Affairs? No."

"How are things between you and your wife?" Gavin really preferred asking in private, but he was afraid that if he suggested having private talks with each of them, everyone would clam up.

Eleanor had said she and Conrad hadn't been intimate in a while. Was it just because they'd been too busy? Too tired? Not enough romance to make it happen? What if Eleanor was the one who was having an affair, and she was projecting on her husband? In her mind, if she was doing it, then he must be too. Why try to kill him? Insurance? Or the prenup clause?

Conrad glanced at Lee. "We're good."

Either Conrad was in denial that he and his wife were having trouble, or he just didn't want to discuss it with Gavin.

"Anybody else have any personal reasons that might make someone want you dead?" Gavin asked.

"No. I still say it could have to do with the fired pilot and the flight company's competitors, and nothing to do with any of us," Lee said.

"I agree," Gavin said. "I think it's very likely that the pilot messed with the plane, but did he act solely out of revenge, or did someone pay him to do it?"

"We were the first group flown out that day," Lee said. "We needed to get an early start if we were going to make it to our first campsite later that day. I'm the only one who is an experienced paddler. Though Conrad and Theodore are getting much better."

Gavin wondered if she always took them on trips where she was good at what she did. He imagined so. That way, she'd always appear to have the upper hand in a situation.

"One other thing did occur to me. If it was for revenge or the competition's plan, making the plane crash when it carried more passengers would have more impact. Make for a bigger news splash. Which might have also been the reason we were targeted and not someone else. Which meant it had nothing to do with any of us," Lee said.

Theodore cleared his throat. "Do you think we're in danger by being here?"

Lee said, "Okay, I first thought I wasn't going to be pushed to leave because of some maniac's actions that didn't have anything to do with us. But it bothers me that you've seen Mindy's husband out here. And that he's been involved in illegal business before. Since that's the case, I want us to head to the next pickup point. It'll take us two days to go forward. I'll call for an early pickup."

"Or return the way you came. It would be a shorter distance, but your pickup could conflict with someone else's. Well, either way, you'll be leaving early," Gavin said. "Another option would be to paddle out of here, and I could have my agency come pick us up in Ely. No flying then."

Everyone looked torn about what to do.

"What would you do?" Theodore asked Gavin.

"I suggest leaving. Mostly because trying to protect a group of people out in the wilderness is difficult to do. And trying to get help is problematic, if something bad goes down. I think it would be best if we let investigators determine what happened without putting anyone at further risk."

"But if this has to do with an insurance policy—particularly with a double indemnity clause—wouldn't it be less likely that he or she would continue to pursue this? The plane 'accident' was one thing. If a person in our group were to die after that, wouldn't it be seen as murder?" Orwell asked.

"I would think so. What if the intended victim does die accidentally? I don't think it's a good idea to risk it. Returning to where you were dropped off is a day and a half's journey." Less, but they'd need more breaks than he did. "It's up to all of you, but I would return there."

Chapter 15

EARLY THE NEXT MORNING, AMELIA GOT A CALL FROM Gavin, right before she had a flight scheduled. The swelling of Slade's eye had gone down significantly. Despite how much better he was doing, her dad said no to him taking anyone up today. Amelia thought Slade could take over for her tomorrow, and he promised to drop her off wherever was closest to Gavin's location.

Amelia was usually so work-focused that she couldn't believe how much she wanted to be with Gavin. He was like the chocolate frosting on a devil's food cake.

"Is it him?" Slade asked when he heard the phone ring. "So sorry about all this."

"It is." She'd worried Gavin would have trouble. She moved away from her brother so she could talk privately. Slade got the message and returned to the office.

"Hey, we're headed back to the place where you and Nina were picked up. It's the closest to us. I spotted Asher Michaels out here yesterday paddling, and I found Lee's group. They weren't where they were supposed to be. In case whoever took the plane down had done so because of one of them, they didn't want him to know where they were. After seeing Asher out here, Lee and I figured it was time to come in. Safer for everyone."

Worried about him and the group, Amelia couldn't have been more surprised. "Asher Michaels is there? That doesn't sound good."

"Yeah, I thought the same."

"Are you and everybody else okay?" She was so glad to hear from Gavin but concerned now that he'd spied Asher out there.

"Yeah. We'll be in tomorrow evening. If you can pick us up the next morning, that would be good."

"You're not worried about me flying?"

He chuckled. "You know, come to think of it, there are too many canoes to haul back in one trip. I'll just paddle back to Ely."

"You *are* afraid of flying with me."

"No. You proved to me that no matter the circumstances, no engine, no nothing, you could still land the seaplane without suffering any casualties."

"All right. I'm coming with you."

He hesitated, and she wondered if the call had dropped. "Gavin?"

"Yeah, the thing of it is, Asher knows I'm out here too. What if I have trouble with him on the way out of here?"

"Did you call your partners?" Amelia was thinking it was time for Gavin to call in more muscle.

"Faith says no one's come back from their jobs yet. I don't want you in the middle of this. It could get ugly."

"I'm coming with you. I'll bring more food, because I'm sure you're getting low on yours after having to share with so many others—Theodore, me, and more if you shared with the rest of the group later."

"Amelia—"

"Do you want to court me? We're starting now. I'm coming with you. Just get ready."

He chuckled. "An Arctic she-wolf after my own heart."

She smiled. She hoped he meant it, because she was

serious. If he was going to bat for them over this whole situation, she'd be there for him. That's what wolves did. They were there for each other. No tucking tail and running. If they were going to see if this worked out between them, she had to be there too.

Of course, she had no plans to tell her father or brother. They'd ruin everything and want to be the one to take her place. Her mother had risked her life for her father a few times while running as wolves in the snow country, as he had for her. It was just part of who they were. It was a natural state of being. If she and Gavin couldn't do that for each other now, what about when they had pups?

She hoped Gavin was really all right with it. That was another thing. If they couldn't be honest about issues, that could be a problem.

"Just bring another Taser gun."

She smiled. "Will do." So he was agreeable. She could have jumped for joy, except that her dad was heading her way. "Okay, let me check on the schedule and get back with you. We might have to come in while it's still dark so we don't have conflicts with the flights later in the morning."

"Okay, let me know. We're just packing up and will be headed out shortly."

"I'll get right back with you."

Her dad reached her and said, "Slade told me you got a call from Gavin. Is he having trouble?" He sounded like he was getting ready to come to Gavin's aid, and Amelia appreciated it.

"Yeah, Lee's group needs to be picked up at the original drop-off place. They'll be there tomorrow night.

I was thinking we could pick them up the next morning before any of your other flights, or even tomorrow night, if they don't get in too late."

"We?"

"Well, you're going to drop me off. Since there would be too many canoes to bring back at once, I'll go with Gavin. We'll paddle to Ely where he can have someone pick us up, and we'll return to the hangar sometime after that to get his vehicle."

"Did something else happen?"

"Nina had to return early due to food poisoning. Then there's this business with the plane. They were so scared that they didn't stick to their itinerary in case someone is after one of them. They finally decided it wasn't worth staying out there and worrying about it. What if something did happen to someone? No one would know where they really were. What if they got lost? They're not from this area, and from what Lee told you and Slade, they've never been out here before. Getting help out there would be difficult if they had an emergency."

"Okay. As long as you'll be all right. Gavin too, of course."

"We will be." She believed in him. And she'd be there to help if he needed her to.

"All right. I'll be on standby. If they get in early enough, I'll fly out to pick them up."

"Okay, I'm going to take this flight out and then go home to get more food ready and pack a few more clothes in case we're out there for a while."

Her father raised a brow.

She smiled back at him, shrugging. "It's a good getting-to-know-you time."

"Then you'd better talk to your mother about meeting him too."

"I will. I've got to go." She was excited about seeing Gavin, but she was also conscious of the fact that they could have problems. She couldn't wait for her last flight of the day. She called Gavin quickly about the flight pickup times.

"You know what I'll be opting for. I'd have to push these folks hard to make it early enough the next night."

She laughed. "Unless it's a life-or-death situation, don't do that to them. I'll talk to you soon."

Gavin told Lee and her people their options, and everyone was willing to push the envelope to reach the dock the next night. They could be on their way home sooner. Gavin really wanted to see Amelia too. He hoped they didn't run into any trouble on the way to Ely.

"I want to paddle with you," Mindy told Gavin.

At first, he was surprised, then he assumed she felt she needed protection from her husband, and he understood that. He really didn't figure her husband would try to kill her for insurance money now. Still, Gavin would remain on guard.

"Are you worried about Asher finding you?"

"Asher? No. He's not here. You have to be mistaken. I just want to be with the man who knows how to get back to the dock."

Gavin didn't believe her. Unless she was so shocked that Asher truly would be here that she was in denial.

They stopped for breaks a couple of times, and when Gavin called Amelia to tell her they would arrive at the dock by five that night, she said, "I'll let Dad know. He's finished with his flight, and I just returned with my last one."

"If it's a go tonight, I'll just set up my tent and a campfire, and we'll keep the rest of the gear by the dock. You don't need to bring any extra food. They aren't going to pack up what they had left to take with them, so we'll have plenty to eat."

"Oh, okay. Wait, here's Dad. Can we pick them up at five?"

"Yeah. That will work. It will still be light out when we return them here."

"Dad said it's a go, if you didn't hear him."

"We'll be ready. And, Amelia, thanks for saying you'd come with me."

"Are you kidding? This is the first real vacation I've had in two years. I'm looking forward to it."

Though everyone was tired from the nearly two days of paddling, they'd picked up their pace when they saw the bay. They were going home to all their creature comforts.

When Gavin and the others finally arrived at the dock, they were even earlier than they'd planned. They pulled their canoes out of the water and unloaded their gear.

Conrad helped Gavin set up his tent, and the others helped make a campfire. For Gavin, this was as much home as his house with all the amenities. He'd always loved the great outdoors, but being a part-time wolf made him appreciate it all the more.

Then they set a lantern on the edge of the dock, though it was still plenty light out. They weren't taking any chances that Henry would have trouble.

As soon as Gavin heard the plane, he began to keep a lookout.

"Do you see anything?" Theodore asked.

"No. I hear it though." Gavin knew Theodore couldn't hear it yet.

Then they both saw the plane, and Mindy said, "Thank God, and all in one piece too."

"Does Asher have a sat phone?" Gavin asked her, suddenly wondering if she could reach him and ask him what he was doing out here.

"Yeah. So?"

"You should try calling him and ask why he's out here."

"Are you joking?"

"Don't tell me you're going to go home and pretend he never came out here."

"I didn't see him. And he never told me he was coming out here. It's just your word that you saw him. You have to be mistaken."

"Play it however you want, but I'd be wary of your ex-con husband."

"Can I use your phone?" Mindy asked Lee.

"Sure." She handed her the sat phone.

Mindy placed a call. "Hey, Asher, it's me. You know that guy that had you arrested and testified against you at the trial? The one looking for his Samoyed pups? Well, he's here in the Boundary Waters, if you can imagine. And you know what he said? He saw you paddling out here."

Gavin heard him laughing on the phone.

"Asher's laughing," Mindy told Gavin. "He's never been paddling and doesn't even know how to swim. He hates the water. He's home, waiting for his loving wife to return. That's what he says."

"Are you afraid of him?" Gavin asked.

She said to Asher, "I told him you were mistaken. I'll see you soon."

Gavin wondered if she was afraid of her husband and suspected she believed Asher was here, which was why she hadn't wanted to paddle with someone else.

"Bye." She handed Lee her sat phone.

"Of course, there could be more to this than meets the eye. You're working on something illegal with your husband, and you don't want anyone to believe he's here." Not that Gavin really thought that. Mindy had been too shocked at hearing the news when he'd first told her.

Mindy folded her arms across her waist. "All right. For whatever it's worth, I believe you. I heard the water lapping at the canoe when he answered the sat phone." She shrugged. "I couldn't admit to him I knew he was out here, but I wanted him to know you had come along and said he was. Just in case he'd been watching us."

"I understand."

Lee patted her shoulder. "If you want, I'll help you get a lawyer and a divorce. If I were you, I'd cancel my life insurance policy."

"Can I have your sat phone back?" Mindy asked.

Lee handed it to her.

Mindy called someone and said, "Hi, I need to have you call my insurance company." She gave the operator the name, and then said a few seconds later, "Hi, this is Mindy Michaels. And I have a problem. I'm in the Boundary Waters on a canoe trip, but someone poisoned my food and sabotaged the plane I was on. I need to cancel my life insurance policy, in case my beneficiary is involved in recent events. Thank you."

Then she gave details to prove who she was and ended the call and returned the phone to Lee. "I believe I'll take you up on your offer of a lawyer's assistance in handling my divorce."

Gavin swore everyone in the group released their collective breaths at once.

As soon as the plane taxied in and parked at the dock, Gavin tied it off and opened the doors to let Henry and Amelia out.

"You take good care of her," Henry warned.

"I will, sir." Gavin smiled at Amelia and gave her a big hug.

Then he hauled out her bags. They were going to enjoy this trip. They both carried the bags off the dock and then helped everyone carry their gear to the plane. It took them some time to load all the gear and the canoes.

"Thank you," Lee told Gavin, "for coming back to take care of us."

Theodore shook Gavin's hand. "I really owe you." He gave Gavin his business card. "If you ever come to Seattle, look me up, will you?"

"Sure, and thanks."

Conrad shook his hand. "Too bad your agency isn't situated in the Seattle area. I might need a PI myself."

Gavin raised a brow in question.

Conrad gave him a dark smile. "Let's just say I might know why you were out here. I don't have anything to hide. On the other hand, she might."

Gavin opened his mouth to speak, to verify that

the "she" he was referring to was his wife, but Orwell came over and shook Gavin's hand. "My wife has been unfaithful for the last five years of our marriage. We had an understanding. We only separated recently because she suddenly didn't like the idea that I would be seeing other women. If you ever want to check out the guys she's been seeing, come out to Seattle and I'll hire you for the investigation."

"He's on my case for now," Amelia said, taking hold of Gavin's hand. "But if it turns out it has anything to do with any of you, we'll be sure to contact you."

"Thank you," Lee said, glancing again at Conrad.

Gavin suspected Lee still wanted to make a play for Conrad, particularly if he suspected his wife was up to no good.

Then Henry gave Amelia a hug, and everyone loaded onto the plane. Gavin thought they looked relieved to be going home. Amelia looked relieved to see them all leaving too. Gavin wrapped his arms around her shoulders as they saw the group off.

"Let's have some hot dogs for dinner, and then we can watch the sunset," Gavin said.

"Now that sounds like a plan."

They fixed hot dogs, and she'd brought brownies for dessert. Afterward, they roasted marshmallows and watched the sunset. "Beautiful," she said. "Sometimes I see the sunset when I'm flying, and it's just mesmerizing. Here with you, it's so much more…romantic."

Anytime spent with her, he couldn't see it any other way. "As wet and chilly as it was the first couple of days we were here together, I thought that was romantic too."

She smiled and snuggled up next to him. "I never thought I'd be in a situation like that, but I agree."

Once the blue hour had passed, the stars dotted the dark night, and Gavin and Amelia admired their simplistic magnificence. "Beautiful."

She was.

They listened to frogs croaking, the sound of a breeze ruffling pine needles and leaves, and an owl hooting nearby. Gavin loved hearing the sounds of nature at night and her heart beating next to his.

"How long will it take for us to reach Ely?" she asked.

"Three days, if we're enjoying the trip and not trying to rush to get there. I called Faith to tell her we'll need a pickup. She said to just call her when we're near, and she'll drive there to get us. She can't wait to meet you. She was upset to hear what had happened to us." The whole pack wanted to know more about Amelia and her family. Faith already knew, without Gavin having to say a thing, that he had fallen for the she-wolf.

"I bet."

"My partners will help us with this too, once they return from their current assignments. If we haven't resolved it by ourselves by then." He sure hoped they'd finish it themselves before anyone else in the agency had to drop what they were doing to help.

"What do you think about Conrad's comment? Did he mean he'd hire you to investigate his wife?"

"I suspect that's what he meant."

"Sounds like you could have a bunch of jobs." Amelia sounded proud of him.

"But then I have the issue with the gray wolf pack there." Not that they would stop him.

"What if this investigation requires you to go to Seattle?"

Gavin took her hand and squeezed. "Then that's where I'll be going. Gray wolf pack or no."

"I'll go with you and give them a piece of my mind," Amelia said. "I'm not newly turned, and if they have issues with me, tough. I'm surprised they gave you and your pack trouble but said nothing to me or my family."

"I suspect they hadn't run across you. You said you lived out a way from Seattle."

"Could be. What about Asher coming after you once you saw he was here? You'd be a witness," Amelia said.

"Mindy's all right. She wasn't hurt. Unless we can tie him to the plane sabotage, the only other reason he might want me dead is for having him arrested. That was over seven years ago. I can't imagine he'd want revenge at this late date."

"How did Mindy act about you seeing him here?"

"Shocked. She canceled her insurance policy."

"Good. Do you think he came in by seaplane or paddled in from Ely?"

"Not sure. If he came by plane, he had to have come with one of the other seaplane services or you would have recognized him, don't you think?" Gavin loved the feel of Amelia's warm body wrapped in his arms. The way her butt was pressed against his cock was making him ramrod stiff. He swore touching her always made it happen.

"I'd say that was more likely. He probably came earlier so he could witness the plane crash. He must have been shaken up to learn Mindy wasn't even on the flight. By the way, my mother told me that if you rescued me from an ice floe, we'd be mated wolves for certain."

"No ice floes around here."

"I think coming to each other's aid in a plane crash counts too." She turned her face up to smile at him.

He kissed her mouth tenderly, enjoying this time with her out here under the stars, but he wanted something more to relieve the sexual tension she had aroused in him. "How does your brother feel about us?" Gavin had been close to his parents and had never had any siblings, so his partners had been like his brothers. He wanted to have good relations with Amelia's parents and her brother, just as much as he knew she'd want the same.

"My brother is happy for me. And he's eager to meet you. I have to tell you, both my dad and my brother wanted to be the one to paddle back with you."

Gavin smiled at her. "It would be nice to get to know them, but I'd much rather share a tent with you." And so much more.

Chapter 16

LATER THAT NIGHT, AMELIA RAN HER HAND OVER GAVIN'S muscular thigh. "It's late and I'm tired. Are you ready to retire to bed?" Amelia didn't really have sleeping in mind, especially not when Gavin's rigid cock was pressed against her backside. Between that and the musky smell of him, she was getting horny.

Gavin rose to his feet and banked the fire. "I am." He hauled the bags into the tent while she turned on a lantern inside.

Worried about the food, Amelia left the tent and looked in the direction of their campfire. "All the food is put away, right?" She didn't want to have to fight with a bear over their food packs again.

"Yeah. Come on." He led her back inside the tent. His gaze was so hotly intense on her that she felt the heat sizzle between them, and he wasn't even touching her.

And then it was like a race to the finish line, both of them feeling the need to get naked and have sex. At least as far as they could go without mating. They yanked off their boots and socks. Shirts and jeans went flying. Neither of them had bothered with underwear, and now they were naked together, standing, kissing, touching.

She ran her hands up his muscled chest, and he drew in a sharp, ragged breath. Then she began to kiss him hard on the mouth. His hands moved to her hips, and he settled her against his crotch. His arousal poked her in the belly, and she was certain he wanted a deeper connection between them like she did.

The air was already thick with their musky, sexy scents, mixing, mingling, preparing them to move forward.

She pulled him tighter and began kissing him again, their bodies snug, their hearts pounding. "You feel so good," she said against his mouth.

"You feel even better."

He lifted her up and settled her on the sleeping bag. He spread her legs with his hand, caressing her inner thigh all the way to her mound, his darkened gaze shifting from her face to his actions. His fingers combed gently through her curly hairs. She barely breathed. The need to feel him touching her, coaxing her into climax, was overwhelming.

But then he swept his hand over her belly, his warming caress heating her. Liquid heat pooled between her legs, preparing her for his penetration, even though they couldn't unless they were going for a mating.

He traced her inner thigh again, drawing closer to the center of her, teasing her. Then he began to stroke her, his mouth kissing a trail up her belly to her breast. His tongue licked a nipple, and she groaned out loud. His fingers were steady, determined, coaxing her bud. She was caught up in the mesmerizing feel of his touches, the way his tongue circled her nipple, wet and warm and gentle, the way his hot mouth sucked.

She was primed for him, eager to agree to anything, spreading her legs further, her pheromones telling him in no uncertain terms that she'd picked him. Of any wolf she could have, he was the one she wanted.

But then the thought occurred to her: Could she deal

with the issue of being mated to a more newly turned wolf?

She had to think of her offspring too. They would have the disadvantage of having mostly human genetics, and her children wouldn't be royals like her. They'd have trouble like he did with not having complete control over shifting during the various phases of the moon.

If she didn't have to think practically about this, about what kind of a life she would be setting up for her children, she wouldn't have cared that he was newly turned.

Then he was kissing her on the mouth again, moving his hard cock against her thigh, riding her, and the whole business of children and newly turned wolf problems melted away, her every sense tuned to him, to his scent, his touch, and his taste. He was such a gorgeous specimen of a man, and a wolf as well.

Her body thrummed with delicious need. His fingers worked harder to bring her to the top, his mouth claiming hers and their tongues intertwining in a lover's dance. Every stroke brought her higher.

He kissed her throat, and she felt the climax coming. She gripped the sleeping bag in her fists and free-fell, as if she'd jumped from her plane without a parachute, the sheer joy washing over her in a heady rush.

She wanted to pull him into her, to seat his cock deep inside her, to feel his hot seed explode into her. Instead, she took hold of him and began to stroke. He lay back on the sleeping bag while she worked her magic on him.

The water lapped at the beach nearby, the bugs singing in chorus, but Gavin's concentration was on the siren stroking him to completion. Her blond hair hung about her shoulders, her beautiful breasts swinging as she stroked him. Her nipples were dark and peaked, her lips parted as she licked them. She was wet and ready for him, and he wanted to finish this thing between them, to mate her, but he knew she was wise to hold back. It was killing him to do so though. Even if he knew it was best to know this was what they really wanted—for all time.

Her fingers were firm on his cock, sliding up and down to the base, her thumb sliding across the wet tip and then stroking him again. He reached his hands to her legs and pulled her so she was straddling him, open to him, as if she was going to ride him next. The image of her splayed above him and her heated strokes brought him quickly to the top, and he climaxed. He groaned and pulled her down to kiss her deeply, her body spread-eagled across his. He swept his hands down her body, cupping her ass.

"You are beautiful."

"You are so hot. Why don't we go skinny-dipping to clean off under the stars?"

"You're so the wolf for me," he said as she climbed off him.

She laughed.

Before she could walk barefooted across the stone-covered beach, he scooped her up and headed out to the water.

And then when he'd carried her out far enough, he let her go, and they splashed around, laughing and enjoying the nighttime swim. "Hope we aren't within hearing distance of any poor souls who are trying to sleep."

"Maybe we'll give them ideas."

———

After breakfast the next morning, Amelia and Gavin headed out on the next day of their journey to Ely.

"Since we never saw any sign of Asher or Heaton, Lee and her party all arrived home safe and sound, and the aircraft investigators are still checking into the downed plane, I want to go to Seattle to check into Conrad and Orwell's situations. Both wanted to hire me," Gavin said.

"Do you need a flying companion?" Amelia asked, not surprised he'd take the jobs.

"I'd love it."

"What about Conrad's wife?"

"I haven't called her yet. I was giving Conrad time to return home. Because he's cut his canoe trip short by several days, if he doesn't tell Eleanor, he might get a surprise himself when he arrives home."

"You mean that she could be seeing someone."

"Correct. In which case he might not need my services."

"Except to document it."

"True. He could hire someone there, less expense for him."

"Did you tell him you were working for his wife?"

"No. That's confidential, but I suspect he knows that's why I was there. I'm not finished with Conrad either. What if he's not having an affair with anyone at work, but he is with someone away from work? Unless Eleanor lied about what she found to be suspicious concerning her husband's actions, it's worth looking into."

"A wolf and his bone."

"I'm always as thorough as I can be."

They spent two days paddling, fishing, running and swimming as wolves, and had another day to go before they reached Ely. They had made love again last night, to the extent they could without a mating, but Amelia didn't know how long either of them would last at it. They'd both had to put on the brakes, but she didn't think it would be long before they took the plunge.

When they camped that night, Gavin called ahead to let Faith know they were getting close to Ely.

"David came in, so he's picking you up when you arrive. Just let him know an hour out, and he'll be there. You know him... He wants to meet the lady wolf," Faith said. "I'm staying here to watch the kids and man the agency phones."

"Did you tell him about her when he was still out in the field?" Gavin asked.

Faith laughed. "Yes. Sorry. Should I have kept it a secret?"

Gavin said to Amelia, "Okay, so David Davis is the other bachelor male in the pack. And apparently he's finagled his way into picking us up."

"Faith is working scheduling and has the triplets to care for. I don't blame her. I assume this worked out better for her. And for David."

Gavin said, "Yeah, I wasn't going to mention that part."

"You didn't have to. New Arctic female wolf shows up in your territory; she's single, he's single. Stands to reason." Amelia put her arms around Gavin's waist. "You don't seem worried."

"Oh, he'll be interested, and he'll hope he has a chance with you. I hope he doesn't."

"He doesn't," Amelia assured him.

He smiled at her, then spoke again to Faith. "I think he's too late if he thought to make a connection with Amelia."

"Oh my. Well, it sounds like we might have some celebrating to do."

"There's something else I meant to mention. We're taking a puppy Saint Bernard into the pack. The kids will love him, but while I'm off on missions, can you look after him?"

"Absolutely. And I'm sure Owen's mate will love to have the company while she's writing her next novel. Is…that some of the reason why you got the girl?"

He laughed. "He was part of our adventure, and he missed going home to a family. He needs some training as far as not running off, but he's a great dog. Big. Much bigger than us when we're wolves. Good-natured."

"The kids will be delighted. They won't be able to wait until he's here."

"Hold on." Gavin said to Amelia, "Do you think your brother could deliver Winston to Faith and Cameron's house?"

"Sure. When you get off the phone, I'll call Slade."

"Amelia will ask her brother when he can bring him." Gavin heard the kids shouting with excitement in the background.

"Hope it's sooner than later!"

"I've got a couple of jobs in Seattle that might relate to this case," Gavin said. "I've already called ahead for a flight for the day after we arrive. That means you'll have to take care of Winston for a while."

"Seattle?" Faith sounded like she didn't care for the idea.

"I've got a couple of jobs there," he reiterated.

"And if the gray pack sees you there?"

"Their tough luck. They're not going to stop us if we have business in the area."

"Maybe David should go with you."

"I believe if it's only me—"

"And me," Amelia said.

"And Amelia." Gavin looked down into her luminous green eyes and saw the eagerness there. "We'll be fine."

"Okay."

Gavin knew Faith was figuring that the changes in his life suddenly had something to do with the she-wolf. Which was true. "We'll be fine."

"I'll let everyone know. And, Gavin, you only have about five days before the moon starts messing with your shifting."

"That's why we're flying out as soon as we can."

"Tell Faith that if you have trouble with shifting, we'll just drive back. I can control the shifting at all times."

"I heard," Faith said. "And tell her I thank her."

"I'm mating her." Gavin didn't see any reason not to state how he felt about Amelia, though he supposed he should have asked her if she wanted it too. The way they'd been so close to throwing caution to the wind and mating last night, he was certain it would be soon, one way or another.

Amelia laughed.

"I guess I should ask her first." Gavin smiled down at her, his fingers combing through her satiny blond hair.

"Gavin, you and your partners." Faith sighed. "Talk to her, and when you can, let me know."

"I'll talk to you soon. She needs to call her brother about the dog too."

When they ended the call, Gavin handed the sat phone to Amelia. She was smiling at him, waiting for him to say something before she called her brother.

He pulled her into his arms, and she set the sat phone down on the grass.

"I love you, Amelia. I thought there must be something wrong with me when I was so glad to see you again. Like I was seeing an old friend, despite the fact that you tased me the last time we met. When I smelled you were a wolf, that made all the difference in the world to me. All the instincts I have as a human, and the deeper ones that are part of our wolf nature, instantly kicked in. Now I know why Owen didn't want the rest of us to meet Candice until they were mated wolves. And why Cameron was so possessive and protective of Faith. Though with both wolf couples, it goes both ways."

"As it should if the wolves are suited to each other," Amelia said, holding him close. She could already feel his cock stirring against her, loved feeling his hard body pressed against her, his arms wrapped securely around her. She knew she should wait and see how he dealt with the issue of not having control over his shifting. She'd never known a wolf who had been turned. She didn't care. If he needed her, she would be there for him every step of the way. As far as kids were concerned, well, they'd all deal with the shifting issues.

Gavin kissed her forehead. "I admire you for being able to fly—without fear, and in extraordinary circumstances, landing so that we survived. Every night you were gone, I breathed in your sexy scent on the sleeping bags and wished we were sharing them again. Every day, I wished you were paddling with me, sharing meals, enjoying the wilderness together. All I could think of was how much I wanted to court you and win you over and, well, hell... Will you mate me?"

She laughed. "I didn't think you'd ever ask. Any man who would put up with me tasing him, then still be good-natured while we were attempting to make it to shore with Winston and all your gear is remarkable. Then you offered to help us learn the truth about the plane, decided to take Winston, and offered your pack's help with anything we might need.

"I hated having to leave you behind when my brother needed me to fly for him, and I hoped you would still need me so I could return here and paddle with you further."

"Are you kidding? I thought of nothing else."

She smiled. "When I went home to an empty bed, I felt like I'd lost my packmate. That's how much I already felt the strong connection between us. And truly, last night, we were well on our way to being mated wolves, so it's happening. Sooner's much better for me."

She pulled him down for a kiss and planted her lips softly against his. "I love you right back, Gavin." Something in the sky caught her attention, and she looked up to see a pale ribbon of green and pink lights that turned into brilliant bands across the night sky. A wolf howled off in the distance, and several more followed suit and sang for several minutes: the gathering of the pack, hauntingly beautiful. The perfect night for mated love between two Arctic wolves.

She pulled away from Gavin, and he started to follow her to the tent, but she said, "We'll do this outside, under the beautiful night sky. With the aurora borealis dancing above us, nothing would make it more special."

He smiled. "It sure will be special."

They brought out the sleeping bag and laid it out under the stars as they both hurried to strip. No one could tell how long the beams of lights would last, maybe up to a half hour, possibly repeating again later. She wanted to do this now. To make this mating even more special than it would already be. Forever, they would remember it this way.

"You're beautiful, you know?" Gavin said, smiling down at her before he pulled her over to the sleeping bag and they climbed into it.

"You are too." Amelia kissed him as they settled into the bag.

For several minutes, she lay wrapped in his arms in the sleeping bag, both of them watching the aurora borealis display overhead, the beauty of the lights reflecting off the glassy water. "Dawn of the north," she said.

Yet no matter how spectacular the lights were, she couldn't stop thinking of Gavin's hot, naked body wrapped around her. The feel of his hard muscles beneath her. The spicy, male wolfish scent that she couldn't help breathing in, filling her with heady delight.

She thought he was watching the lights just to please her, to show how romantic he could be, but she kept wanting to slide her hands all over his body and feel his cock thrusting inside her. What if he really wanted to watch the lights? She didn't want to ruin it for him.

He started caressing her arm, and she moved her hand down his body, touching his rigid cock, and she smiled. He was always ready for her.

He kissed her forehead, but she moved against his body so she could kiss his mouth. He parted his kissable masculine lips to her and drew her inside. She kissed him long and deep, straddling his leg, rubbing her mons against his thigh. It didn't take much of touching him, feeling his heat, and smelling his sexy scent before her body reacted in a primal, needy way. Sharing her own scent that said she craved the wolf. She ground her body against him, trying to find her own release.

He raised his knee so his thigh was firmer beneath her spread legs, his hands combing through her hair, his mouth on hers, his tongue plunging, taking, until they had to come up for air.

"Beautiful," he whispered against her ear, the light stubble on his face brushing against her cheek as he nuzzled her.

And then he was moving her onto her back where she got a glimpse of the gorgeous light display overhead. He only smiled at her and wickedly began to stroke her, as if to say the northern lights couldn't hold a candle to the way he'd make her feel.

He would be right as he stroked her into oblivion. She felt like she was shooting into the dancing lights and burning up with them. Then his mouth was on hers again, and he had her wrapped in his arms, his knee spreading her thighs apart before he slid his cock into the center of her being and held still while she adjusted to his size, the hot, hard length of him.

This was it. The mating. Taking care of each other, their offspring, loving each other until the end. This felt right. And she loved him for it.

Then he began to thrust, and she saw the love in his

eyes as he gazed down at her, and she felt the love for him as she gazed up at him. He kissed her nose, her eyes, her cheeks, and her mouth.

Their tongues tangled while he drove his cock into her, and she thrust her pelvis to make a deeper connection. Then she locked her ankles around his legs and enjoyed the ride as he took her up to that brilliantly colored starry field above and she cried out in exaltation.

It occurred to her that people could hear her a mile away, if humans were staying that close by. Gavin came inside her, the heat of his seed warming her as he finished and then sank against her. "Beautiful," he said, then re-situated them so they could continue to watch the light show.

"Wow," she said, his arms wrapped around her as she held on to him and enjoyed the night show. "You are one hot wolf. And I love you with all my heart."

"So are you, and I love you right back. If you're not too tired, maybe later tonight, the lights will appear again, and we can repeat what just happened to make it even more memorable."

She laughed. "You've got a deal."

Chapter 17

AFTER MAKING LOVE AGAIN LAST NIGHT AND DOING JUST what Gavin suggested—watching more of the northern lights on full display—they got up late the next morning and had oatmeal for breakfast. Gavin pulled out the sat phone and called Eleanor, knowing Conrad would have been home long before this. "This is Gavin Summerfield. I lost the sat phone and had no cell reception in the Boundary Waters," he said, leaving a message on Eleanor's answering machine. "I didn't see any evidence of what you were looking for. If you want me to investigate further, I can." The message machine cut off, and Gavin called again. "The party returned home, but I had no way to contact you. The charges will be just for the first couple of days. I'm headed home now. Let me know if I can be of further assistance." The message machine cut off.

"You had to leave a message," Amelia said.

"Yeah. So we'll see if she calls back to have me do any further investigation."

"How much do you want to bet she won't?"

"I agree with you there. I keep thinking about her wanting me, no one else, to investigate Conrad. And she wanted to make sure I was flying, not paddling in."

"You didn't say that before. The part about not paddling in."

"I just can't see how she could be connected to Heaton. I mean, why would she want me dead?"

"And Red wanted me dead?" Amelia asked.

"I would think if that were the case, she was involved in the jewelry heist. That's the only connection between you, me, and Red."

"She's an heiress. If she was the one who hired the men to do the heist, why would she need the money?" Amelia asked.

"Maybe she's not that financially set. I just assumed she was because she was worried about divorcing Conrad and losing some of her money in the settlement. But maybe that's the reason she's afraid of losing it. She isn't as well off as I'd imagined. She's also living in Seattle, where the jewelry heist occurred."

"When we have better access to the internet, maybe we can learn more about her."

"Yeah. I just couldn't see the connection, but maybe it wasn't about Conrad at all. We were loose ends in the heist. Come on. Let's get on our way. While we're in Seattle, I want to do some digging into her background."

After packing up, they had paddled a couple of hours when they heard angry voices arguing on an island nearby. Gavin recognized the one canoe as the kind Asher had rented. "That could be Asher's canoe."

"Who in the world would he be arguing with?" Amelia whispered.

"Some hapless camper, probably."

They pulled their canoe onto the shore.

"I'd feel better if you stayed with the canoe," Gavin said, hoping she'd go along with the suggestion. "Unless he's just angry with another paddler, if it's Asher, this might have something to do with our case."

"I'm sticking with you." Amelia grabbed the camera, her Taser, and the sat phone.

"All right, but if there's real trouble, you duck into the woods, get naked, and shift."

They hurried toward the sound of voices just ahead, careful to be as quiet as humanly possible.

"You were supposed to take down the first group of passengers," Asher said, his voice hot with anger. "My wife and her lover along with it."

Gavin's adrenaline was already filling every cell, and now he was angry. Whoever was out here had been in on the plot to kill Asher's wife.

"I planned the whole thing that way, damn it! Based on the schedule, I had the timer set correctly. Your wife's boss screwed everything up by arriving early and flying an hour earlier than scheduled. I mean, hell, how could I have predicted that? Flights might leave later or on time, but they don't leave an hour earlier than scheduled—normally." *Heaton!*

"Hell, that's how I missed seeing the plane crash! I thought the flight hadn't arrived yet, so I paddled there late and then had to see for myself who made it to shore," Asher said.

"The PI said someone stole Amelia's raft. Was that you?" Heaton growled.

Asher snorted.

"What the hell for?" Heaton sounded like he was still carrying a torch for Amelia.

"The bastard was involved with the police and put me away the first time. I figured if they were stranded on the island, they'd never know who did it and wouldn't run into me later either. I heard them returning and had to drop the canoe."

Gavin and Amelia moved into the brush, close enough that they could get a glimpse of the two men— Heaton and Asher Michaels—while being hidden from their view. Why wasn't Gavin surprised? Obviously, Heaton had never left the Boundary Waters like he said he was going to. The men were facing each other, offering Gavin and Amelia a clear view of the gun Asher had pointed at Heaton.

"From what I hear, someone else paid you to take the plane down too. Maybe someone with more money. Maybe someone who was targeting a different passenger or group of passengers."

"I don't know what you mean." Heaton looked nervous now, like that's exactly what had happened and he'd been caught up in the scam.

Gavin had to wait and listen, to learn what he could of the truth before he could attempt to take them down. Then he saw that Amelia was recording everything on his camera.

"I had drinks with one of the pilots who works with you, and he said he figured his manager hired you to take it down. The manager wouldn't care who was on it as long as the old man was flying it. So a second person paid for the job, other than me?" Asher asked.

Heaton looked as pale as if he was going to pass out. "Will you put the gun down?"

"We had a deal. You kill my wife, along with everyone else on the plane to make it look accidental. At the same time, you'd get rid of the guy who fired you. I get rid of my unfaithful wife and her lover. And you'd do it so it looked like a damn accident. You said you'd be able to. No problem."

"I would never have double-crossed you. Do you think I have a death wish?"

"My wife has gone home, and I've lost the chance I had to make this look like an accident. She'll be wary of a second attempt now. No telling what she'll do— leave notes with her family, saying to suspect me if she dies accidentally, probably. She'll most likely cancel her insurance policy. I can see coming home to sign divorce papers. Which is not where this was supposed to go. Now aircraft investigators are looking into the accident. What if they implicate you? You said no one would ever consider it any more than pilot error. If they decide you did it, then where does that leave me? I'll tell you where that leaves me. They'll question you, and who will you say paid for this? Me."

"I didn't have anything to do with the change in schedule. And I swear they'll never be able to figure out that it was sabotaged."

"You're a loose end I can't afford."

Before Gavin could take Asher down to stop him, Asher fired five shots at Heaton.

As soon as Gavin broke through the brush to tackle him, Asher turned the gun on him. Heart racing, Gavin dove for cover and quickly rose to shoot Asher twice in the shoulder. Crying out, Asher dropped the gun, cursing, and Gavin rushed forth to retrieve it before Asher could regain it. Gun secured, Gavin shoved Asher to the ground and pinned his good arm behind his back. Heaton was gasping for air. He sounded like he didn't have long to live.

"Sorry," Heaton croaked out to Amelia. That was the last breath he would take.

Amelia had been video recording all of it to protect themselves and document the confessions, but once Gavin had taken Asher down, she'd rushed forth to check on Heaton. She shook her head at Gavin. "Asher killed him." She pulled out the sat phone and called the sheriff's office with a report about the shooting and their location. "Yes, my boyfriend's a former Seattle cop and a private investigator in the area. He's got the suspect pinned down for now. I need to run and get some rope to tie him up with," she said to someone on the phone.

She dashed off, leaving the camera with Gavin as she continued to talk to the authorities.

"Feels like déjà vu, me taking you down, only this time, it's for cold-blooded murder instead of dognapping," Gavin growled at Asher, furious with the man. "Maybe you'll stay in the slammer for longer this time. Like for life."

Forever, Gavin was hoping.

When Amelia returned with the rope and the first aid kit, Gavin tied Asher's hands in back of him.

"Damn it, you're killing me." Asher scowled at him.

"Yeah, tell someone who gives a damn." Even though Gavin and Amelia had assumed some of what had happened might be true, hearing it for real had to be upsetting to Amelia. Gavin gave her a hug and saw the tears in her eyes. "I'm sorry about Heaton."

She nodded. "Though he deserved what he got."

Gavin knew she meant because he was a wolf who had intended to kill her father and the others for money and revenge. Gavin bandaged Asher's shoulder.

"I'll get the emergency blanket in case he goes into shock." She raced off again.

"And some water!" Gavin called out to her. They'd have to wait a considerable time before anyone could reach them, but he suspected they'd be better off paddling to a location where Heaton and Asher would be picked up.

"Okay!"

After a few minutes, Amelia returned with water and a blanket. "The Lake County Sheriff's Office told me that with 2,300 square miles to cover, they have only three duty stations. They have to call the U.S. Forest Service, because they fly in to remote areas from a seaplane base. The seaplane is out on another mission. An injured teenager whose canoe flipped over in rapids. He was caught between the rocks and has been in the water for eight hours. Three others with him are still in the water too. No one has been able to reach them yet."

"Okay, so what does that mean for us?" Gavin asked.

"You shouldn't have shot me! That's what it means," Asher growled.

"The sheriff's office is calling a Minnesota State Patrol helicopter team, or MART, that works rescue missions with the Saint Paul and Brainerd fire departments. They need two hours' notice to get everyone on board. They'll have to get as close as they can to our site, portage, then go by canoe the rest of the way here. Seaplanes just can't get into some of these lakes, like this one. I'd say we should take him to be picked up earlier, but we can't leave Heaton here, or a bear or wolves might find him and think he's supper."

"He's dead," Asher reminded them.

"We can't split up. I don't want you alone with Asher, and I don't want you staying here with Heaton, should a bear or a pack of wolves show up. We stay together," Gavin said, determined to protect her at all costs.

"And I could die. Then that would be on your head," Asher said.

Gavin snorted. "Not something I'd lose sleep over."

"I have the camera recording that proves exactly what happened and shows Gavin acted in self-defense. If you die, no great loss to the world," Amelia said.

"How about we carry Heaton's body out in one canoe, you in the other?" Gavin asked.

"I'll go with the woman." Asher had to be crazy if he thought he had any say in this.

Gavin shook his head. "You'll go with me."

"He doesn't want to go with the dead body. Some boyfriend he makes," Asher gritted out.

"Okay, so how are we going to get them there?" Amelia asked.

"I'll tie Asher's hands in front, and he can help me carry Heaton to the beach."

Asher grunted. "Over my dead body."

"That could be arranged." Gavin didn't want to untie Asher. He didn't trust the man, and he wasn't sure what kind of a shot Amelia would be if Asher tried to fight him. Gavin didn't think she could help him carry Heaton. Even if she could, they would both have their hands full. On the other hand, Asher was human. Gavin didn't trust that he could wait it out on the island for an emergency crew to get to them before Asher could be in real medical distress.

"I'll call the sheriff's office to let them know where we're headed."

"Okay. After you do that, keep the gun on him and shoot him if he tries anything," Gavin said.

She conveyed the information to the sheriff's office about where they were and where they were going and that they would meet up with them in four hours.

When she ended the call, Gavin handed his gun to Amelia. She slipped Asher's gun and the sat phone in the camera bag. Thankfully, she'd had enough presence of mind that she'd used the bottom edge of her shirt to handle the weapon.

"Don't shoot me by accident," Asher warned her.

"Don't worry. I'll only shoot you on purpose, if it's necessary."

Gavin untied Asher's wrists, then retied his hands in front of him. "Okay, let's get going." Gavin had Asher carry the upper part of Heaton's body, while Gavin carried his legs so he could keep an eye on Asher.

"You can take our canoe," Gavin said to Amelia as she followed behind the men. If Asher did anything stupid, like trying to tip over his canoe, Gavin wanted to make sure they didn't lose their possessions.

"Do you need my help with Heaton?" she asked.

"No. We're good."

"Speak for yourself," Asher said, grunting.

With Asher stumbling under the weight of Heaton, it seemed to take them forever to reach the canoes and load Heaton into his own canoe. "I'll tie Heaton's canoe to mine," Gavin said, not wanting Amelia to have to deal with it. He made up a towrope, MacGyver style. "Come here, Asher."

"This isn't necessary. I can help you paddle."

"Like hell you can." Gavin could just imagine getting a paddle upside the head.

After retying Asher's hands in back, Gavin helped him into the front of Asher's canoe. Then he waited while Amelia got into hers. "We'll push hard to get there by tonight. Hopefully, the EMTs will arrive and the police, and they can take care of these two."

"Okay. The gun's easily reached, so if Asher tries something, I'll just add another hole or two," Amelia warned. "Or I could use the Taser."

"As if I'm going to do anything."

Amelia lifted her paddle. "Are you sure I shouldn't tow the canoe? You've got more deadweight in yours, and you're dragging the other one behind you."

"We'll be fine. And, Asher, if you begin feeling light-headed, lie down in the canoe," Gavin said.

"I'm surprised you would be concerned."

"Why? Though we have the camera recording of all that you said and did, we still want you to pay for your crime," Gavin said, damn serious.

"And you don't want them investigating you for shooting me."

"It was self-defense, pure and simple. Of course they'll take my gun and check my story as part of the routine investigation."

"You didn't have to shoot me twice!"

"You didn't drop the gun the first time I shot you. I wasn't waiting for you to shoot me. Then what a mess we would have been in!"

After they were ready to leave, they paddled for hours. The EMTs would have to use the portage to join them, unless they could convince Asher to carry his own gear and canoe, but he probably wasn't in any shape to do it.

"Are you doing all right?" Gavin asked Amelia. She looked tired.

"Yeah. Maybe we can stop and eat soon."

Asher was now lying down on the bottom of the canoe, sleeping or out of it.

"Is he all right?"

"Sleeping, I think. Let's paddle to the beach over there, and we can grab something to eat and check on him."

"How far do you think we have to go?"

"Another six miles."

"Okay, that's good. I can do another two hours after we eat some lunch."

They pulled onto the beach, and Gavin woke Asher up. "We're having lunch. How are you doing?"

"I'm dying."

"So melodramatic. Maybe next time you'll think twice before you pull a gun on a former cop."

Amelia made them tuna fish sandwiches, and after they ate, they were on their way again.

Asher lay back down in the bottom of the canoe, and a couple of hours later, they finally reached the island where they'd meet the police and EMTs. No one was there when they arrived. Gavin hoped they were just taking longer to get here and hadn't been confused about the meeting location. Another hour passed, and Amelia was about to call the EMTs and police when they saw four canoes headed their way.

Amelia wanted to jump for joy at seeing them. She

waved vigorously instead. They'd helped Asher onto his own sleeping bag and had taken care of him the best they could.

After the EMTs stabilized Asher, they took him in one canoe, and some of the police towed Heaton in the other.

The police questioned everyone thoroughly, while Gavin and Amelia explained the business with the downed plane, the shooting, and the confession. Amelia hadn't wanted to give the camera to the police, though they needed to use the video-recorded confession on it. She wanted to send a copy to Gavin's and her email to ensure the video recording didn't get "lost." But they had no internet out here, so she couldn't do it. And they needed to give the video to the police so they could see she and Gavin were innocent of any wrongdoing.

Gavin identified the location where the shooting had taken place, and the police were heading there to get any evidence from the scene that they could. Then they released Gavin and Amelia so they could be on their way.

They were so tired from staying up so late last night that they stopped early, had dinner, and retired. Being newly mated, they managed only a catnap before making love.

The next morning, they got up even earlier to make up for stopping early the night before.

When they finally arrived in Ely, David was waiting for them. He hurried to greet them, giving Amelia a warm hug as if they were old friends. "I can't believe Owen, and now you, found a beautiful Arctic she-wolf to mate." He said to Amelia, "Faith said you don't have any sisters."

"Sorry, no."

"That's a shame." David helped them carry their gear and the canoe to the Suburban. "Faith and I picked up your vehicle, Gavin, and it's at your home now. She said you were flying out to Seattle. Are you sure you don't want me to go with you? Those gray wolves could eat you alive."

"I really think too many of us would catch their attention. I don't plan to stay long."

"You're taking Amelia?"

"Yes," she said. "I've been part of this whole fiasco from the beginning, and I want to learn the truth too."

"Do you need me to drive you to the airport? Or home?" David asked.

"Home. Thanks, David. We'll repack, get washed up, and head out again. That way, we'll have the car for when we return."

David said, "Faith and the kids are going to pick Winston up. They can't wait. And frankly, everyone else is excited too. It feels like Christmas in summer around here. Winston will be here with us when you return. Owen and Candice have already said they want equal time with the pup. You may never get to see him."

Amelia laughed. "I'm so glad the other family didn't get him. Sounds to me like he's got several families to love on him." She was so grateful Gavin had wanted Winston to join their family.

"A whole pack," Gavin agreed.

She was a little apprehensive about this new mission and hoped they learned the whole truth about what was going on with the sabotage of the plane. She also hoped she was a help to Gavin and not a hindrance.

She still couldn't believe Heaton had planned to kill her father. Glad he couldn't hurt anyone further, she just hoped Asher was put away for a very long time.

When they arrived at Gavin's home, a log cabin sitting in the woods on a lovely lake, Amelia couldn't have been more excited.

David helped Gavin with his bags and the canoe, while Amelia carried her bags to the door. A dog woofed inside, startling her. "Winston?"

David smiled but didn't say anything.

Gavin unlocked the front door and pulled it open. Winston bounded out to greet them, startling her.

Then several people inside shouted, "Welcome to the pack, Amelia!"

And that was Amelia's first meeting with all the pack members. She'd been worried whether she'd fit in. Now she was sure that wouldn't be a problem as Cameron and Faith's two boys and girl all gave her a hug. Everyone else in the pack hugged her after that, Gavin finally giving her a whopper of a kiss while everyone hooted and hollered. She was both embarrassed and thrilled.

They had a big dinner of grilled steaks, corn on the cob, green beans, watermelon, and ice cream, while everyone told wolf stories. And Amelia knew as she sat with Gavin on a stone patio, Winston at their feet, with the others sitting about on the various chairs around a fire pit, that she was finally home.

Faith said, "We've been talking about how Amelia and her family are Arctic wolves and royals and how this could be beneficial to us. At the same time, we don't want to be a burden to them if we're having difficulty controlling our shifting during the full moon. We want your family to feel as though they're part of ours, and anything we can help you with, we're here for you."

"Thank you," Amelia said. "I've got to say that having a larger group of Arctic wolves as friends is a good thing."

"Some of us met your family when we went to get Winston. We couldn't wait to get him. They're lovely. We've already talked among ourselves about having them join our pack, though we hadn't had a chance to discuss this with Gavin or you yet."

"I'm sure they would be interested, but I can't speak for them," Amelia said, glad that Gavin's pack wanted to include her family but not sure her parents would like being told what to do.

"We're completely democratic in our rules. Though Cameron and I have been kind of running the pack, we've discussed having your parents take on the pack as our leaders."

Amelia's eyes misted. She couldn't help it. Not only was it a great honor, but her parents had never been asked to do such a thing.

"We know you have to leave for Seattle, but when we get together the next time, we'd like to propose this to your parents, if you think they'd be agreeable," Cameron said.

"Of course." Amelia thought they would be, but she couldn't speak for them.

Everyone began talking about plans for the fall, and Amelia caught Gavin smiling at her. She took hold of his hand and squeezed.

Despite loving the reception she'd gotten and enjoying this festive time with the pack, Amelia was eager for everyone to leave because she wanted to try out a real bed with Gavin instead of a sleeping bag on hard ground. He was still smiling at her as if he knew just what she was thinking, and then, as if the whole pack could read their minds, everyone began to clear out, congratulating the two of them and leaving them alone.

Except Faith, who made them an offer. "I know you have to leave for Seattle, and you might want some time alone. We wouldn't mind taking Winston with us."

The kids looked so eager that Amelia laughed. "That would work out great. Give him all your loving, and we'll pick him up when we return."

Winston was everyone's dog, and he went eagerly with the kids and everyone else.

"You'd better have a soft mattress, Gavin" was all Amelia said as she dragged him into the house and down the hall, looking for his bedroom.

Chapter 18

"I LOVE YOUR HOME," AMELIA SAID, PEEKING INTO THE TWO spare bedrooms, one made into a game room, the other a guest room. When she reached his master bedroom, she'd expected something fairly utilitarian. Instead, she found a nicely decorated masculine setting of forest greens and dark pine wood, with pictures of shaded forest trails and the sunset on the lake. A cushy green love seat sat against one wall of the spacious bedroom. A chest of drawers, a highboy, a king-size bed, and bedside tables furnished the rest of the room.

"*Our* home, and you can make any changes you want."

She checked out his huge walk-in closet, only half-full, and smiled. "Looks like there's plenty of room for me."

"I'll make more room for you if there's not enough."

"You know just the way to a girl's heart." Then she checked out the lavish bathroom. A glass-surrounded shower stall, a jet whirlpool tub, a separate closet for the commode, a black marble countertop, two sinks, and a wall of mirrors. Now that was perfect for the queen.

She really needed a shower before they ended up in bed. Though they'd gone swimming both as wolves and humans in the lake and the river, so they weren't that dirty.

He rubbed his hand over her back. "Tub or shower?"

"Which do you prefer?" she asked.

"Whichever one you're planning to be in."

She laughed and began stripping off her clothes. "I have a laundry basket in my bathroom at home, so I don't usually just throw my dirty clothes on the floor."

He was jerking off his clothes just as fast. "We can set up things any way you want so you'll feel right at home."

She was still unfastening her bra when he started the shower. She tossed her bra on the sea-green tile floor and joined him. He shut the door, and with the shower massager spray sluicing down their skin, he cupped her face and began to kiss her.

Water ran down their faces, and they licked and kissed each other's mouths, their hands exploring their slippery, wet bodies. He reached back to a built-in shelf and grabbed a bottle of body wash, then squeezed it onto her, the pearly, lime-scented soap sliding over her skin. As soon as she poured some on his, they began running their hands over each other's slippery skin. She loved feeling his muscles beneath her fingertips as much as she loved feeling his hands caressing her breasts.

When his fingers soaped her mons and then began to stroke her clit, she about melted under the heated water. She slid her hands down his hard-muscled chest and reached his erection and began to wash and stroke him. He quickly pinned her against the wall, pulling her hands above her head, kissing her lips with passion, seeking entrance and spearing her mouth with his tongue.

His body was doing wicked things to hers, his penis rubbing against her belly, his hands shifting so he held both of her wrists with one and began stroking her clit with his free hand. She realized he didn't want to come in her hand. He wanted to finish inside her but was intent on bringing her to climax first.

She could go along with that plan. She nipped his lip, her body moving against his fingers, begging for completion.

"You are so hot and wet for me," he whispered against her ear, licking the curve of it.

"Oh God, Gavin, finish it."

He smiled and kissed her mouth, stroking her harder, faster. She hadn't expected him to grab her ass and lift her. She wrapped her legs around him, and he drove his cock into her. She was still thinking of cleaning up and making love on that very soft mattress he'd better have.

When she felt his hard erection fill her to the hilt and he began thrusting into her, she figured he just couldn't wait for the bed. She couldn't either, his thrusting and rubbing hitting all the right nerves. She shot straight to the moon, crying out, before he followed with a satisfied half growl, half groan.

"I couldn't wait," he said, kissing her mouth, still holding her to him. The wolf had stamina.

"Me either," she had to agree.

They took it slow then, him separating from her, then setting her on the floor. She began washing his hair while he washed hers. Then they washed the rest of their bodies before finally turning off the water and grabbing a couple of towels.

Once they'd finished drying each other, her hair still damp, he carried her to the bed.

"It better be soft." She realized he hadn't said if it was or wasn't. Not once. Good sign or bad?

He just smiled at her, pulled the covers aside, and dropped her on the pillow mattress. As soon as she fell against the ultrasoft mattress, she felt it surround her like a nest.

She moaned with ecstasy. "I think I'm in heaven."

He joined her on the mattress, covering her with his hard body. "Not yet. Soon." And he began kissing her all over again.

———

When Gavin and Amelia arrived at their Seattle hotel the next afternoon—a posh, five-star hotel, so different from camping in the wilderness—they had a welcoming committee: two of the gray wolves who served as the enforcers for the Seattle pack.

"We've told you before you can't be here," Rock Rockledge said, his black, bushy brows pinched into a perpetual scowl.

"We have business here, investigating a case. We're not moving into your territory. We have our own," Gavin said.

"Make it quick. We know you don't hold your shape during some of the phases of the moon. And it's getting close to being trouble for you." Rock glanced at Amelia. "I remember you. Your family moved into the area. Before we could tell you that it was our territory and to go back to where you came from, you packed up and left."

She folded her arms. "We had no intention of causing problems for you. We're royals. We can shift at will. Can you?"

"We're counting the days that you're here," Rock said to Gavin. "So get your business done and get out of here."

"We'll be here as long as it takes." Gavin wasn't going to be pushed around by these wolves. It was one thing to live among them, quite another to visit a city for either pleasure or work and be told you couldn't ever be here. He and Amelia were going to get the job done. He didn't know any other wolf pack as disagreeable as this one.

Gavin swore the guy cast him an elusive smile. Maybe the gray pack had been waiting for the Arctic wolves to make a stand. Or maybe they planned to kill them if they didn't listen.

Then the two men left.

"Are you going to look into Orwell's wife's situation? You said you had two cases," Amelia said, kissing his cheek.

"I will, but first we have to see what's going on with Eleanor Dylan." Gavin felt the early onset of the urge to shift into his wolf, and he groaned. "Skip that. First, I'm going to shift." He was glad the gray wolves hadn't seen that he was having trouble with this already. He just hoped Amelia didn't regret that she'd hooked up with a wolf who wasn't a royal.

"No problem, Gavin. Shift, and I will too."

He smiled at her. She was the perfect wolf mate for him. He could hold off and not shift for a couple of hours sometimes, once he began getting the urge. But he'd rather do this now, while they were safely in a hotel room, and hopefully turn back into his human form fairly quickly.

Amelia hung out the Do Not Disturb sign, then locked the door and joined him before he could remove anything more than his boots. She pulled his T-shirt over his head and kissed his chest. Then she began working on his belt.

He slid his hands down her back, smiling down at his beautiful she-wolf, and for the first time, he wasn't annoyed about having to shift when he wanted to complete a mission. The mission could wait. Being with his mate as a wolf couldn't.

They helped each other undress, and then they kissed and moved apart, shifted, and leaped onto the bed. She shifted back, and he watched her as she turned on the TV, selected a conspiracy theory movie, and shifted, curling up with him to watch the movie as wolves.

—∿∿—

For two days, Gavin and Amelia followed Eleanor Dylan around in a rental car while she had her hair done, got a facial, manicure, and pedicure, shopped for clothes, lunched out, and more. In the meantime, Amelia was doing searches on the internet. "Hey, I looked up the jewelry-store heist and dug deeper into the background on the store. Guess who the owner of the jewelry store is."

"Who?"

"Megabucks Eleanor Dylan."

"Now *that's* too much of a coincidence."

"You didn't remember this?"

"I wasn't working the case. Too personally involved. And I was off for a while, broken leg, physical therapy. When I went back to work, I was stuck in the office for months, running down leads on other cases. I never gave it much thought. They'd captured all but one of the bad guys."

"Except for the pilot," she reminded him.

He smiled at her. "I'm glad you made it home safely and sent your dad and brother to rescue me."

"Me too. It says here she's got tons of businesses to diversify her income."

"She's on the move again."

This time, Eleanor stopped at a restaurant and used valet parking.

Gavin dropped Amelia off at the front door so she could see where Eleanor got a seat while he parked the car. When he joined her, she'd asked for a booth on the other side of where Eleanor had been seated. The wall was topped with silk flowers and plants that divided them so they couldn't be seen, but they could hear Eleanor if she joined anyone.

"Will she recognize you if she sees you?" Amelia asked Gavin, her voice hushed.

"No. We don't have pictures on the website. Unless she was involved in this business all along and read the newspaper accounts about the cop who was taken hostage."

"Well, she doesn't know me."

"I'm waiting for someone, thank you," Eleanor said to the server.

Gavin hadn't officially taken the job Conrad offered him to see if Eleanor was having an affair. He needed to learn if she was involved in paying Heaton to sabotage the plane, and if so, why. If he learned she was also having an affair? He figured he wouldn't charge Conrad for the information.

"Are you all right, Gavin?"

He knew she meant about his issue with shifting, but he'd shifted late last night and the day before, both times when he and Amelia were able to stay in their hotel room, safe from prying eyes. Both times, Amelia had shifted with him to be a wolf too, as if this was perfectly normal for her. For now, he was fine. "Yeah, honey. Doing great."

"You're late, Cheryl," Eleanor said to a woman.

"I'm sorry. Traffic was horrendous, and your husband kept me late," Cheryl said.

"He didn't suspect anything, did he?" Eleanor sounded worried.

"No. Conrad's clueless."

"Good. Take a seat."

"Mrs. Dylan." Cheryl paused as a waitress came to take her drink order.

"She's not staying," Eleanor told the waitress.

Gavin shared a look with Amelia. He wondered if Eleanor believed Cheryl was having an affair with Conrad, and she was going to straighten her out.

"Mrs. Dylan," Cheryl said again, "you know I've tried to get him interested in me. That's not working, and he said he'd fire me if I keep trying. And Lee even offered him a promotion, but he's not biting."

What the hell? Eleanor was trying to force an affair on her husband?

"Lee assured me that would do the trick," Eleanor said. "I can't believe that damn private investigator went to your campsite. He said he'd be discreet."

"He was discreet. Lee and I didn't know you were using a PI to get proof of Conrad's infidelity. Though we assumed it when he told us he was a PI who happened to be on the sabotaged plane and was helping the seaplane company to investigate it. But he began questioning us about who might have a reason for someone wanting them dead, and he asked if anyone was having an affair. I mean, no one else knew—Orwell, Theodore, Nina, Conrad—that he was there for more than determining who was involved in the plane crash. After the plane went down and Theodore got lost and Gavin went to help locate him, what can you expect?"

"For him to be discreet, damn it. His job should have been his top priority. Nothing else mattered!" Eleanor growled.

"Yes, but he wanted to know if anyone had a reason for someone wanting them dead. Gavin asked Conrad if he had a reason anyone would want to see him killed, but he said no." But Cheryl had to be wondering if Eleanor had been behind the plane crash.

"Go. Keep trying. If you get a commitment from him, let me know, and I'll make it worth your while."

"Of course. I'll keep trying." Cheryl got up and left.

Gavin had never expected this turn of events.

The server dropped off soup and a salad for Eleanor.

Their own server returned, and Gavin and Amelia ordered shrimp scampi and iced tea. He thought of how enjoyable these stakeouts were with Amelia. She was a real go-getter. She was always looking for information while they were sitting in the car, waiting for something to happen. Even now, she was searching for information on Eleanor on her phone. "Omigod, guess who owns the greeting-card company that Lee is the CEO of."

"Don't tell me. Eleanor."

"Yes!"

"Well, I'll be damned."

Another quarter of an hour passed, and someone else approached Eleanor's table.

"Red, what are you doing here?" Eleanor asked, setting her empty salad dish aside.

"Red?" Amelia whispered. She chanced peeking through the plants. "It's him," she told Gavin. "The guy who wouldn't fly with me. The one who was involved in the jewelry-store heist."

And that had Gavin thinking back to what had happened between him and Eleanor—her insistence he be the PI to take on the mission. No other. Lee had arrived early with her team, so they flew to their destination before the timer went off on the plane. Not even Heaton had accounted for Eleanor's treachery.

The waitress brought Gavin's and Amelia's shrimp scampis and iced tea.

Red took a seat at Eleanor's booth, even though Eleanor hadn't offered one. At least verbally.

"I imagine they're business associates. Not lovers," Gavin said. "Or he works for her."

"I can't imagine with the wealth she has that she would hire a thief for any reason. To hit her jewelry store?"

"She probably makes claims against the insurance company and sells the stolen jewelry. She pays the thieves their cut after they've delivered the goods, or they'd take off with them."

"So he's here for another job?" Amelia asked.

"Maybe. I need to check with a couple of buddies still at the police department to see what Red's been doing for the last few years."

"What are you doing here?" Eleanor asked Red.

"Asher Michaels said he wants in on the new job. He

said something he was working on didn't pan out, so he wants the job."

So neither Red nor Eleanor knew Asher had been arrested for killing Heaton.

"You still think he's reliable?" she asked Red.

"He's got a good track record for making money. The only one of us who got away clean the last time after that bitch crashed the plane. And he turned over his share of the loot to you for a tidy sum. So yeah."

"Some was missing."

"That was Clayton's score. He buried it. No one ever discovered where."

"No criminal record for anything since then?"

"Just minor. I sent you the details. Hell, you didn't tell me Conrad was joining you for lunch."

"He wasn't. Go. Now. Before he sees you."

Red hurried out of the restaurant as Gavin and Amelia stared through the foliage in disbelief.

"So Asher was the other thief, the one who got away. Conrad can't be involved in this whole business, can he?" Amelia asked Gavin.

"I hope not. I was beginning to like the guy."

"Why, Conrad, how did you know I would be here for lunch?" Eleanor asked in a coy way.

"Your secretary said she made a reservation for you here. I had a stopping point in my work and thought I'd join you because Lisa said you weren't meeting anyone."

"Well, how nice. It's not like you to want to join me. What made you decide to do so?"

"The truth is I'm quitting my job."

Gavin and Amelia exchanged glances. That was a shock, and Gavin suspected it would be a shock to Eleanor.

After a moment, Eleanor said, "What? You can't!"

"Don't worry. I won't be living off you. I've taken a much-better-paying job in Manhattan. Better promotional opportunities. I can't work for Lee any longer. You wouldn't believe how she sexually harasses me on the job. I'll give her notice when I return to work. I'll start the new job in two weeks."

"What…what about us?"

"That's up to you. Well, I have to get back to work. I'll be home later than usual tonight. Don't wait up for me." Conrad left.

Eleanor got up and stalked out of the restaurant.

"It feels like one of those celebratory moments to me." Gavin motioned to the server and asked for the dessert menu. "What would you like?"

Amelia smiled. "Carrot cake and a cup of coffee."

"All right." He told the server, "One carrot cake and one slice of cheesecake."

When she left to get their dessert, Amelia asked Gavin, "Why would Red meet Eleanor in such a public place?" To her way of thinking, the woman was playing with fire. Then again, she had seemed above suspicion all along.

"From the sound of it, she was surprised to see him. It appeared that she'd only meant to meet with Cheryl. In any event, Eleanor probably didn't believe anybody would be watching her. Maybe Red doesn't trust her to meet somewhere less…private."

The server returned with their cakes and refilled their drinks, then left.

"They must not know Asher killed Heaton and is currently incarcerated." Amelia sliced into her cake. "Okay, so she hires you, tells you which plane service Conrad used, then you're supposed to learn if her husband is unfaithful. She pays off—or promises to pay off—Cheryl and Conrad's boss to create a scene to make it appear he's having an affair. He won't take the bait. Why would the thief be there, making us fly the sabotaged plane?"

Gavin cut off a piece of his cheesecake. "It all goes back to the heist. It's been seven and a half years. I've been thinking about that. Lee got her people there an hour early, so we took the plane. What if this was all orchestrated by Eleanor? Lee was working for her, Cheryl too, and Red."

"So *you* were the intended victim."

"Or both of us."

"It was over seven years ago, but you and your friends were turned since then. You've been moving, no real office for a while, right?"

"You're right. We didn't open a brick-and-mortar until a few months ago."

"And it could have taken her that long to figure out I had been dating Clayton and that I was a pilot and where I'd ended up. He might not have ever mentioned my name to the other men. We moved back to Alaska right after that, so if they were searching for a female pilot in Seattle, they wouldn't have located me. Somehow, they must have figured it out."

"And Eleanor set up this trip for Lee's company. She had me investigating her husband. Red, another employee of hers, made you fly the other plane. Heaton was hired to tamper with it. And we were supposed to crash. Not the company's people. Heaton thought he was taking your dad down, not you. I'm sure that much is true."

"And *Asher* had paid Heaton to crash the plane when the company's people were onboard to get rid of his wife and Orwell. Which means Heaton had intended to do that too. Take my dad out and the company's people. Eleanor was working behind the scenes, having Red and Lee mess that up. She thought she could get out of a divorce settlement to Conrad because Cheryl and Lee were both going to be there on the camping trip and trying to seduce him. But then she would have needed you, the PI, to document it. You were supposed to be dead."

"Maybe she intended to have everyone there witness his infidelity and have them testify to that. Only it didn't work out the way Eleanor planned," Gavin said.

"That sounds like it. Except now we need to get proof to turn this over to the police."

After they finished their dessert, they headed over to the police department.

Gavin met with his friends, and one of them, Harvey Smith, said, "Yeah, Red, he got out of prison two weeks ago. Don't tell me he's looking to do another job already."

"That's what we're trying to learn."

"He's been in prison since the heist?" Amelia asked.

"Yep. The whole time."

"And the others?" Gavin asked.

"Still in."

After speaking with the officers, Amelia and Gavin returned to the hotel.

"I was thinking about giving some swimming lessons in a nice heated pool," Gavin said.

Before Amelia could agree, Gavin got a call from Conrad. "Hey, don't worry about investigating my wife. I've got a new job in New York, and I'll be leaving in two weeks."

"Separation? Divorce?"

"Separation for sure. Divorce after that. If she doesn't trust me enough to be faithful, that's her problem."

"If she finds fault with you?"

"I'm not doing anything wrong, so she can make up whatever story she wants. After the incident with the plane?"

"We think that might have more to do with me and Amelia than you."

"Oh?" Conrad sounded really surprised to hear that.

"Yeah. Do you know anything about your wife's jewelry store?"

"She has six of them in the Seattle area alone."

"The one I'm thinking about was robbed seven years ago."

"Wait a minute. Gavin Summerfield. You're…the former cop who was taken hostage. Yeah, I remember. What would that have to do with the sabotage of the plane in Minnesota?"

"Your wife just met with one of the bank robbers involved in that heist at Charlie's Seafood and Steakhouse."

"You can't be serious. Wait…you were at the restaurant?"

"Yeah. We overheard you telling Eleanor you had a new job and were leaving. Not only that, but Eleanor met with Cheryl before you arrived."

"Cheryl? For God's sake. Don't tell me Eleanor

read her the riot act, thinking Cheryl is having an affair with me."

"No. Apparently, she and Lee have been trying to seduce you, without success, both at the behest of your wife. They're on her payroll. So is the bank robber," Gavin said.

Conrad didn't say anything for a moment, and then he laughed. "Well, hell, am I glad I found a new job. Tell me what I owe you, and I'll send you a payment. You're off the hook."

"No charge. I think I'll stick around. Did you know she owns the company you work for?"

Conrad was silent for several seconds. "Hell."

"I need to prove she's the mastermind behind the jewelry heist."

"I can help you with that, if I can get her to confess on camera. We have security cameras everywhere. I don't know if it would work, but we could give it a shot. If she doesn't get wise to it, the video would be admissible in court. I'll wear a wire even. The wire wouldn't be admissible in court, but you can hear the truth at the same time. And just in case she tries to shoot me? You can come in and rescue me. Who knows what she's capable of. I never thought she would have done anything like this." Conrad sounded eager to help.

Gavin smiled. "I have some police friends who would be glad to help."

Chapter 19

BEFORE THE BIG SHOW, GAVIN SLIPPED OFF TO THE HOTEL WITH Amelia to have some wolf time with her. The full moon was now waning, but he was still feeling its pull. He sure as hell didn't want to be sitting in a police van with two officers and fighting the urge to shift. Sometimes, he could shift like this, and the need wouldn't occur again until hours later. Not in the beginning after he'd been turned though. Back then? If he had to shift, it was fast, and he could be stuck like that for hours. No anticipating it. No control over it at all. So he was getting much better at this.

He smiled at Amelia as she turned on a show for them, then shifted and joined him to watch the movie as a wolf. She definitely was the one in charge of the TV controller during these times.

Then it was the real showtime.

That night, Conrad went home earlier than planned. The police and Gavin had given him tips on what to say to try to get his wife to confess to the burglary and the sabotage of the plane.

The two policemen, Gavin, and Amelia were listening from a van near the house. They'd wired Conrad and shown him a picture of Red. Since Red had met with Eleanor at the restaurant and Conrad had shown up after that, he was going to use that as his lead-in.

"I thought you were going to stay out real late tonight," Eleanor said, sounding highly aggravated when Conrad entered the home earlier than expected.

"If you're mad I'm home, sorry. I thought I'd have to stay late at the office, but once I told Lee I was leaving in two weeks, she didn't bother to ask me to stay late like she usually does. I should have done this a long time ago. Do we have anything to eat?"

"Who is she?"

"Who is who? Are *you* having an affair? Because I sure as hell am not. When I went to meet you at the restaurant, I saw a redheaded guy sitting with you at your table. Surprised the hell out of me. So who is he?"

"Someone who's done some work for me."

"Ah, okay. I wouldn't think you, of all people, would meet an employee at a restaurant. Then again, I wouldn't think you'd be consorting with criminals either."

"What?"

"Why do you look so surprised that I know what's going on? The guy was involved in the theft at your jewelry store. I remember seeing his mug in the paper. Either he's giving you the missing jewelry back after having found it wherever they stashed it—which I highly doubt—or you've got another job for him."

Frowning, one of the police officers leaned back in his chair in the surveillance van and folded his arms.

Amelia thought that meant this wasn't going the way they thought it should. Conrad was doing all the talking, and Eleanor wasn't incriminating herself.

"What I don't understand is why you intended to murder Gavin Summerfield. The poor guy was nearly killed in the first plane crash that your thieving crew took up, and then you hired Heaton to crash the plane carrying Gavin to investigate me in the Boundary Waters? Oh, don't look so surprised. You don't think he would have switched his focus from investigating *me* to investigating *you*? Hell, he's already spoken with the police about you and Red. If you don't recall, he used to be a cop on the force here, and he's still friends with a lot of them."

The other police officer shook his head. The first groaned.

Gavin was frowning, but he didn't appear overly anxious or annoyed that Conrad was ruining any chance they might have of getting the truth out of Eleanor.

"I didn't have anything to do with any of it."

"All except for one thing. The guy who set up the heist? Clayton Drummer? You learned his girlfriend was Amelia White. He took Amelia hostage to fly the plane. Except while he was in pain and dying in the woods, he told her how much he really loved her and how much he wanted to make it right with her. Which meant he told her who had masterminded the whole setup. *You.*

"So guess who was flying the plane over the Boundary Waters? None other than Amelia. You had learned who she was and where she was located. She wasn't flying the plane that was tampered with. Her father was. And you had to fix that. So one of your burglars, Red, was there to ensure the right people were in the right place, and he refused to fly with Amelia. She switched planes with her dad, and the rest is history."

Gavin rubbed Amelia's back.

"This is all preposterous."

"The police have Red down at the station now. He doesn't want to go back to prison. He's giving you up, dear wife. Oh, and I know all about you paying Lee and Cheryl to try to seduce me. Then you'd have dirt on me and wouldn't have to pay me any money in a divorce settlement. What did I ever do to deserve you?"

"Why, you ungrateful—" Something crashed.

Everyone in the surveillance van was on their feet in an instant.

"Temper, temper. I imagine when you learned the robbers didn't get away with any of your jewels, you were devastated. Just think of how much money you could have had, from the insurance payment on the jewelry that had been stolen and the reselling of it at retail—marked up, of course. Then again, you did get a hefty sum for some of the jewelry that wasn't recovered. It was recovered, wasn't it?"

"You're crazy."

"To have trusted you? Yes. Oh, and Heaton was arrested for tampering with the plane. He's spilling his guts. Asher Michaels has been picked up for questioning concerning the next job you want them to do. I'll tell you what though. I'll give you an airtight alibi if you'll agree to a divorce with a full settlement like you agreed upon in the prenuptials. If I'm not in the wrong and you are, you'll pay me a tidy sum."

Gavin and Amelia smiled at his words. They'd told him what to say because of what they'd overheard Eleanor talking about, and the police had kept a tight lid on the story with regard to Asher and Heaton.

"I haven't done anything wrong. So I don't need an alibi."

"Have it your way. I won't offer again." Conrad started to walk off.

"Ah hell," one of the police officers said.

"We know it's always a gamble," the other said.

"All right, Conrad," Eleanor said.

Everyone was quiet in the van, waiting with expectant breaths.

"Why in the world would you even do something so risky?" Conrad asked. "You can't need the money."

"How do you think I have so much money? Do you think the inheritance I had would last forever? Not all my investments have turned a profit."

"Now he's got her," the one officer said.

"I was making enough," Conrad said, sounding annoyed.

"You can never have enough."

"Didn't you worry about working with these guys? They're hardened criminals. They would just as soon slit your throat if you crossed them than give up the money."

"Don't be so melodramatic. Clayton Drummer came up with the idea. He'd never been in jail, but he knew some great thieves."

"How in the world did you meet him?"

Eleanor didn't say anything.

"Aw hell, you were lovers?"

"Like you would really care! We've barely had sex for years!"

Gavin glanced at Amelia and squeezed her hand. She couldn't believe it! Her boyfriend had been screwing Eleanor and then pretending to want to be a wolf mate with Amelia someday in the future? Amelia knew Clayton had been using her, but she really hadn't expected to learn this. She didn't think he would have turned Eleanor. He must have been just using her too.

"*That's* why you wanted to get rid of Amelia. It

wasn't just because she could implicate you in the crime. You learned he was having intimate relations with her too. And you couldn't deal with it."

Eleanor didn't say anything. Then she finally said, "She took the rest of the jewels!"

"So it was not only vengeance, but you were afraid Amelia would be able to identify you. She never has," Conrad said to his wife.

"I've been trying to locate her and the former cop all this time. They were loose ends. I couldn't rely on them never coming forth with whatever they knew. I had to get them together to take care of them at the same time. I really didn't think you were having an affair, or I would have divorced you. I just had to have a really good excuse for Gavin to take the plane trip to the Boundary Waters. Heaton was just a blessing because he'd gotten fired from his job and was eager to earn some extra cash. I still couldn't believe you wouldn't have an affair when two women were so eager to be with you."

"What time frame do you need to have an alibi for?" Conrad asked.

"I'll give you the times, and we'll have to work something out," Eleanor said.

"Come on, let's give the guy a break." One cop headed for the van door.

"Her lawyers will be all over this," the other said.

"If he's right, we've got her testimony on video, so that should be good enough. Let's make the arrest, get the search warrant, and go from there."

"You must feel as used as I did," Amelia told Gavin as he drew her into his arms.

"All that matters is that it brought us together again. Only this time, we're staying together."

"Even if I'm flying us somewhere."

"Hell, yeah."

Conrad turned over the video to the police, Eleanor was arrested, and the Minnesota police investigated Heaton's new employer, who revealed that the manager of Flying Right Adventure Tours had also paid Heaton to sabotage the plane. Heaton had gotten plenty of money out of the deal: an advance from Eleanor, one from his new boss, and one from Asher Michaels. Too bad he didn't live to spend any of it.

"We miss having you on the force," one officer said to Gavin.

"You were always good at getting your man," the other said, winking at Amelia, "or in this case…woman."

But they had one more job to do. Gavin contacted Orwell and learned where his wife lived. And then Gavin and Amelia set up surveillance to learn what they could about any guys Orwell's wife was seeing. Before long, they were able to document that she was actually dating three men. They shared the information with Orwell so he could use it in his defense when he had to go to court over the divorce. And then Gavin and Amelia were all set to go home and start living as a mated couple, though they were thinking of a small gathering of the pack and her family for a wedding too.

When they returned to Minnesota, Amelia learned that her dad had bought her a new plane. Her brother told her, "So that's how you get a new plane around here."

"Be my guest to go through what I did to get it, Slade."

"Yeah, but you got a mate out of the deal too."

She only smiled. Now *that* was totally worth it.

When they arrived at Gavin's home, Amelia was so ready to move in. What really surprised her was the meeting the pack had set up to discuss leadership with her at Cameron and Faith's lakeside home in the woods. Amelia supposed she should have remembered about it, but she'd been so busy with Gavin and his investigations that she'd forgotten.

Winston was eager to greet them and welcome them home. Amelia gave him a big hug, and so did Gavin.

All the pack members' homes were within walking distance of each other, and Amelia loved how Gavin's place was situated on the water like the other homes. That meant she'd have ample opportunity to learn to swim better.

Before they had breakfast, Cameron started by saying, "We're so glad to have you in our pack, Amelia. We mentioned before that we really haven't had a pack where we had true leaders. Everyone just kind of assumed Faith and I were running things. We've always done everything democratically. With Amelia joining us, I'd like to officially extend an offer to her parents and brother to join us, so we can offer our protection and for all the fun we can have with it. Since Henry and Lolita and their offspring are royals, I wanted to ask one last time if anyone objects to having them run the pack. This would be up to them as well. I don't see things changing much, but with their age and wisdom, and their ability to shift whenever they want, I think it would be a viable option."

"I'm sure my parents would be honored," Amelia said. "Surprised too. If everyone agrees with this, I'll ask them."

Gavin nodded, then reached down and scratched Winston's head. "I agree. As long as we still have a democratic voice in matters, we can all help each other out."

Owen said, "That works for me."

"And me," Candice said.

"I'm all for it," David said. "Though it would have been better if I'd gotten the girl." He winked at Amelia.

She laughed.

Faith got them refills on their coffee. "We're all behind this, if your parents and brother agree."

After breakfast, Amelia called her parents, still surprised the wolf pack would trust them to run the pack. It was such an honor, but her mother and father might believe it was too much work. "Mom, I need to ask you and Dad a question. Is he there?"

"Yes, dear. I'll put this on speaker."

"Gavin's pack wants you to join us. Not just join as pack members. The group unanimously voted to have you and Dad run the pack as the pack leaders, if you agree."

Her mother snuffled, and her father cleared his suddenly gravelly throat.

Amelia blinked back tears. She knew they were overwhelmed by the offer, yet she knew they would make great pack leaders.

"They run it democratically, just like you have with us since we've become adults. They don't expect a lot of changes, but since you're older and wiser, and you're royals, they thought it would work out great."

"We would be honored," her father said, his voice just as emotional.

Her mom was sniffling in the background. "We would," her mother said, her voice tearful.

Tears spilled down Amelia's cheeks, and she quickly brushed them away, but everyone was watching to see what her parents had to say. She hadn't put it on speaker, so she could give them some privacy in coming to a decision. She smiled at the group to let the pack know it was good news.

They all clapped and cheered, telling her parents in no uncertain terms this was a good thing, a new beginning for them, and a cause for celebration.

Winston jumped up and woofed, and Amelia laughed and hugged him. She put the phone on speaker and told her parents, "You can tell the pack the news yourself."

And then they set a date for the celebration and ended the call with her parents. Then everyone wanted to learn about the case Gavin and Amelia had just finished, and they explained everything that had happened.

"What about the bag of jewels that was never found in the woods?" Cameron asked.

"Someday, I was thinking we might take a trip there and check it out," Amelia said. "Of course, we'll have to turn it in. On the other hand, what if the police thought I had hidden it there and came back for it?"

"If that was the case, you wouldn't be turning it in," Gavin said to Amelia. "I think that would be the best thing to do and finally find closure in the case. In the meantime, are you ready to take a swim in the lake?"

The water was warm, the sun shining, the day was beautiful, and he wanted to spend the rest of it and the night with Amelia, soaking up every bit of her until they had to return to work.

"Yeah, let's go. Thanks to everyone," Amelia said.

They all said their goodbyes, reaffirming how thrilled they were to have more Arctic wolves in the pack.

As Amelia and Gavin walked back to his house, his arm draped over her shoulder, Winston running beside them, she said, "I told you it was a conspiracy. Eleanor, Asher, and the manager of the competitor airplane service were all in on it, albeit with their own agendas."

"And one dead wolf was at the root of it."

"Yeah, between Heaton and Clayton, I sure knew how to pick 'em. What are we going to tell our kids someday about how *we* met? My parents met on the ice floe, and Dad saved her. It was so romantic."

"You saved me during a jewelry heist. Here I thought my fellow police officers would come to my rescue. A beautiful she-wolf did instead. One that I love and adore."

"And to think you were only a human back then, and now see where we are? I love you, you sexy old wolf, you. Race you home and into the water!"

"I'll do one better." And with that, Gavin swept her into his arms and jogged home with her and Winston.

"You are such a show-off."

"I didn't want you to beat me."

She laughed, loving him—the cop, the PI, and the wolf that he was. She was glad she could be there for him, sharing every blessed moment as wolf or woman, whatever he needed.

Gavin couldn't have been more ecstatic to find the right wolf for him. She was everything he could have asked for in a mate and more. He had worried she might change her mind when the full moon was out and he wouldn't know when the need to shift would occur, or when the new moon was here and he couldn't shift. She had assured him she would love him no matter what and had proved it to him while they spent time in the hotel, watching movies together as wolves. For the first time, he'd faced the uncertainty during the changing moon, knowing he'd have his wolf mate by his side. He couldn't love her more.

The Arctic pack was officially a wolf pack, still called the MacPherson Pack in honor of Cameron, who had been the first of them turned against his will. The pack was now led by royal Arctic wolf leaders and had increased in number by four more pack members, with more sure to be on their way whenever little ones began to come onto the scene.

Slade swore he'd have to return to Alaska to find a mate, and David said if they had more Arctic she-wolves up there, he was tagging along for the ride.

For now, Gavin was happy to have Amelia as his mate after she'd kept dropping into his life. He knew it was karma. Just like she knew that it was with him and couldn't be happier with her wolf mate. And Winston? He was in dog heaven with all kinds of wolves and wolf pups and humans to play with.

"Ready to go for a ride?" Amelia asked Gavin. Only she wasn't flying this time. Her brother was. She and Gavin were returning to their special alcove to make new memories, just like they'd said they would when this was all said and done.

"Yeah, and lots of swimming."

"And fishing."

"And stargazing."

"And loving."

"And loving." For a lifetime—and for a wolf shifter, that was a very long time.

*Read on for a sneak peek at book 8
in Terry Spear's Silver Town Wolf series*

ALL'S FAIR
IN LOVE AND
WOLF

Coming soon from Sourcebooks Casablanca

"WE'LL CAPTURE THE FUGITIVE, MOM. I'LL FIND HIM."
Jenna St. James was eager to locate Sarandon Silver,
promptly arrest him, and turn him over to the police
before her mom had to forfeit the bond she'd put up
to ensure he'd appear in court. He'd been charged with
numerous counts of identity theft, mail fraud, and pos-
sessing stolen property in Colorado Springs, Colorado,
and the judge had let him out of jail on bond. Afterward,
the suspect cut off his ankle GPS monitor and ran. It was
time for him to return to jail and stay there until his trial
date. Jenna just hoped she—or the police—could catch
him before her mother had to pay the bond in full.

She considered Sarandon's driver's license photo
again and thought it was a shame he was a crook—or at
least a suspected crook. He was a handsome guy, his hair
dark brown and wavy, his dark-brown eyes smiling, his

manly lips curved up just a hint, and his jaw sturdy and square. She imagined that his good looks and smooth moves could manipulate just about anyone. Good thing he wasn't a wolf like her and her family, because she was going to enjoy bringing him down.

"I don't want you to take any risks with this guy," her mom said. Victoria St. James had taken over as bail bondswoman from her dad when he'd died, and she'd run the business successfully for decades.

Jenna's triplet sisters, Crystal and Suzanne, and their father, Logan, were all in other parts of the state on fugitive recovery jobs so Jenna had to do this on her own.

"I'll be careful, Mom. No problem." She continued to pack a couple of bags. "Piece of cake. He's never committed any crimes before this… Well, at least that we know of. His current charges aren't for violent crimes, just sneaky and despicable ones. I'll wear a bulletproof vest, just in case. I'll take my 9 mm semi-automatic pistol, rifle, Taser, boot knife, and pepper spray. I'll be ready." She figured Sarandon couldn't be all that dangerous, or her father would have insisted on handling the case.

Her family had one of the most successful fugitive recovery agencies in the state of Colorado—which made sense since they each had a nose for tracking suspects. One with a gray wolf's keen sense of smell.

"Yeah, that's what your dad said when he attempted to bring that one man in. Logan was armed to the teeth, just in case. The bail jumper wasn't the problem."

"His brother was. I remember." Jenna had been ten at the time. Her dad had come home with the bullet stuck to his bulletproof vest. "I'll be fine. How many years have I been doing this now?" Jenna knew she didn't have to remind her mother, but they seemed to be having this discussion a lot lately.

"Nearly fifty. Your dad had been doing it for seventy years when he got shot. Thankfully, the bulletproof vest saved his life, but even then, the bullet broke a rib and bruised him badly. At least the bullet didn't tear through the vest and hit any vital arteries."

Bleeding out could be a problem for any of them. But being a wolf helped her father to heal faster than a human so he was able to return to work fairly quickly.

"That's why I'm wearing a vest. Just in case. I'll be fine, Mom. Really. If I get into trouble, I'll call on the local law-enforcement agency." Jenna already knew there was a sheriff's office in Silver Town. She gave her mom a hug. "You've posted a reward for information concerning his whereabouts, right?"

"Yes. First thing, always. We certainly would rather pay someone a reward for turning these guys in than have to pay the full bond."

"Okay, good." The fastest turnaround they'd ever had on one of their bail jumpers was an hour, when a mother called them about her son, picked up the reward money, and got him out of her house so she wouldn't be in trouble for harboring and abetting him. Best case ever.

Jenna wished that was the situation with this guy, but he'd already been gone for four hours. No one had turned him in, and he hadn't turned himself in. "I need to finish packing, Mom. I'll let you know when I'm on my way." Jenna already had a good lead, but she wondered if the guy had picked the name Silver as an alias based on the name of the place where she thought he was living. Silver Town. At least, that was the address on his driver's license.

No matter what, she didn't want her family to get stuck paying the $150,000 bond. A brother named Eric Silver had given them the title for undeveloped land as collateral for the bond. Once Sarandon Silver fled, further investigation revealed that the deed had been falsified, and there was no such property in Eric Silver's name. Sarandon was going down as soon as Jenna could catch up to him.

Eric Silver slapped Sarandon on the back as they met for lunch at the Silver Town Tavern before Sarandon took off for a vacation at the family cabin in the mountains. "Hey, Brother. I tell you, if you want to spice up your life a bit, you need to find a she-wolf to hook up with. Pepper has definitely made a world of difference in my life."

Sarandon was thinking more along the lines of finding a new and exciting adventure to take tour groups on. He was already booked for butterfly photo groups, bird photo ops, mountain climbing, wildflower hikes, white-water rafting, and hikes into the backcountry. He was always trying to think up the next fun adventure. Which was one of the reasons he was headed to their mountain cabin retreat between tours. He often had returning customers who'd enjoyed his excursions but were looking for any new activities he might be offering.

"If you find a hot, sexy she-wolf who loves the outdoors and wants to visit me at the cabin, send her along."

Of course, Sarandon was kidding. Not that there weren't a few she-wolves like that, but any who lived nearby were seeing other wolves or too busy with their own lives. And he'd never met one he'd really connected with.

Eric laughed. He was the eldest of the quadruplet brothers, Sarandon the next oldest, and the two of them had always been the best of friends. They were close to their younger brothers too, but Brett and CJ, the youngest, always hung together. Their cousin, Darien, and his mate, Lelandi, were the pack leaders. Darien and his brother Jake had been pals with the older boys, while Tom, the youngest of that set of triplets, had been Brett's and CJ's friend.

All in all, they were the Silver Town wolves, their ancestors having established the town in the beginning, and they continued to run the town as a pack.

Sam, the owner and bartender of the tavern, brought them roast beef sandwiches. "What I wouldn't give to go up into the mountains for a couple of weeks with Silva for a vacation. Now that she runs her tea shop in the afternoons, and we run this place in the evenings together, we just don't have the time to get away."

"You know, you'd have a ton of volunteers willing to take over for you at both places. And they'd do a good job. Just ask Darien," Sarandon said. That was one nice thing about having a pack-run town: they always had plenty of pack members who were willing to help out if they needed it.

"I guess I will. Do you need anything else?"

"No. Thanks, Sam. The sandwiches look as good as always," Eric said.

Sam nodded and headed off to another table, carrying a tray of drinks.

The door opened, and they saw the trio of men from the ghost-hunter show walk in with their cameraman. "Don't tell me they think the tavern is haunted," Sarandon said, still unable to keep from feeling animosity toward the brothers for wanting to take the hotel away from the three MacTire sisters who had purchased it.

"Sam will throw them out on their ears if they pull that in here. Who knows what story they're chasing this time."

The three ghost-hunter brothers waved at Sarandon and Eric, who inclined their heads in greeting.

"All right," Stanton Wernicke, the eldest and the darkest-haired of the three brothers, said to his blond-haired cameraman. "Listen, it's all right to take an emergency trip somewhere, but hell, let us know." They took seats near where Eric and Sarandon were sitting at the pack leader's table. The Silver cousins or Darien's brothers often used it when Darien and Lelandi weren't there.

"Sorry, man. I left a message on your voicemail," the man said.

Stanton narrowed his blue eyes at him. "That's not good enough, Burt. You need to clear it with us first, if there's a next time. We had a production schedule to meet, and we had to find another cameraman to fill in. You're the best at your job and you're a wolf, which is what we need, so just ask us next time, okay? If it's an emergency, we'll work around it. We've got a gig at that new lodge up on the slopes tonight, so no slacking off."

Sarandon wondered how Stanton and his brothers had found ghosts at the new lodge. No one had ever spied ghosts on the ski slopes or at the ski hut. And the lodge was brand new.

The men ordered hamburgers from Sam.

Eric cleared his throat to get Sarandon's attention. "You told Darien where you're going for the next couple of weeks, right?" Eric and his mate led their own pack located four hours from Silver Town. But serving as a park ranger in the state park nearby, Eric stopped in regularly to check on how things were going back home, as if he couldn't give up his old pack. Or felt the need to monitor what his brothers were doing.

"I told Darien. When would I not tell him?" Sarandon asked. He knew it was important to keep the pack abreast of where he would be.

Not that Darien or Lelandi micromanaged the pack. They just didn't want to send out search parties if they didn't have to. They had set up the protocol that anyone leaving the area for longer than a day would let Darien or Lelandi know. Even though Eric wasn't Sarandon's pack leader, he was still his older brother and him looking out for Sarandon seemed to be something that would never change between them. That was okay too.

Sarandon sighed, thinking of the invitation Eric had given him. "Okay, sure, I'll come to the Spring Fling that your pack is having. No setting me up with a date. I'll come as I am." All the brothers and their cousins were mated now, and that meant everyone was trying to find Sarandon a mate, as if he couldn't be as happy as they were without having one of his own.

Eric smiled. "Good. Pepper will be thrilled. I've got to run to see Brett to make sure he puts the notice in the paper properly."

That meant outsiders—those who weren't members of either the Silver Town pack or Eric's Grayling pack—wouldn't have a clue where or when the Spring Fling was. Everyone else would know by the cryptic message in the paper. Sure, they could just email or text everyone, but they had fun sharing interesting tidbits without letting the humans in on the secret.

"Have fun," Eric said.

"I will. See you soon."

Sarandon returned home to finish his last-minute packing. His phone rang as he loaded the last bag into the Suburban. When he saw the call was from Lelandi, he figured she had pack-leader business to discuss with him. "Yeah, Lelandi, what do you need?"

"Jake's out on a wildflower shoot for a new art exhibit. He didn't realize you were going to the Elk Horn cabin this soon. The Bear Creek, Wolf River, Eagle's Nest, and Beaver Bay cabins are all booked. I just wanted to mention he might drop in on you for a day or two so you won't be too surprised," Lelandi said. "I couldn't get ahold of him to tell him about your plans. My mistake."

"No problem. I'd love the company. We can take a wolf run. Maybe he can help me brainstorm some ideas. We'll have fun. No worries."

"Okay, I just wanted to let you know in case he suddenly arrives."

"Thanks, Lelandi."

Looking forward to seeing Jake there, Sarandon climbed into the Suburban and took off. This might be even more fun than he had planned.

Sarandon headed into the wilderness, and after a couple of hours, he finally reached the Elk Horn cabin. He parked, got out, and stretched. Taking a deep breath of the pines and Douglas firs, he embraced the peace and

quiet, the sound of a river flowing nearby, birds twitter-
ing in the trees, and the breeze fluttering the leaves.

Once he'd hauled all his supplies inside, he started a
fire in the fireplace and planned to go for a run, something he couldn't do while acting as a tour guide. Not
unless he was taking a wolf group out.

Within minutes, he'd stripped off his clothes and
shifted, then pushed through the wolf door. He dashed
through the woods, exploring and scent-marking, letting
any animal in the area know a wolf was on the prowl and
this was his claimed territory.

The sound of a car's tires crunching on the private
gravel road, heading toward the cabin, caught his attention. He stopped and listened from the shelter of the trees
and brush. There was nothing out here but wilderness.
And the cabins and the land were private property. He
could tell by the engine's purr that the car wasn't Jake's
or anyone else's he knew in the pack. The car parked,
and the engine shut off in the distance.

If the driver were a hunter, Sarandon didn't want
to be caught in his wolf coat and end up getting shot.
Cursing mentally to himself, he waffled about what to
do. Hidden in the undergrowth in the woods, he could
check out the person leaving the car, or he could run
back to the cabin, shift, dress, arm himself with his rifle,
and then see who it was and what he or she was up to.

Sarandon opted for returning to the cabin first and
ditching his wolf coat. That way, he could tell the tres-
passer to leave.

When he reached the cabin, he dove through the wolf
door, shifted, and rushed to dress. He removed his rifle
from the locked gun cabinet and left the cabin, locking it

behind him. Listening for any sign of where the person was, Sarandon headed down the road to where he'd heard the car park.

A quarter of a mile from the cabin, he stopped dead in his tracks. A woman was standing off the road, partially hidden in the woods, holding a rifle aimed at him. The way she was holding it, she looked like she knew how to use it. And he'd thought running as a wolf could cause him trouble!

"Hey, I'm just camping up here at one of my family's cabins. I don't have any intention of hurting you," Sarandon said, trying to put the woman at ease, even if she was in the wrong. "This is private property."

"Carefully, put the rifle down!" she commanded in an authoritative, no-nonsense way.

Well, *this* was bizarre. She was trespassing and pointing a rifle at him, and yet she was telling him to disarm himself when he belonged here? He considered her attire: black cargo pants, a black windbreaker, and boots. She didn't look like a half-crazed criminal or a hunter either. He wasn't afraid of her; he'd be much warier of a man holding a rifle on him than a woman. He just figured he'd spooked her.

"All right. All right. You don't have to be afraid of me." Being the nice wolf he was, Sarandon set his rifle on the ground, figuring the woman was going hiking, albeit on private property, and didn't know privately owned cabins were located here, though signs were posted in the area. But the fact that she was carrying a rifle made him suspect something else might be going on. "I run photo-op tours, hiking, mountain climbing, and white-water rafting guided tours, one-on-one tours, and group tours." He thought if he told her what he did, she would realize he was employed, not some mountain man living out here in the wilderness alone, and that his occupation meant he was one of the good guys who liked working with people. "Whatever customers might be interested in," he continued.

She was someone he was interested in. If she was a wolf and would put the weapon down. Something about her straightforward and confrontational attitude appealed. He swore it was the wolf in him.

"Sarandon Silver?" she asked, her brow arched.

Learning that she knew his name surprised him. If she knew who he was, why was she pointing the rifle at him? Then he wondered if this had something to do with his brothers. Maybe they'd sent her as a plant, a way to get him to meet a new she-wolf, believing the standard boy-meets-girl routine wouldn't cut it with him. Especially since he'd said he was trying to come up with an idea for a new adventure.

"Yeah, I'm Sarandon Silver. Do you want to tell me how you know me and why you're still pointing a weapon at me?" She had to be his brothers' idea, but he wondered where she was taking this.

If this was for real, he didn't recall anything he'd done that would have aggravated anyone to the extent that she'd pull a weapon on him. He hadn't taken a mate and pissed off her family. He hadn't lost anyone on one of his excursions. His dad was the only one who'd ever committed any crimes in the family, and he'd paid for his sins with his life.

"Come this way, nice and slow," she said, her voice firm and resolved.

He frowned at her. She sounded like a cop. He looked her over again, but her clothes didn't indicate that. He couldn't see what was underneath the jacket, though from the slight bulk underneath the material, it looked like she might have a sidearm holstered there. She hadn't said she was a cop though. Plus, if she were, she wasn't in her own jurisdiction. Her car was a silver Ford Expedition, with no indication it was a cop's vehicle.

She was a beautiful brunette, her hair cut short and bouncy, her eyes a crystal-clear blue. If his brothers — and maybe his cousins — had put her up to this... Well, he didn't want to appear as though he couldn't take a joke. She'd share with them how growly he'd been, and they'd all have a good laugh over it — at his expense.

"Am I under arrest?" he asked with good humor, smiling a little. He couldn't help it. He couldn't take this seriously.

She narrowed her eyes, looking warier than before, as if his acting like her actions were funny made her think he believed he had the upper hand. "Yes, you're under arrest, and I'm taking you in. I'm a fugitive recovery agent. Jenna St. James."

"Fugitive?" Bounty hunter? No way.

She smiled, albeit sarcastically. "Recovery. Agent. Wow, you're really good at this."

"At this?" He began to walk toward her as she'd ordered him to. If she wasn't a wolf, that would mean his brothers hadn't put her up to this. And she was for real. He had to smell her scent, and the breeze wasn't cooperating.

"Yeah — suave, polished, great at manipulation. If I hadn't been doing this for a number of years, I might even think you weren't the right guy, and you were innocent of any wrongdoing."

"I am. *Innocent* of any wrongdoing." Since she was still holding the rifle on him, he figured he should at least ask for her credentials. "Have you got some ID?"

"Hold it right there. Lie down on the ground and put your hands behind your head. I'll show you my ID once your hands are secured."

"You're serious." He still didn't believe this was anything other than a joke. "You have to play by the rules. You show me a badge, and I'll do whatever you ask of me." He was certain she wouldn't because she didn't have a badge.

"Down. On. Your. Belly. *Now*."

Every bit of his wolf nature rebelled at the idea that he'd get on his stomach for her or anyone else he didn't know. Even if it was a joke. "Or what? Are you going to shoot me? You can't. I'm unarmed, and I haven't done anything threatening. So then *you* would be guilty of a crime." Though he hoped it wouldn't go that far. "By the way, what am I supposed to have done?"

"All right, I'll play your game."

His game?

"You weren't supposed to leave the city. You removed your GPS ankle monitor. And you ran. As if you didn't know, you're wanted for identity theft and financial fraud." She gave him a wide berth as she tried to move behind him. "Keep your eyes straight ahead."

"I wasn't supposed to leave Silver Town?" He knew if she said yes, it was just a gag.

"*Don't* play dumb. You left Colorado Springs."

"Colorado Springs? I haven't been there in ages."

He turned to watch her. "No ID, no can do. I know my rights. You could be a dangerous criminal, looking to steal from me."

As soon as the breeze caught her scent and carried it to him, he could smell her floral fragrance. And more. She was a wolf. He'd begun to worry that maybe this was a case of mistaken identity, and she *was* the real deal.

"I can tase you first, and then you'll be compliant," she warned, reaching for something around her neck, the object hidden by her T-shirt. When she pulled it out, he saw it was a Taser.

Okay, now she had him worried. For a second, he imagined her taking him down, but how would she be able to load him in her car? Still, he wouldn't be able to fight back, and she could confine his wrists in the meantime.

He lunged forward and tackled her, taking her to the ground before she had time to react. If this was the game, he was ready to play. If she was for real, he couldn't let her tase him and confine him. The fall knocked the breath out of her, but at least she hadn't hit anything except for leafy bushes that cushioned her fall.

Eyes wide, she took a deep breath, smelling his scent like any good wolf would, and struggled to get out from underneath him. "You're a wolf!" She sounded shocked.

What the hell was going on? If his brothers and cousins had put her up to it, she would have known just what he was. She wouldn't play dumb.

"My brothers didn't send you?" He breathed in her she-wolf fragrance, floral and woman, wolf and the woods. *She* could really spice up his life, if she wasn't trying to arrest him. "You really *are* here to take me into custody?" He couldn't believe it.

"Yes." Still lying beneath him, she read him his rights from memory as if she were in charge.

Smiling a little, he got a kick out of her gutsy actions. No woman, wolf or otherwise, had ever attempted to take him down like this. Feeling her heat and soft curves pressed against him, he felt his wolfish male interest in her waken.

She felt it too. Her eyes rounded and she tried to dump him off her, but he calculated the thrust with her pelvis and balanced himself to take the full brunt of her action so she didn't win the round. All her wriggling around underneath him turned him on even more, when he was fighting damn hard to keep that part of his wolf-ishness at bay. Hell, even his pheromones had leaped to the forefront, telling her in no uncertain terms just how intrigued he was with her. She couldn't deny that her own pheromones were reacting to his in the same fascinated way.

"Okay, so whoever the guy is you're supposed to arrest, do you know if he's a wolf?" The way she had reacted to learning Sarandon was one made him think she was clueless about that part. And that meant she had the wrong guy. Well, of course she had the wrong guy. He wasn't the one she was looking for, no matter what she thought. He needed to get this cleared up.

"I haven't met him—*you*—before."

"Well, that's for damn sure…about me. You would have known I'm not the one you're looking for, if you'd met the guy you're really after. You would know the difference in our scents, for one thing."

"You look just like your picture, and you have the same name."

"Which should tell you something right there. If I were on the lam, why would I be using the same name?"

"It's your MO? You're arrogant enough to believe you won't get caught?"

She was cute in an exasperating way. "I'm afraid you've got the wrong man." Damn glad too.

They heard something moving in the woods, and Sarandon turned his head to get a look at what it was, worried she might have backup and he'd *really* be in trouble. She took advantage of his distraction. Lifting her hip and grasping his shoulders with her hands, she flipped him onto his back, surprising him with her agility and strength.

She was seated on top of him, her hands holding his wrists against the ground, her jacket parted, her breasts close to his face in the formfitting black T-shirt. Her heart was racing, and he liked the way she was sitting on him, like she hoped to do more than just take him into custody. Which was why he didn't flip her onto her back to take charge of the situation.

That's when Sarandon saw Jake headed in their direction, camera bag slung over his shoulder, and Jake laughed. Hell, his cousin was supposed to come to his aid, not find humor in the situation. Though Sarandon had to admit if the roles had been reversed, he would have reacted in the same way.

Looking determined, Jenna pulled his arms forward to tie them. She wouldn't be successful, not without his cooperation, and he wasn't giving it. He flipped her onto her back again, straddling her.

"I didn't know you'd be up here," Jake said to Sarandon, smiling, folding his arms, watching.

"Lelandi told me you might come by," Sarandon said to his cousin. "Great timing."

Jake shook his head and joined them, looking down at the two of them. "I thought I might be interrupting something. I certainly never expected to see a she-wolf we don't know out here with you. I'm Jake Silver. Sarandon's my cousin. And you are?"

"I'm Jenna St. James, a *fugitive* recovery agent. And if you know what's good for you, you'll help me talk some sense into Sarandon. He has to come back with me to face criminal charges. We have offered a reward for his apprehension. Everyone will be looking for him so they can turn him in for the reward money. If you don't want to face tons of police and reporters and have to explain your own complicity in helping him to avoid being returned for trial, you'll do what's right."

"Well, Jenna, if you're not Sarandon's brothers' idea of a joke, you have to know that as a wolf, he can't be taken to jail." Jake folded his arms across his chest and smirked down at them. "He's right though. You've got the wrong man. The whole pack will vouch for him."

She scowled at Jake. "I knew there'd be a problem once I learned he's a wolf. A pack? Sure. Protect a pack member who's nothing more than a common thief."

"Listen, we'll take you to meet Darien and Lelandi Silver, the pack leaders. Darien's my brother and Sarandon's cousin. We'll help you in any way we can to straighten out this mistake," Jake said. "He's not who you're looking for, and if someone from our pack has committed a crime, he *will* do the time."

As if Jake had any authority over Sarandon, Jenna said, "Tell him to get off me."

Jake raised a brow at Sarandon, asking in his silent way if his cousin would agree.

Sarandon didn't trust her one bit. They'd have to disarm the lady and put the plastic ties on her, or he wasn't letting her up.

"She's armed and dangerous," Sarandon said, smiling. And she was one hot, little firecracker of a she-wolf who had made the trip to Elk Horn cabin all the more worthwhile. As long as they cleared up this business of him being a fugitive.

Chapter 2

"I NEED TO CALL MY BOSS," JENNA SAID AS THE TWO WOLVES walked her toward a cabin, the smoke curling up from its chimney. She and her sisters never referred to the bail bondswoman as their mother. They thought it might not sound professional. Jenna couldn't believe the men had taken her hostage, or the bind she was in.

Once she realized Sarandon was a wolf, she should have known others in his pack could be lurking about. Were they all involved in the identity theft and financial crimes?

Even if they weren't, she knew they wouldn't offer him up to pay his debt to society. Not only because he was a wolf and going to jail could be problematic. Pack members often defended one another against outsiders. They took care of their own, including handling rogue wolves who were bad news for the pack and for humans.

The problem was that her mother would have to pay the $150,000 bond if Sarandon didn't show up for court. He could be looking at a fifteen- to thirty-year sentence if found guilty. Jenna wasn't going to allow the wolf to get away with this. At the very least, he'd have to pay the bond. Even if he did pay it, he'd still be a wanted man. Unless he could prove his innocence.

Wriggling her hands proved how futile it was get rid of the ties on her own. She let out her breath in exasperation. She couldn't believe she was disarmed and tied up with her own plastic ties. *That* was humiliating.

How was she going to get herself out of this predicament? She had to convince them she was right and they needed to go along with her plan. Once she located a fugitive, she could often use psychology to control the suspect. Not all suspects could be influenced that way, but many could. She hoped it would work here. But given what had already happened, she suspected it wasn't going to be that easy. Not only did she have the problem with the two wolves, but she also had to deal with a whole wolf pack who would unite behind Sarandon.

Jake had taken her rifle, 9 mm pistol, and Taser, but they didn't have her pepper spray or boot knife. They'd confiscated her driver's license, badge, car keys, and phone too.

The fact that Sarandon was a wolf raised new questions. She needed to call her mom and ask more about him. Had her mom sent one of Jenna's sisters to get the bail bond paperwork from him at the jail when he had been arrested and confined for a few hours? If so, then whoever went to see him would know what he smelled like, and Jenna would be assured he was the right man when she brought him in. But if her mom had received the information in an email or fax, none of them would know him by scent.

Mainly, she needed to know if the man who had been arrested was a wolf. Then again, if her mother had known he was, she would have told Jenna. If Jenna had known that, she would have been even warier when trying to arrest him.

Since her mother didn't tell her the man was a wolf, that meant either he wasn't a wolf and Jenna had the wrong guy, or this guy was the right one, and no one had met him in person.

The suspect was a mastermind at identity theft. What if he wasn't Sarandon but had used Sarandon's ID to claim his identity? She couldn't have gone after the wrong man, could she?

"Is this really necessary?" she asked, raising her hands to indicate the plastic ties.

"Once we're at the cabin, we'll release you," Sarandon said. "And you can share everything you know with us."

"That you don't already know?"

"Absolutely. Because this is all news to me. In the business you're in, haven't you ever been tied up before?"

She smiled a little. Of course she had. So she could learn how to get herself out of a bind if this was done to her. Not that she'd ever had to. Until now.

"During your training? To know how it would feel to be the hostage? I mean, the captive suspect?" He smiled. Sarandon had the most devilishly disarming smile.

"No."

"Not even to learn how to get out of the tie if a suspect turned the tables on you? Am I right?" Sarandon lifted his brows. When she didn't answer him, he laughed. "Don't play poker."

She needed to school her expressions more. Or maybe he could read her so well because he was a wolf.

Jenna couldn't believe Sarandon had taken her down. Suspects had punched, kicked, and knocked her out, but not once had the wanted suspect taken her to the ground and held her there, acting…well, interested in her.

To top that off, he'd become aroused, as if he had nothing to worry about as far as being arrested. And instead was just totally intrigued with her, which she attributed to them both being wolves. Even her attempt at overpowering him had seemed to be a turn-on. As far as her attraction to him, she couldn't help that he was as attractive as sin. No suspect should be that good-looking. Then their pheromones were singing to each other, which had to do with a wolf's biological need. She couldn't believe it. As if her wolf was telling her that no matter who this was or what he had done, that wolf part of her was eager to mate with him. Physical attributes came in at a ten. Willingness to have offspring with him? Check. That was her wolf's nature telling her what to do. Her human nature was in total conflict. Arrest him and turn him over to the police for their disposition. End of story.

Never had a perp taken *her* hostage either! If she made it through this okay, her sisters would *never* let her live it down. Not that she had any intention of letting the family know how he'd gotten the best of her, once she had him under control.

As they got closer, she could see that the log cabin sat near the river, with a dusty black Suburban parked beside it. She worried where Sarandon and his cousin intended to go with this, particularly when they had to know she wasn't leaving peaceably without taking Sarandon with her.

"I need to make a call," she said, her voice rising a bit in annoyance as she scowled up at Sarandon.

"To the bail bondsman you work for?" Sarandon's hand grasped her arm firmly, and he wasn't easing up.

At least her wrists were tied in front, which could afford her a better opportunity to free herself, if she had the chance. All she'd need to do was reach her boot knife, make short work of the ties, and run. Then she'd have to get back to town, contact the sheriff's office, and have them help her take Sarandon into custody.

He was carrying his rifle over his shoulder. Jake walked beside them, a pack on his back, her rifle and Taser in his hand, her ID and cell phone in one of the backpack's pockets.

Irritated to the max, Jenna was trying to figure out a way to get all her stuff back. She had no intention of seeing the pack leaders. Trying to take on two male wolves at the same time and forcing Sarandon to return with her might be more than she could handle on her own though.

Yet, she was making the attempt the first chance she got. She'd never let her family down before, and she wasn't about to now.

———

Jenna St. James truly was armed and dangerous. Not to mention that she was wearing a bulletproof vest beneath the black windbreaker, and a black fugitive recovery agent T-shirt underneath that. She must have thought Sarandon was really dangerous. She even had a badge, which surprised the hell out of him. They checked her driver's license and compared it with her badge and her appearance, verifying she was who she said she was.

She still had the wrong man.

She was petite, compared to Sarandon's height and his muscular build. He guessed the only way she would have been able to get the upper hand would have been to tase him. He was glad he'd taken her down before that.

He knew she didn't like the idea of meeting with Darien and Lelandi, but she didn't have a choice. He suspected that if she could, she'd try to get free, take him into custody, and drive him to Colorado Springs. The bond money was too important for her to risk losing him. He didn't blame her for what she thought she had to do.

"Do you have a sat phone?" she asked.

Sarandon glanced at her. She was scowling again. "In the line of work you're in, you ought to have one. The guy you're after could turn out to be really bad news—"

"Like you?" She arched a brow.

Sarandon smiled at her. "Like any of the real criminals you are after. *Not* like me."

"I don't have a satellite phone. Just a cell phone."

"There's no cell reception this far into the wilderness," Sarandon told her.

"Naturally."

"Well, I'm not the man you're looking for," he said. "Which means he's apparently still out there using my identity. Unless he's afraid of getting caught, in which case, he'll be using someone else's identity." That made Sarandon want to turn into his wolf and take the guy down permanently. Stealing someone's identify could cause problems with work, family, and friends—and for a wolf, real trouble if they were jailed. What if this guy impersonated a wolf who didn't have a whole pack to back him up? And who was more newly turned and couldn't control his shifting?

Sarandon wondered how the real suspect had managed to steal his identity. Was it someone he knew?

He unlocked and opened the door to the cabin for Jenna. She walked inside and glanced around at the living room furnishings, taking a deep breath to smell all the wolf scents left there. A large, velour-covered sofa bed sat in front of a warm fire, comfortable recliners on either side of it. A love seat was in one corner, and big pillows stacked on the floor offered ample seating for several people. Beyond the living room was a kitchen, and a table with eight chairs sat in the dining room between the two other rooms. "The cabins have four bedrooms and we can accommodate six to ten pack members, if we have guests. Like you."

"Where are the antlers or the poor dead elk head? It's Elk Horn cabin, right? At least that's what the plaque said on the door."

"We prefer steaks on the grill. No dead animals hanging on the walls. No wolves feasting on elk carcasses. Just photos Jake took of the elk in the forests or in the meadows full of flowers."

"They're beautiful, Jake," Jenna said, sounding like she really did admire them.

"Thanks. I'm a photographer. Mostly a wildlife photographer, but lately, I've been doing a lot of family portraits." Jake laid her weapons on the dining room table. Then he pulled out her ID, badge, phone, and car keys and put them next to the rifle. He slung his backpack with his camera equipment over the back of a chair.

"Well, they're wonderful."

Sarandon sat her down on the couch, then removed the plastic ties around her wrists and rubbed them gently, knowing the reddened skin would be perfectly fine in a few minutes because of their fast-healing wolf genetics. She frowned up at him. "You could make this easy on yourself."

"On you, rather? Why would you have an innocent man turn himself in, pretending to be a criminal? It's not happening. When the police learned the truth, you'd be embarrassed that you'd caught the wrong man, and a wolf at that. In the meantime, you would've let the guilty man go."

"I doubt that the police would deny I had the right man."

"That issue aside, how did you ever think you could take me down and haul me off?" He still couldn't believe her gumption.

"The Taser would have done the job."

He folded his arms and considered her slight build. "And then what? You would never have been able to get me into your car."

"I would have managed."

Sarandon highly doubted it. "You must be new at this." Either that, or he'd rattled her because she hadn't expected him to be a wolf.

"No, I've been doing this for years, and I've never had any trouble. The man, or woman, gives up without a fuss, or I have to use a little extra encouragement. But I've always caught my guy. You're the first who has been a real problem."

Jake was standing in the dining room, listening to them but staying out of the way. He knew two male wolves might intimidate her too much, and they had to learn what was going on.

"How many wolf suspects have you taken down?" Sarandon suspected none, or he wouldn't have startled her so.

"One."

Wondering how she'd managed that without getting herself in serious trouble, he raised a brow, wanting to hear the whole story. Maybe the guy had been a beta or omega wolf.

"Well, one still in progress. I'm working on it. Currently."

He smiled. "Me?"

"If you've got the situation under control, I'll bring her car up to the cabin," Jake said, smiling. He grabbed her car keys off the dining room table.

"Where's your car, Jake?" Sarandon asked, wondering how his cousin had gotten there.

"Alicia dropped me off. She was going to pick me up in a couple of days at the cabin." Jake frowned at Jenna. "If you've been doing this for some time in Colorado, you may know other bounty hunters. My wife is one. She was trying to hunt down some mobsters when I met her—and we fell in love. She was working for a bail bondsman while she tried to track the criminals down."

"Alicia Silver?" Jenna shook her head. "Never heard of her."

"Alicia Greiston, maybe?" Jake asked.

Jenna's jaw dropped. "She was human when I met her."

"Same here when I first met her. She was eyeing these mobsters in a restaurant, and I believed she needed some protection. Anyway, one thing led to another. One of the mobsters turned her, and eventually we were mated. Best thing that could have ever happened to me. When the kids came, she wanted to be a stay-at-home mom. I was glad for that. Not that I wasn't proud of what she was doing, but I worried about her because she was so newly turned."

"And you needed someone to take care of your kids."

"We have a pack to help out. So no problem there."

Sarandon knew Jake preferred for Alicia to stay home and not risk her life trying to apprehend potentially dangerous suspects.

He caught Jenna glancing again in the direction of her Taser, making a calculated risk assessment. He didn't trust that she wouldn't make a go for it. Could she get it before he tackled her again? Not with two men in the cabin, but maybe when Jake left to move her car.

"Let me lock these away first." Sarandon hauled the rifles, Taser, and pistol into the bedroom where they had a locking gun cabinet.

In the meantime, Jake said to her, "You know that you have the wrong man. We'll help you track down the right guy."

"For a price," Jenna said skeptically.

"No. We're wolves, Sarandon's part of our pack, and someone's using his identity to break the law. This is something we would get involved in anyway."

Sarandon finished locking the weapons in the gun cabinet, then shoved the key into his jeans pocket. He rejoined them in the living room. "Weapons are secure." He smiled down at Jenna, but she looked so vixen-like that he wondered if she knew a secret he didn't. He reached down and took hold of her arm and pulled her to stand. "I didn't think we needed to pat you down, not after confiscating all your other weapons. I didn't figure you'd be armed with anything more than that. Maybe that's a mistake."

"Is that how you get your jollies?" she asked, sounding highly annoyed.

Ignoring her comment, he patted her down, having to admit that touching her sure stirred up his pheromones again, when he was trying hard to keep this impersonal. When he reached her jeans pockets, he found a can of spray. "Well, well." He handed it to Jake and continued patting down her pants legs until he came to her boots. He smiled to see a knife tucked inside. "Really, girls shouldn't play with knives." He pulled it free and gave it to Jake.

Jake tsked. "How did you miss those the first time?"

"We *both* missed them." Sarandon hadn't thought she'd be carrying anything more than what they'd already taken.

"I'll lock it up and then get the car." Jake took the knife and pepper spray and headed into the bedroom. All the Silver wolves had a key to the gun cabinet, just in case. And they never left their rifles when they weren't staying there.

Once Jake had locked them up, he left the cabin.

Feeling sure she wouldn't pull anything, Sarandon helped her to sit back down, then went to the kitchen. "Do you want something to drink?"

"A beer."

"You're on a job." Sarandon was amused she'd ask for a beer when she was working a case.

"It appears I'm taking a break. Can I have my phone back?"

"Sure." Since she couldn't call for reinforcements from her company or the police, he brought her a beer and her phone, then took a seat on a chair across from her.

"You're not going to join me in a drink?"

"When Jake returns."

"Okay, do you want me to tell you what I know?" Jenna took another sip of her beer and set the bottle down on the wolf coaster on the coffee table.

"Why don't we wait until Jake returns so he can hear the whole story."

"What are you planning to do with me?"

"Take you to the outskirts of Silver Town. We'll meet with Darien and Lelandi at their home out in the country to talk this over. For now, I want to know all about this, then you can ride with me in my car and Jake can take yours into town."

"Then what? Lock me up? You can't do that because I'm a wolf too."

"Newly turned or royal?"

"Royal."

He smiled.

"Yeah, yeah, so my family has been wolves for generations, and we don't have any trouble with shifting. You still can't lock me up. If you tried to make up a story that I was tailing you, or pulled a gun on you and threatened to shoot you—"

"On my own property? We could charge you with trespassing, for starters."

"As a bounty hunter, I have the power to enter your home and even effect an arrest. Since Jake's married to a bounty hunter, he must know his wife can break into a home and arrest a suspect, when the cops can't do that without a warrant."

"True, but I'm not your suspect. And this business about a warrant? We run the town."

Her eyes widened. "A wolf-run town?"

"Yep. From its inception. We have no problem

incarcerating our own kind in the town jail. In your case, I don't think you have to worry about it though."

"The sheriff's office is…is wolf-run?" She let out her breath. "You're going to detain me?"

"You bet. You're not calling other law enforcement officials to tell them to come pick me up. Like Jake said, we'll help you find the right guy, but I'm not turning myself in and going to trial. Alicia became a bounty hunter to take down the men who killed her mother. How did you get involved in this line of work?"

She took a deep breath and let it out. "Okay, while we're waiting on your cousin, I'll tell you about us. My mom, Victoria St. James, is the bondswoman for the family company but she was a bounty hunter before that. My dad, Logan, saw her on a case when he was an FBI agent. He fell in love wither her, left the FBI, and got his bounty hunter accreditation so he would work for her family. By then, she was the bondswoman for the company. She hired him on the spot. Dad's great at the job. They make a wonderful team. You know, I kind of imagined I might meet a wolf like that someday. It's never happened."

"Maybe looking for a wolf bounty hunter isn't what you need. Maybe a potential suspect is more your style."

She snorted. "Like you? I don't go for the bad boys. I prefer taking them into custody." She took another sip of her beer.

"I take it you wanted to follow in your father's footsteps and trained to be a fugitive recovery agent."

"Uh, no. Not exactly." Jenna had seemed proud of her parents and what they were doing when she'd been talking about them, but her expression had darkened when Sarandon mentioned how *she* got into this business.

He hoped that didn't mean she'd been forced into it and hated it. He didn't even know her, yet he was ready to rescue her.

"I…had a mate." She slipped some of her hair behind her ear. "And I was four months pregnant when the car my husband was driving was hit by a drunken driver. My husband died, and I lost the twins as a result of my injuries. A hit-and-run fifty years ago. Once I'd recovered physically, I was ready to take down the suspect. Emotionally, not so much though."

"I'm so sorry, Jenna. Did they catch the bastard?"

"Later. Yes. He was caught and given bail for another hit-and-run DUI case, before they realized he was the one who had killed my mate and my babies. Will and I had been mated for five months after a whirlwind romance of a month. And then suddenly, both he and my babies were gone. I'll never forgive the man for taking them from me." She frowned. "Having Cavendish run off to avoid standing trial was my reason for becoming a bounty hunter like my father. And my two sisters. We're triplets, and while I was physically recovering from the accident, they immediately enrolled in fugitive apprehension training."

"And your mom was fine with it?"

Jenna shook her head. "Dad had to convince her that my sisters and I could do this. That it would be a family affair. Mom was worried it would be too dangerous, even though she'd been a bounty hunter earlier on. My sisters and I knew what was at stake, and we wanted to help. Since I completed my training and began working with my dad and sisters, I've always caught my man."

"The wrong one *this* time." Sarandon wondered if

she'd ever picked up the wrong man before. "I hope the guy who hurt you is still in prison or died some time ago."

"I don't know. After my dad apprehended him, the perp stood trial, and a jury found him guilty, but he only received twelve years' incarceration."

"Hell. There's no justice in that."

"I agree."

Jake entered the cabin and said, "Okay, what did I miss?"

"Grab us some beers. Jenna's going to tell us what this is all about." Sarandon wasn't going to share the rest of what she'd told him. It wasn't his secret to tell.

Jenna turned on her phone while Jake grabbed a beer for him and for Sarandon. She began looking at her screen. "Okay, so you were in Colorado Springs when you were caught with five different credit cards, three passports, and three different driver's licenses."

"And he said he was Sarandon Silver," Sarandon ventured, ready to wring the man's neck.

"Right. The guy had never been fingerprinted before, and if you're not him but aren't in the police database either, no connection would have been made."

"So, he picked my name from one of his stolen identities. I've never been fingerprinted, so there's no way to verify I'm not him—unless I go in and prove my fingerprints don't match his."

"Exactly! If my mother had sent one of the other agents to get the forms from him, she would have smelled his scent. When she smells yours, she'll know you're not him. *If* you're not. I need to get ahold of her to learn if the forms were sent that way, or someone picked them up from the jail. Sarandon Silver is an unusual name. There isn't another one that I could find like that anywhere. Not online. Not in our database that we use for running people down. The guy in Colorado Springs didn't have any family or friends to speak of. He gave your address, which was verified by the driver's license.

"You own a house and an SUV, no mortgages. Everything was easy to check. The suspect paid for the bond himself. When I arrived at the home in Silver Town listed on your driver's license, I found you weren't there. A man saw me returning to my car, pulled into the driveway, and told me where I could find you. Here. At the family cabin...the Elk's Horn cabin."

"A man? A wolf, you mean?" Sarandon asked.

"I didn't smell his scent, but the way the breeze was blowing, he might have smelled mine and known I was a wolf." She smiled a little. "Maybe he thought you had a new girlfriend. Hope it doesn't get you in trouble with a real one."

"Hell." Sarandon didn't believe Jenna was all that worried she might have caused trouble for him with a girlfriend. He also couldn't believe one of his pack members had sicced her on him. The guy probably thought Sarandon's stay at the cabin had something to do with meeting the beautiful she-wolf up there.

"Since he doesn't have a girlfriend, that will sure start some tongues wagging," Jake said, amused. "I wonder who you spoke with."

"Hell, it'll probably be in tomorrow's paper," Sarandon said. "It makes me wonder when the person stole my identity. What did he have of mine, exactly? You said my driver's license. Anything else?"

"A credit card."

"And the police didn't suspect that all of the identities he had on him were someone else's? That the real Sarandon Silver's ID wasn't his own?"

"His mug shot looks so much like you that I'm sure the police didn't give it a second thought." The more Jenna talked to Sarandon, the more her suspicions were raised that he really was a victim of identity theft. She finished her beer and said, "Okay, let's go to see your pack leaders. I'll call my…uh, boss, and learn if the man they incarcerated was a wolf."

"I'm not missing any credit cards. I only have one and have never applied for more." Sarandon pulled out his wallet. "And my driver's license is good." He showed her both.

She examined each of them. "That doesn't mean you don't have any more credit cards or a duplicate driver's license. The police have the others as evidence, so I don't have them to show you, but they said the items were legitimate."

"Let's go then. I have my name to clear." Sarandon went to the gun cabinet to retrieve the weapons, but he gave them to Jake to carry in her car.

Then Sarandon drove his car, with Jenna in the passenger seat, to Lelandi and Darien's house. Sarandon didn't confine her wrists this time. He suspected she realized she might have the wrong man after all. At least he hoped so.

"So your mom is really the boss, eh?"

"Uh, yeah. We don't usually reveal that to bail jumpers. It's a family affair."

"Makes sense with you being wolves. Do you live in Colorado Springs?"

"Outside it. So we have room to run in the forests. Have you always lived here?"

"Always. And I wasn't in Colorado Springs recently. The last time I was there, it was a few years ago. I went with Jake when he had a new photography exhibit at an art gallery in Colorado Springs."

Jenna assumed Sarandon would let her call her mother as soon as she could get a signal on her phone. "When will I get a cell signal?"

"Could be anytime now. Don't call the cops."

"Just my mom." Jenna kept calling, trying to get ahold of her mother until they were finally closer to town and she was able to reach her. "Mom, listen... Yes, I'm on my way to Silver Town. I have to know, did you send either Suzanne or Crystal, or Dad even, to the jail to pick up the bail bond forms from Sarandon Silver?"

"No, he emailed the forms to me. Why? What difference would this make? Have you located him?"

"I've located Sarandon Silver. And he's *all* wolf."

Sarandon smiled.

Acknowledgments

Thanks so much to my beta readers, Donna Fournier and Dottie Jones, who are such a help. I couldn't do it without you! And to Deb Werksman, who has believed in me all these years! Ten years, and we were having so much fun that it just flew right by. And to the cover artists, who give readers a visual hottie to enjoy. Thanks to Stephany Daniel, who helps me to promote all my titles.

About the Author

Bestselling and award-winning author Terry Spear has written over sixty paranormal romance novels and seven medieval Highland historical romances. Her first werewolf romance, *Heart of the Wolf*, was named a 2008 *Publishers Weekly* Best Book of the Year, and her subsequent titles have garnered high praise and hit the *USA Today* bestseller list. A retired officer of the U.S. Army Reserves, Terry lives in Spring, Texas, where she is working on her next werewolf, jaguar, and cougar romances, continuing with her Highland medieval romances, and having fun with her young adult fae novels. When she's not writing, she's photographing everything that catches her eye, making teddy bears, and playing with her Havanese puppies and her first grandbaby. For more information, please visit terryspear.com, or follow her on Twitter @TerrySpear. She is also on Facebook at facebook.com/terry.spear. And on Wordpress at Terry Spear's Shifters: terryspear.wordpress.com.

Also by Terry Spear